GHOSTS

RAINA TELGEMEIER

GHOSTS

WITH COLOR BY BRADEN LAMB

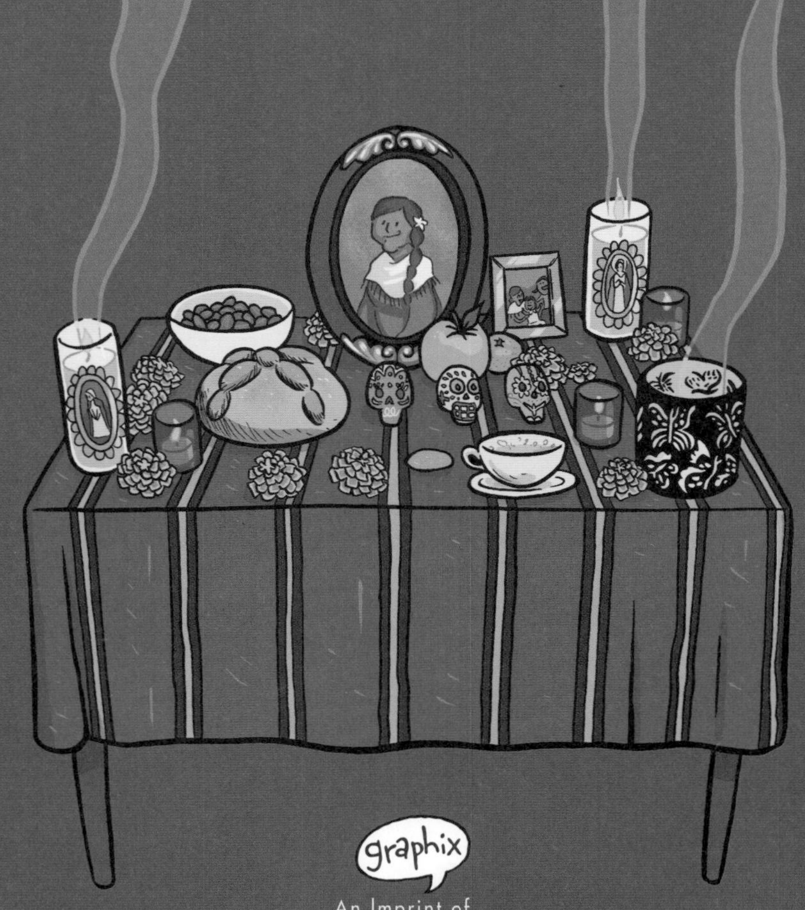

graphix

An Imprint of

SCHOLASTIC

Library of Congress Cataloging-in-Publication Data

Names: Telgemeier, Raina, author, illustrator.
Title: Ghosts / Raina Telgemeier ; with color by Braden Lamb.
Description: First edition. | New York : Graphix, an imprint of Scholastic, 2016. | © 2016 |
Summary: Catrina and her family have moved to the coast of Northern California for the sake
of her little sister, Maya, who has cystic fibrosis—and Cat is even less happy about the move when
she is told that her new town is inhabited by ghosts, and Maya sets her heart on meeting one.
Identifiers: LCCN 2016004672 | ISBN 9780545540612 (hc) | ISBN 9780545540629 (pb)
Subjects: LCSH: Sisters—Comic books, strips, etc. | Sisters—Juvenile fiction. | Ghosts—Comic books,
strips, etc. | Ghost stories. | Moving, Household—Comic books, strips, etc. | Moving, Household—
Juvenile fiction. | Families—California, Northern—Comic books, strips, etc. | Families—California,
Northern—Juvenile fiction. | California, Northern—Comic books, strips, etc. | California, Northern—
Juvenile fiction. | CYAC: Graphic novels. | Sisters—Fiction. | Ghosts—Fiction. |
Cystic fibrosis—Fiction. | Moving, Household—Fiction. | Family life—Fiction. | California,
Northern—Fiction. Classification: LCC PZ7.7.T45 Gh 2016 | DDC 741.5/973—dc23
LC record available at http://lccn.loc.gov/2016004672

10 9 8 7 6 5 4 3 2 1   16 17 18 19 20

Printed in China   62
First edition, September 2016
Edited by Cassandra Pelham
Lettering by Jenny Staley
Book design by Phil Falco
Creative Director: David Saylor

FOR SABINA

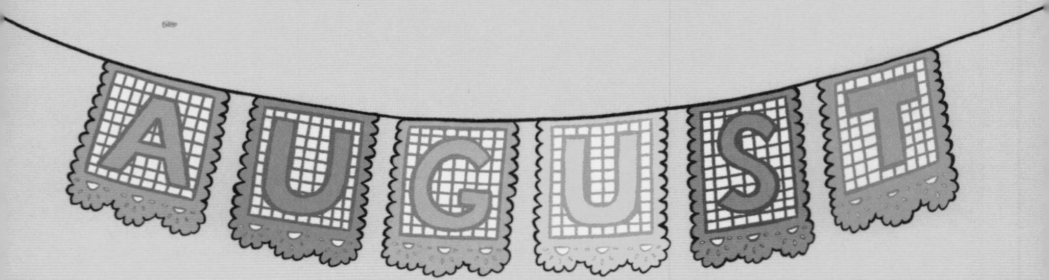
AUGUST

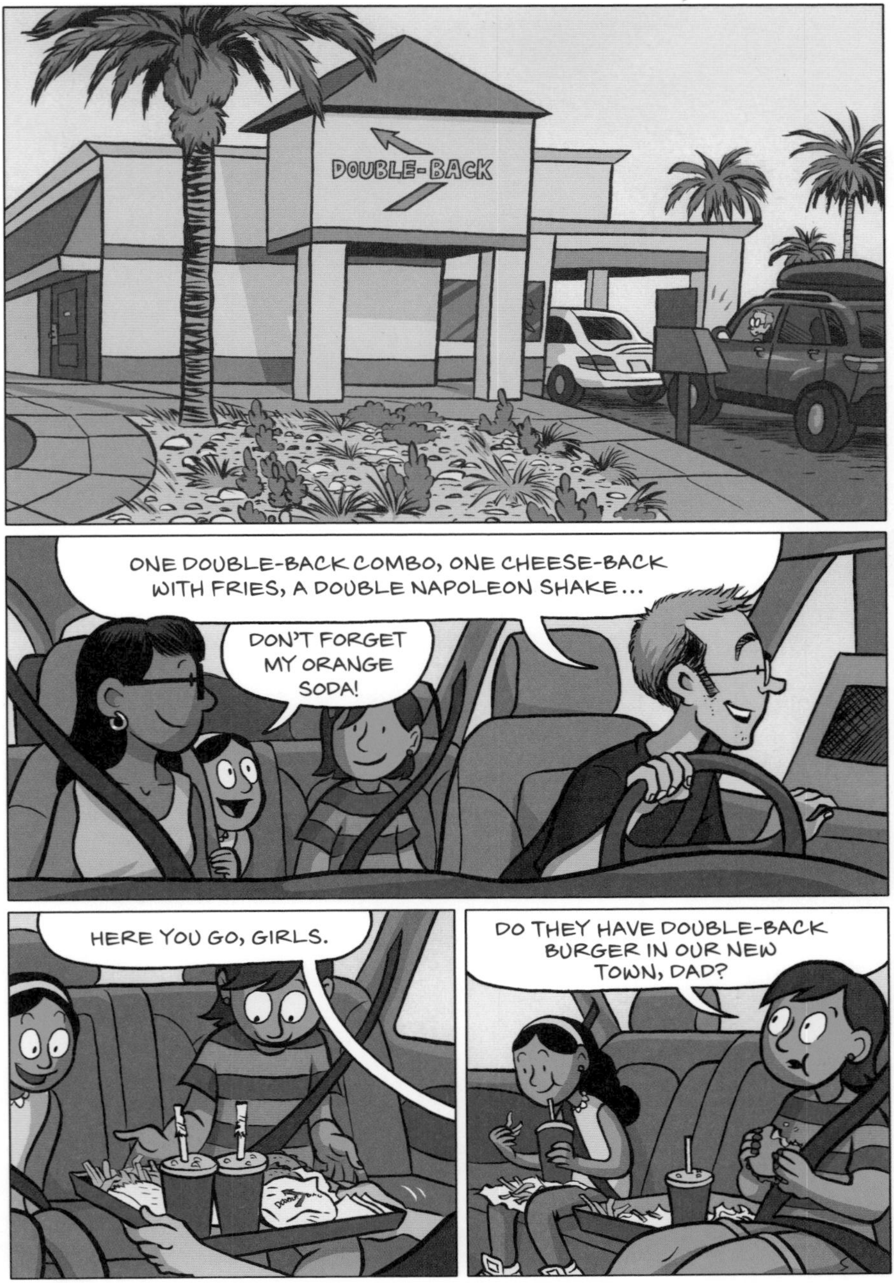
DOUBLE-BACK
ONE DOUBLE-BACK COMBO, ONE CHEESE-BACK WITH FRIES, A DOUBLE NAPOLEON SHAKE…
DON'T FORGET MY ORANGE SODA!
HERE YOU GO, GIRLS.
DO THEY HAVE DOUBLE-BACK BURGER IN OUR NEW TOWN, DAD?

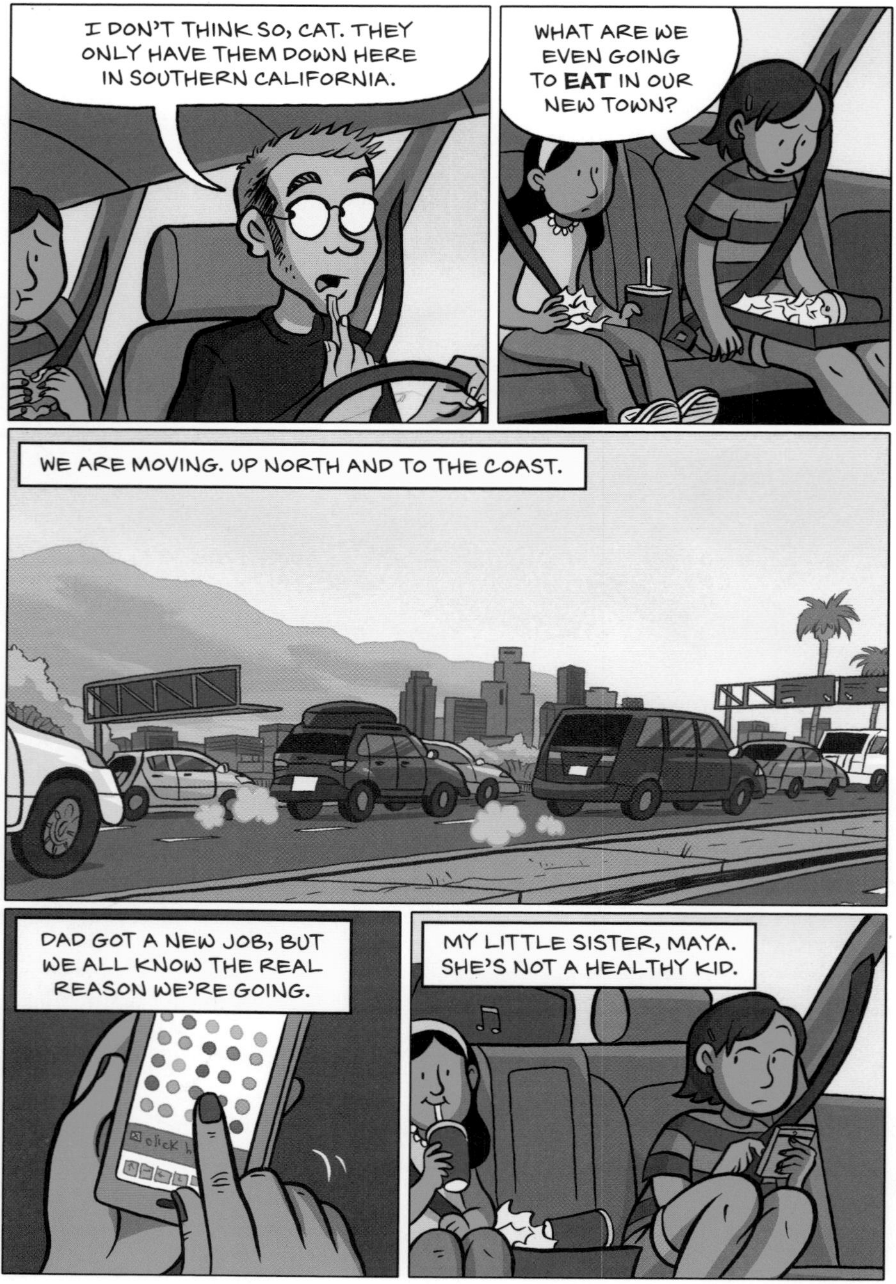
I DON'T THINK SO, CAT. THEY ONLY HAVE THEM DOWN HERE IN SOUTHERN CALIFORNIA.
WHAT ARE WE EVEN GOING TO EAT IN OUR NEW TOWN?
WE ARE MOVING. UP NORTH AND TO THE COAST.
DAD GOT A NEW JOB, BUT WE ALL KNOW THE REAL REASON WE'RE GOING.
MY LITTLE SISTER, MAYA. SHE'S NOT A HEALTHY KID.

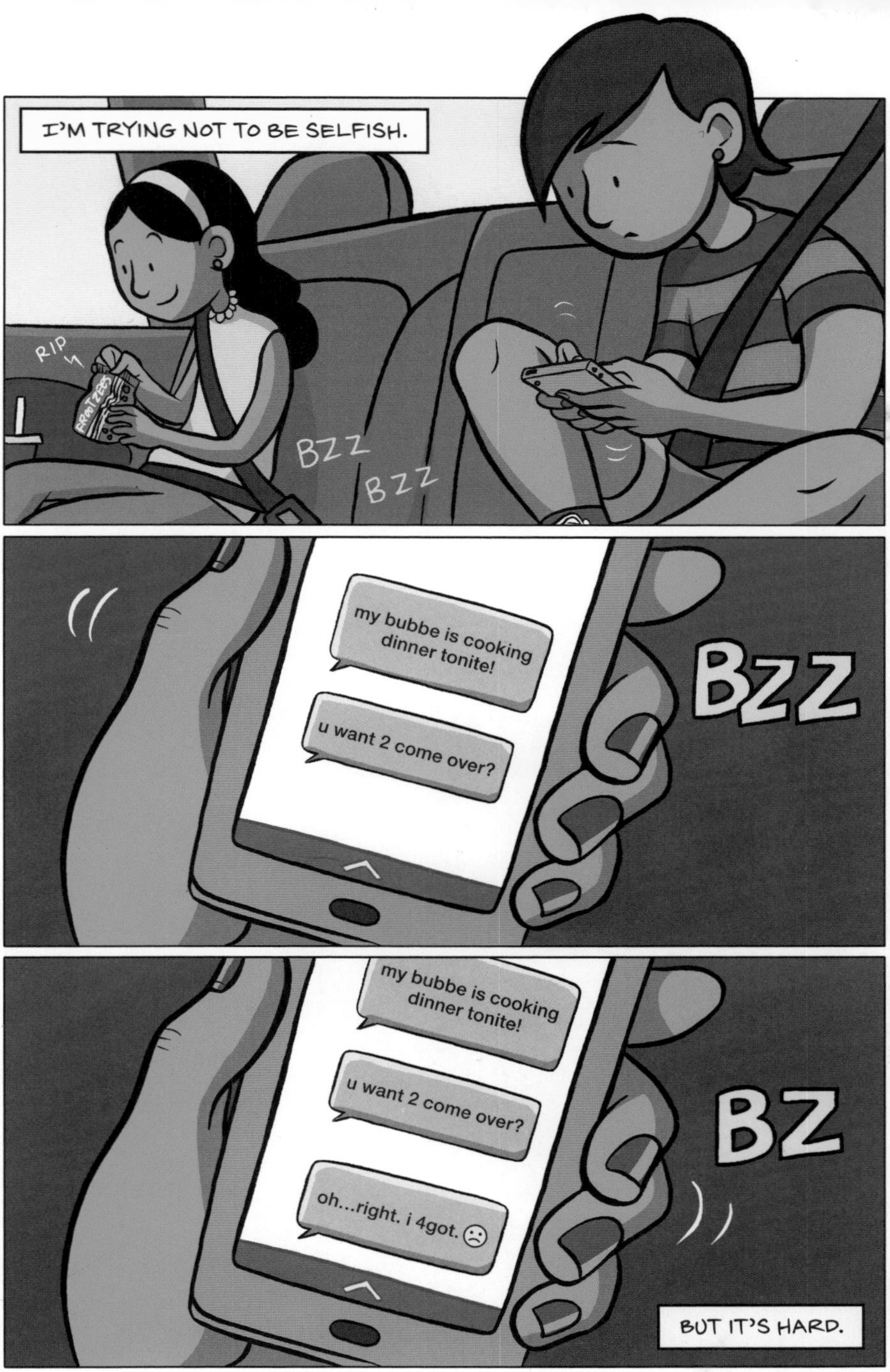
I'M TRYING NOT TO BE SELFISH.
RIP
FROOTZEES
BZZ
BZZ
my bubbe is cooking dinner tonite!
u want 2 come over?
BZZ
my bubbe is cooking dinner tonite!
u want 2 come over?
oh...right. i 4got. ☹
BZ
BUT IT'S HARD.

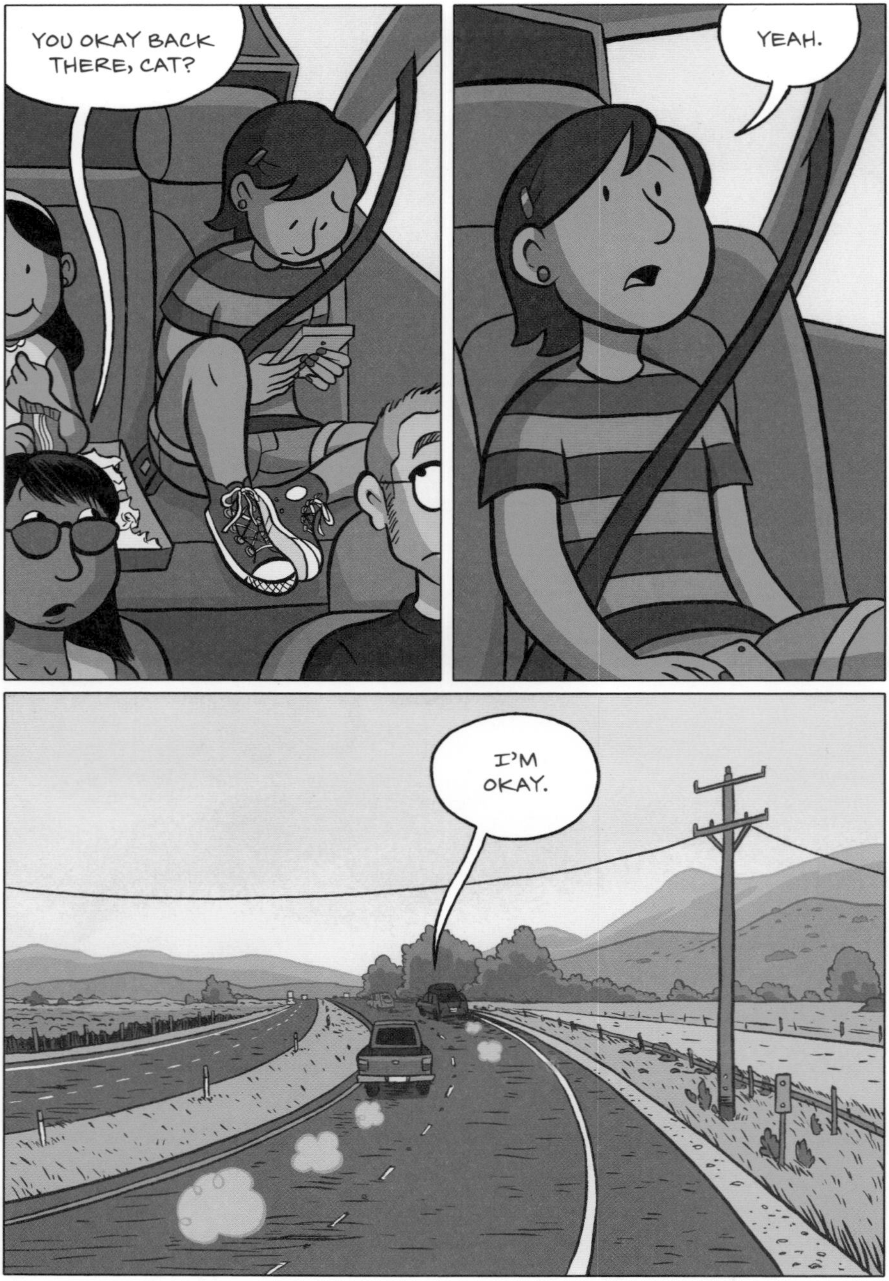
YOU OKAY BACK THERE, CAT?
YEAH.
I'M OKAY.

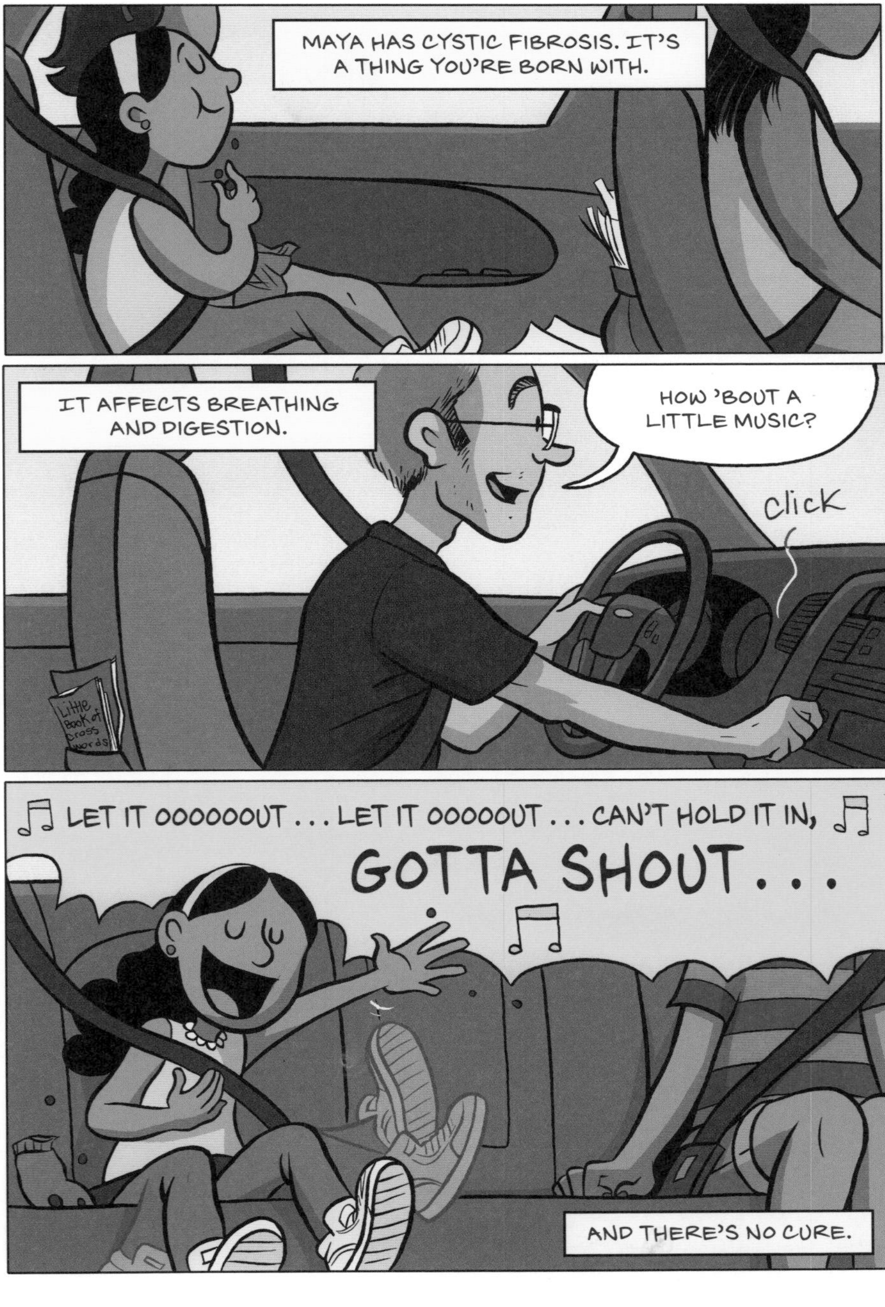
MAYA HAS CYSTIC FIBROSIS. IT'S A THING YOU'RE BORN WITH.
IT AFFECTS BREATHING AND DIGESTION.
HOW 'BOUT A LITTLE MUSIC?
Click
Little Book of Cross words
♫ LET IT OOOOOOUT . . . LET IT OOOOOUT . . . CAN'T HOLD IT IN, ♫
GOTTA SHOUT . . .
AND THERE'S NO CURE.

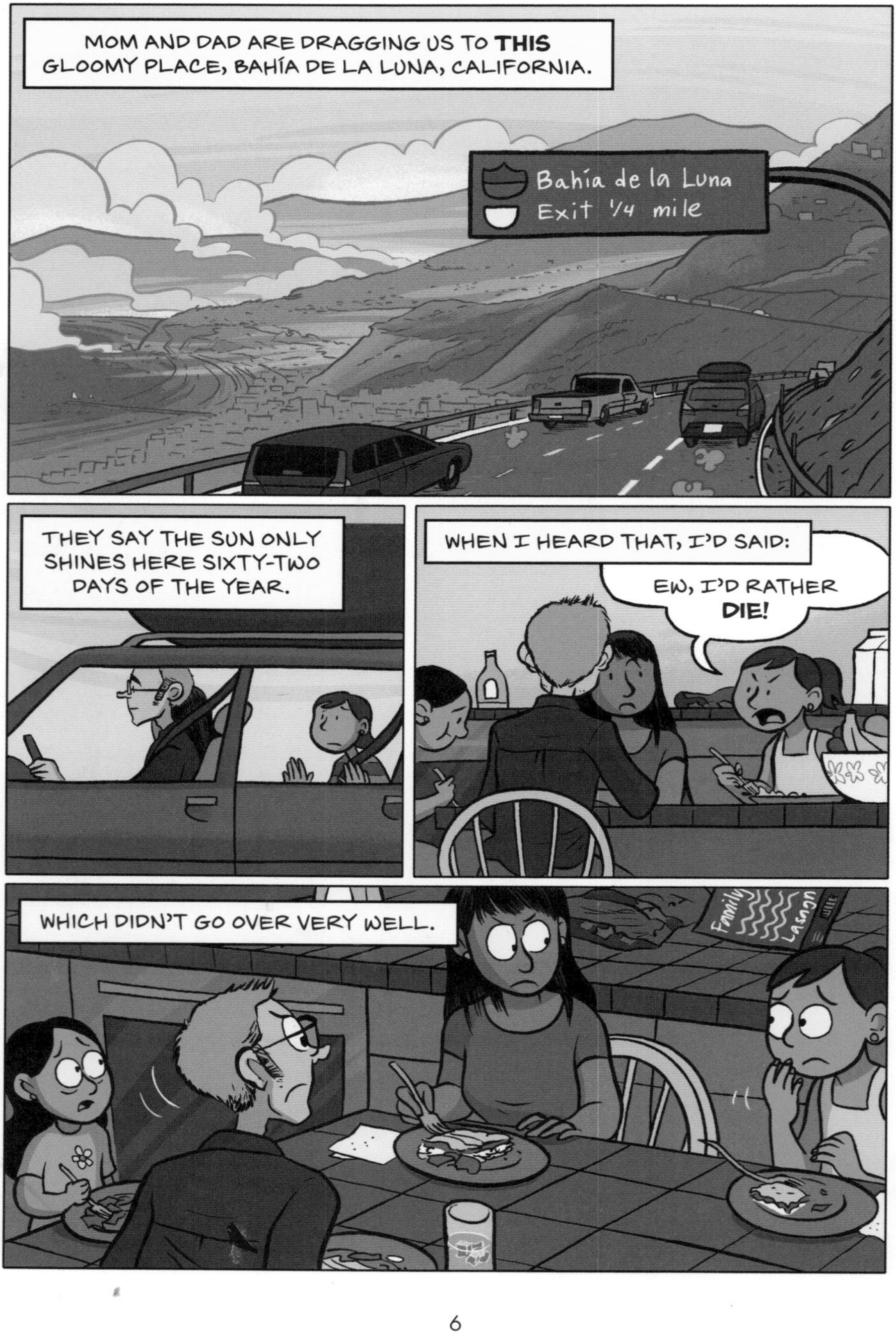

MOM AND DAD ARE DRAGGING US TO **THIS** GLOOMY PLACE, BAHÍA DE LA LUNA, CALIFORNIA.
Bahia de la Luna
Exit 1/4 mile
THEY SAY THE SUN ONLY SHINES HERE SIXTY-TWO DAYS OF THE YEAR.
WHEN I HEARD THAT, I'D SAID:
EW, I'D RATHER **DIE!**
WHICH DIDN'T GO OVER VERY WELL.
Family Lasagn

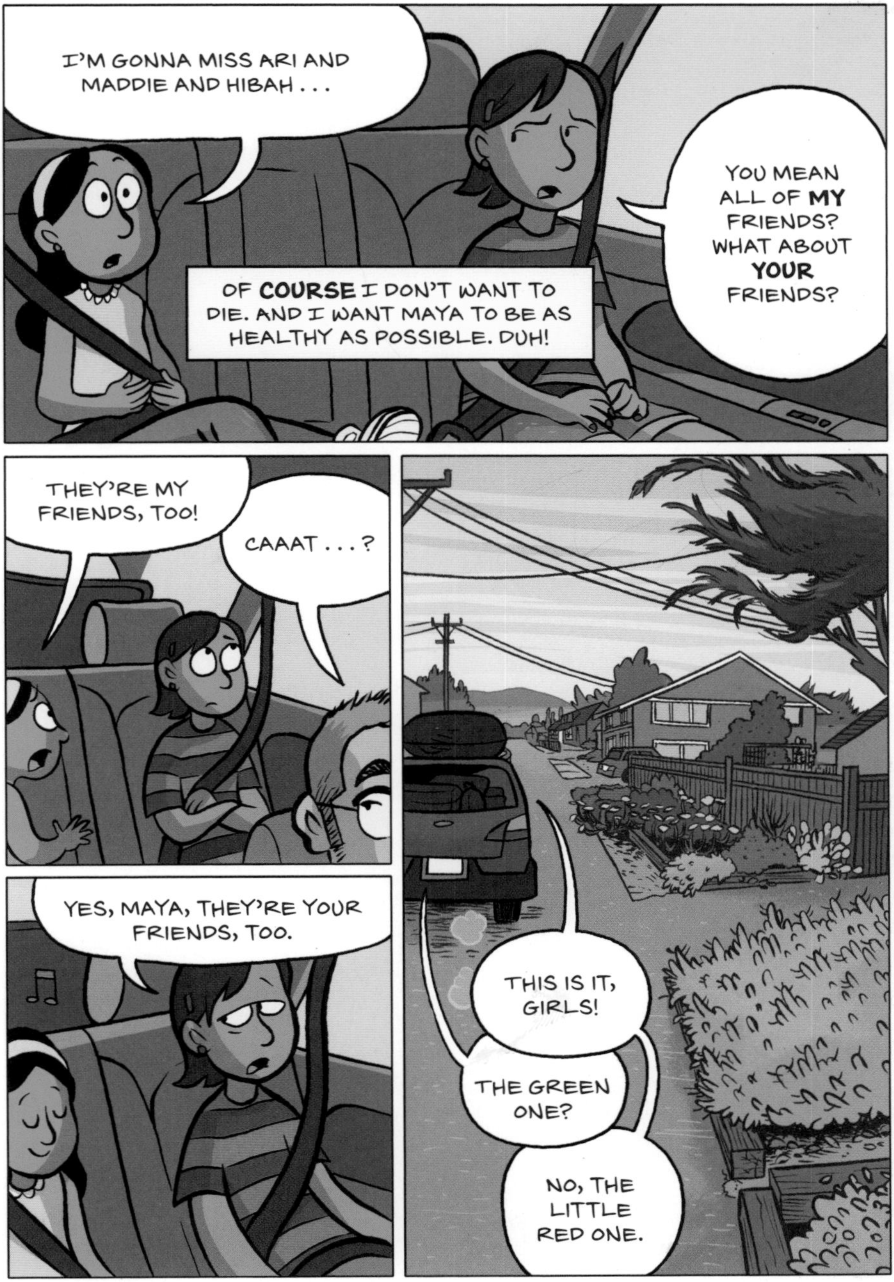
I'M GONNA MISS ARI AND MADDIE AND HIBAH . . .
YOU MEAN ALL OF **MY** FRIENDS? WHAT ABOUT **YOUR** FRIENDS?
OF **COURSE** I DON'T WANT TO DIE. AND I WANT MAYA TO BE AS HEALTHY AS POSSIBLE. DUH!
THEY'RE MY FRIENDS, TOO!
CAAAT . . . ?
YES, MAYA, THEY'RE YOUR FRIENDS, TOO.
THIS IS IT, GIRLS!
THE GREEN ONE?
NO, THE LITTLE RED ONE.

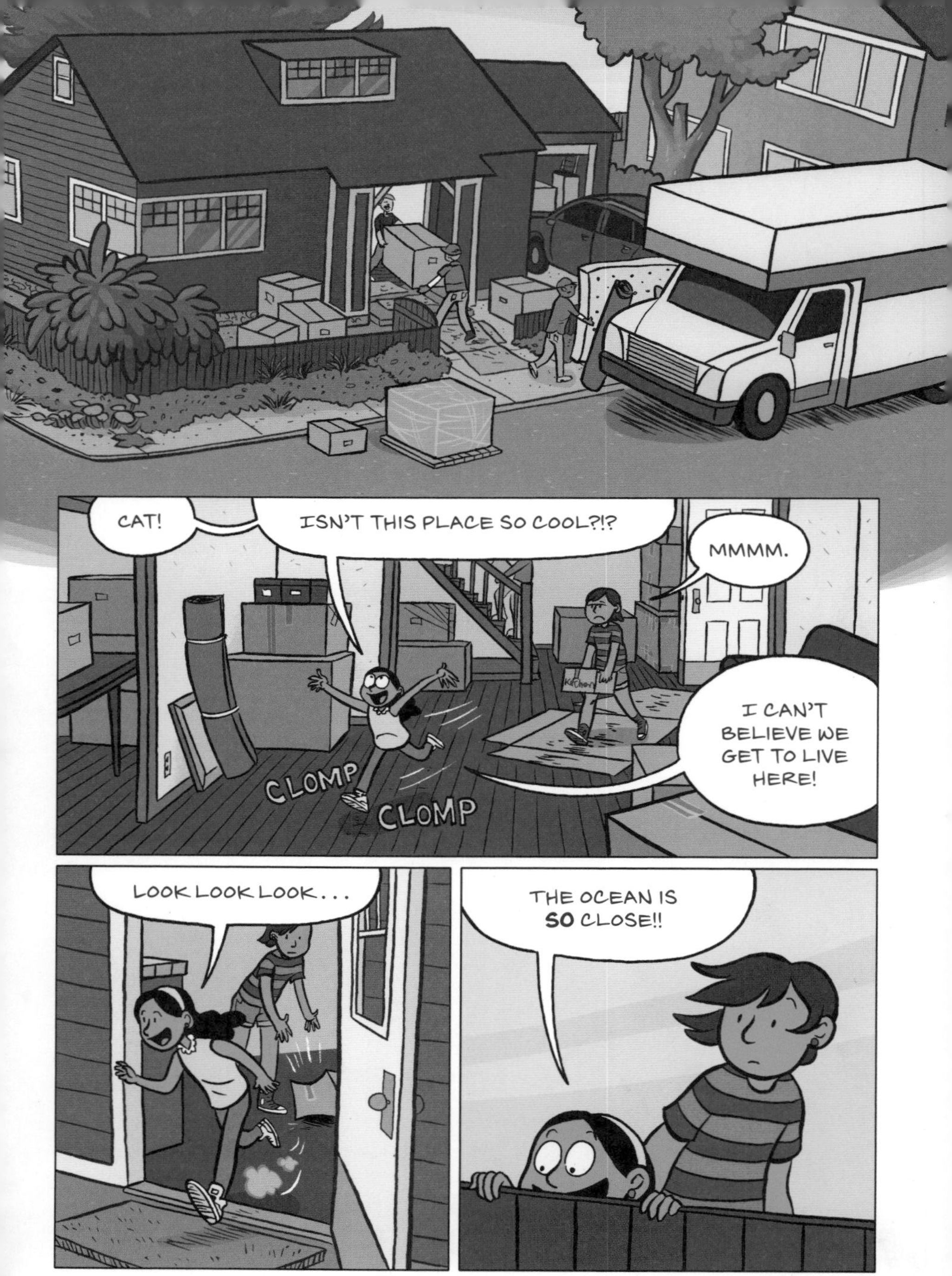
CAT!
ISN'T THIS PLACE SO COOL?!?
MMMM.
I CAN'T BELIEVE WE GET TO LIVE HERE!
CLOMP
CLOMP
LOOK LOOK LOOK . . .
THE OCEAN IS **SO** CLOSE!!

WHOOOOOOOOOOSH

IT'S FREEZING. I'M GOING INSIDE.

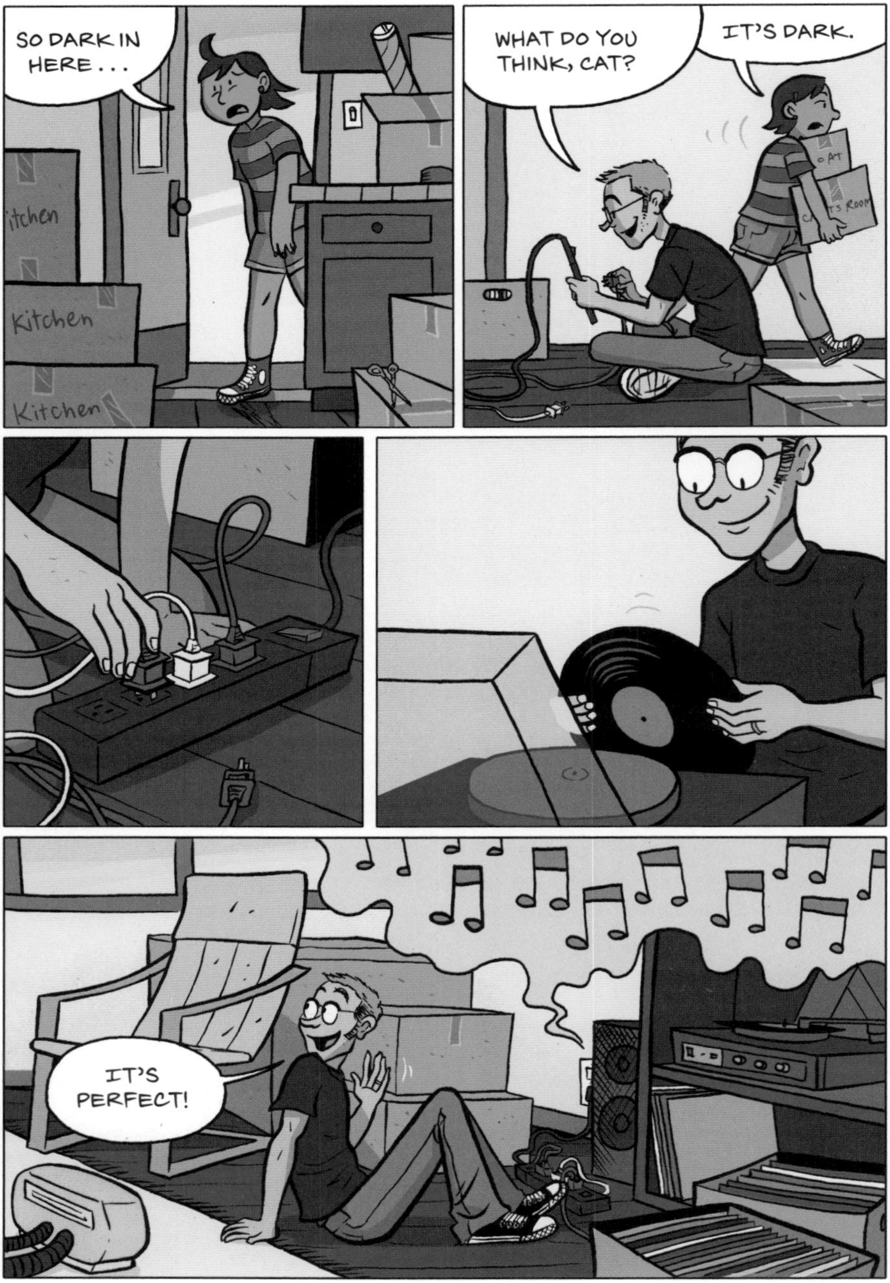
SO DARK IN HERE . . .
Kitchen
Kitchen
Kitchen
WHAT DO YOU THINK, CAT?
IT'S DARK.
IT'S PERFECT!

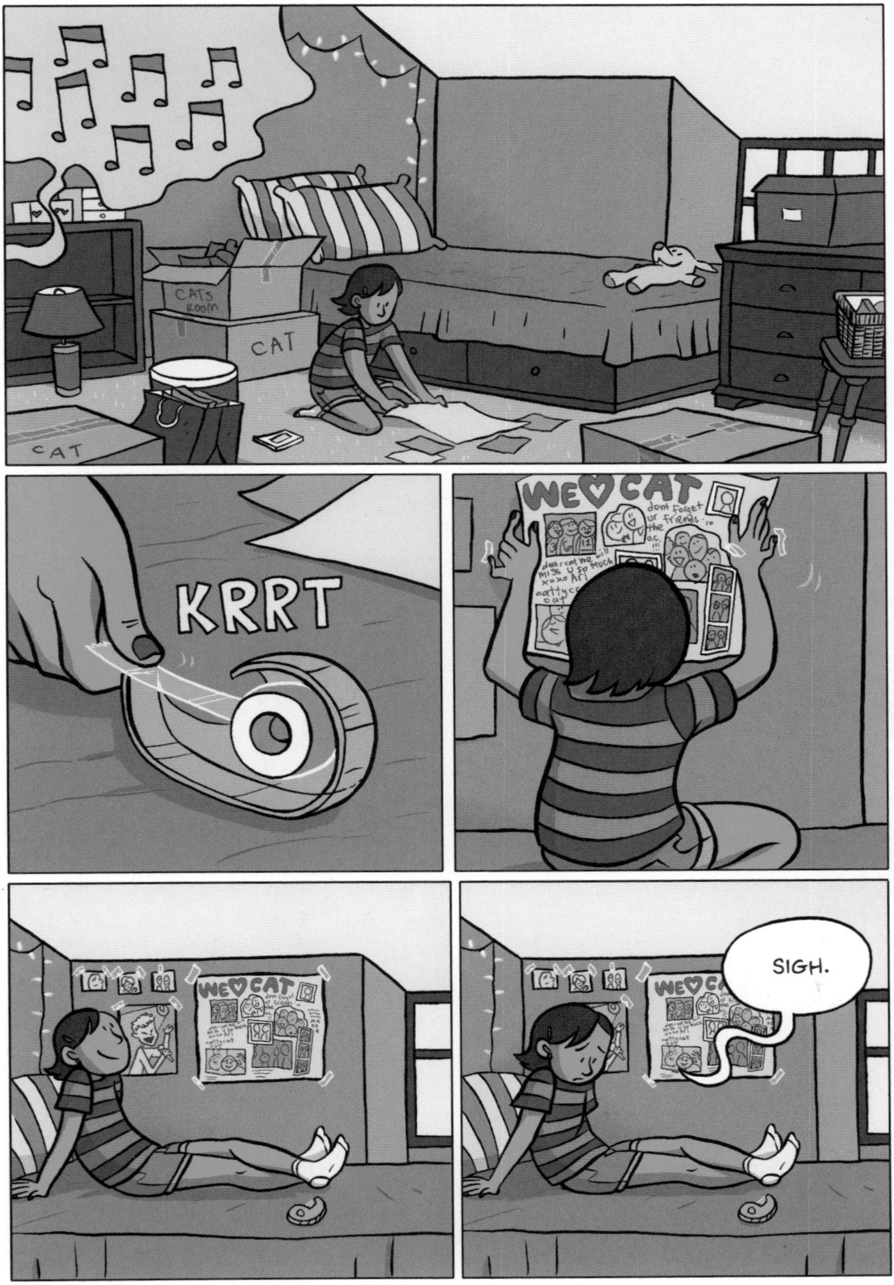
CATS ROOM
CAT
CAT
KRRT
WE ♥ CAT
dont forget ur friends in the o.c. !!!
dear cat we will miss u so much xoxo Ari
SIGH.

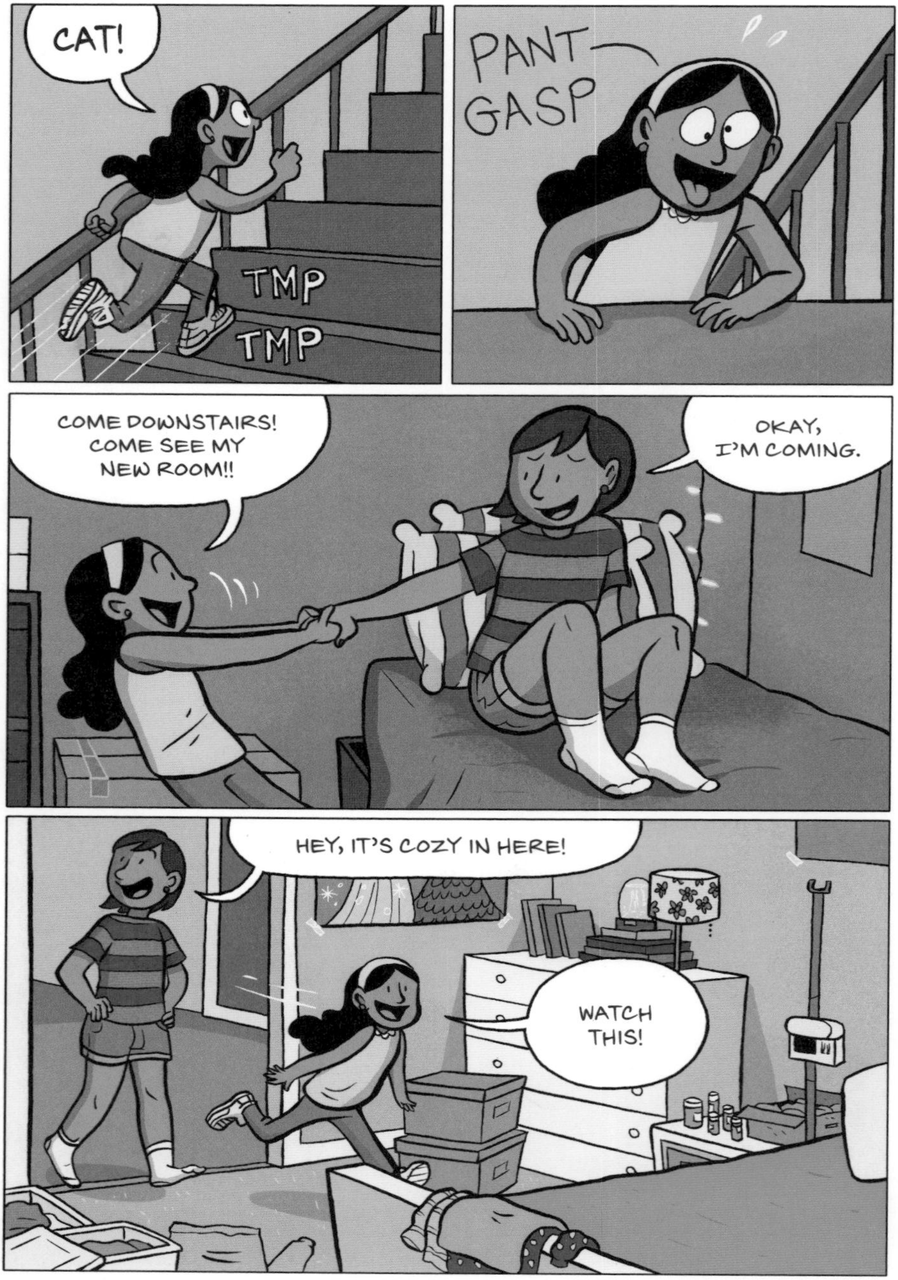
CAT!
TMP
TMP
PANT
GASP
COME DOWNSTAIRS! COME SEE MY NEW ROOM!!
OKAY, I'M COMING.
HEY, IT'S COZY IN HERE!
WATCH THIS!

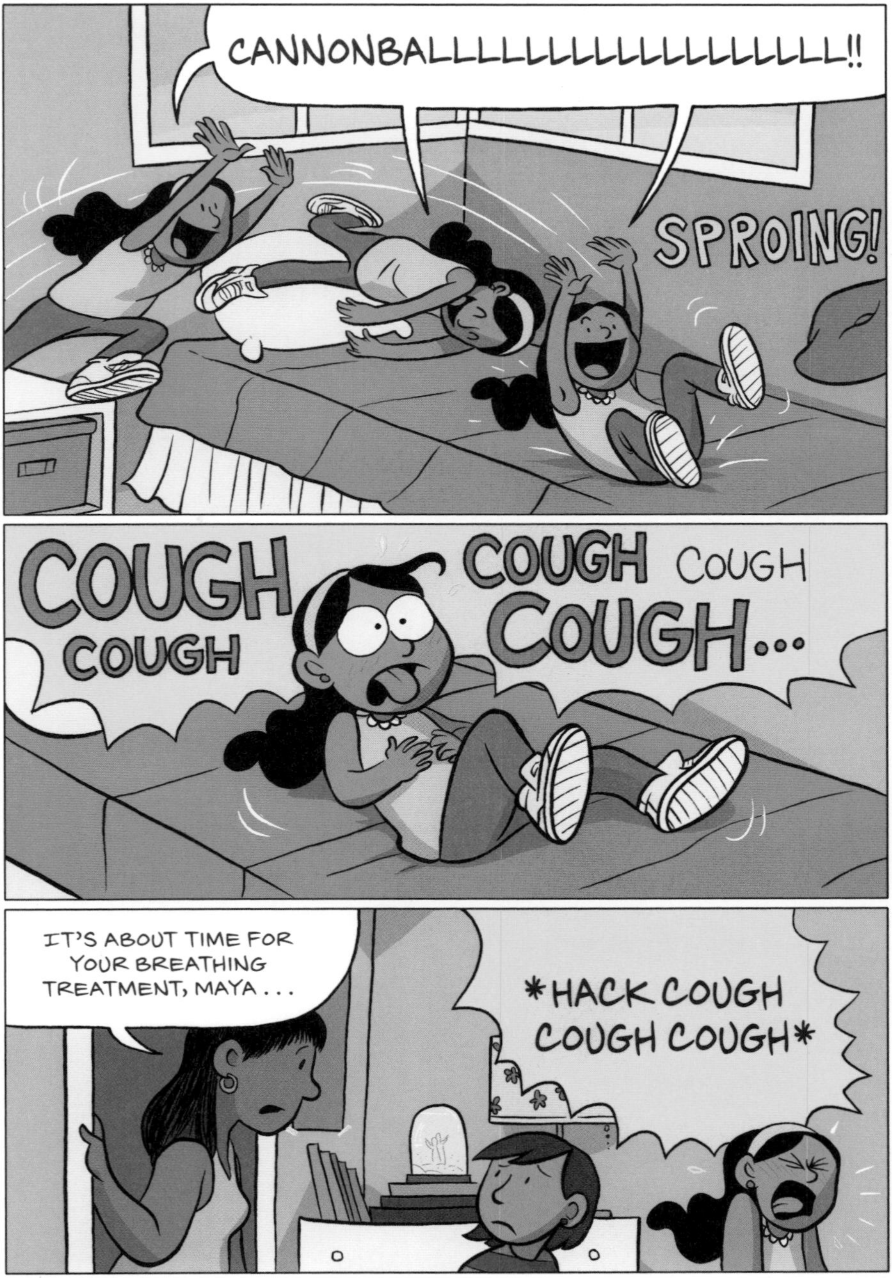
CANNONBALLLLLLLLLLLLLLLLLL!!
SPROING!
COUGH
COUGH
COUGH COUGH
COUGH...
IT'S ABOUT TIME FOR YOUR BREATHING TREATMENT, MAYA . . .
HACK COUGH COUGH COUGH

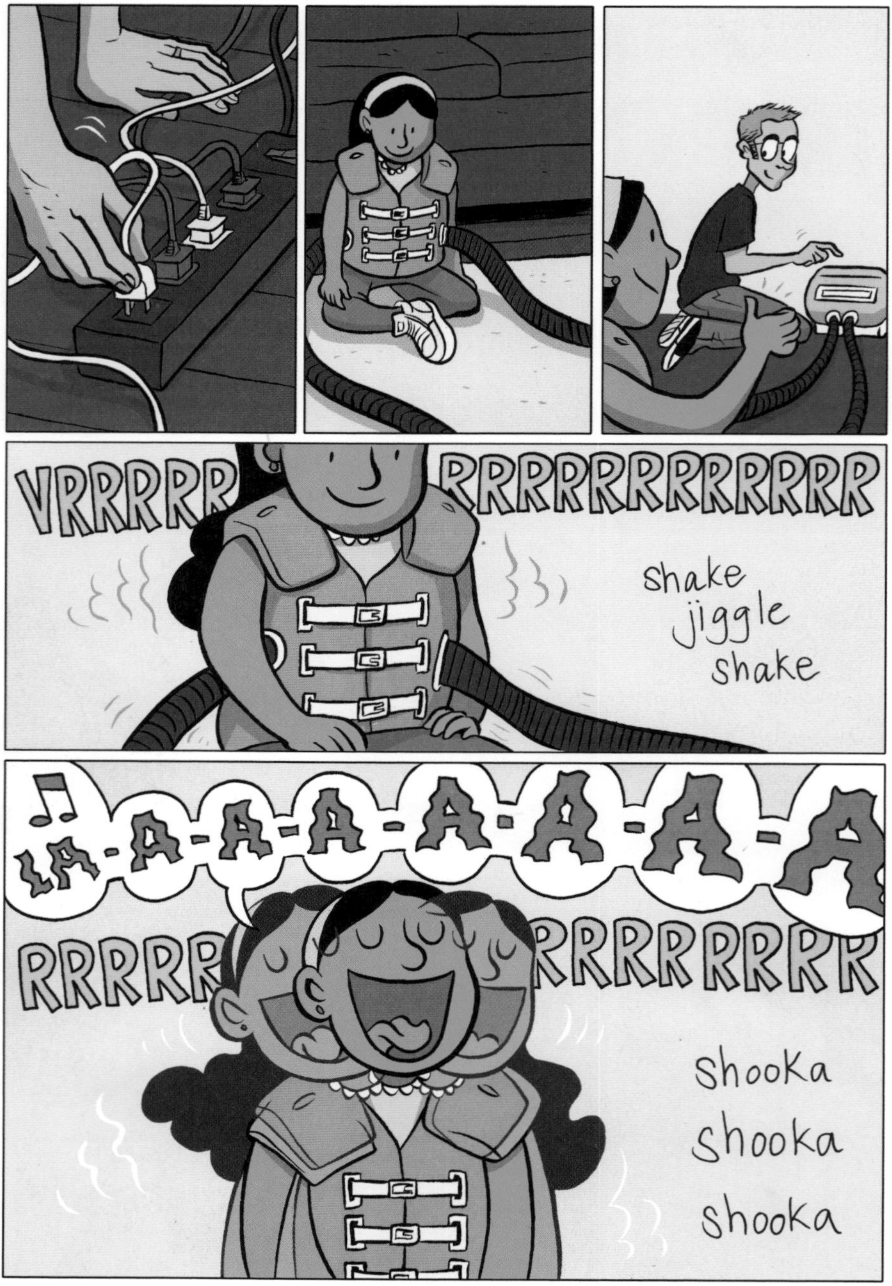
VRRRRR RRRRRRRRRRRR
shake
jiggle
shake
LA-A-A-A-A-A-A-A
RRRRR RRRRRRRRR
shooka
shooka
shooka

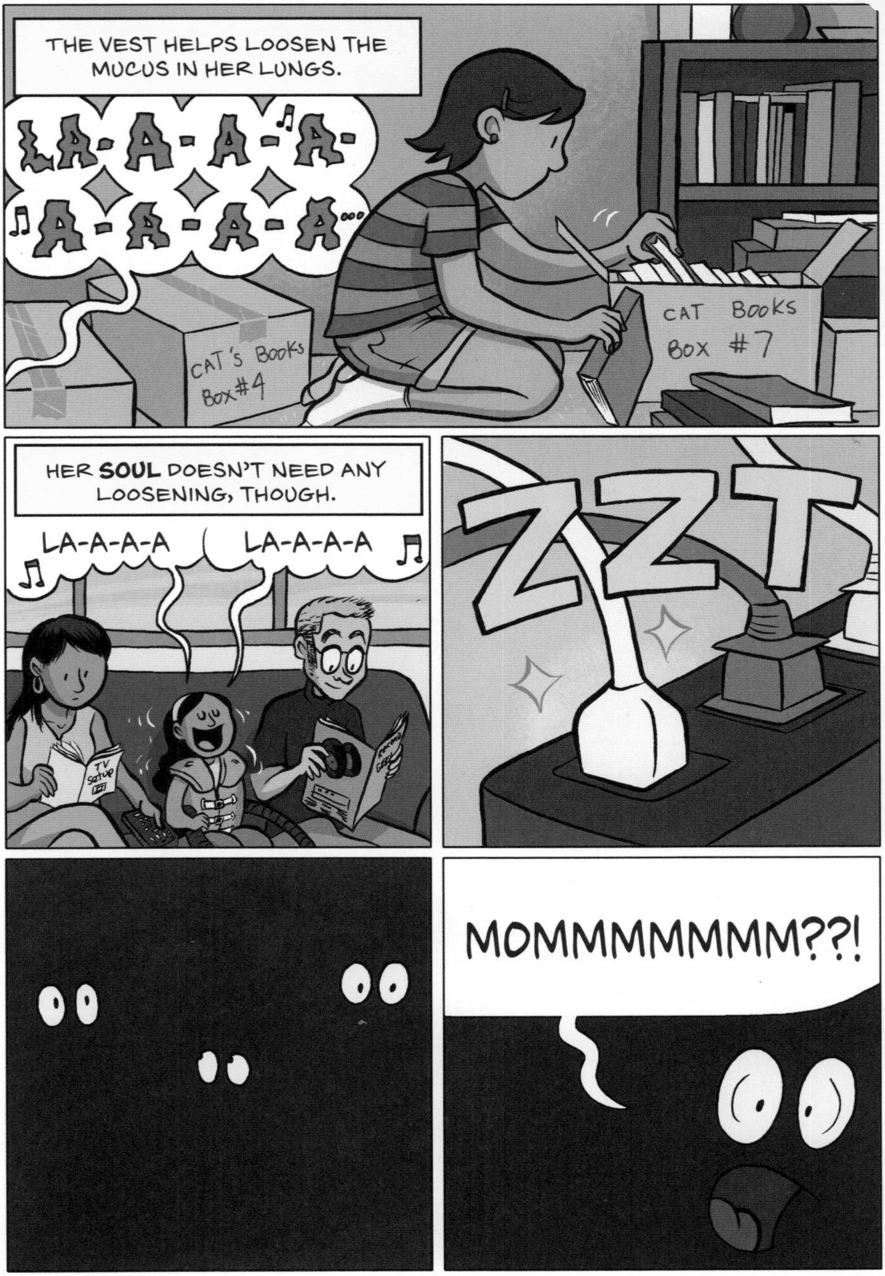
THE VEST HELPS LOOSEN THE MUCUS IN HER LUNGS.
LA-A-A-A-A-A-A-A...
CAT'S BOOKS BOX #4
CAT BOOKS BOX #7
HER SOUL DOESN'T NEED ANY LOOSENING, THOUGH.
LA-A-A-A
LA-A-A-A
TV SETUP
RECORD GEEK
ZZT
MOMMMMMMM??!

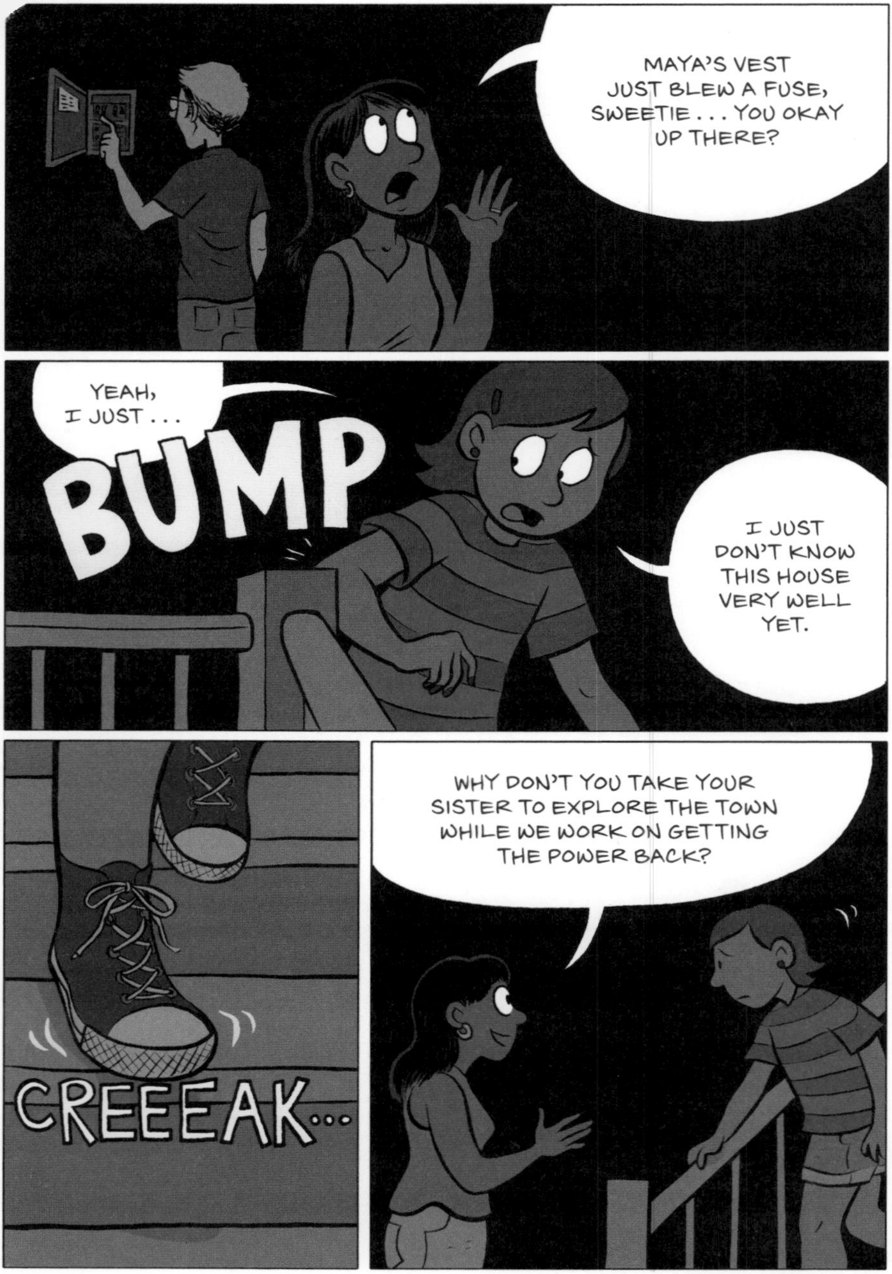
MAYA'S VEST JUST BLEW A FUSE, SWEETIE . . . YOU OKAY UP THERE?
YEAH, I JUST . . .
BUMP
I JUST DON'T KNOW THIS HOUSE VERY WELL YET.
CREEEAK...
WHY DON'T YOU TAKE YOUR SISTER TO EXPLORE THE TOWN WHILE WE WORK ON GETTING THE POWER BACK?

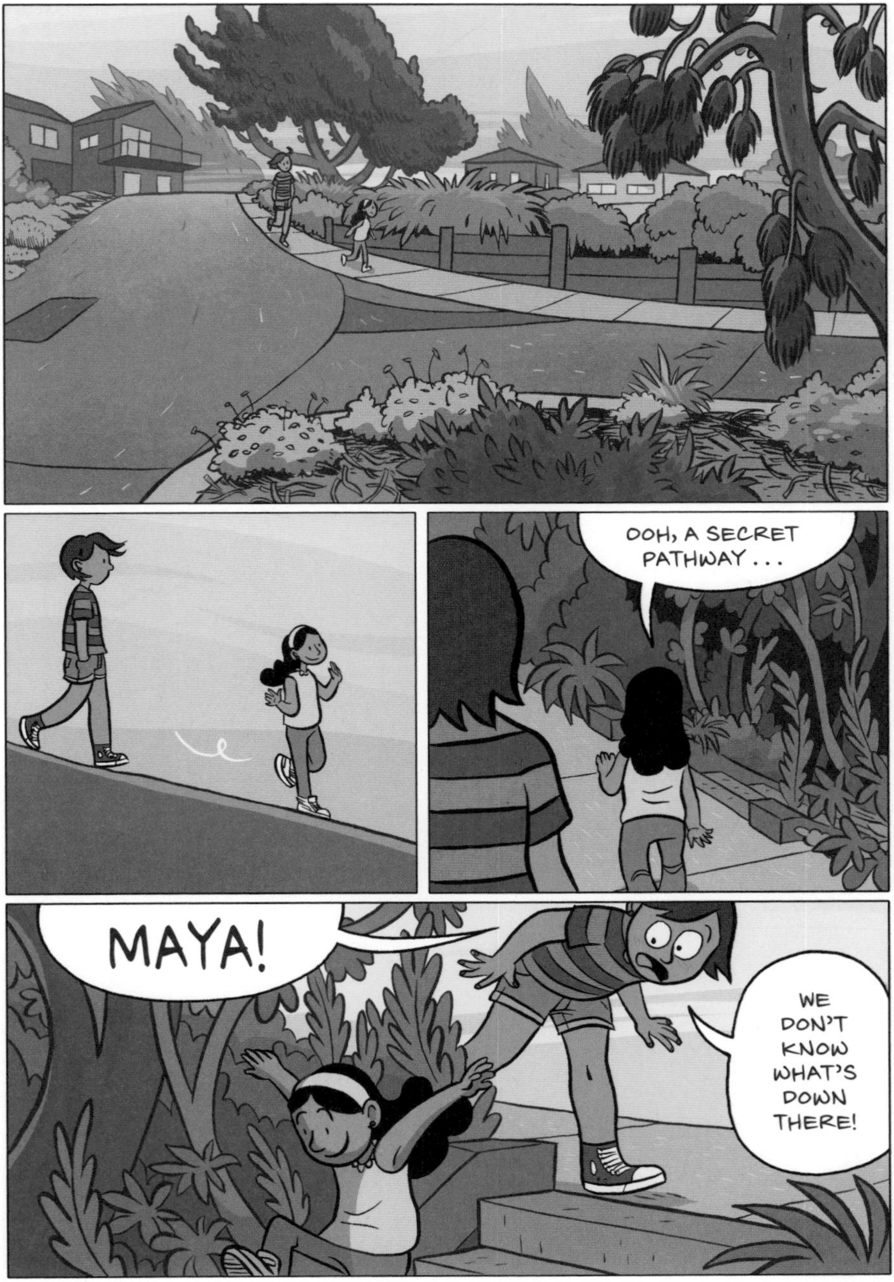
OOH, A SECRET PATHWAY . . .
MAYA!
WE DON'T KNOW WHAT'S DOWN THERE!

SIGH . . .

giggle!

WHHHHHHHHHHHHHHHHHsssssssssSHHH

MAYBE THIS PATH WILL LEAD US TO --

Rustle

KITTY!!

Rustle

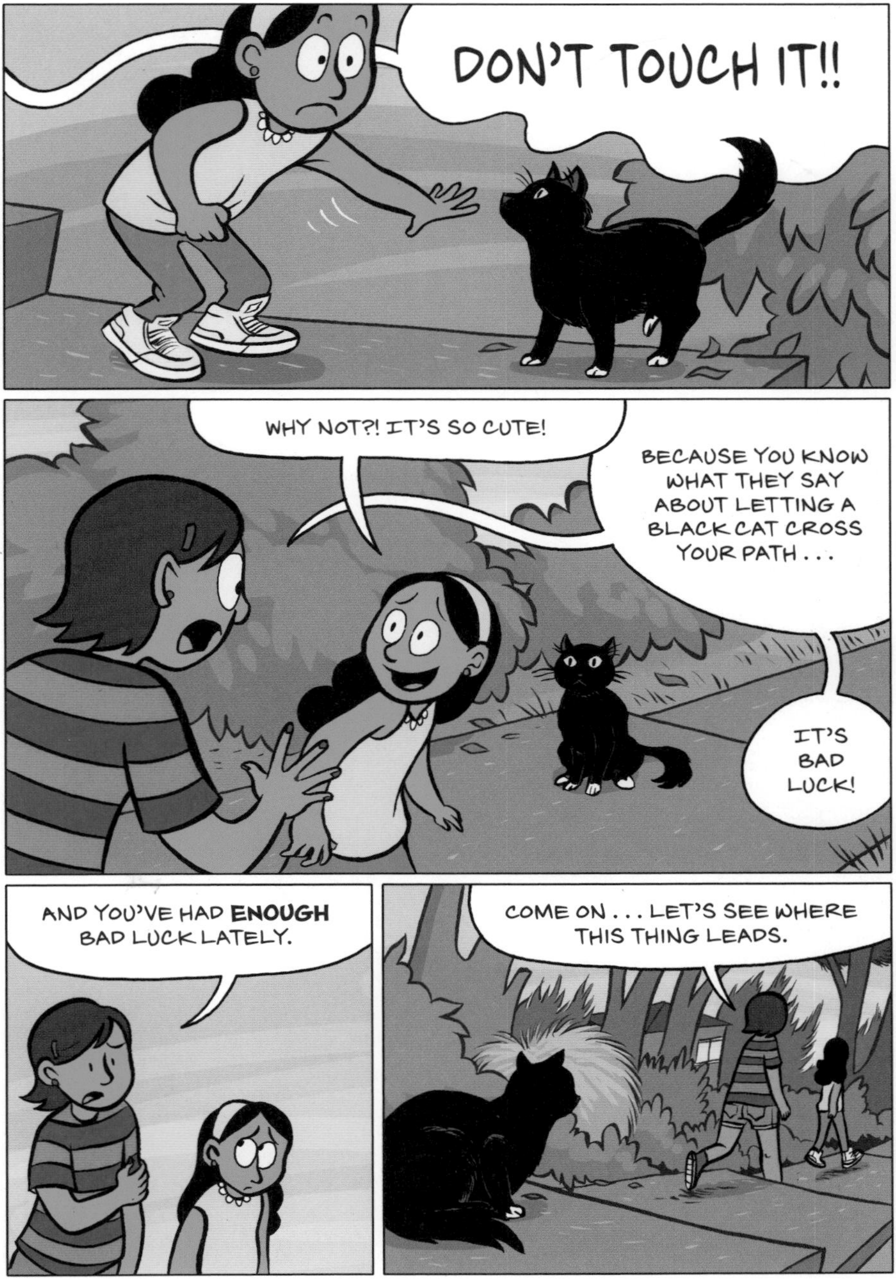
DON'T TOUCH IT!!
WHY NOT?! IT'S SO CUTE!
BECAUSE YOU KNOW WHAT THEY SAY ABOUT LETTING A BLACK CAT CROSS YOUR PATH . . .
IT'S BAD LUCK!
AND YOU'VE HAD **ENOUGH** BAD LUCK LATELY.
COME ON . . . LET'S SEE WHERE THIS THING LEADS.

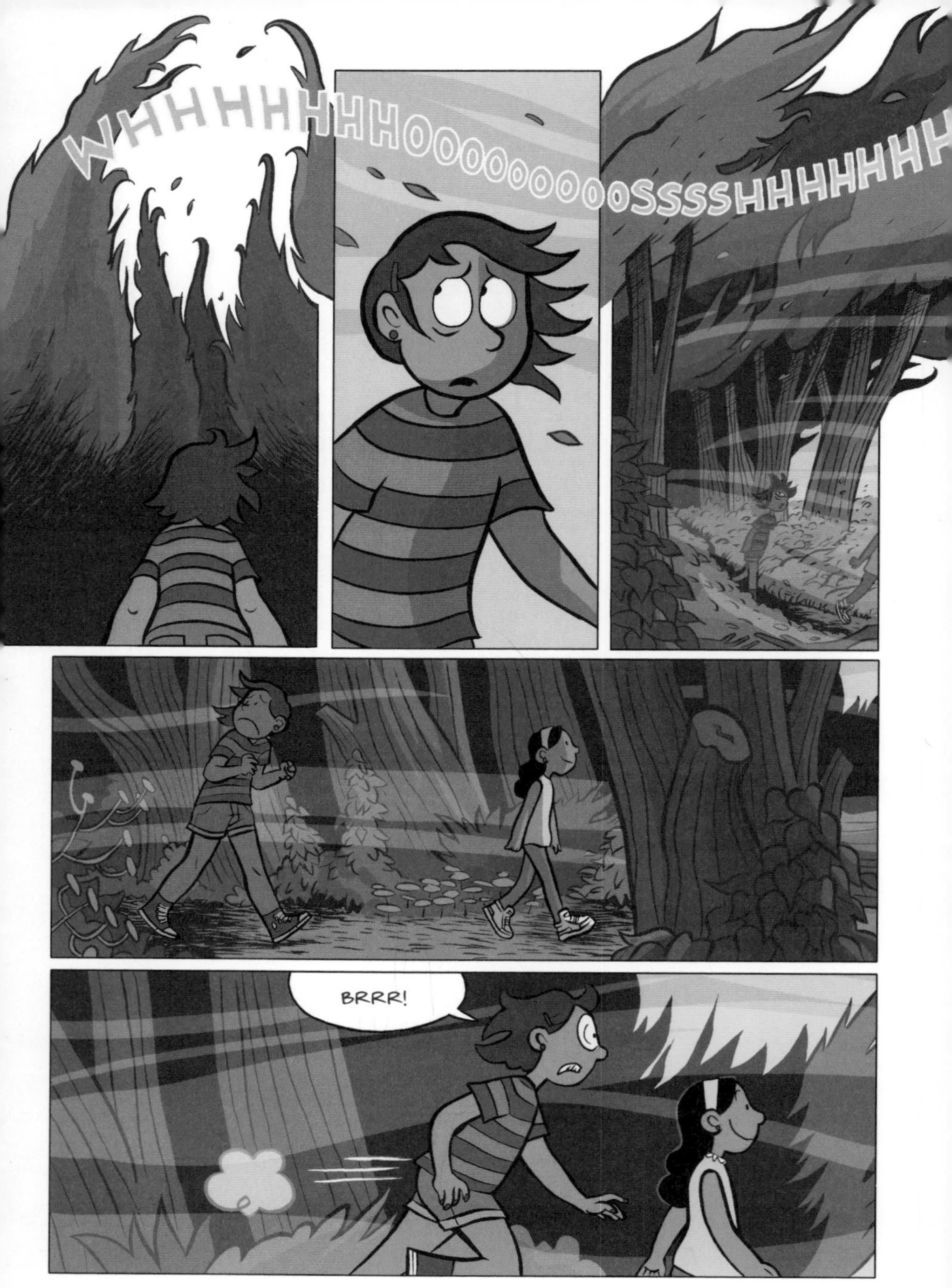
WHHHHHHHOOOOOOOOOOSSSSHHHHHHH
BRRR!

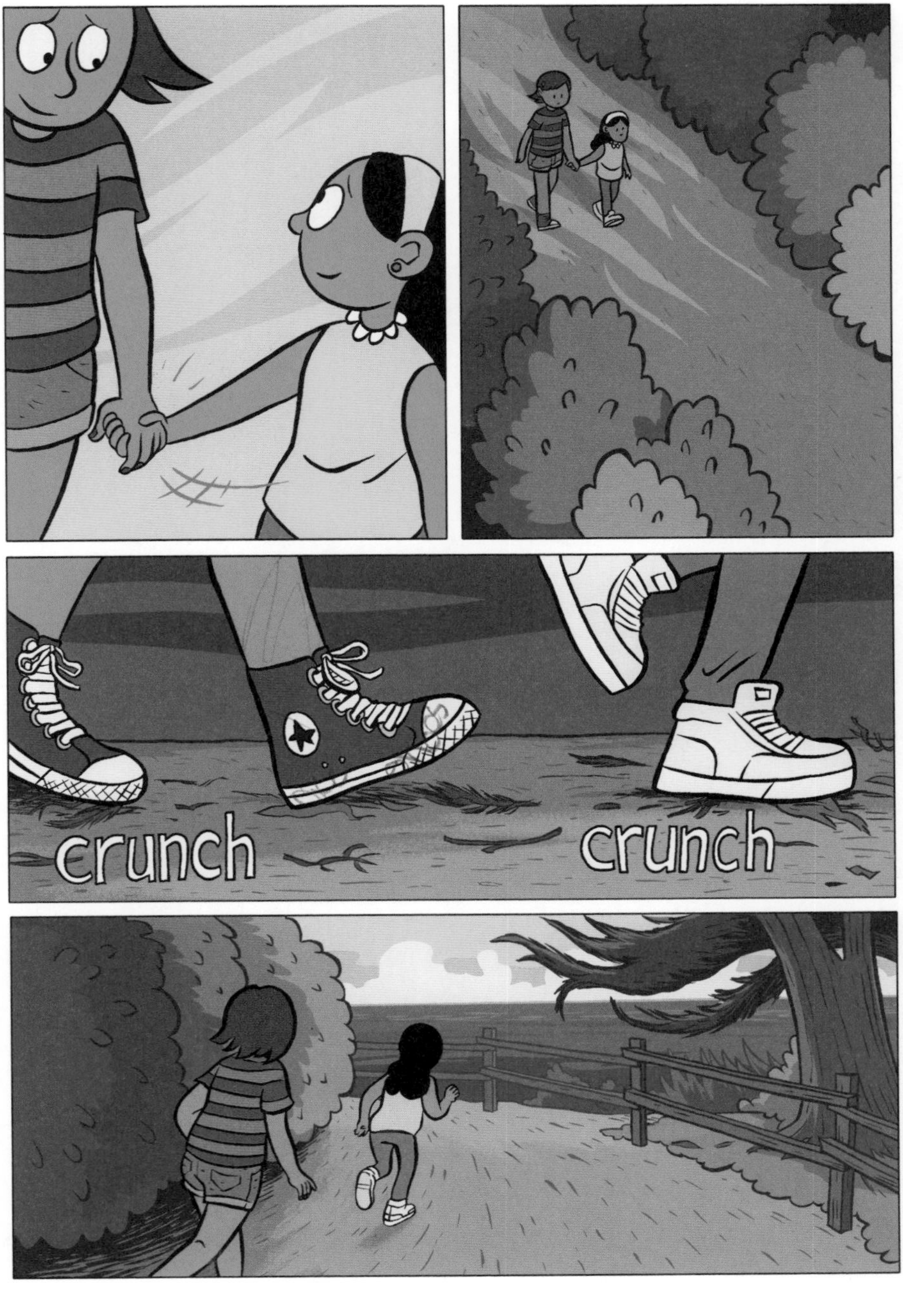
crunch
crunch

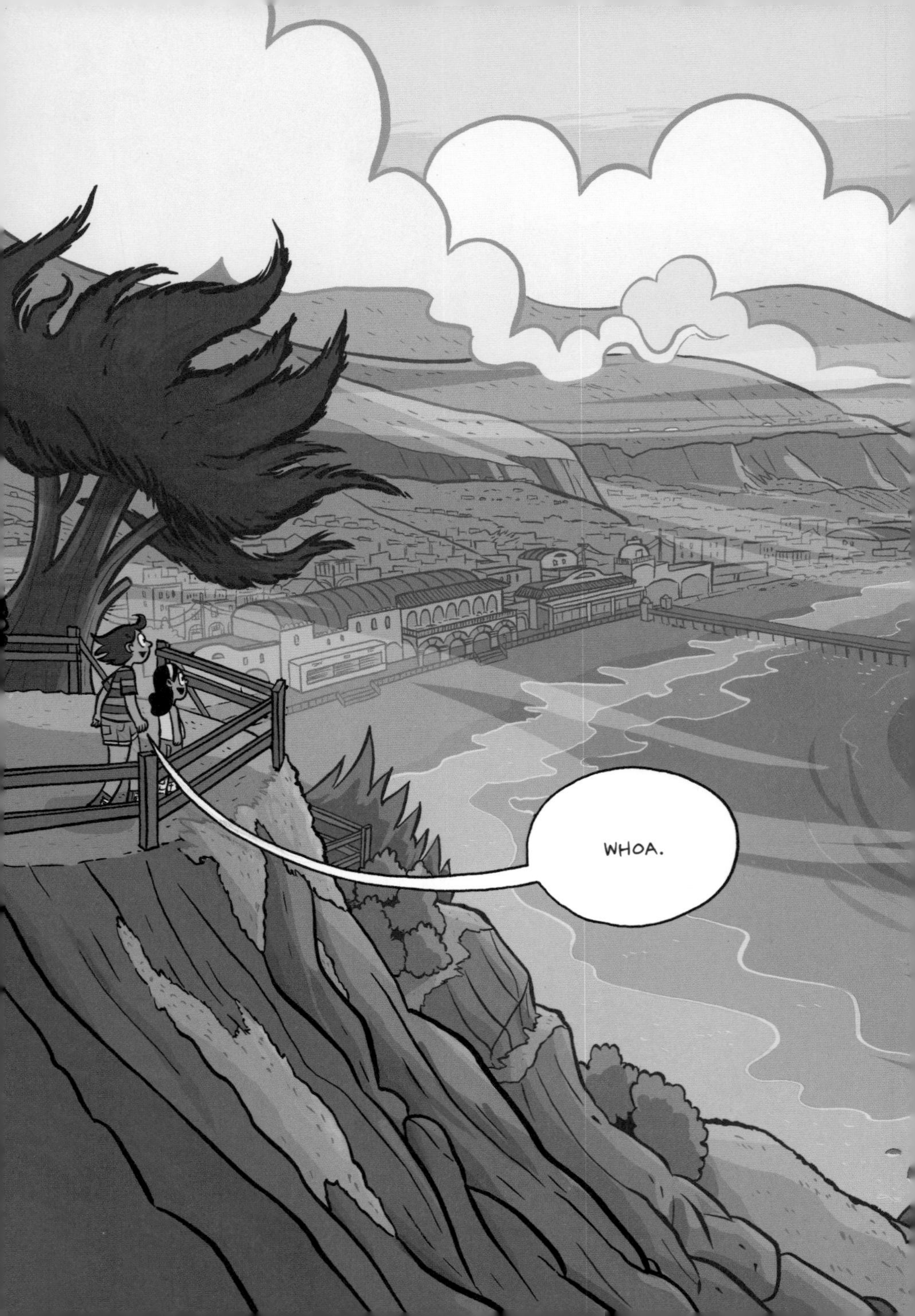
WHOA.

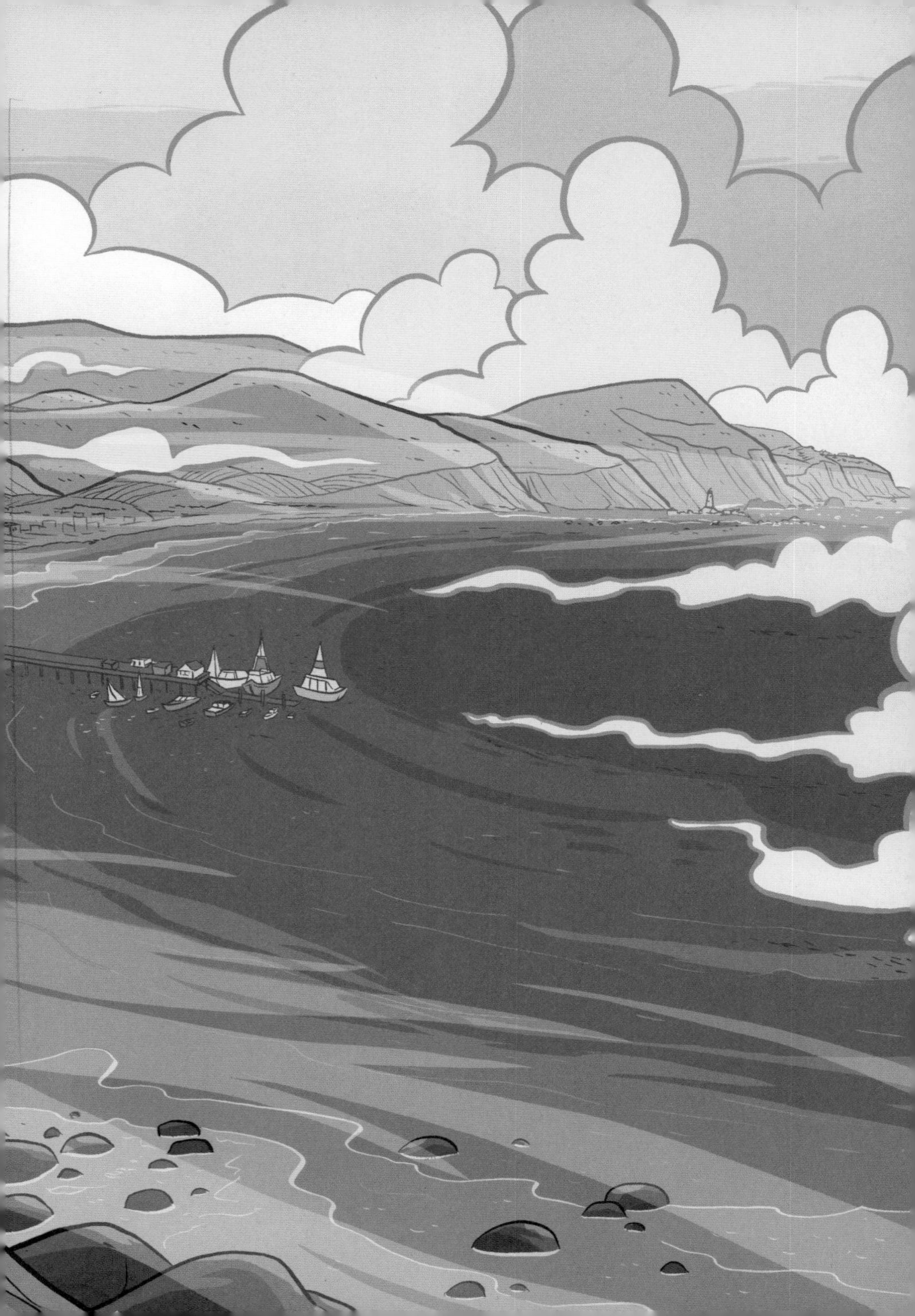

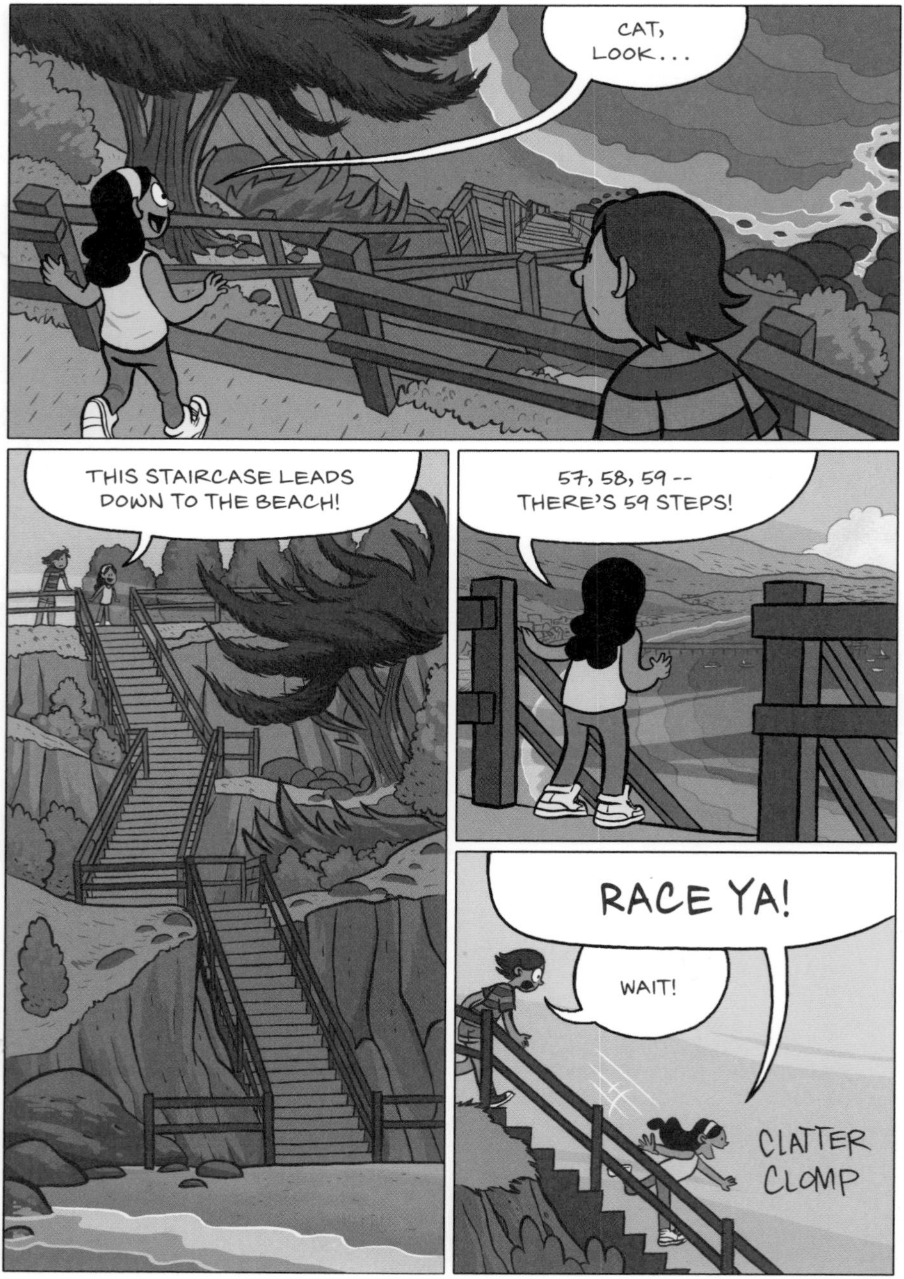
CAT, LOOK...
THIS STAIRCASE LEADS DOWN TO THE BEACH!
57, 58, 59 -- THERE'S 59 STEPS!
RACE YA!
WAIT!
CLATTER CLOMP

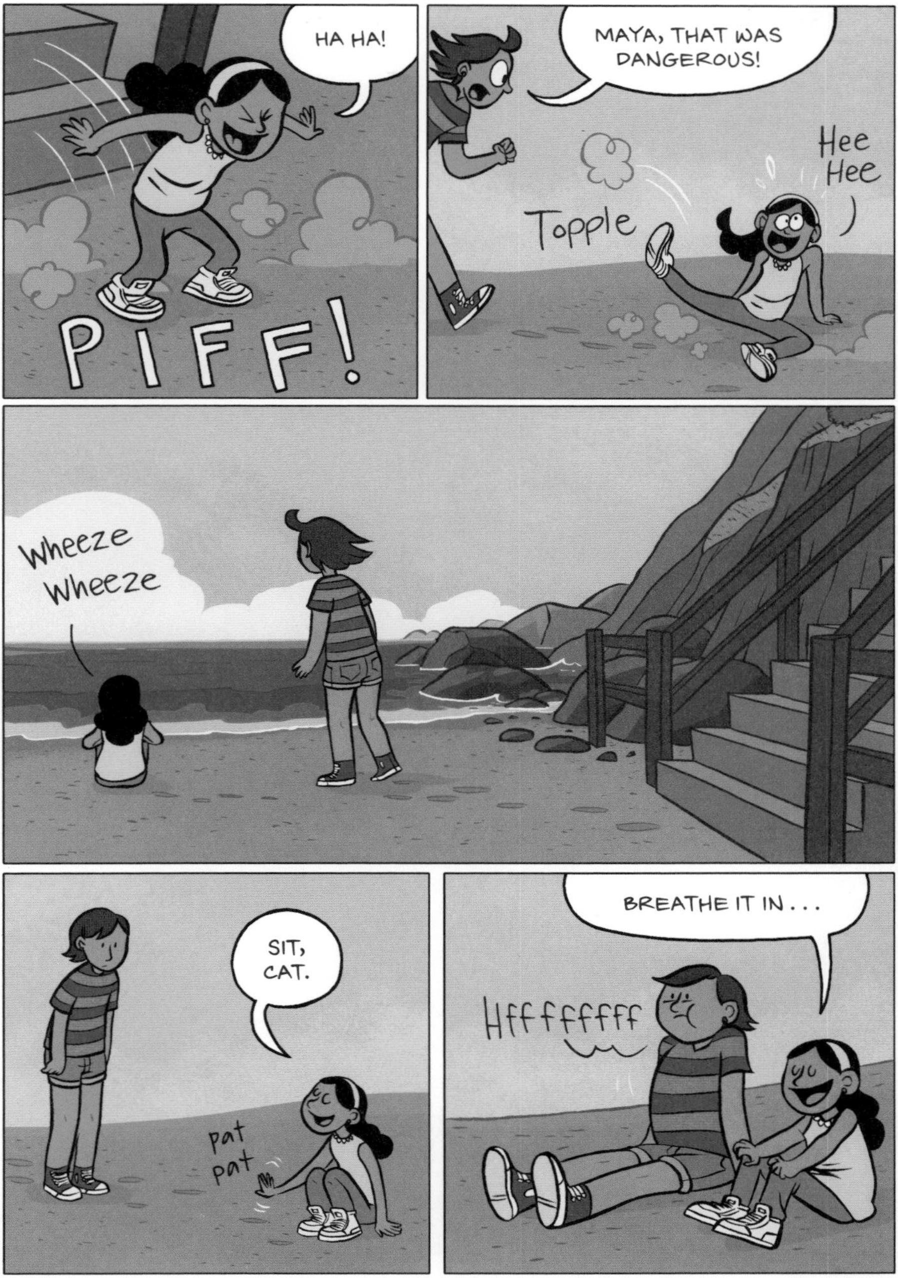
HA HA!
PIFF!
MAYA, THAT WAS DANGEROUS!
Topple
Hee Hee
Wheeze Wheeze
SIT, CAT.
pat pat
BREATHE IT IN . . .
Hffffffff

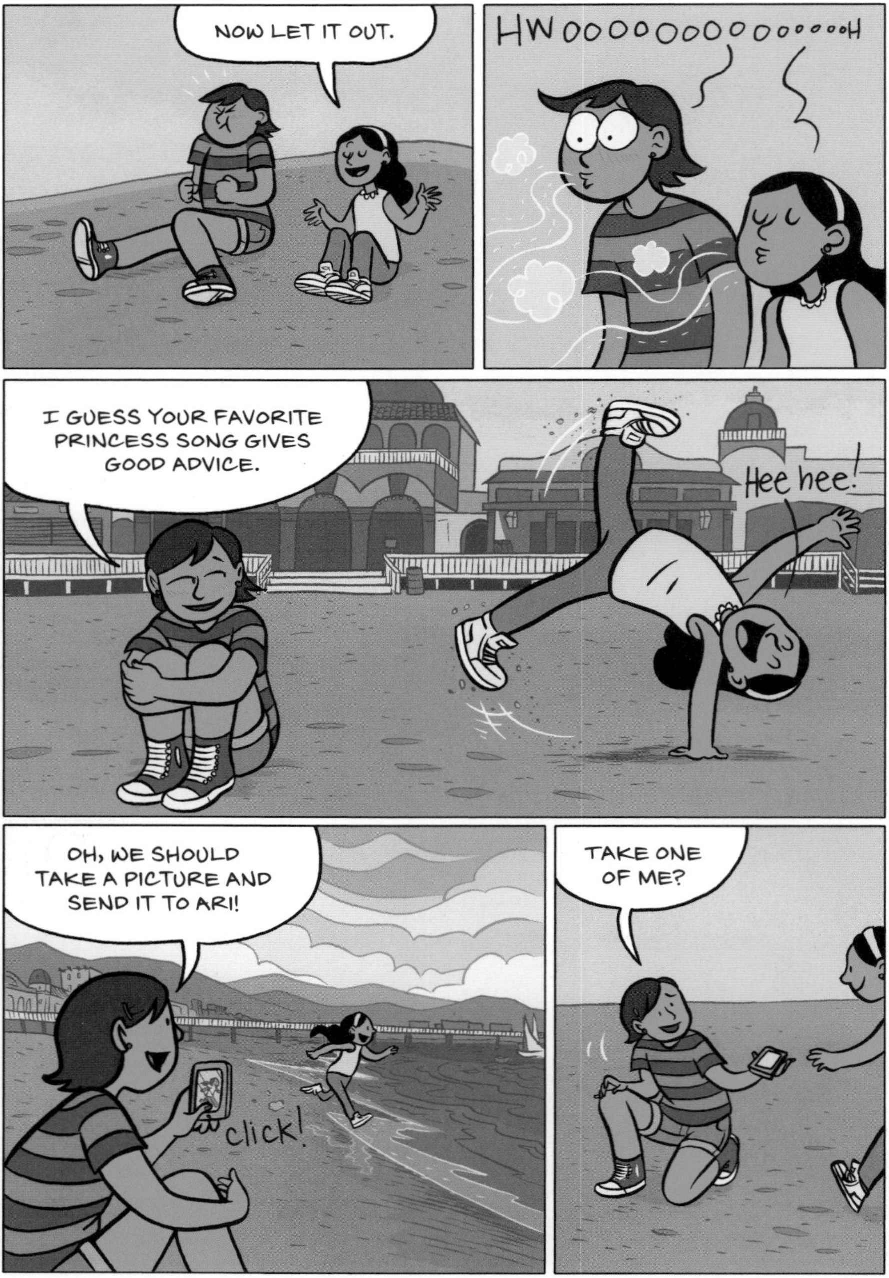
NOW LET IT OUT.
HWOOOOOOOOOOOOOOH
I GUESS YOUR FAVORITE PRINCESS SONG GIVES GOOD ADVICE.
Hee hee!
OH, WE SHOULD TAKE A PICTURE AND SEND IT TO ARI!
click!
TAKE ONE OF ME?

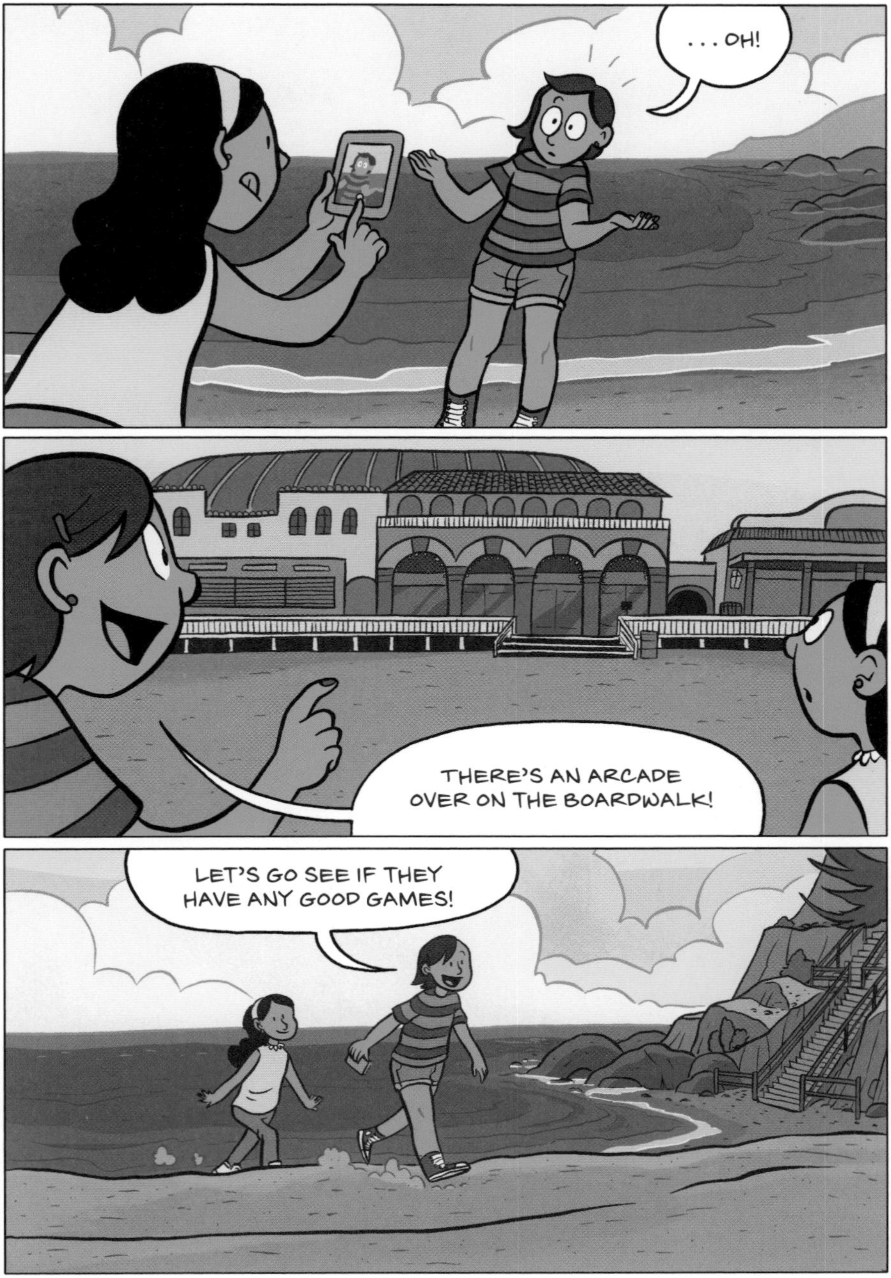
. . . OH!
THERE'S AN ARCADE OVER ON THE BOARDWALK!
LET'S GO SEE IF THEY HAVE ANY GOOD GAMES!

NEVER MIND. IT LOOKS CREEPY AND DARK IN THERE, ANYWAY.

LET'S JUST GO HO--

MAYA?

MAYA?

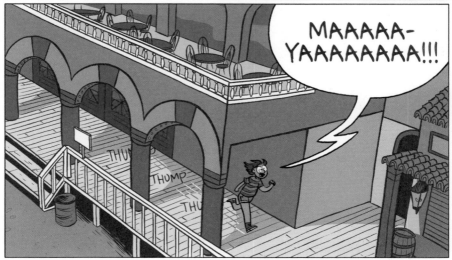

MAAAAA-YAAAAAAAA!!!

THUMP

THUMP

THU

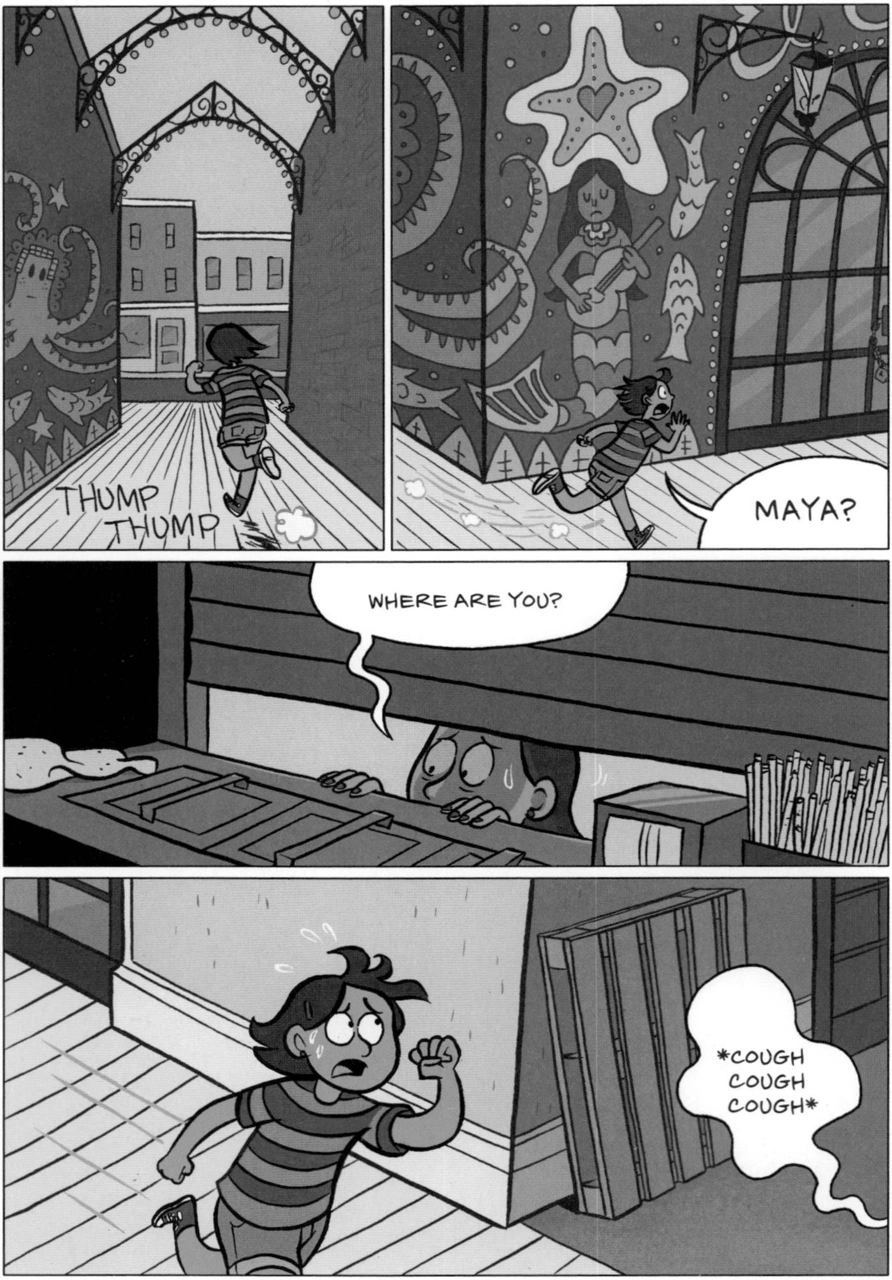
THUMP
THUMP
MAYA?
WHERE ARE YOU?
*COUGH
COUGH
COUGH*

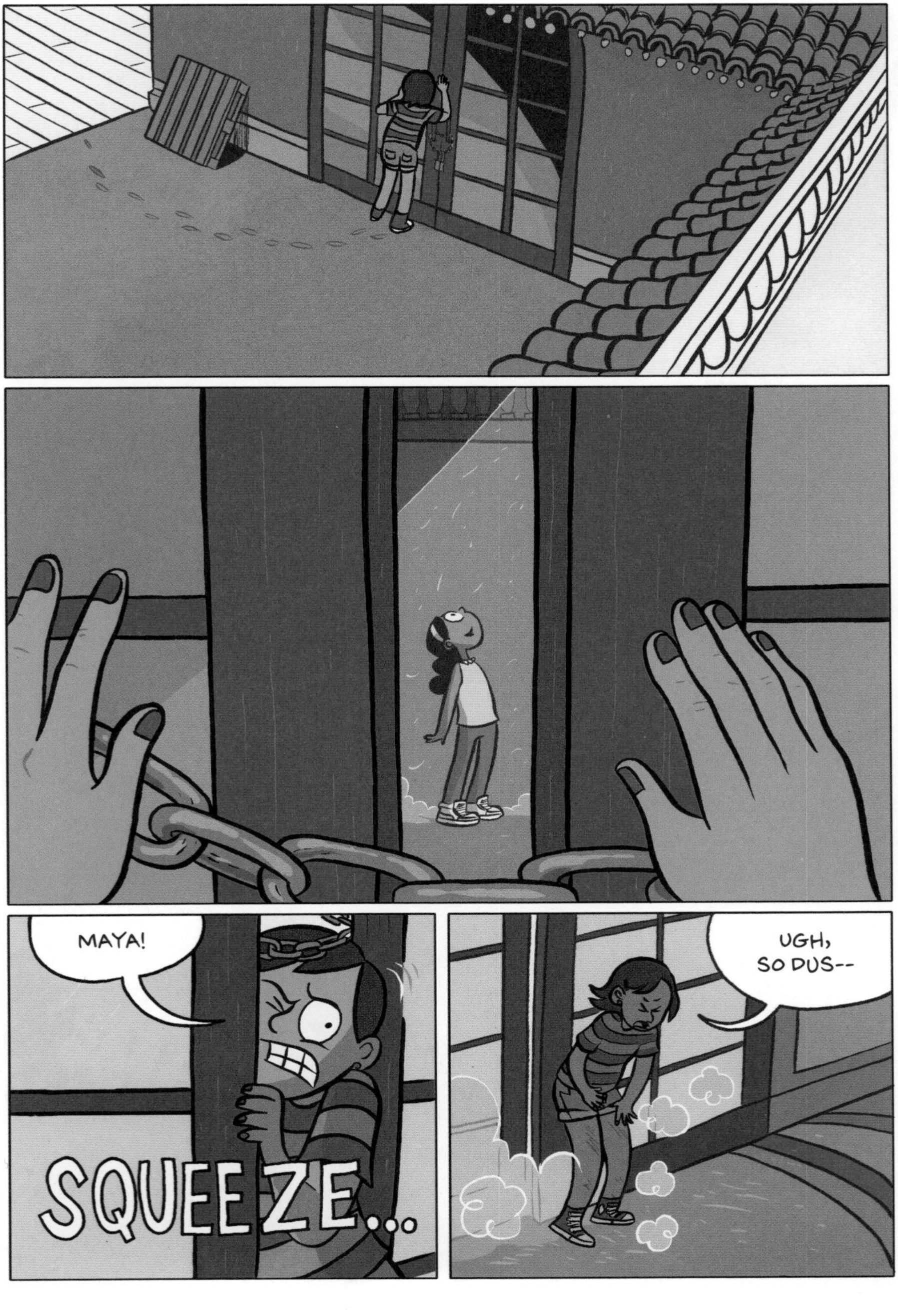
MAYA!
SQUEEZE...
UGH, SO DUS--

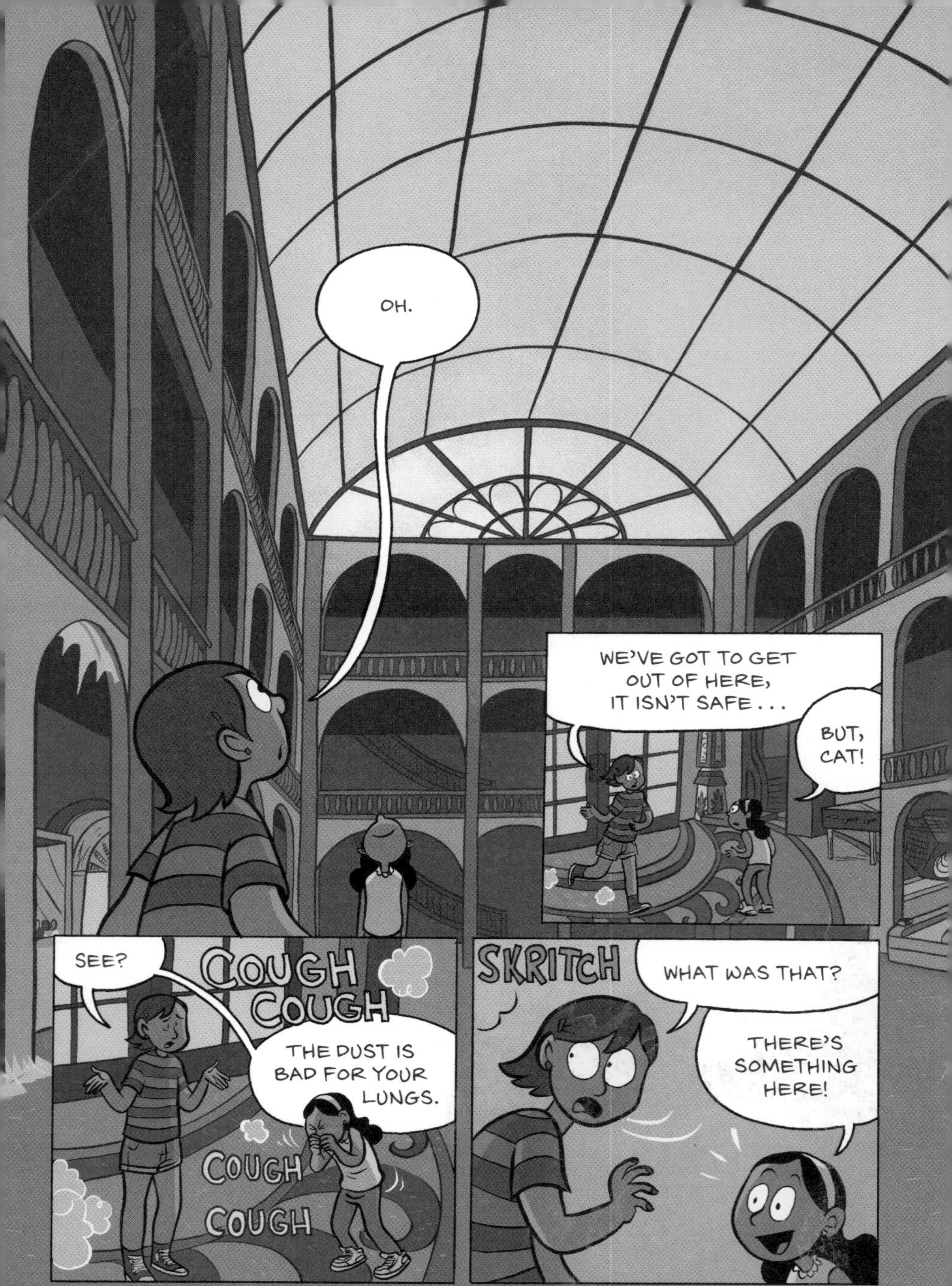

OH.
WE'VE GOT TO GET OUT OF HERE, IT ISN'T SAFE . . .
BUT, CAT!
SEE?
COUGH COUGH
THE DUST IS BAD FOR YOUR LUNGS.
COUGH
COUGH
SKRITCH
WHAT WAS THAT?
THERE'S SOMETHING HERE!

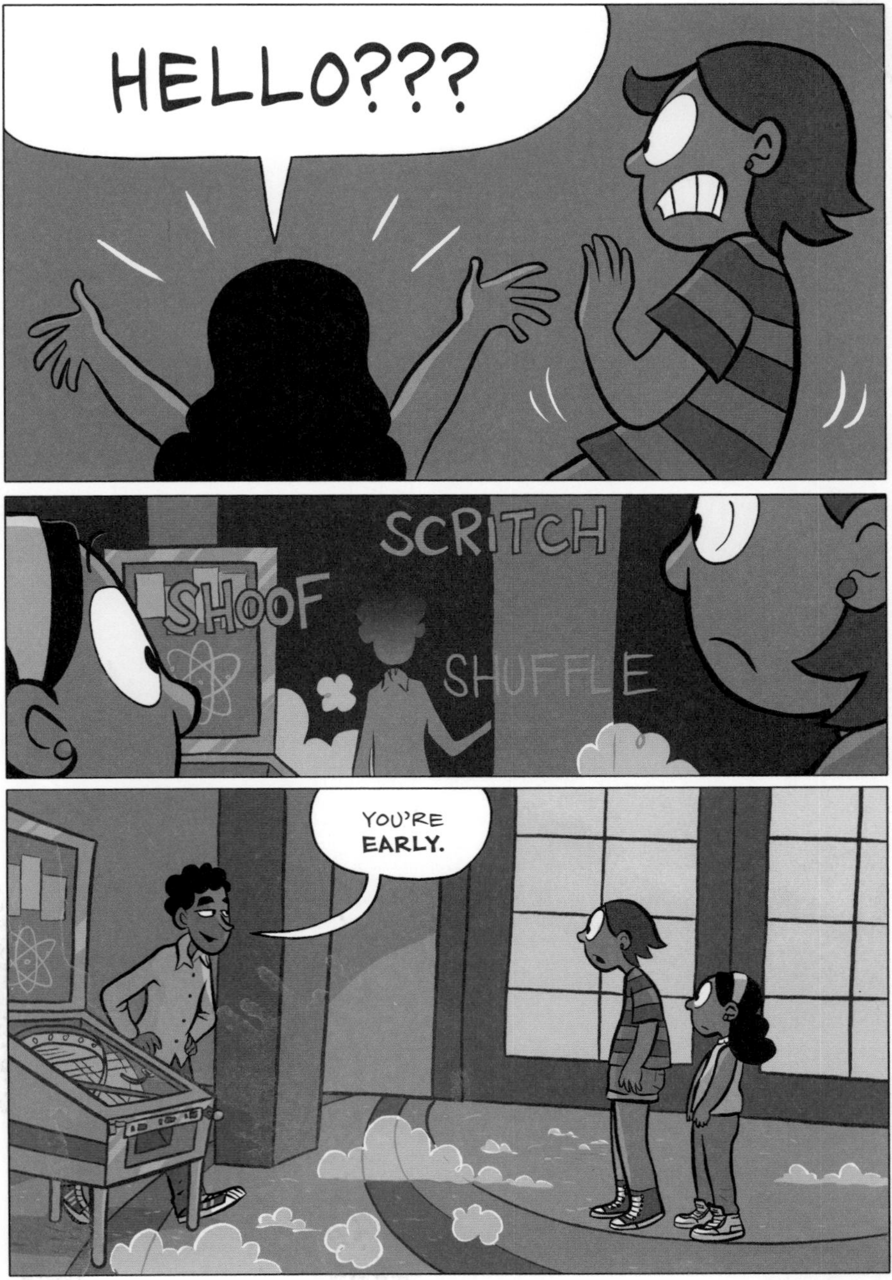
HELLO???
SCRITCH
SHOOF
SHUFFLE
YOU'RE EARLY.

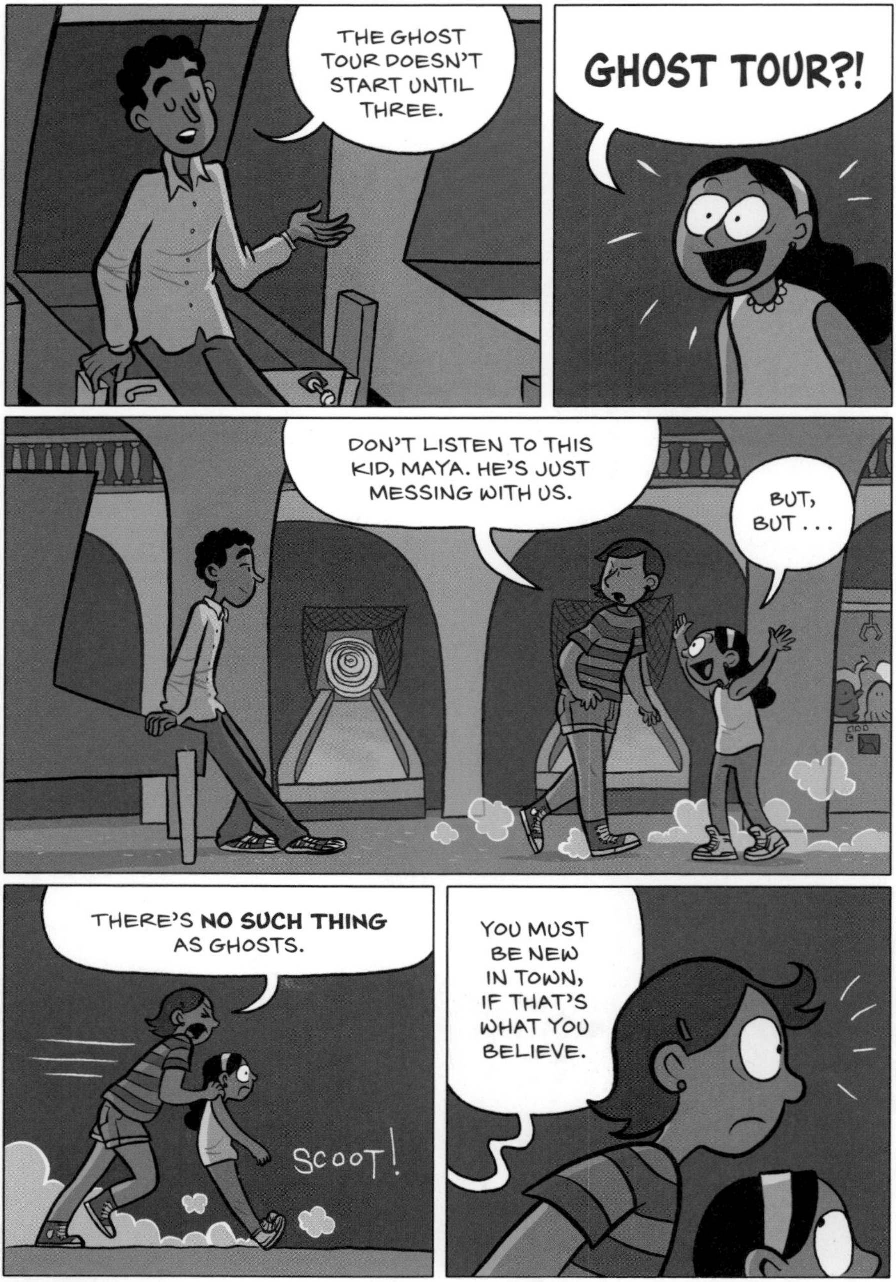
THE GHOST TOUR DOESN'T START UNTIL THREE.
GHOST TOUR?!
DON'T LISTEN TO THIS KID, MAYA. HE'S JUST MESSING WITH US.
BUT, BUT . . .
THERE'S **NO SUCH THING** AS GHOSTS.
SCOOT!
YOU MUST BE NEW IN TOWN, IF THAT'S WHAT YOU BELIEVE.

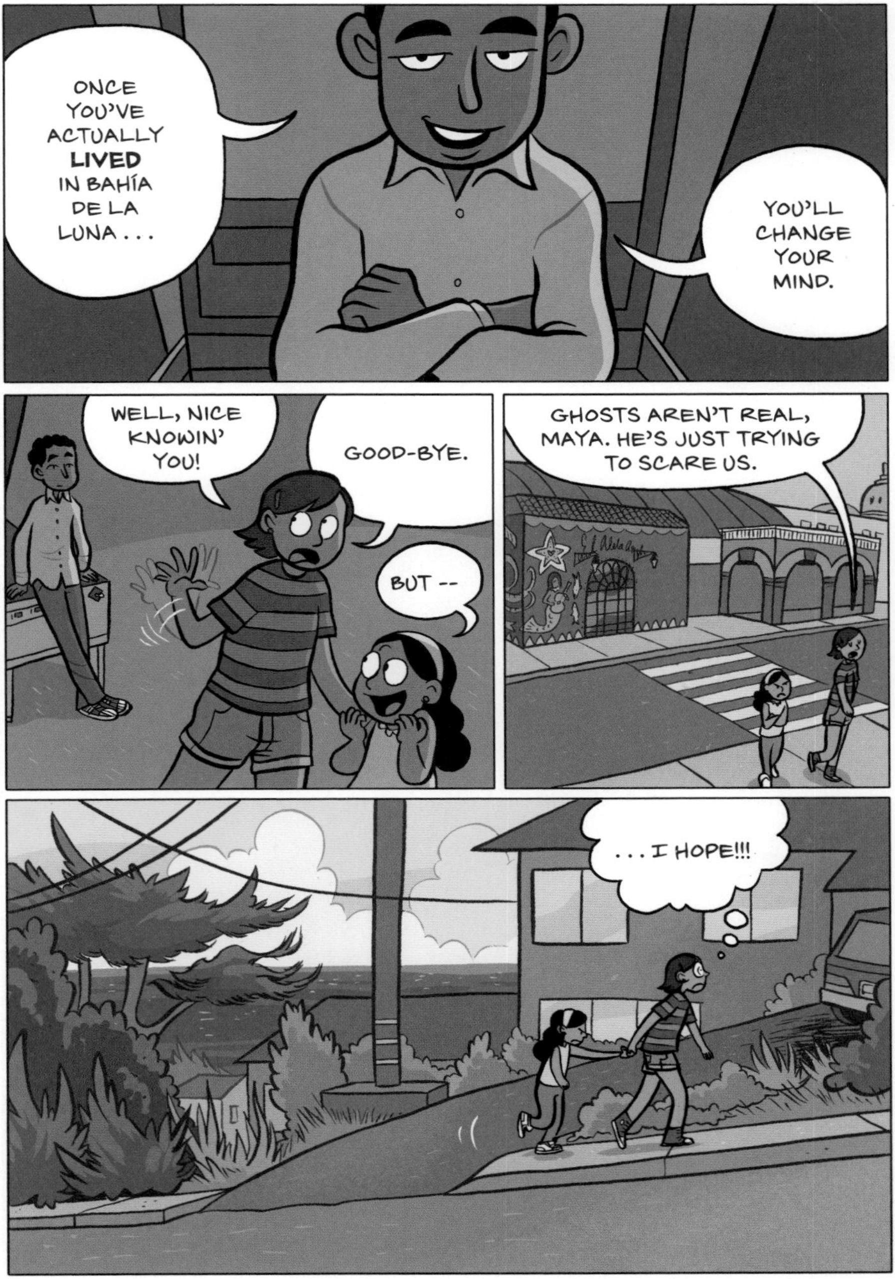
ONCE YOU'VE ACTUALLY LIVED IN BAHÍA DE LA LUNA . . .
YOU'LL CHANGE YOUR MIND.
WELL, NICE KNOWIN' YOU!
GOOD-BYE.
BUT --
GHOSTS AREN'T REAL, MAYA. HE'S JUST TRYING TO SCARE US.
. . . I HOPE!!!

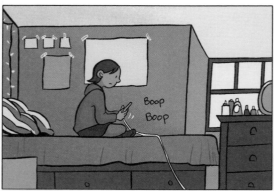

Boop
Boop

freezing!

its sunny
back home ☹

did u get new
clothes 4 school

maya and i met this
weird boy yesterd

QWE
ASD

CATRINA!
LET'S GO!

WHERE ARE WE
GOING, AGAIN?

I TOLD YOU -- THE
NEIGHBORS INVITED US
OVER FOR DINNER.

AWW,
DO I
HAFTA
GO?

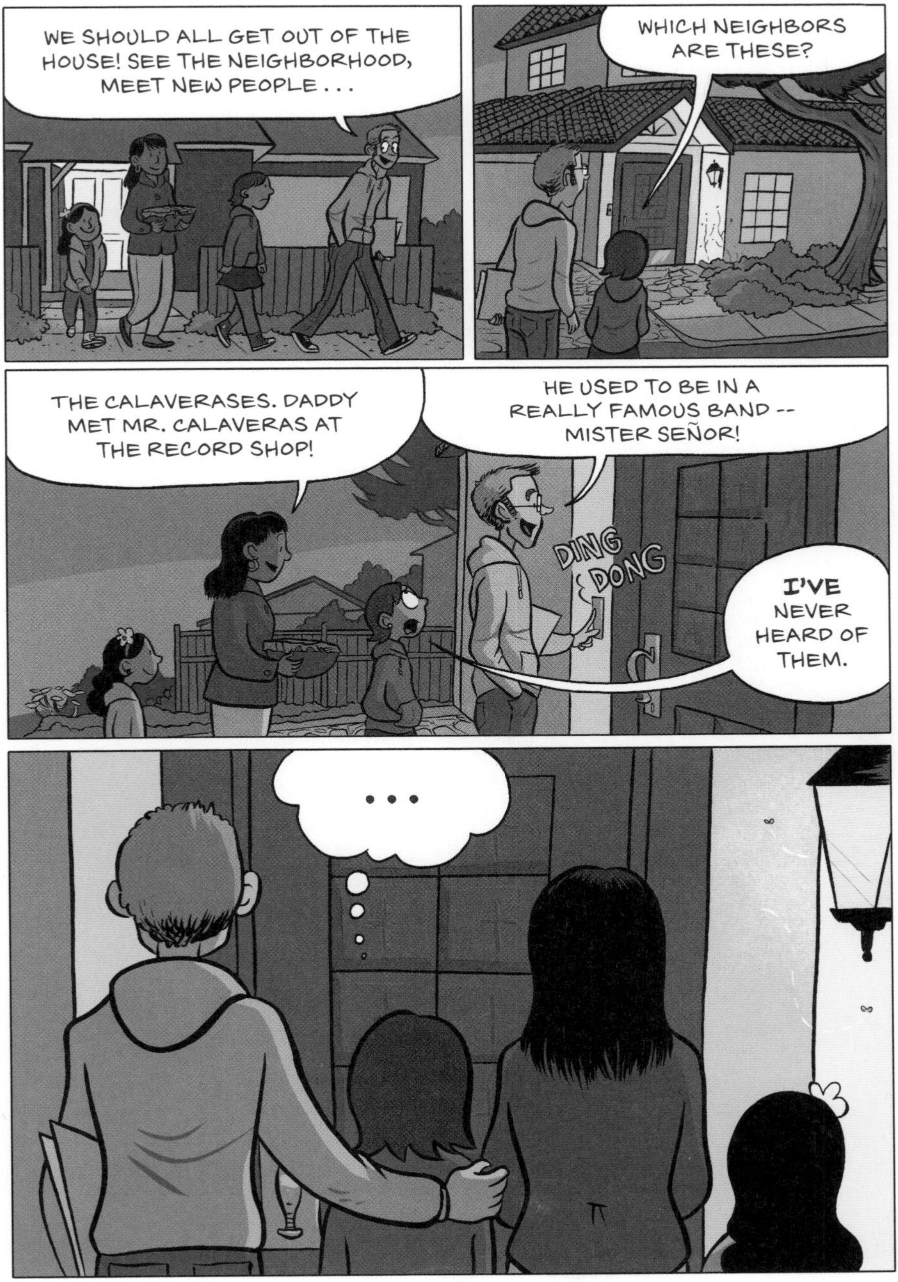

WE SHOULD ALL GET OUT OF THE HOUSE! SEE THE NEIGHBORHOOD, MEET NEW PEOPLE . . .
WHICH NEIGHBORS ARE THESE?
THE CALAVERASES. DADDY MET MR. CALAVERAS AT THE RECORD SHOP!
HE USED TO BE IN A REALLY FAMOUS BAND -- MISTER SEÑOR!
DING DONG
I'VE NEVER HEARD OF THEM.
. . .

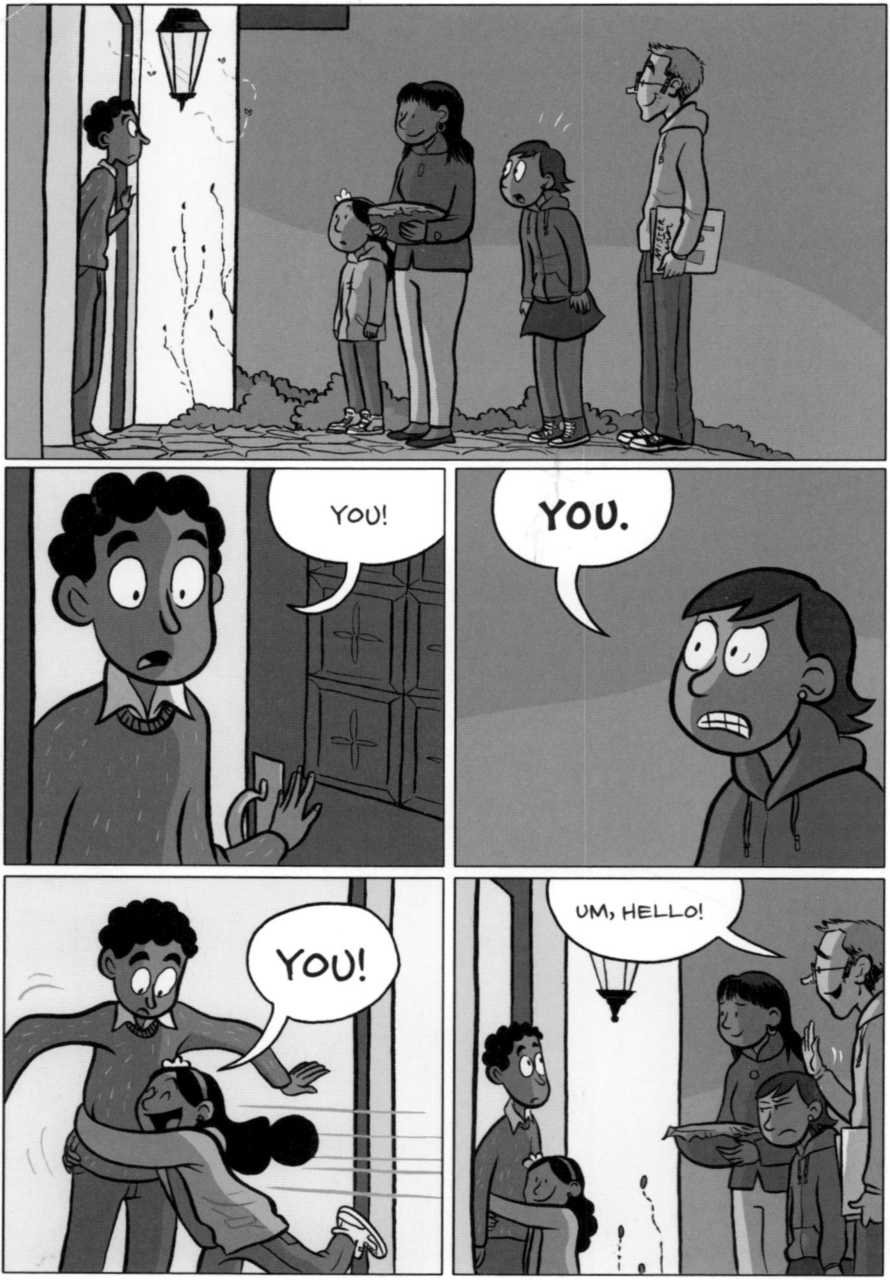
MISTER
YOU!
YOU.
YOU!
UM, HELLO!

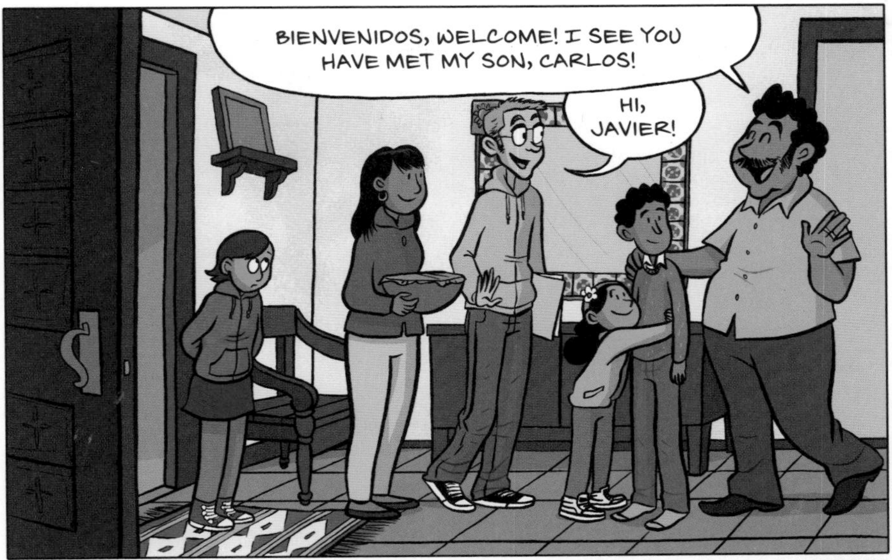
BIENVENIDOS, WELCOME! I SEE YOU HAVE MET MY SON, CARLOS!
HI, JAVIER!

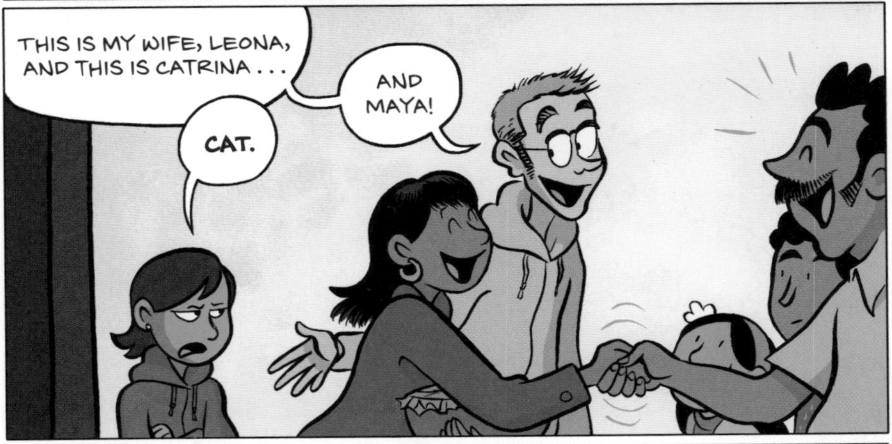
THIS IS MY WIFE, LEONA, AND THIS IS CATRINA . . .
CAT.
AND MAYA!

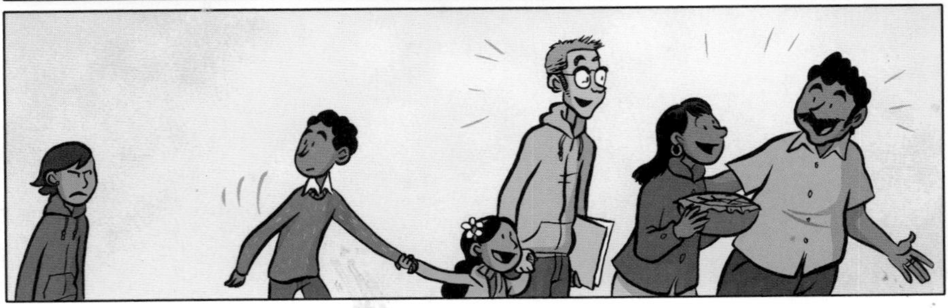

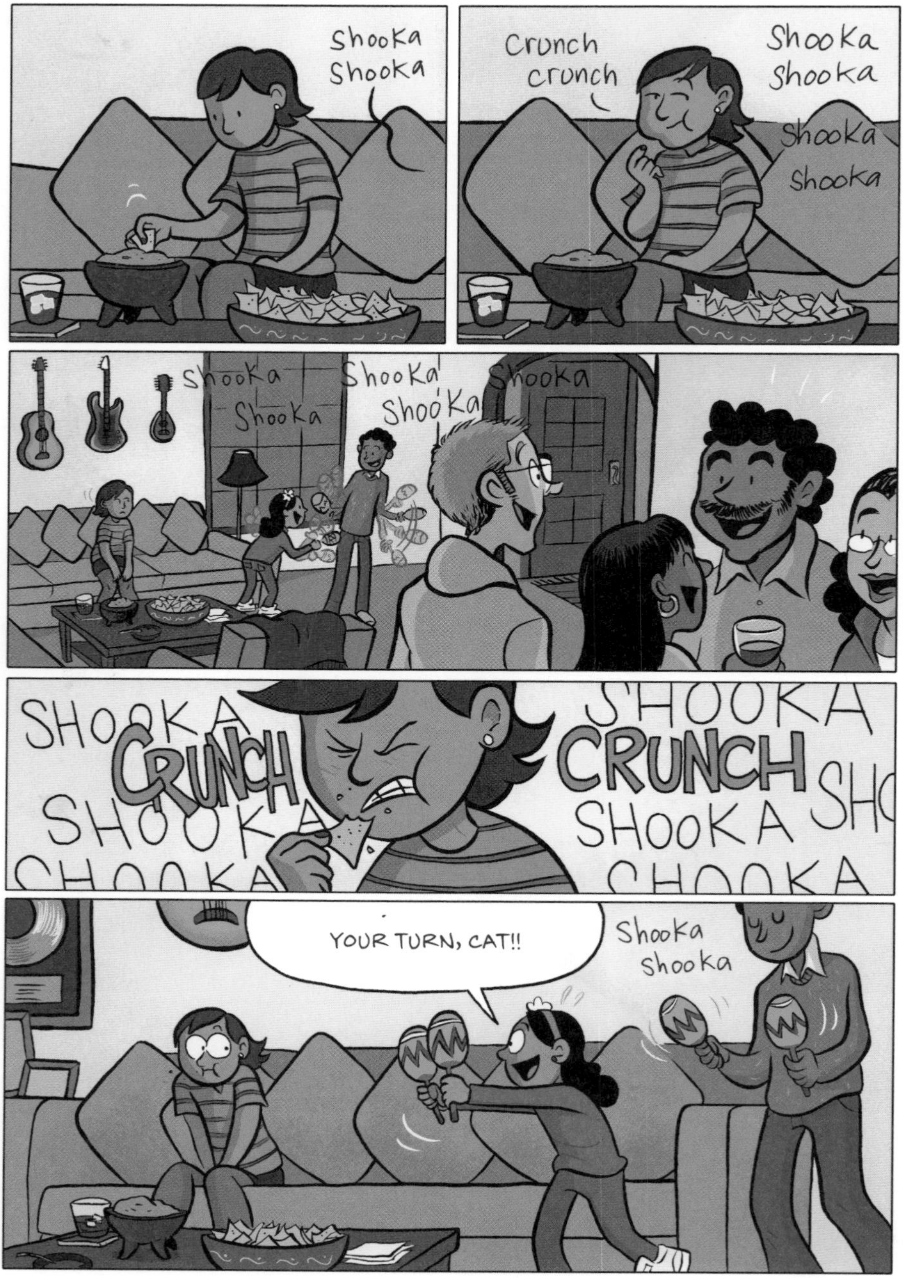
Shooka
Shooka
Crunch
crunch
Shooka
shooka
Shooka
shooka
Shooka
Shooka
Shooka
Shooka
Shooka
SHOOKA
CRUNCH
SHOOKA
SHOOKA
CRUNCH
SHOOKA
YOUR TURN, CAT!!
Shooka
shooka

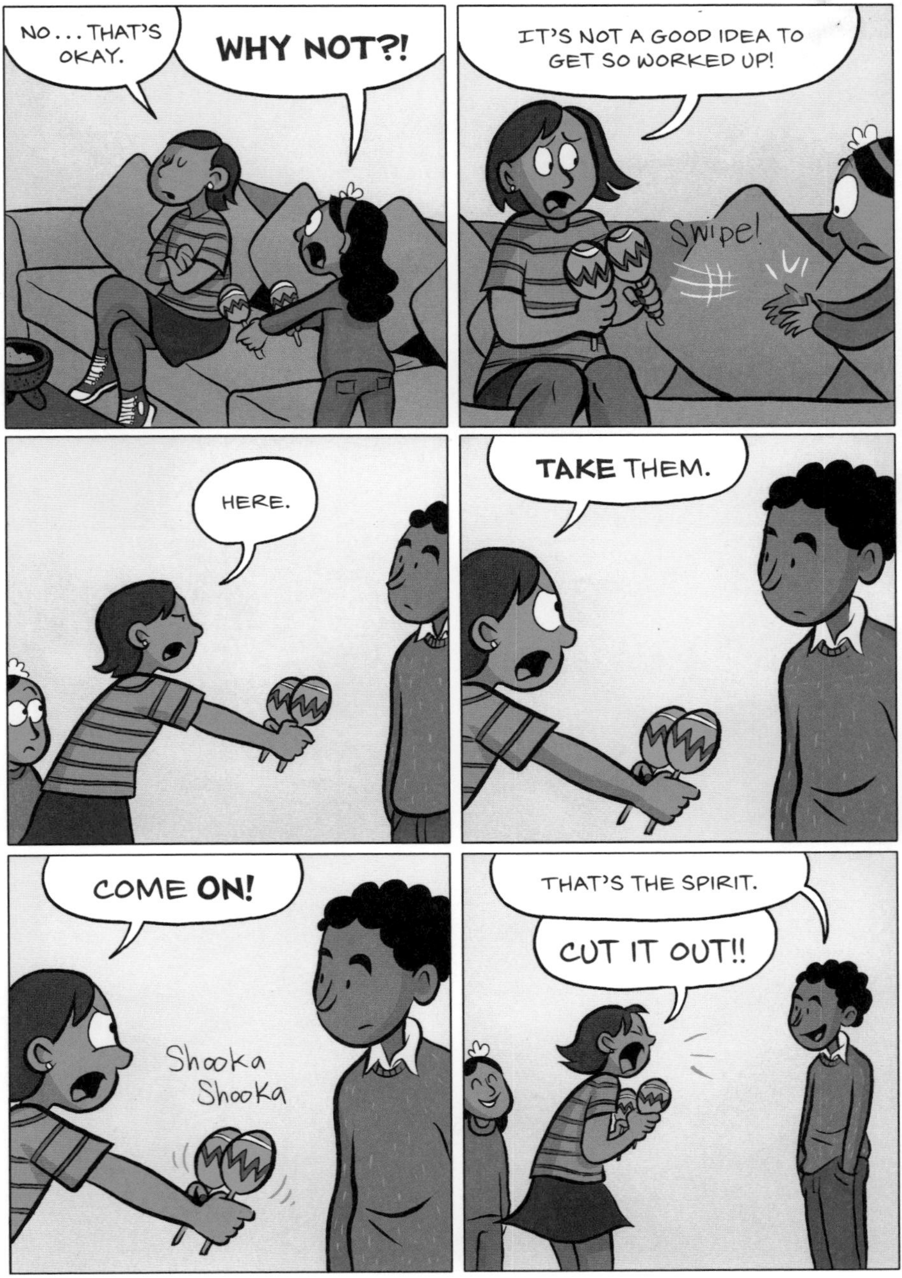
NO . . . THAT'S OKAY.
WHY NOT?!
IT'S NOT A GOOD IDEA TO GET SO WORKED UP!
Swipe!
HERE.
TAKE THEM.
COME ON!
Shooka Shooka
THAT'S THE SPIRIT.
CUT IT OUT!!

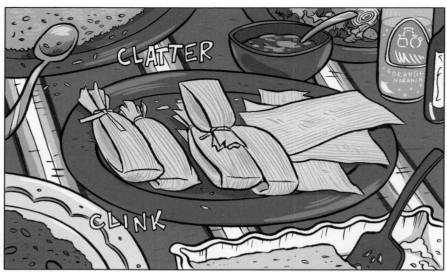

CLATTER

CLINK

This is delicious.

Yum.

Mmm.

OH **WOW.**

IT'S GOOD, RIGHT? MY MOM MAKES THE BEST TAMALES IN TOWN.

...THEY'RE OKAY, I GUESS.

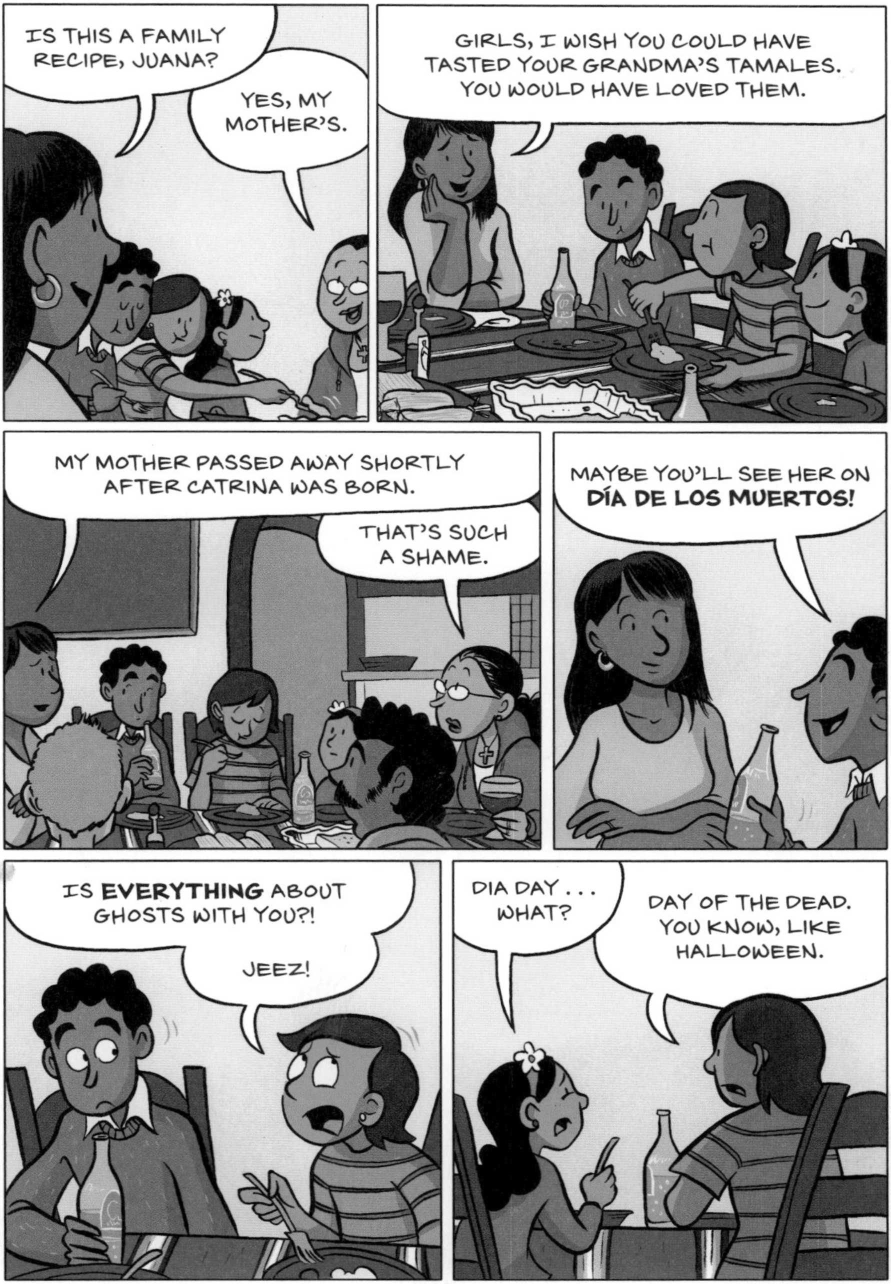
IS THIS A FAMILY RECIPE, JUANA?
YES, MY MOTHER'S.
GIRLS, I WISH YOU COULD HAVE TASTED YOUR GRANDMA'S TAMALES. YOU WOULD HAVE LOVED THEM.
MY MOTHER PASSED AWAY SHORTLY AFTER CATRINA WAS BORN.
THAT'S SUCH A SHAME.
MAYBE YOU'LL SEE HER ON **DÍA DE LOS MUERTOS!**
IS **EVERYTHING** ABOUT GHOSTS WITH YOU?!
JEEZ!
DIA DAY . . . WHAT?
DAY OF THE DEAD. YOU KNOW, LIKE HALLOWEEN.

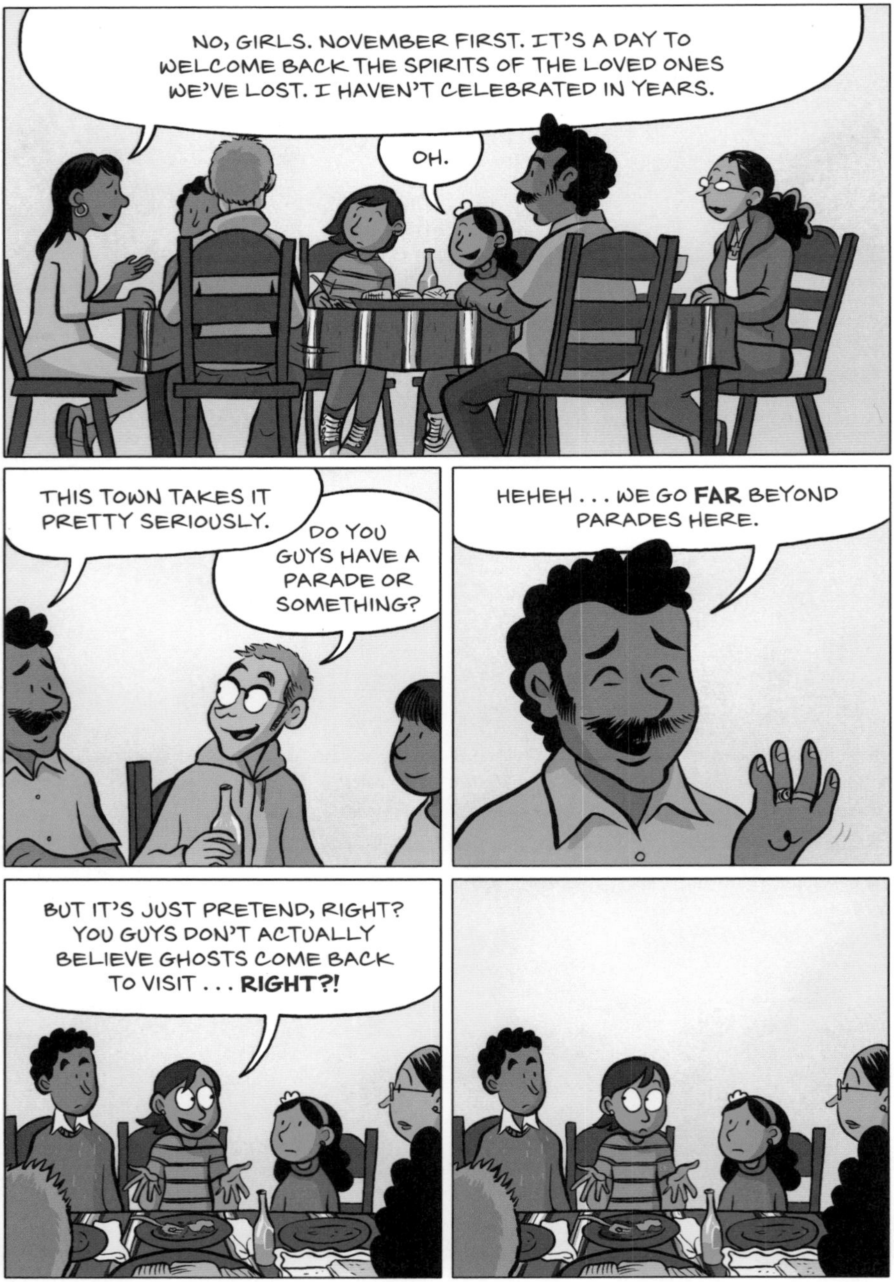
NO, GIRLS. NOVEMBER FIRST. IT'S A DAY TO WELCOME BACK THE SPIRITS OF THE LOVED ONES WE'VE LOST. I HAVEN'T CELEBRATED IN YEARS.
OH.
THIS TOWN TAKES IT PRETTY SERIOUSLY.
DO YOU GUYS HAVE A PARADE OR SOMETHING?
HEHEH . . . WE GO **FAR** BEYOND PARADES HERE.
BUT IT'S JUST PRETEND, RIGHT? YOU GUYS DON'T ACTUALLY BELIEVE GHOSTS COME BACK TO VISIT . . . **RIGHT?!**

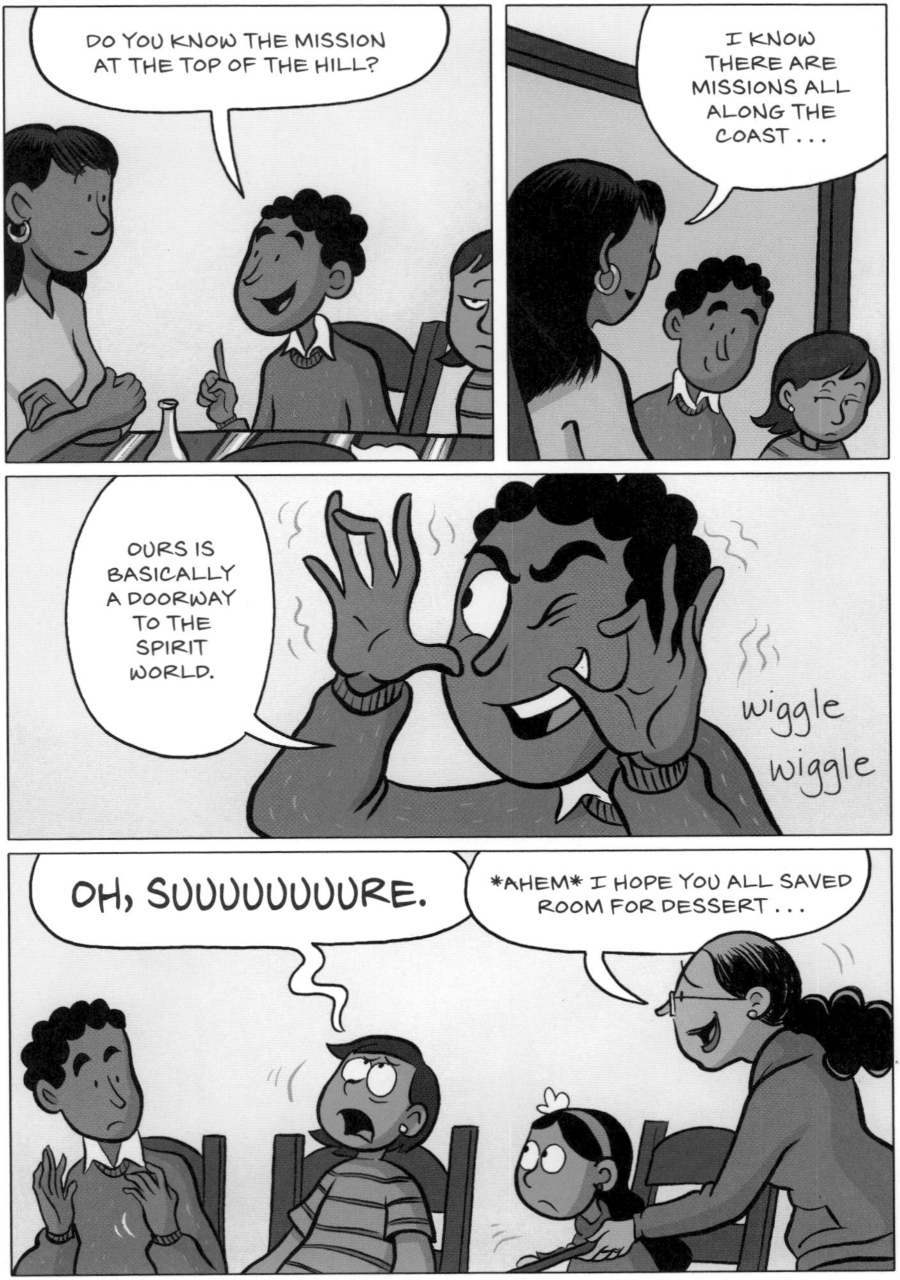
DO YOU KNOW THE MISSION AT THE TOP OF THE HILL?
I KNOW THERE ARE MISSIONS ALL ALONG THE COAST . . .
OURS IS BASICALLY A DOORWAY TO THE SPIRIT WORLD.
wiggle wiggle
OH, SUUUUUUUURE.
AHEM I HOPE YOU ALL SAVED ROOM FOR DESSERT . . .

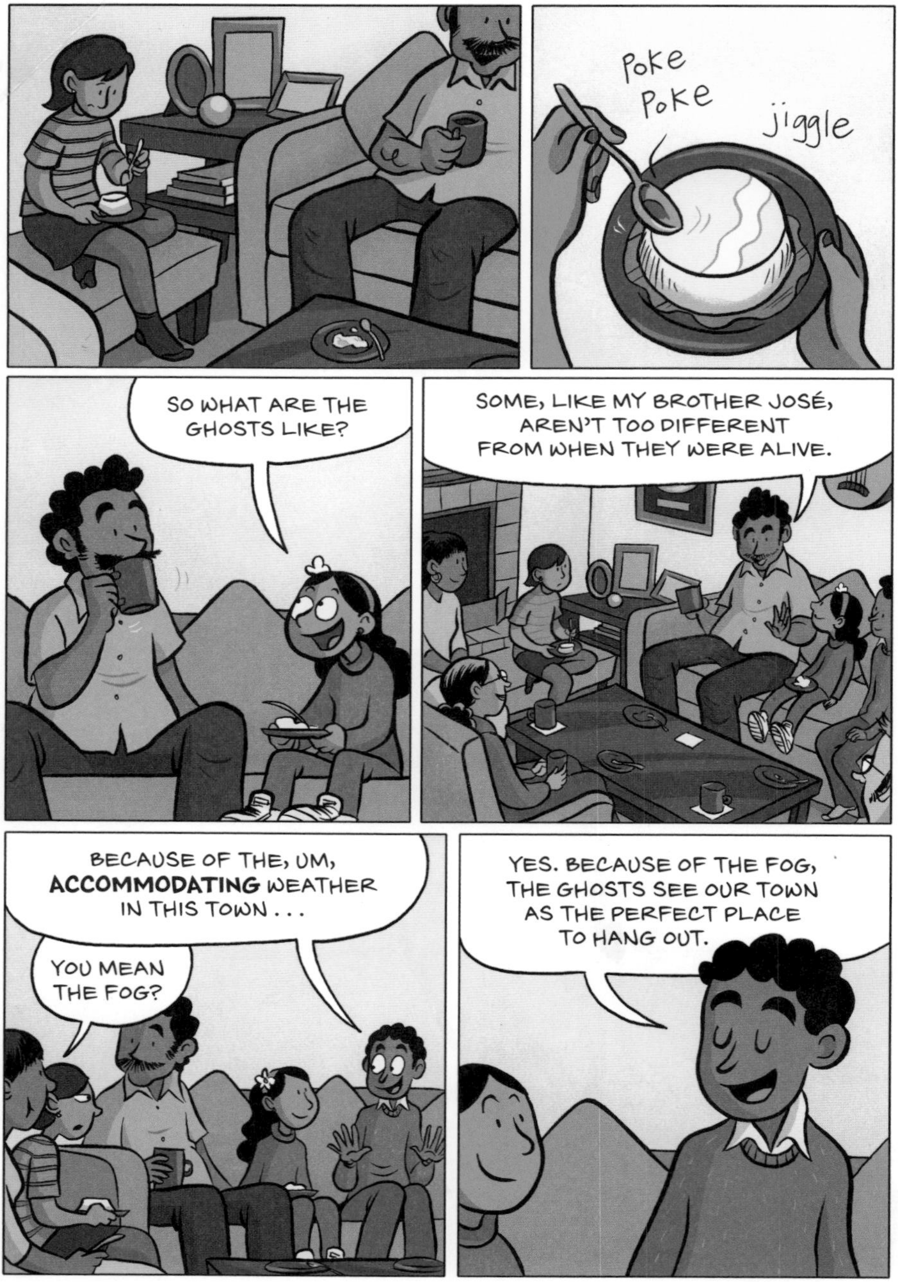
Poke
Poke
jiggle
SO WHAT ARE THE GHOSTS LIKE?
SOME, LIKE MY BROTHER JOSÉ, AREN'T TOO DIFFERENT FROM WHEN THEY WERE ALIVE.
BECAUSE OF THE, UM, **ACCOMMODATING** WEATHER IN THIS TOWN . . .
YOU MEAN THE FOG?
YES. BECAUSE OF THE FOG, THE GHOSTS SEE OUR TOWN AS THE PERFECT PLACE TO HANG OUT.

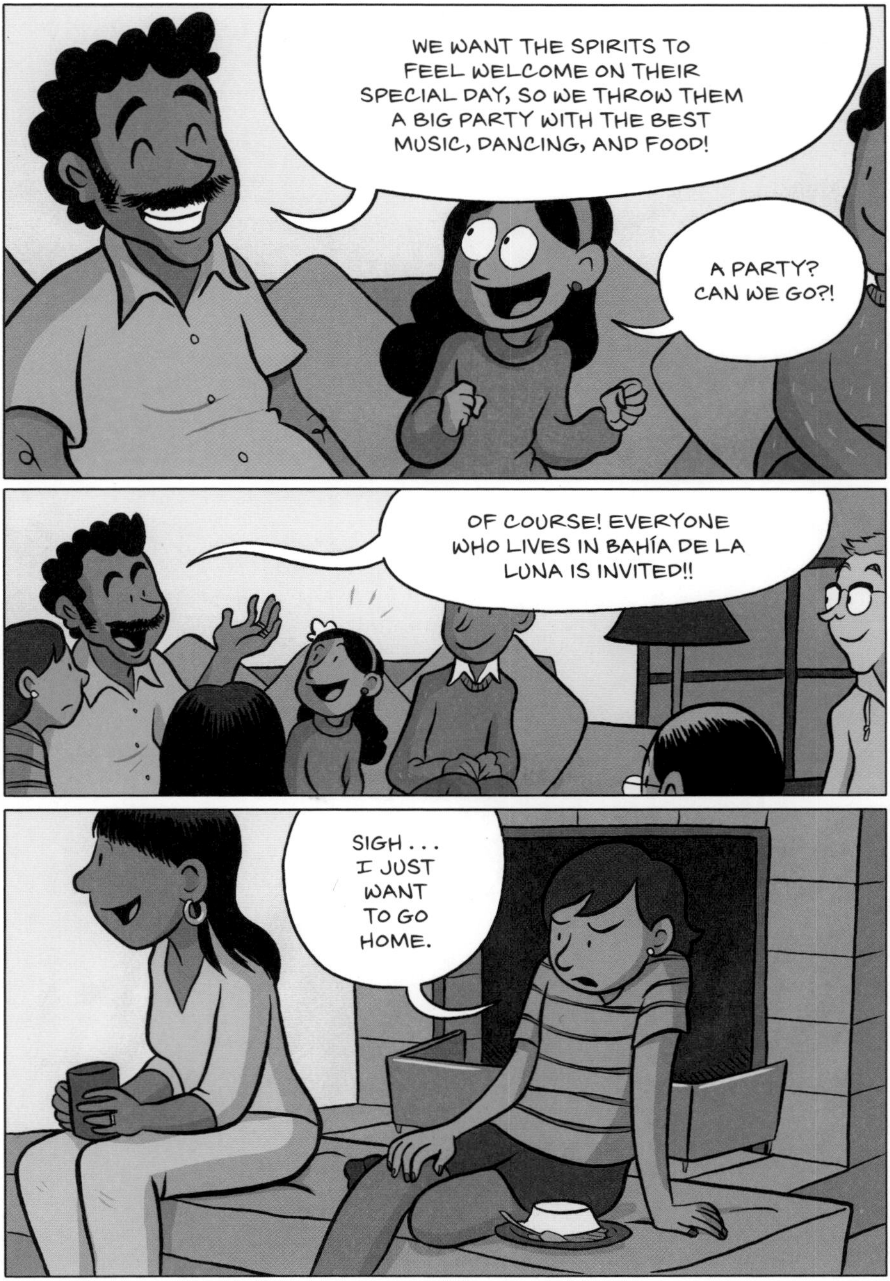
WE WANT THE SPIRITS TO FEEL WELCOME ON THEIR SPECIAL DAY, SO WE THROW THEM A BIG PARTY WITH THE BEST MUSIC, DANCING, AND FOOD!
A PARTY? CAN WE GO?!
OF COURSE! EVERYONE WHO LIVES IN BAHÍA DE LA LUNA IS INVITED!!
SIGH . . . I JUST WANT TO GO HOME.

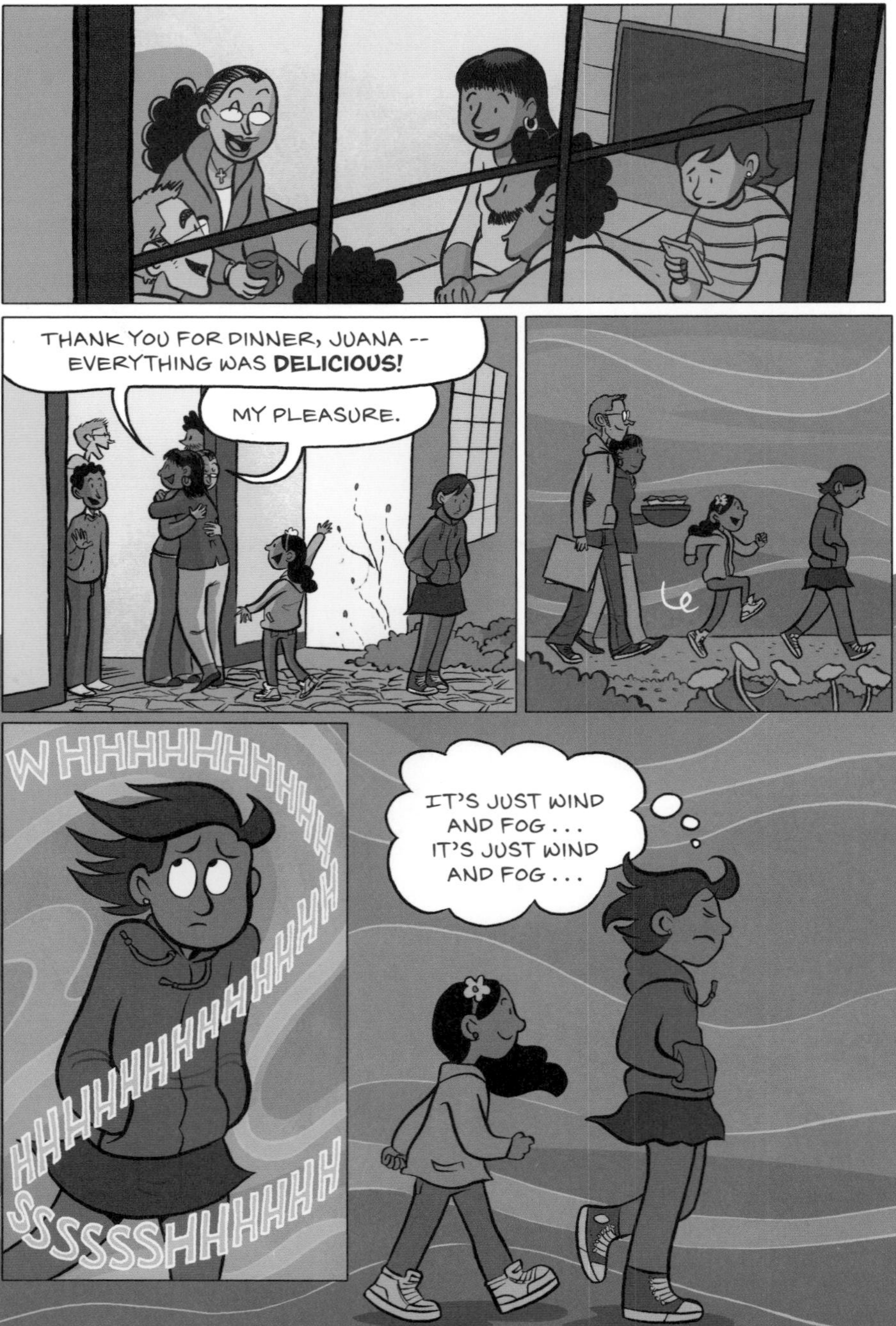
THANK YOU FOR DINNER, JUANA -- EVERYTHING WAS DELICIOUS!
MY PLEASURE.
WHHHHHHHHHHHHHHHHHHHHHHHHHHHHHHHHHHHHH SSSSSHHHHHHH
IT'S JUST WIND AND FOG . . . IT'S JUST WIND AND FOG . . .

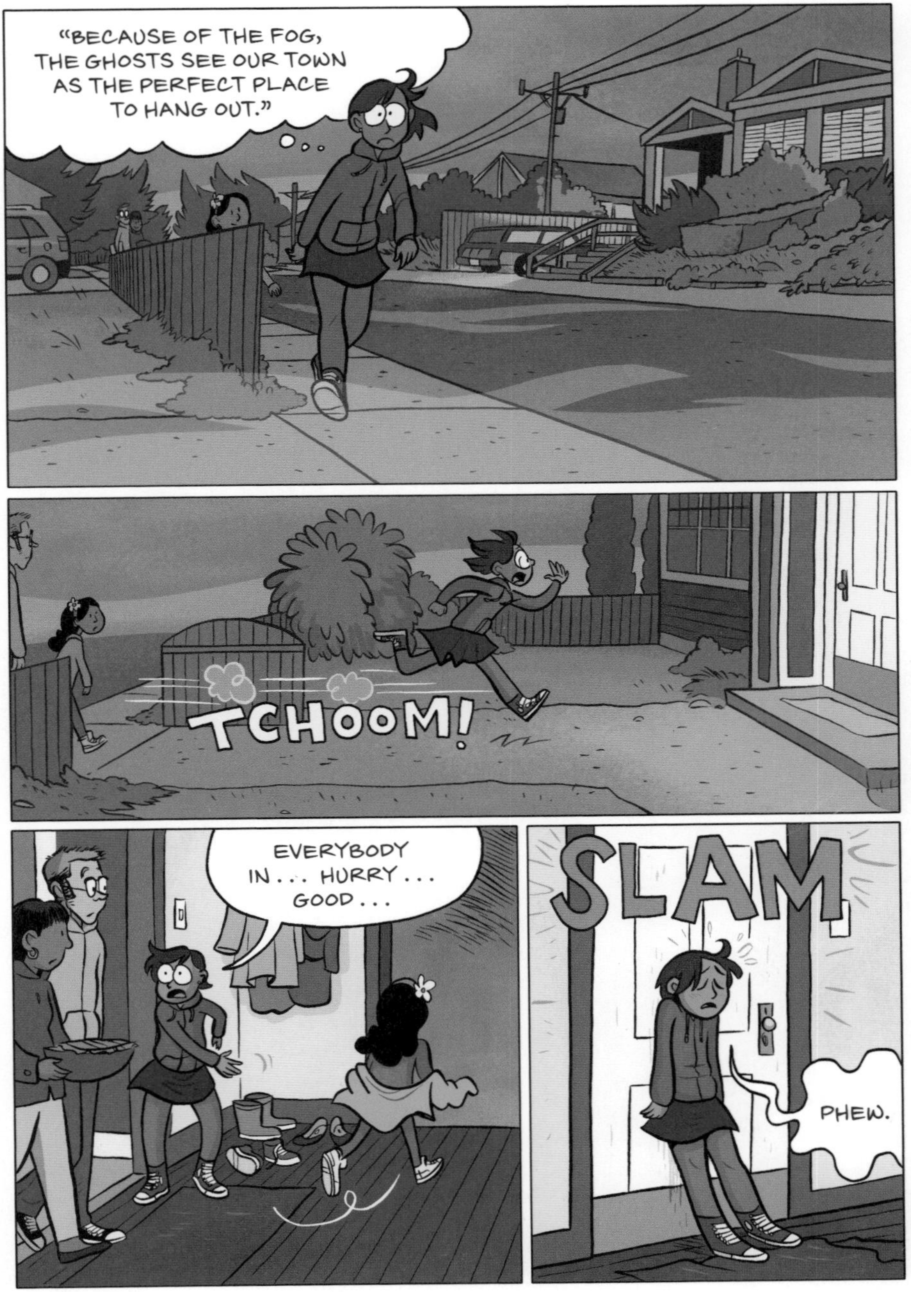
"BECAUSE OF THE FOG, THE GHOSTS SEE OUR TOWN AS THE PERFECT PLACE TO HANG OUT."
TCHOOM!
EVERYBODY IN . . . HURRY . . . GOOD . . .
SLAM
PHEW.

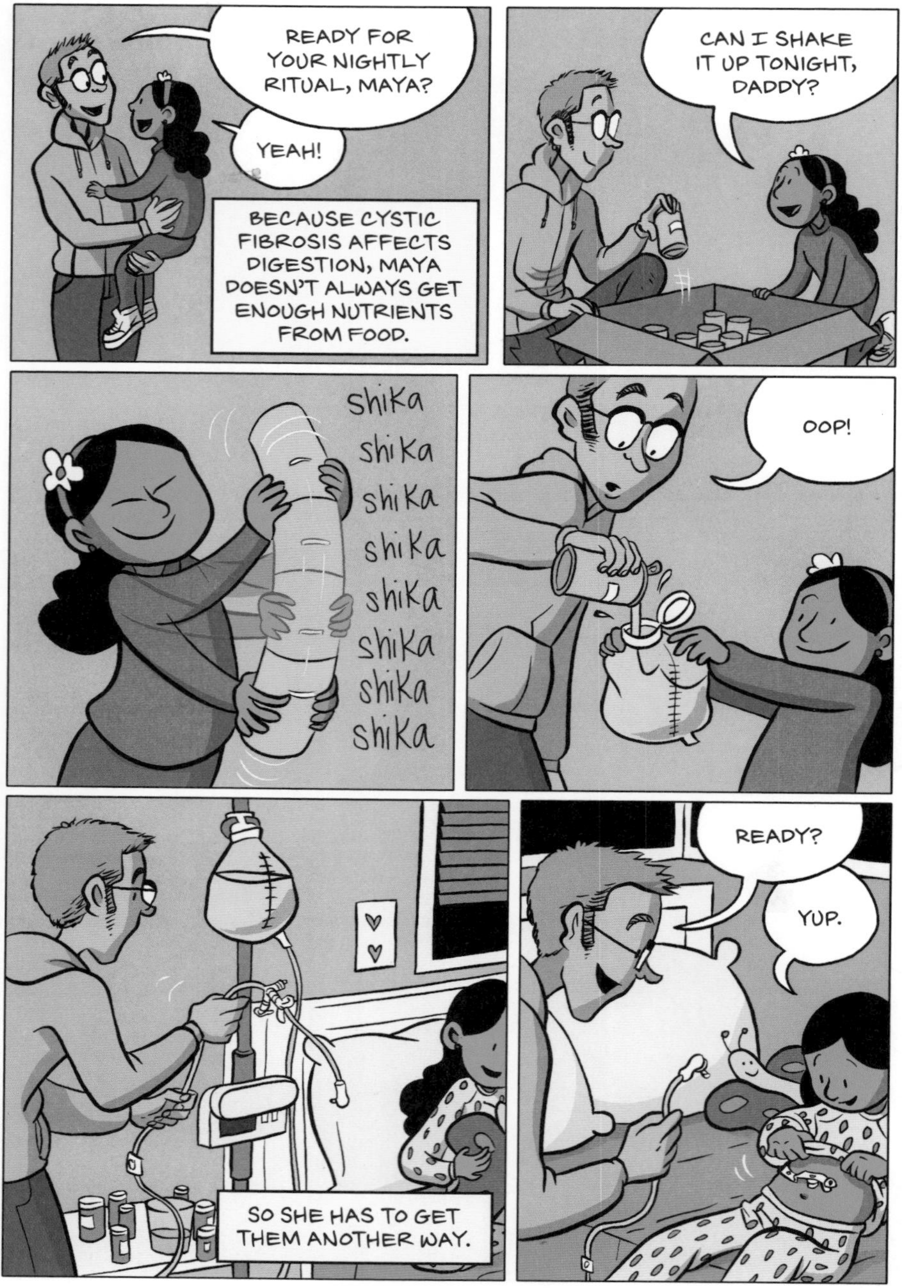
READY FOR YOUR NIGHTLY RITUAL, MAYA?
YEAH!
BECAUSE CYSTIC FIBROSIS AFFECTS DIGESTION, MAYA DOESN'T ALWAYS GET ENOUGH NUTRIENTS FROM FOOD.
CAN I SHAKE IT UP TONIGHT, DADDY?
shika shika shika shika shika shika shika shika
OOP!
SO SHE HAS TO GET THEM ANOTHER WAY.
READY?
YUP.

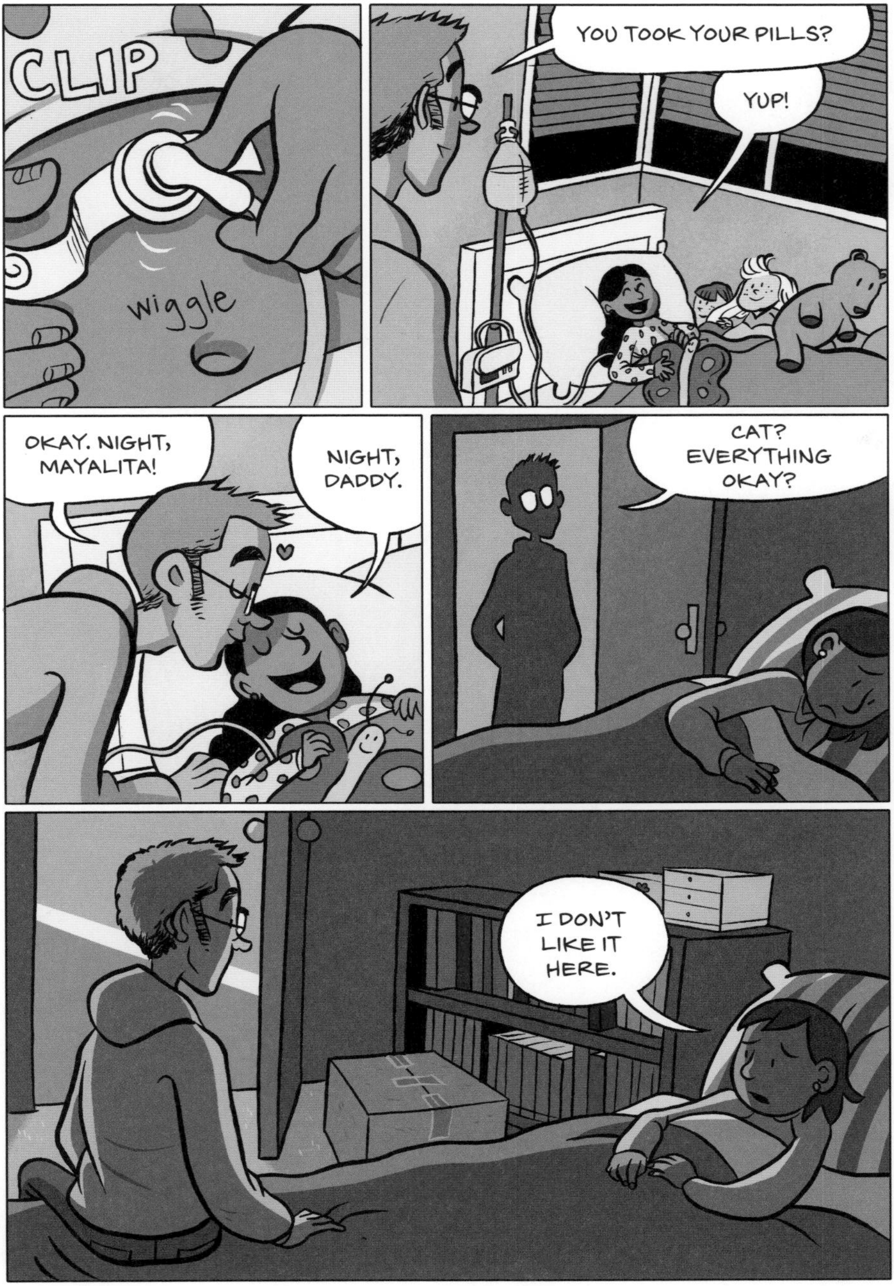
CLIP
wiggle
YOU TOOK YOUR PILLS?
YUP!
OKAY. NIGHT, MAYALITA!
NIGHT, DADDY.
CAT? EVERYTHING OKAY?
I DON'T LIKE IT HERE.

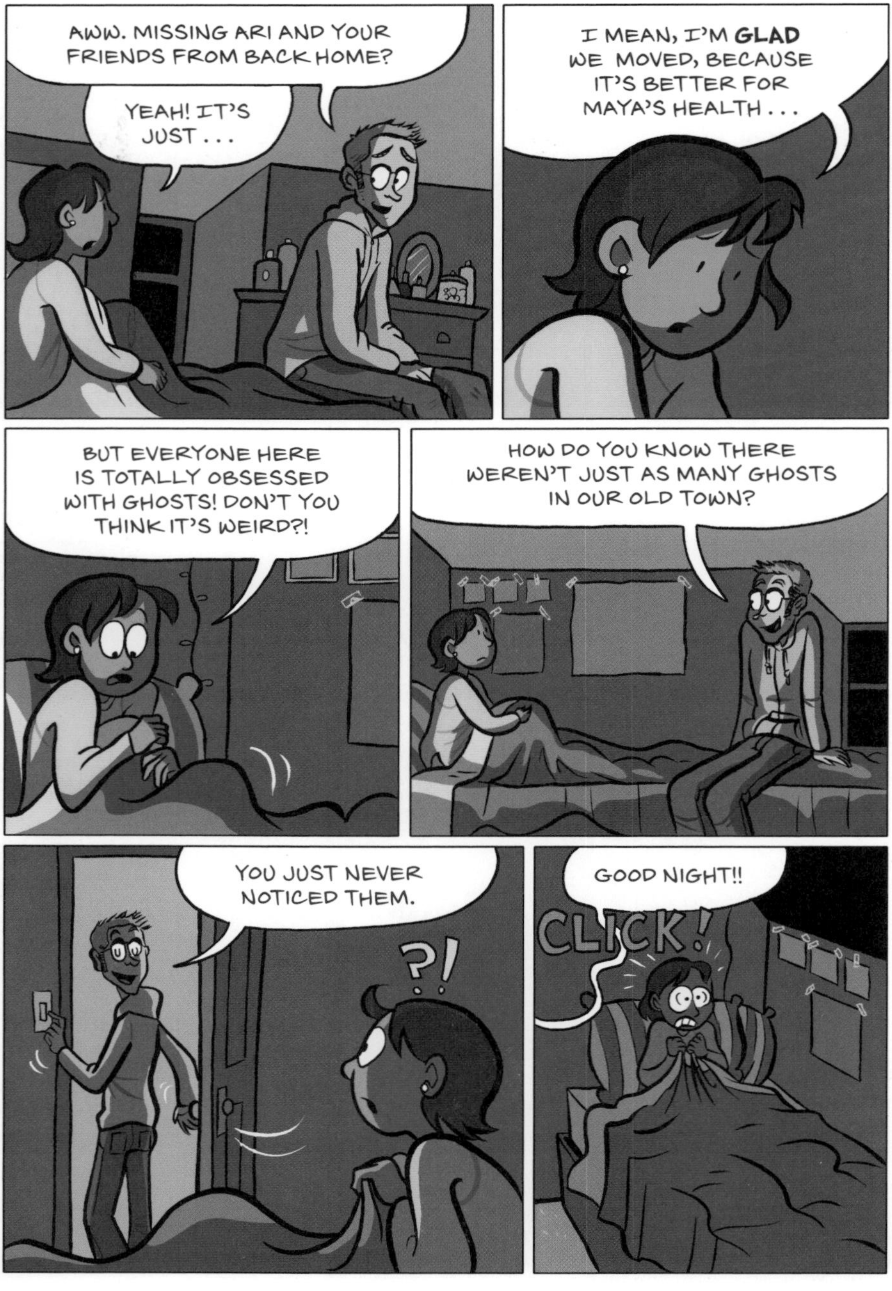
AWW. MISSING ARI AND YOUR FRIENDS FROM BACK HOME?
YEAH! IT'S JUST . . .
I MEAN, I'M **GLAD** WE MOVED, BECAUSE IT'S BETTER FOR MAYA'S HEALTH . . .
BUT EVERYONE HERE IS TOTALLY OBSESSED WITH GHOSTS! DON'T YOU THINK IT'S WEIRD?!
HOW DO YOU KNOW THERE WEREN'T JUST AS MANY GHOSTS IN OUR OLD TOWN?
YOU JUST NEVER NOTICED THEM.
?!
GOOD NIGHT!!
CLICK!

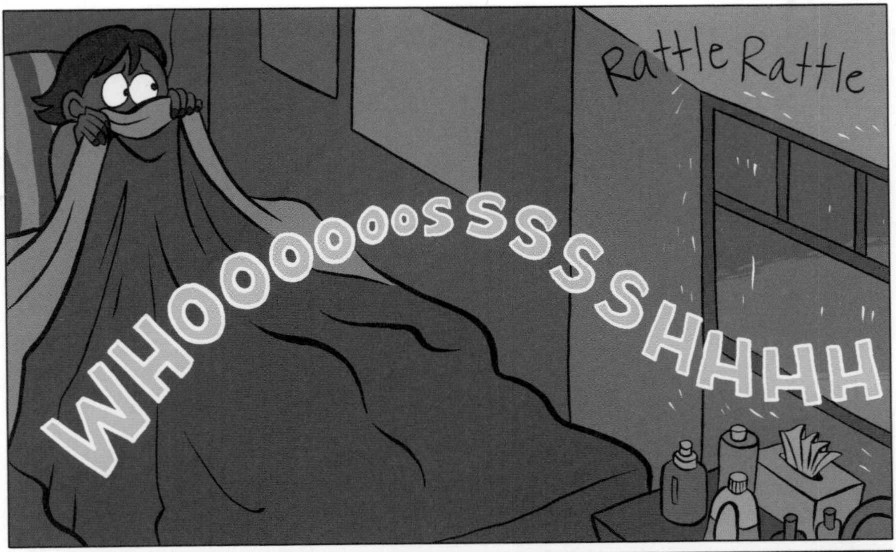
Rattle Rattle
WHOOOOOOOoSSSSSHHHH

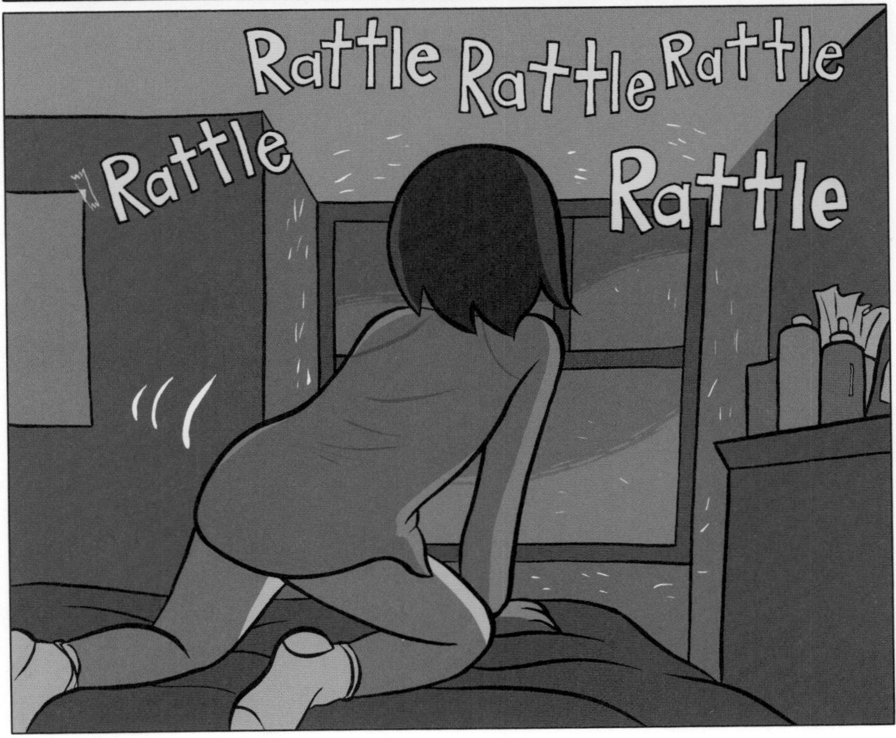
Rattle Rattle Rattle
Rattle
Rattle

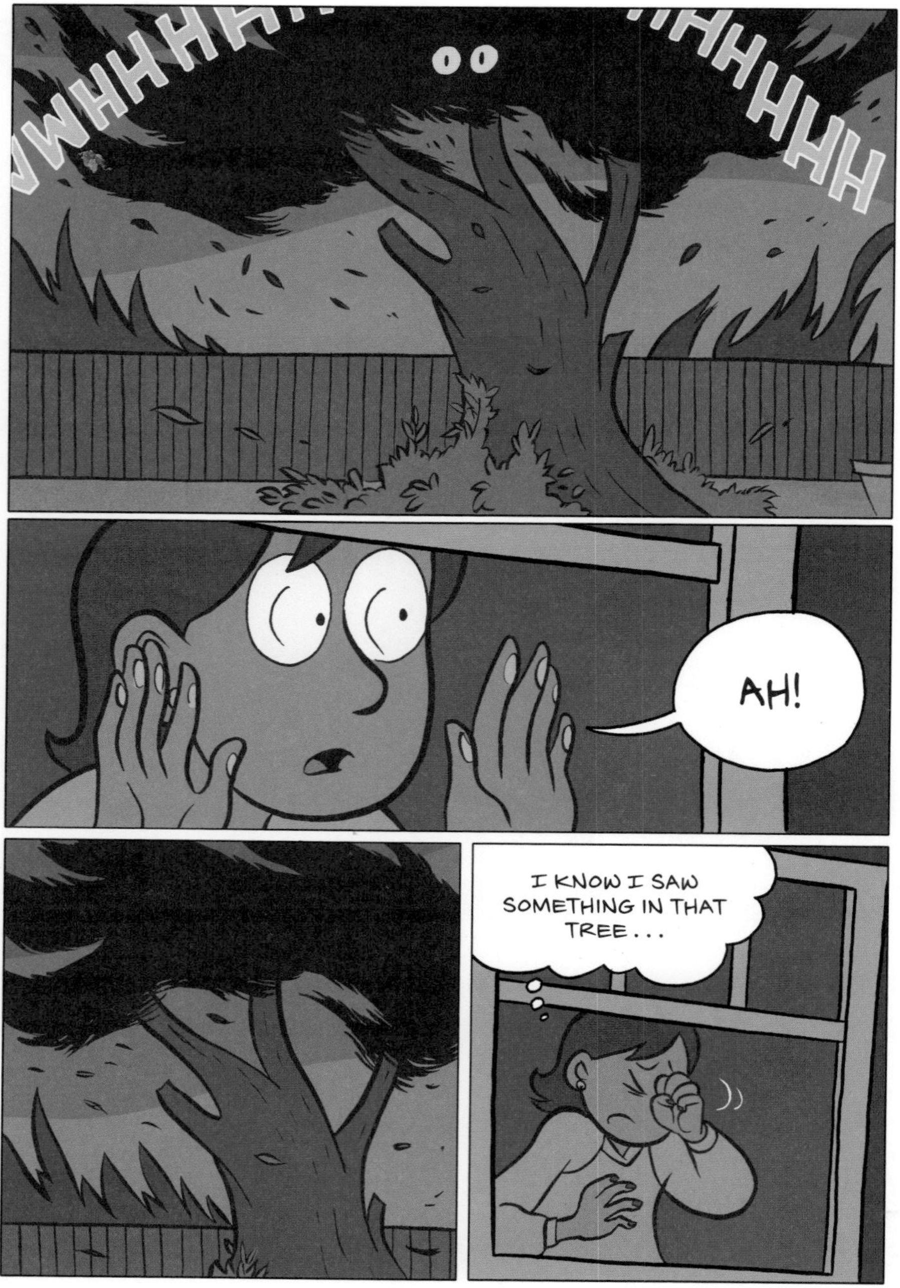
AH!
I KNOW I SAW SOMETHING IN THAT TREE . . .

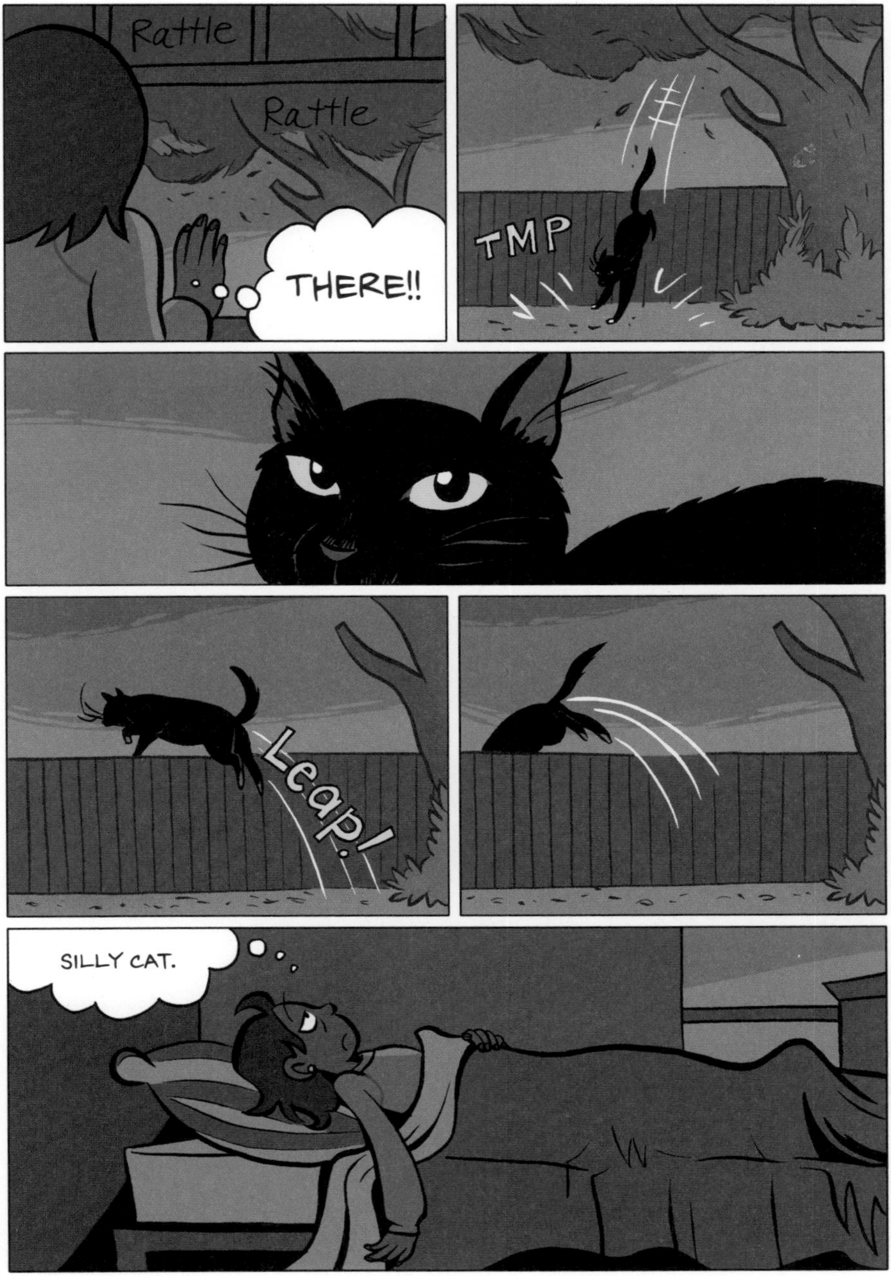
Rattle
Rattle
THERE!!
TMP
Leap!
SILLY CAT.

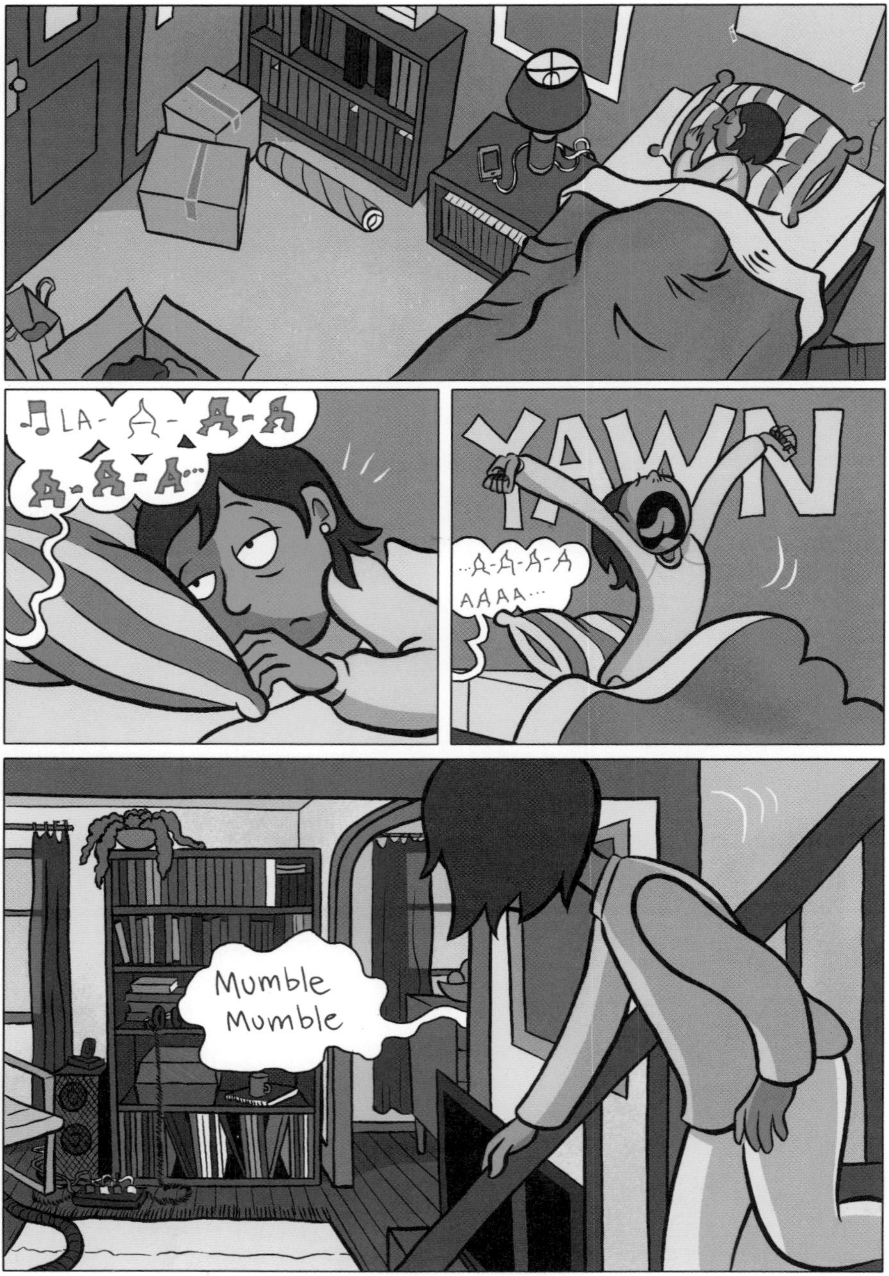
LA-A-A-A
A-A-A...
YAWN
...A-A-A-A
AAAA...
Mumble
Mumble

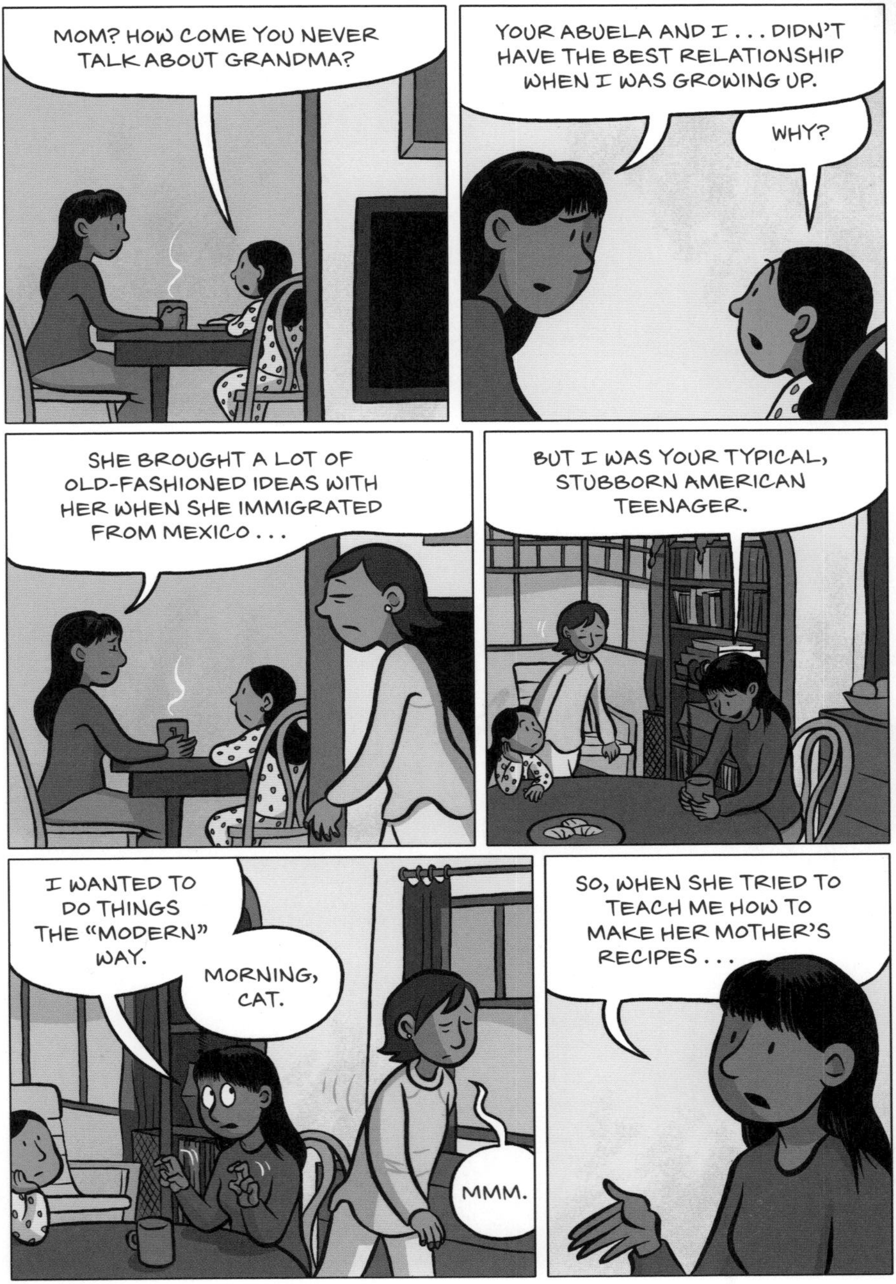
MOM? HOW COME YOU NEVER TALK ABOUT GRANDMA?
YOUR ABUELA AND I . . . DIDN'T HAVE THE BEST RELATIONSHIP WHEN I WAS GROWING UP.
WHY?
SHE BROUGHT A LOT OF OLD-FASHIONED IDEAS WITH HER WHEN SHE IMMIGRATED FROM MEXICO . . .
BUT I WAS YOUR TYPICAL, STUBBORN AMERICAN TEENAGER.
I WANTED TO DO THINGS THE "MODERN" WAY.
MORNING, CAT.
MMM.
SO, WHEN SHE TRIED TO TEACH ME HOW TO MAKE HER MOTHER'S RECIPES . . .

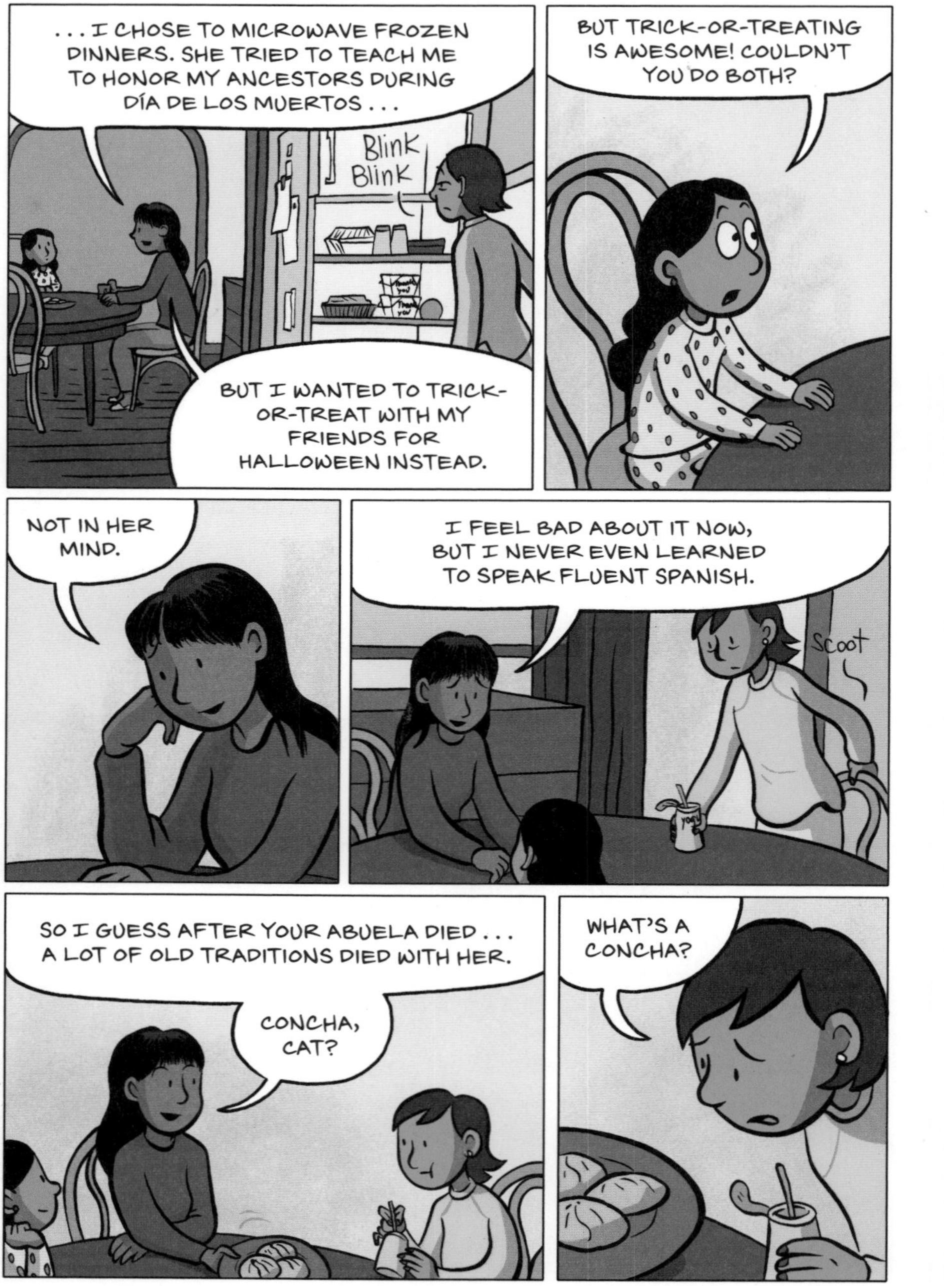

. . . I CHOSE TO MICROWAVE FROZEN DINNERS. SHE TRIED TO TEACH ME TO HONOR MY ANCESTORS DURING DÍA DE LOS MUERTOS . . .
Blink Blink
BUT I WANTED TO TRICK-OR-TREAT WITH MY FRIENDS FOR HALLOWEEN INSTEAD.
BUT TRICK-OR-TREATING IS AWESOME! COULDN'T YOU DO BOTH?
NOT IN HER MIND.
I FEEL BAD ABOUT IT NOW, BUT I NEVER EVEN LEARNED TO SPEAK FLUENT SPANISH.
SCOOT
SO I GUESS AFTER YOUR ABUELA DIED . . . A LOT OF OLD TRADITIONS DIED WITH HER.
CONCHA, CAT?
WHAT'S A CONCHA?

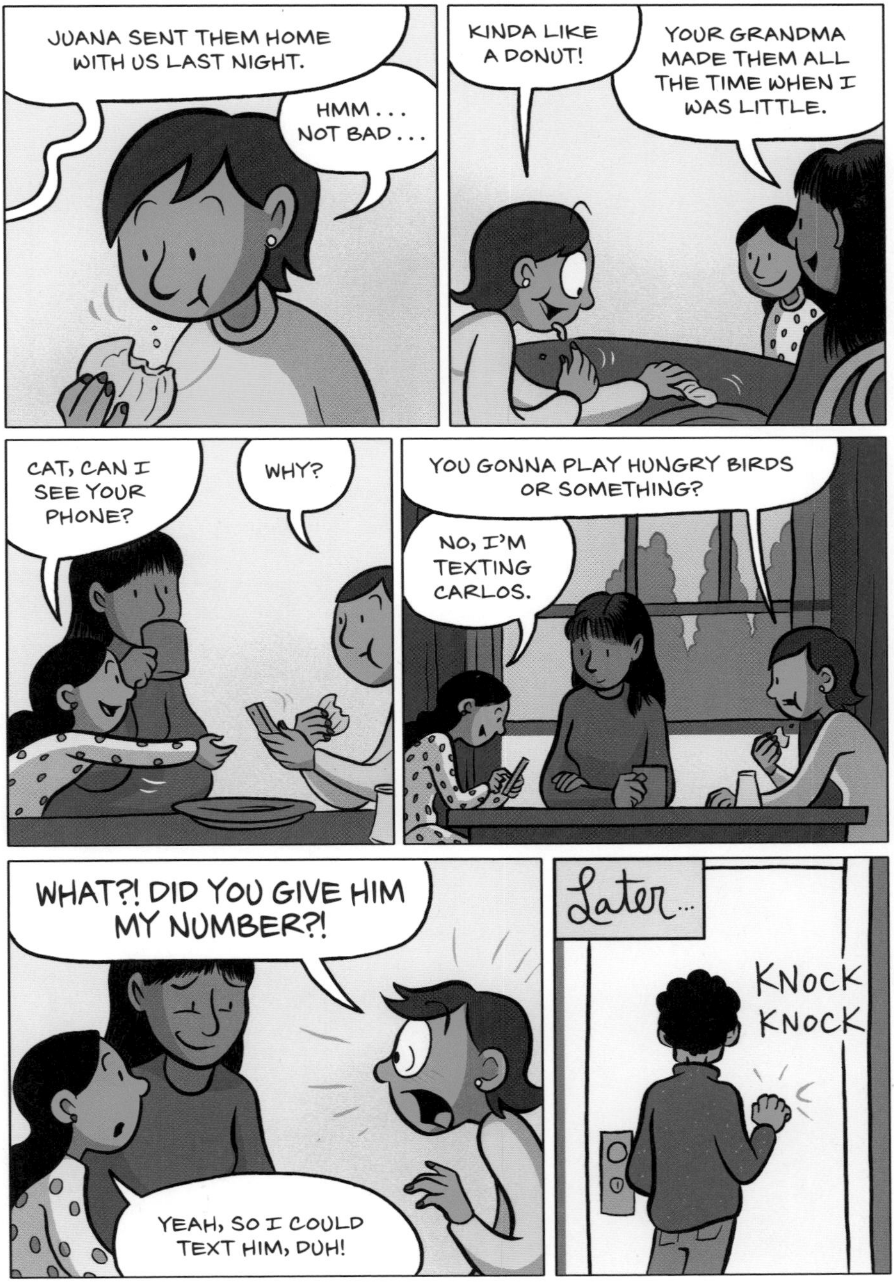
JUANA SENT THEM HOME WITH US LAST NIGHT.
HMM . . . NOT BAD . . .
KINDA LIKE A DONUT!
YOUR GRANDMA MADE THEM ALL THE TIME WHEN I WAS LITTLE.
CAT, CAN I SEE YOUR PHONE?
WHY?
YOU GONNA PLAY HUNGRY BIRDS OR SOMETHING?
NO, I'M TEXTING CARLOS.
WHAT?! DID YOU GIVE HIM MY NUMBER?!
YEAH, SO I COULD TEXT HIM, DUH!
Later...
KNOCK KNOCK

hi 😊😊😊 u shud come ovr 😊😊😊 lol

MAYA'S HANDIWORK. I'M A BETTER TEXTER THAN **THAT**.

WHAT'RE YOU GUYS UP TO?

CARLOS! WE'RE MAKING AN OFRENDA* FOR OUR ABUELA! COME SEE!!

VERY NICE.

BUT AN OFRENDA NEEDS MORE DECORATING.

OOOH! YEAH!

*AN ALTAR FOR A DECEASED RELATIVE

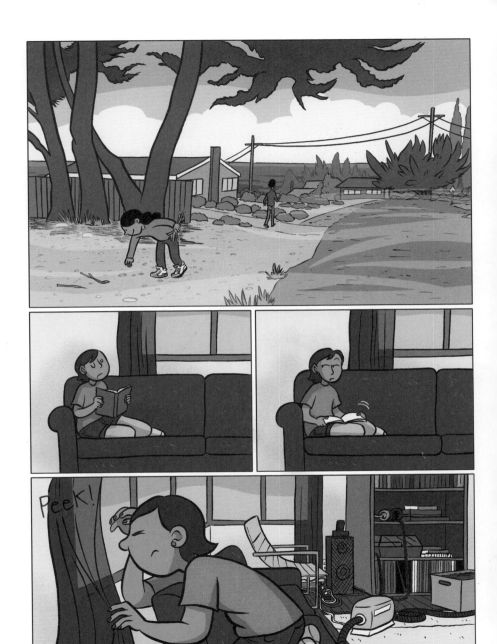

PeeK!

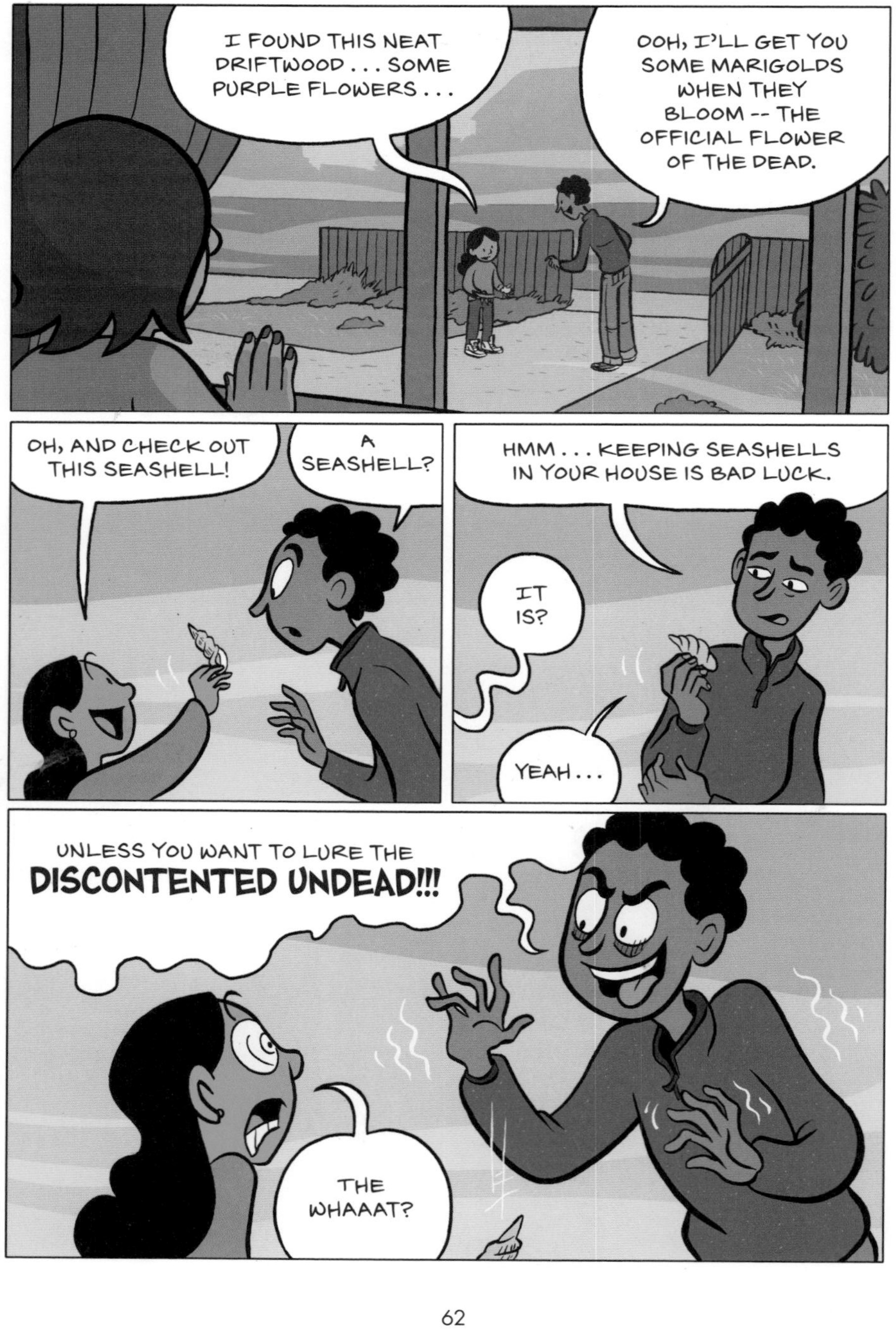
I FOUND THIS NEAT DRIFTWOOD . . . SOME PURPLE FLOWERS . . .
OOH, I'LL GET YOU SOME MARIGOLDS WHEN THEY BLOOM -- THE OFFICIAL FLOWER OF THE DEAD.
OH, AND CHECK OUT THIS SEASHELL!
A SEASHELL?
HMM . . . KEEPING SEASHELLS IN YOUR HOUSE IS BAD LUCK.
IT IS?
YEAH . . .
UNLESS YOU WANT TO LURE THE DISCONTENTED UNDEAD!!!
THE WHAAAT?

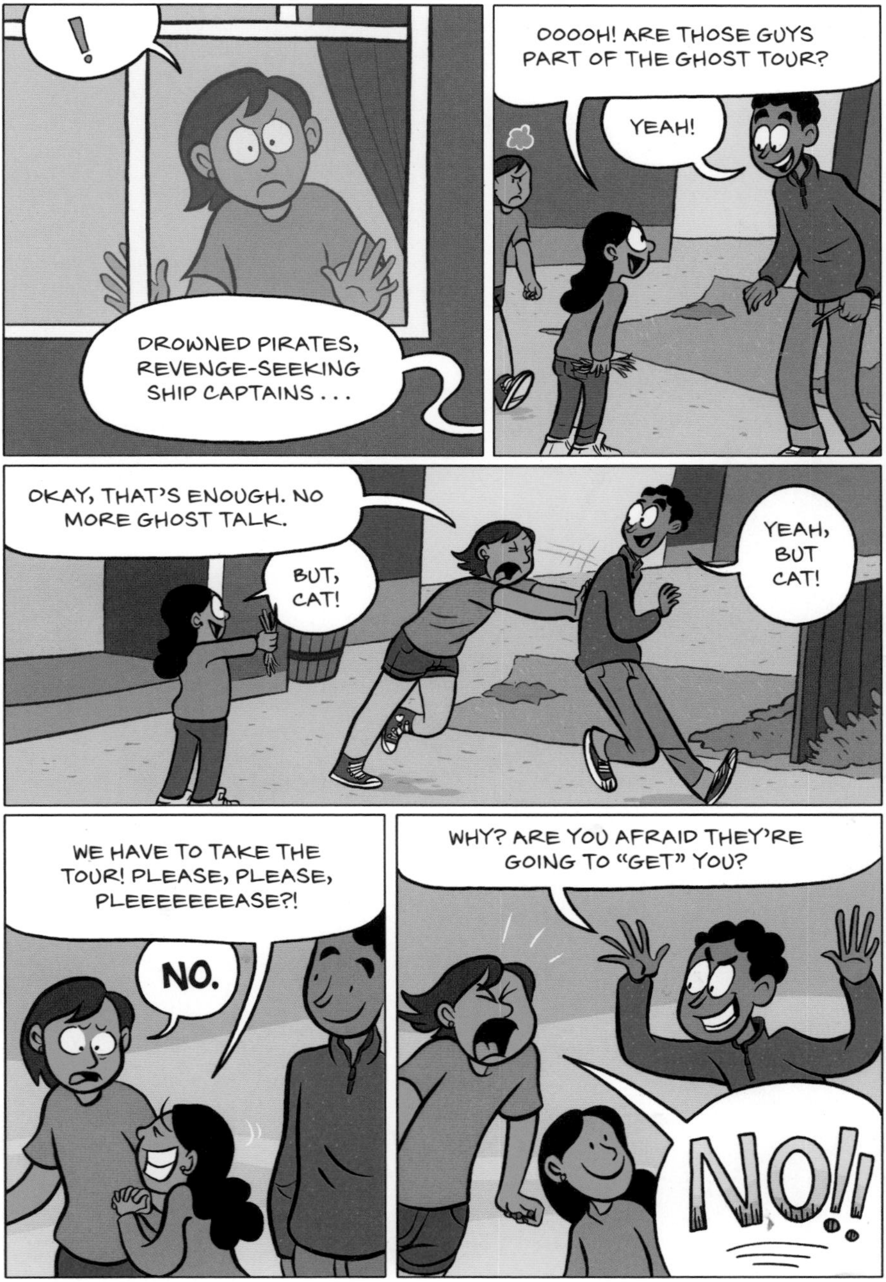
!
DROWNED PIRATES, REVENGE-SEEKING SHIP CAPTAINS . . .
OOOOH! ARE THOSE GUYS PART OF THE GHOST TOUR?
YEAH!
OKAY, THAT'S ENOUGH. NO MORE GHOST TALK.
BUT, CAT!
YEAH, BUT CAT!
WE HAVE TO TAKE THE TOUR! PLEASE, PLEASE, PLEEEEEEEASE?!
NO.
WHY? ARE YOU AFRAID THEY'RE GOING TO "GET" YOU?
NO!!

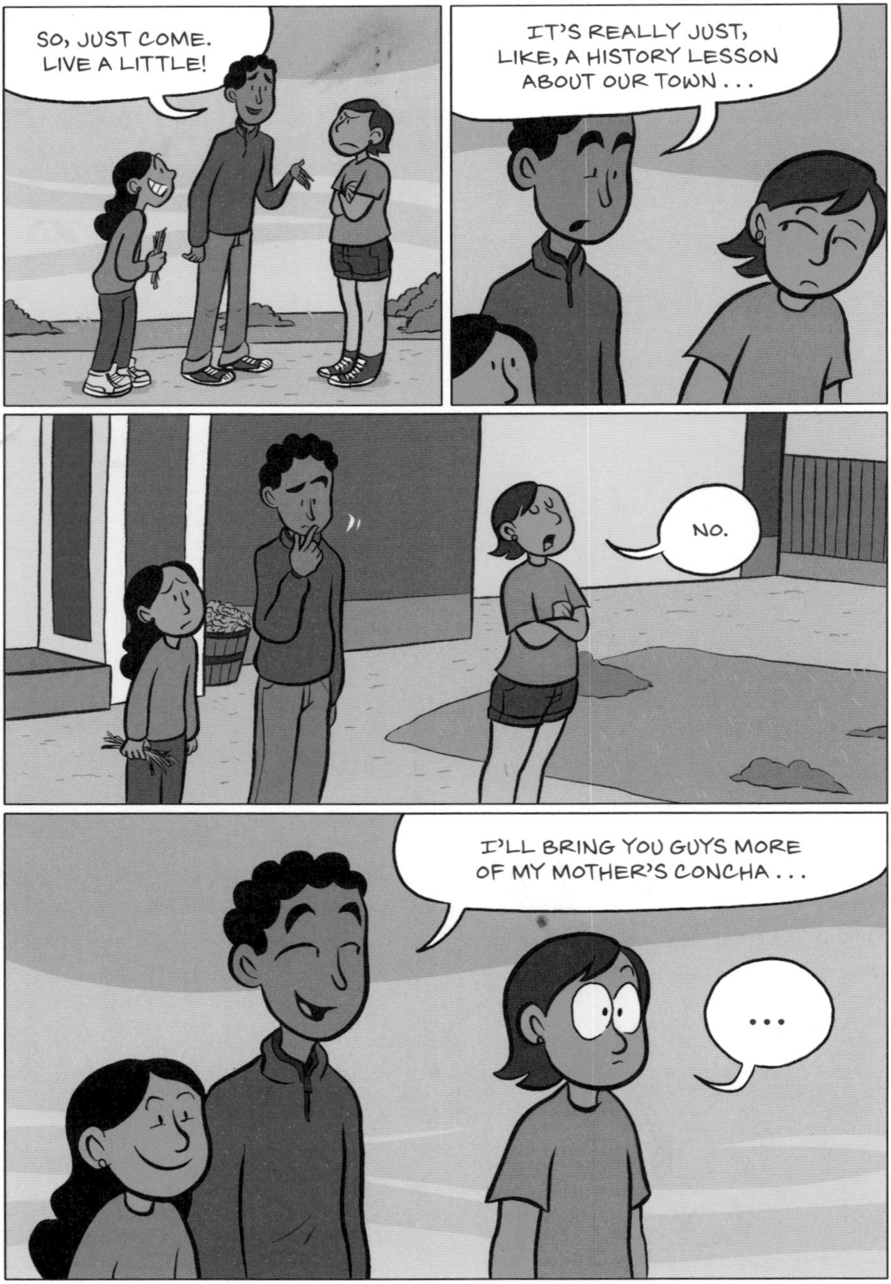
SO, JUST COME. LIVE A LITTLE!
IT'S REALLY JUST, LIKE, A HISTORY LESSON ABOUT OUR TOWN . . .
NO.
I'LL BRING YOU GUYS MORE OF MY MOTHER'S CONCHA . . .
. . .

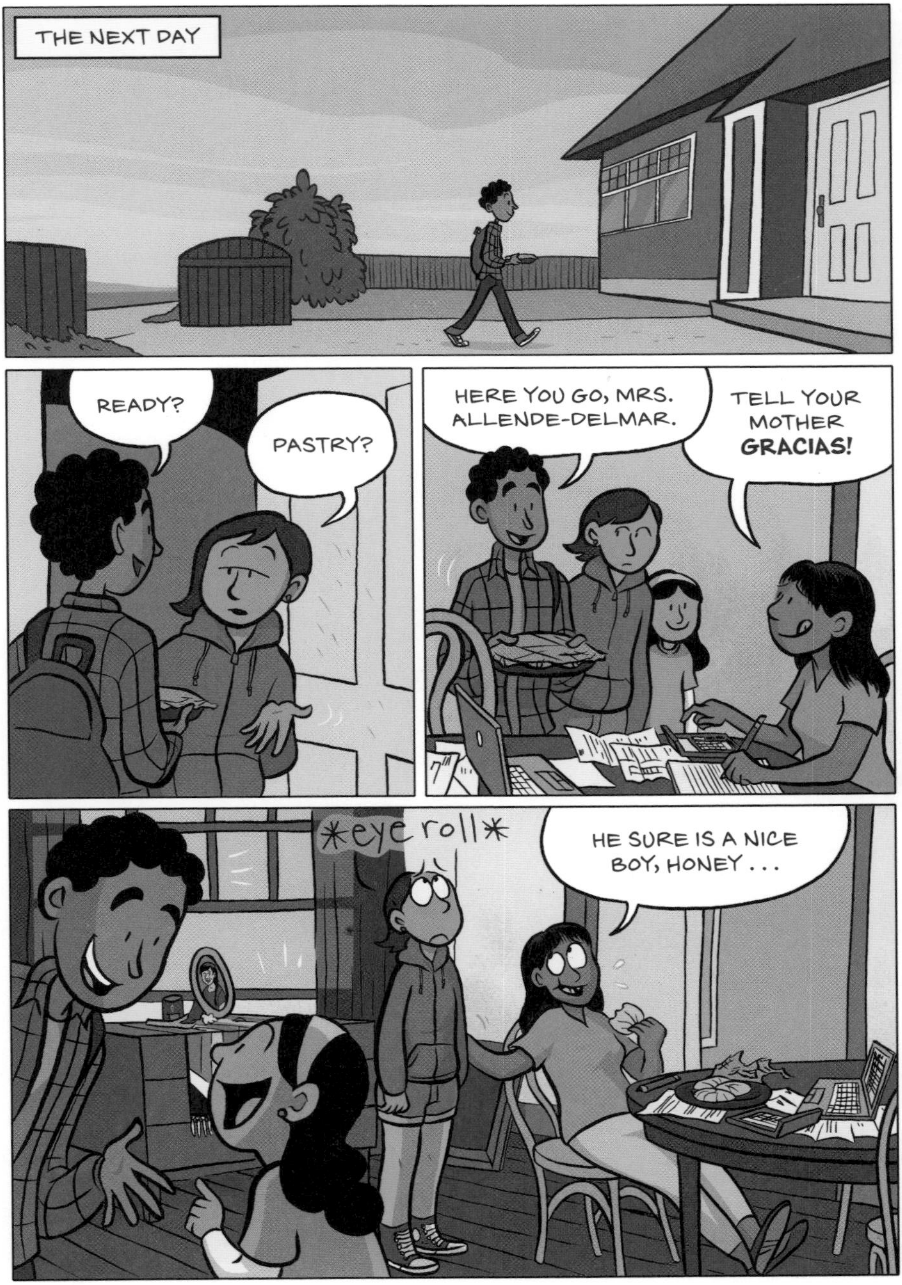
THE NEXT DAY
READY?
PASTRY?
HERE YOU GO, MRS. ALLENDE-DELMAR.
TELL YOUR MOTHER **GRACIAS!**
eye roll
HE SURE IS A NICE BOY, HONEY . . .

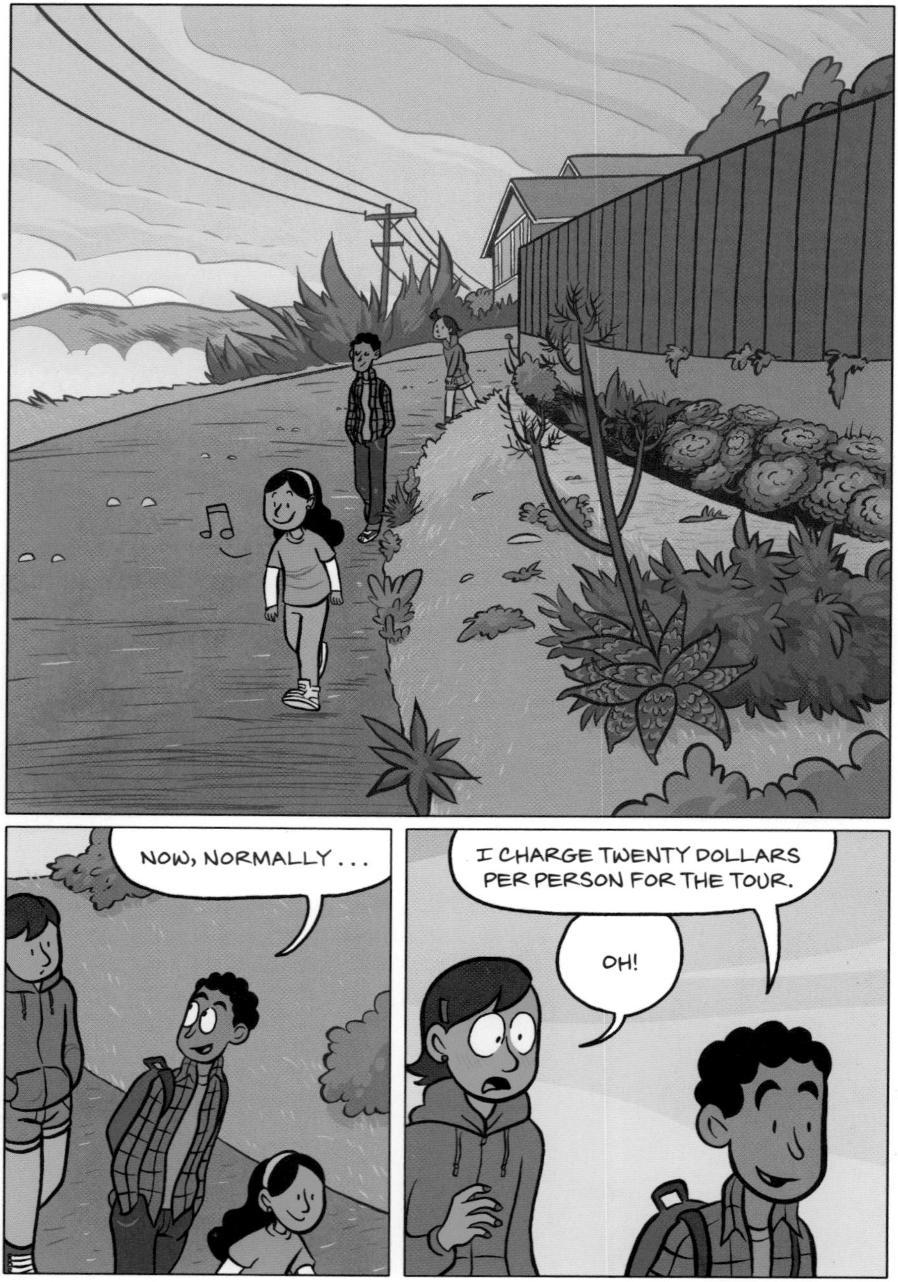
NOW, NORMALLY . . .
I CHARGE TWENTY DOLLARS PER PERSON FOR THE TOUR.
OH!

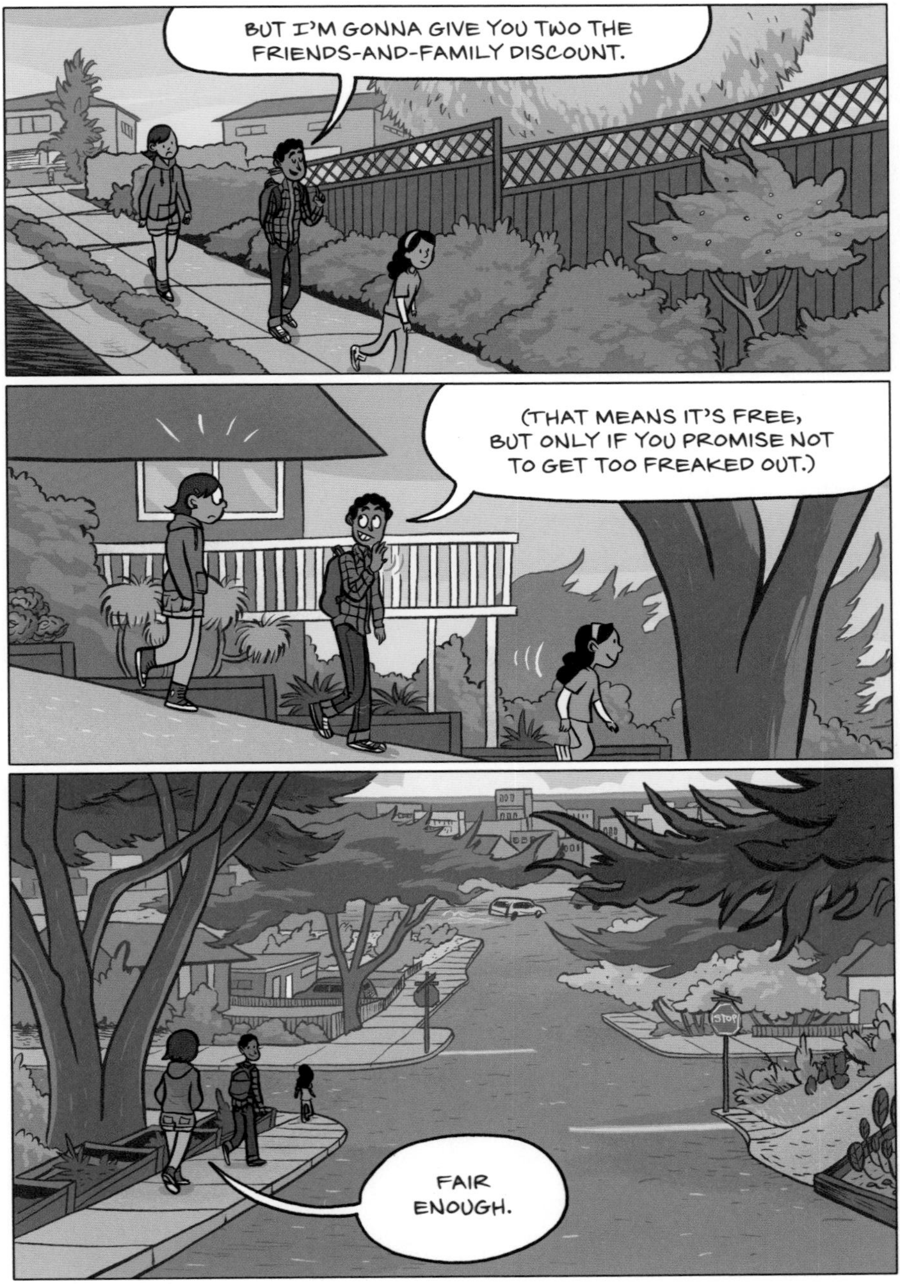
BUT I'M GONNA GIVE YOU TWO THE FRIENDS-AND-FAMILY DISCOUNT.
(THAT MEANS IT'S FREE, BUT ONLY IF YOU PROMISE NOT TO GET TOO FREAKED OUT.)
STOP
FAIR ENOUGH.

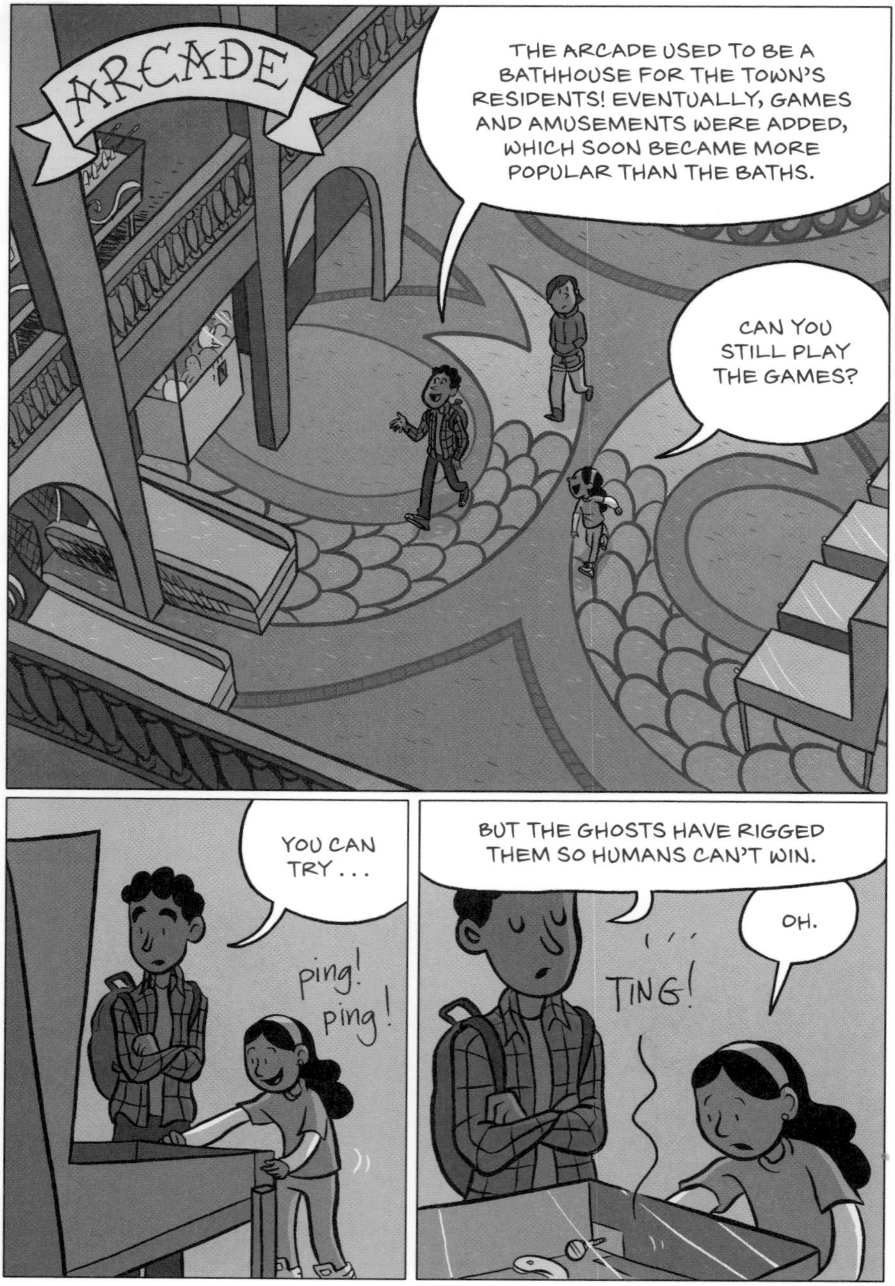
ARCADE
THE ARCADE USED TO BE A BATHHOUSE FOR THE TOWN'S RESIDENTS! EVENTUALLY, GAMES AND AMUSEMENTS WERE ADDED, WHICH SOON BECAME MORE POPULAR THAN THE BATHS.
CAN YOU STILL PLAY THE GAMES?
YOU CAN TRY . . .
ping! ping!
BUT THE GHOSTS HAVE RIGGED THEM SO HUMANS CAN'T WIN.
TING!
OH.

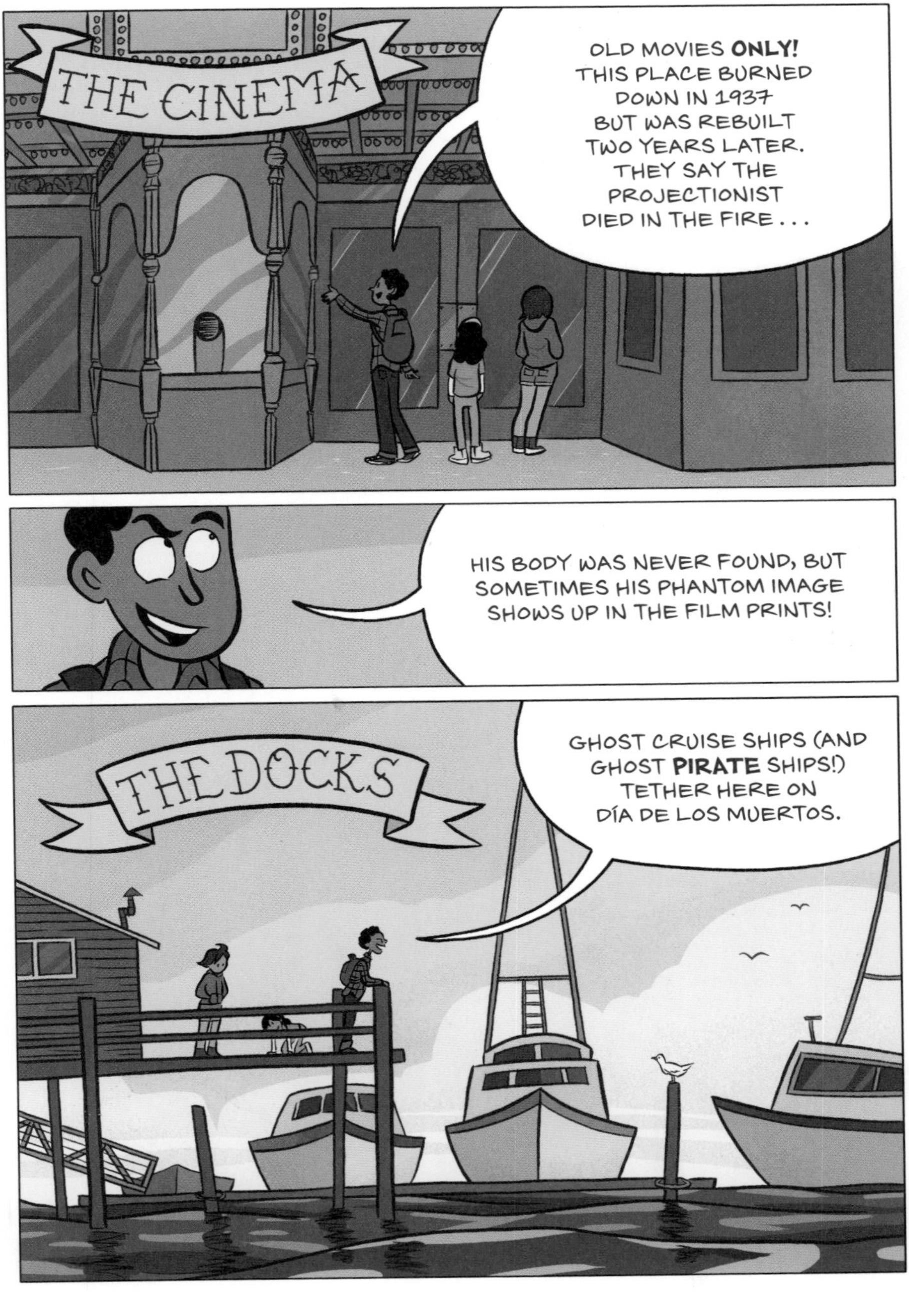
THE CINEMA
OLD MOVIES **ONLY!** THIS PLACE BURNED DOWN IN 1937 BUT WAS REBUILT TWO YEARS LATER. THEY SAY THE PROJECTIONIST DIED IN THE FIRE . . .
HIS BODY WAS NEVER FOUND, BUT SOMETIMES HIS PHANTOM IMAGE SHOWS UP IN THE FILM PRINTS!
THE DOCKS
GHOST CRUISE SHIPS (AND GHOST **PIRATE** SHIPS!) TETHER HERE ON DÍA DE LOS MUERTOS.

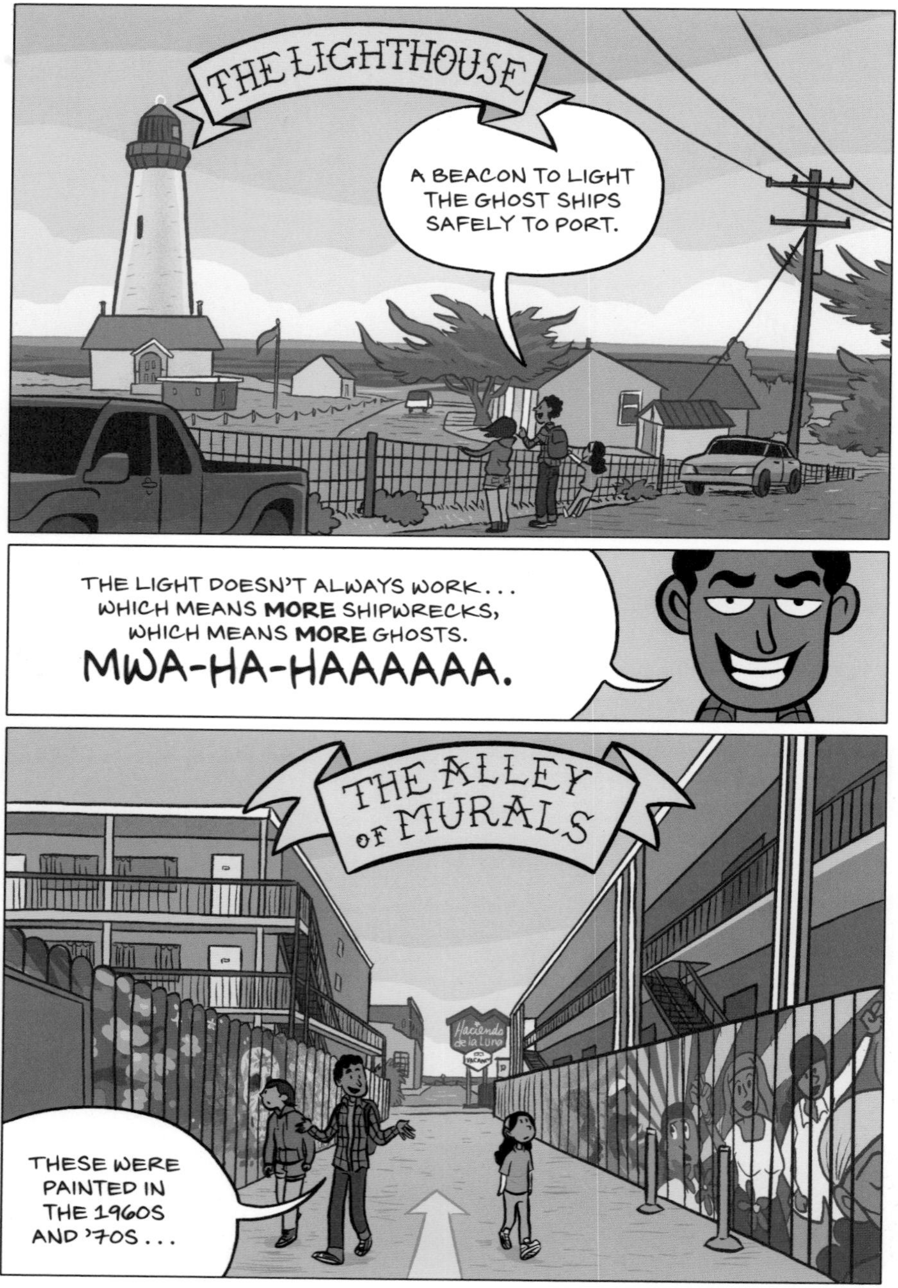
THE LIGHTHOUSE
A BEACON TO LIGHT THE GHOST SHIPS SAFELY TO PORT.
THE LIGHT DOESN'T ALWAYS WORK... WHICH MEANS **MORE** SHIPWRECKS, WHICH MEANS **MORE** GHOSTS.
MWA-HA-HAAAAAA.
THE ALLEY OF MURALS
Hacienda de la Luna
THESE WERE PAINTED IN THE 1960S AND '70S...

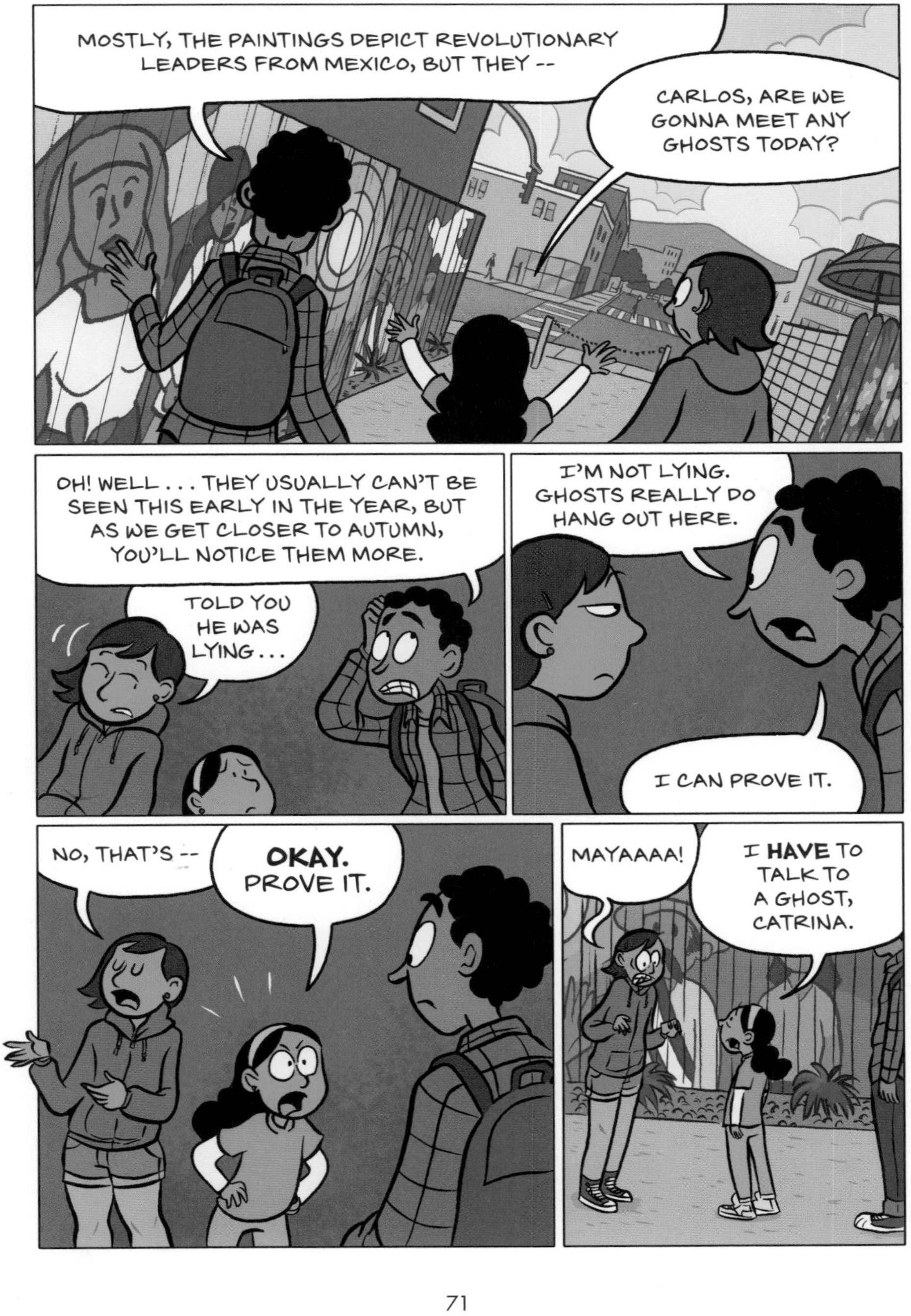

MOSTLY, THE PAINTINGS DEPICT REVOLUTIONARY LEADERS FROM MEXICO, BUT THEY --
CARLOS, ARE WE GONNA MEET ANY GHOSTS TODAY?
OH! WELL . . . THEY USUALLY CAN'T BE SEEN THIS EARLY IN THE YEAR, BUT AS WE GET CLOSER TO AUTUMN, YOU'LL NOTICE THEM MORE.
TOLD YOU HE WAS LYING . . .
I'M NOT LYING. GHOSTS REALLY DO HANG OUT HERE.
I CAN PROVE IT.
NO, THAT'S --
OKAY. PROVE IT.
MAYAAAA!
I **HAVE** TO TALK TO A GHOST, CATRINA.

WHAT DO YOU WANT TO ASK IT ABOUT?

Hffffff

I WANT TO KNOW WHAT HAPPENS WHEN YOU DIE.

UH-HUH, AND **I** WANT TO FLY, BUT IT'S NOT LIKE **THAT'S** EVER GOING TO HAPPEN.

DYING ISN'T PRETEND, CAT.

IT'S REAL.

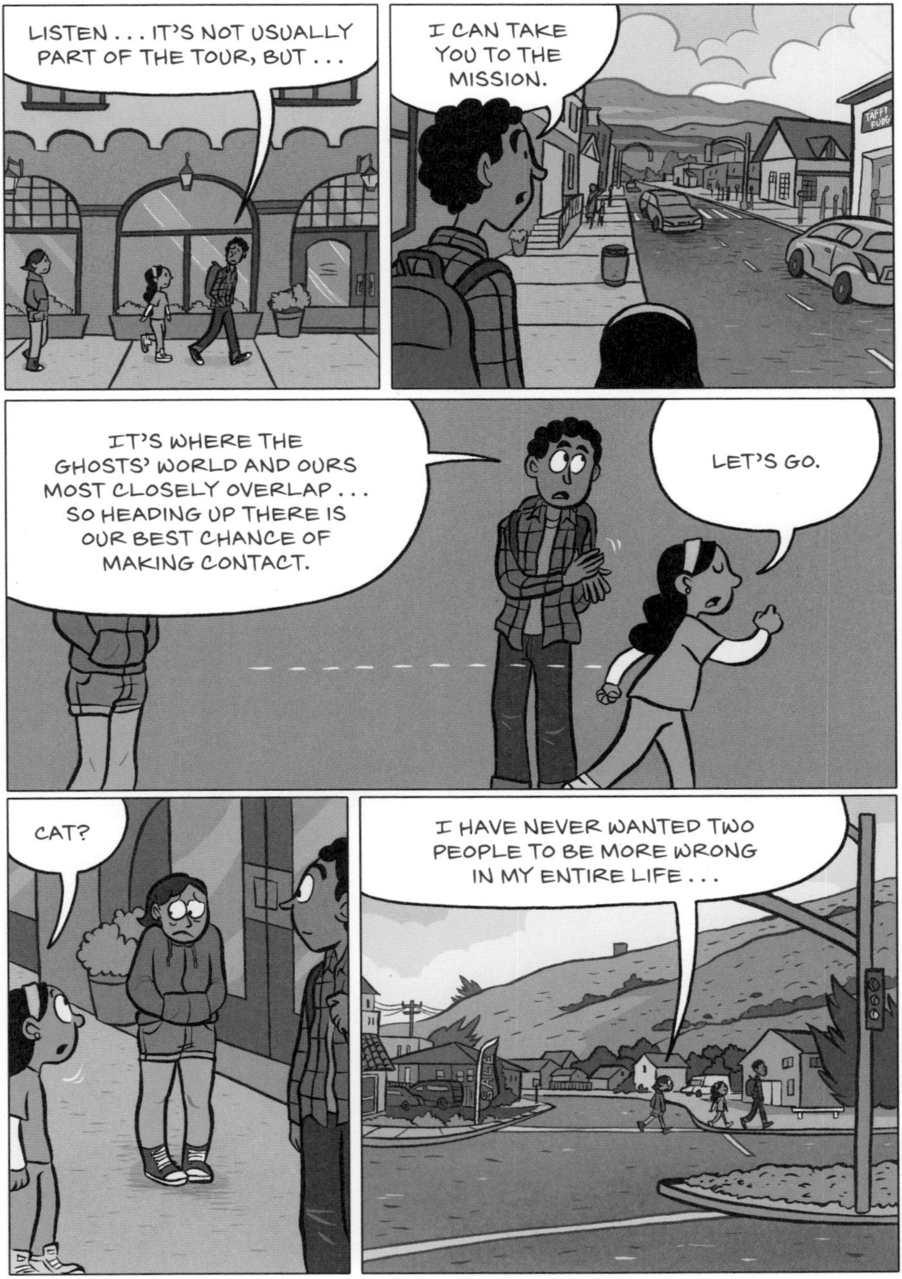
LISTEN . . . IT'S NOT USUALLY PART OF THE TOUR, BUT . . .
I CAN TAKE YOU TO THE MISSION.
TAFFY FUDGE
IT'S WHERE THE GHOSTS' WORLD AND OURS MOST CLOSELY OVERLAP . . . SO HEADING UP THERE IS OUR BEST CHANCE OF MAKING CONTACT.
LET'S GO.
CAT?
I HAVE NEVER WANTED TWO PEOPLE TO BE MORE WRONG IN MY ENTIRE LIFE . . .
SALE

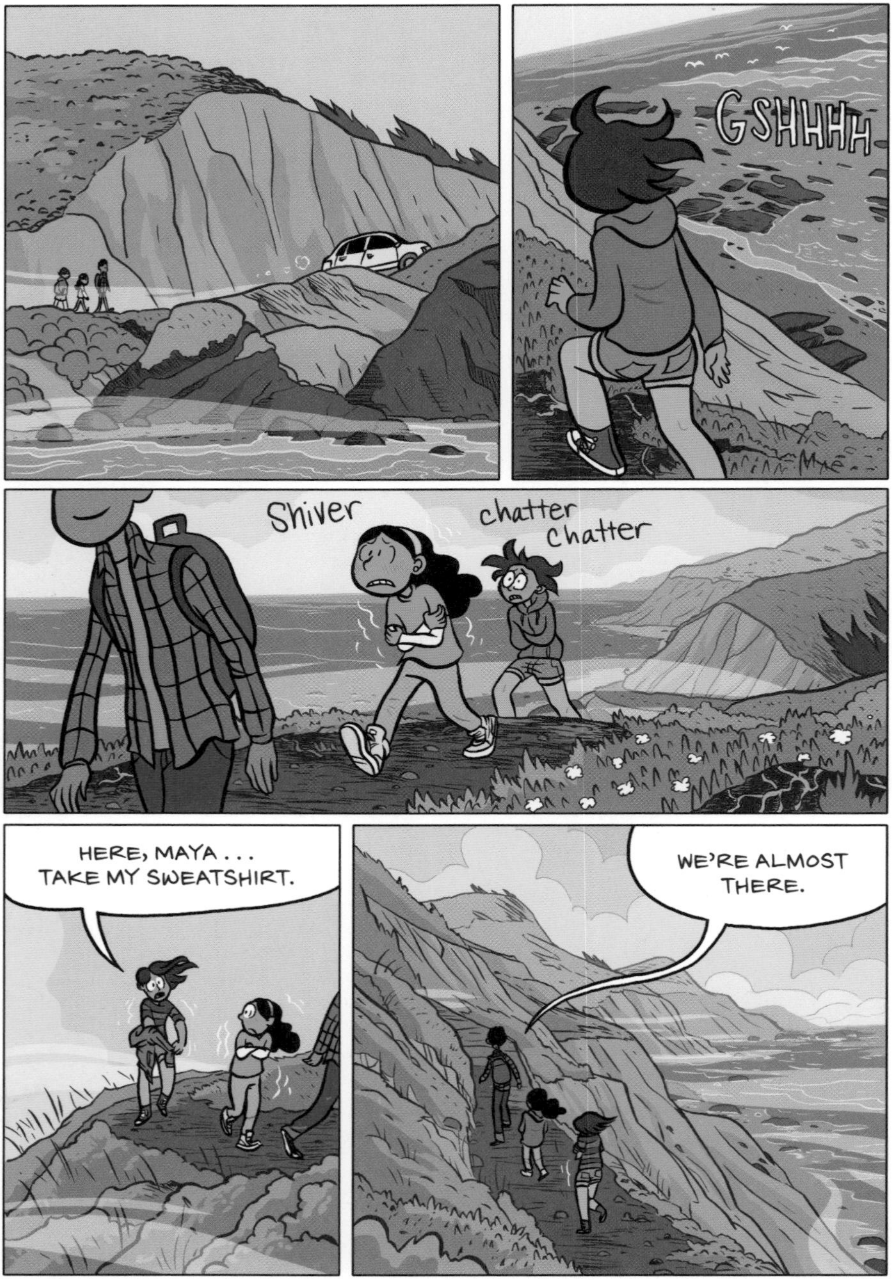
GSHHHH
Shiver
chatter
Chatter
HERE, MAYA . . .
TAKE MY SWEATSHIRT.
WE'RE ALMOST
THERE.

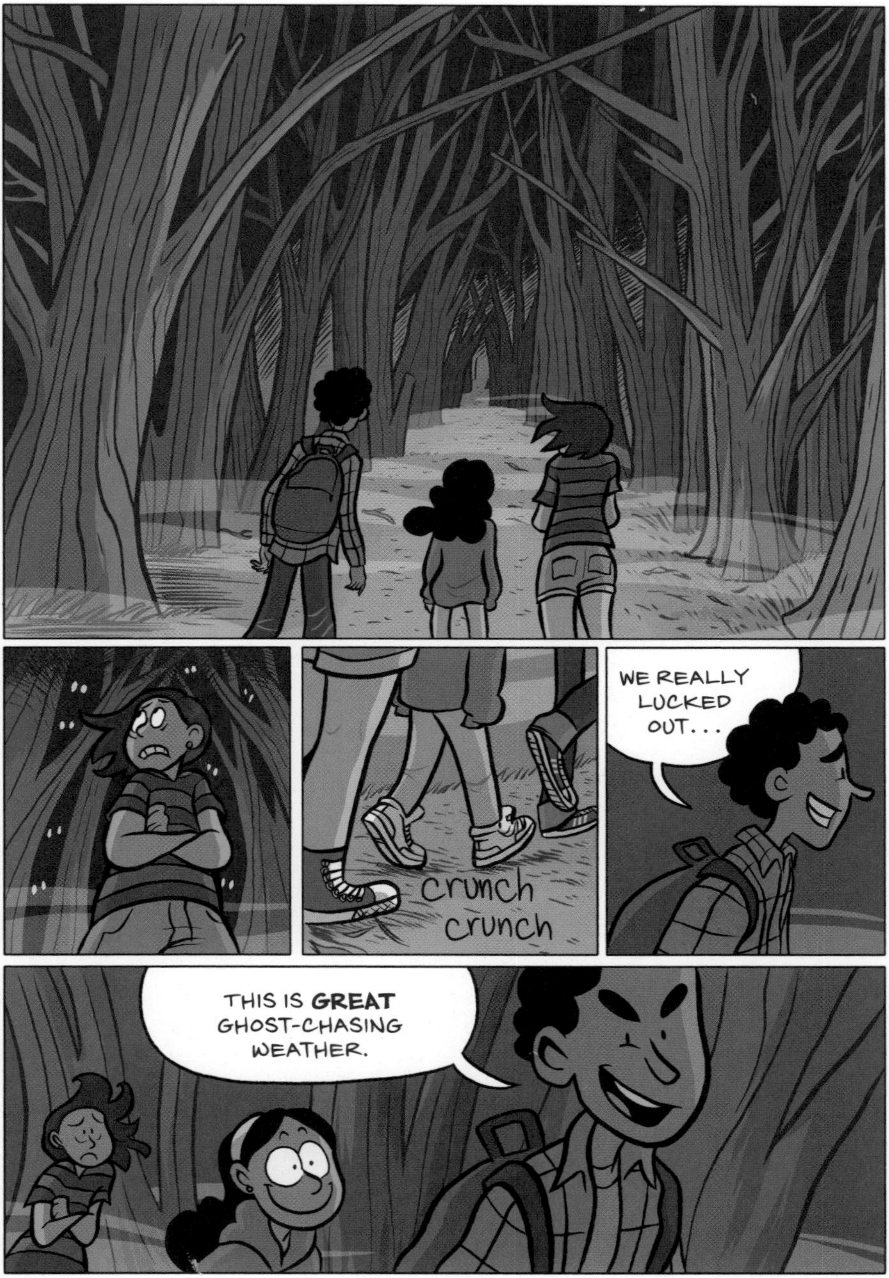
crunch
crunch
WE REALLY LUCKED OUT...
THIS IS **GREAT** GHOST-CHASING WEATHER.

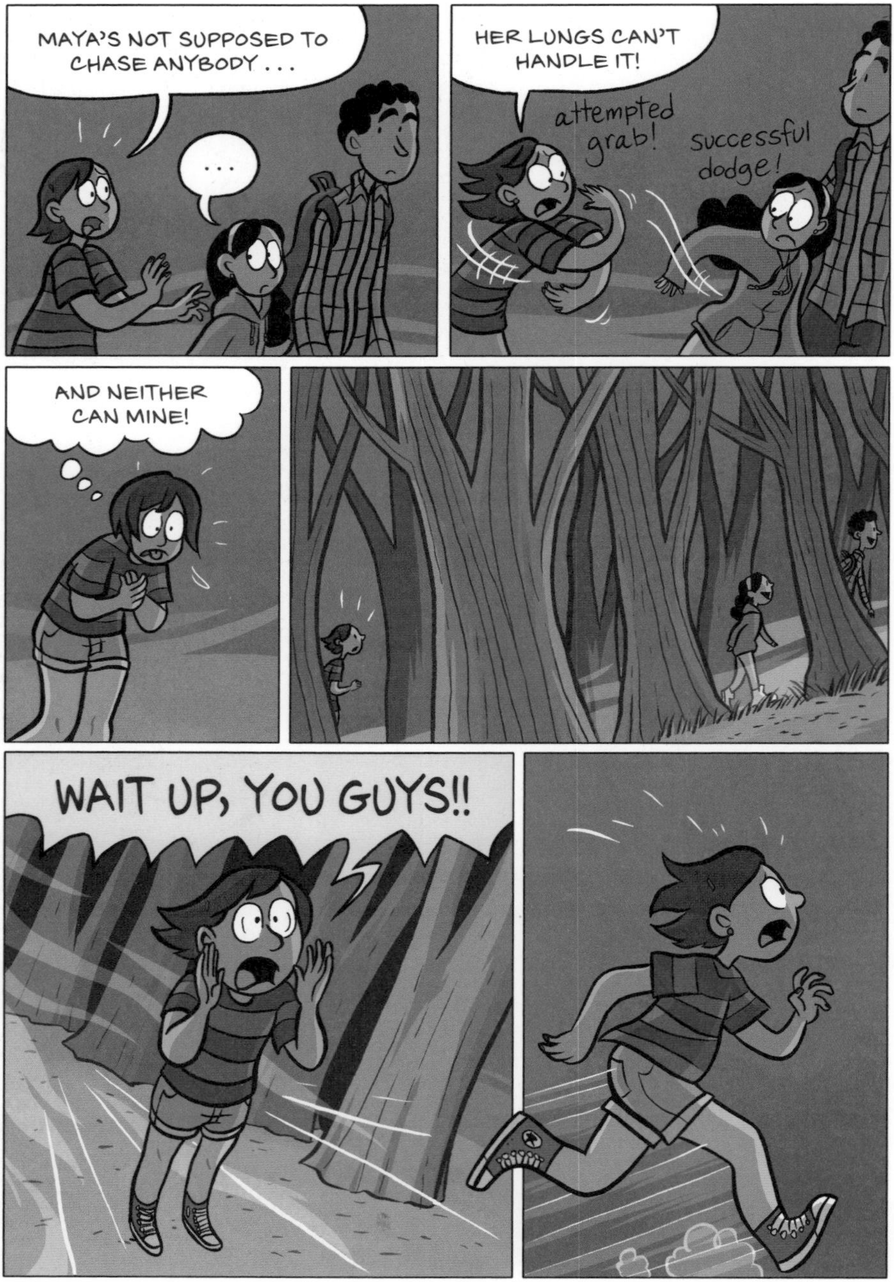
MAYA'S NOT SUPPOSED TO CHASE ANYBODY . . .
. . .
HER LUNGS CAN'T HANDLE IT!
attempted grab!
successful dodge!
AND NEITHER CAN MINE!
WAIT UP, YOU GUYS!!

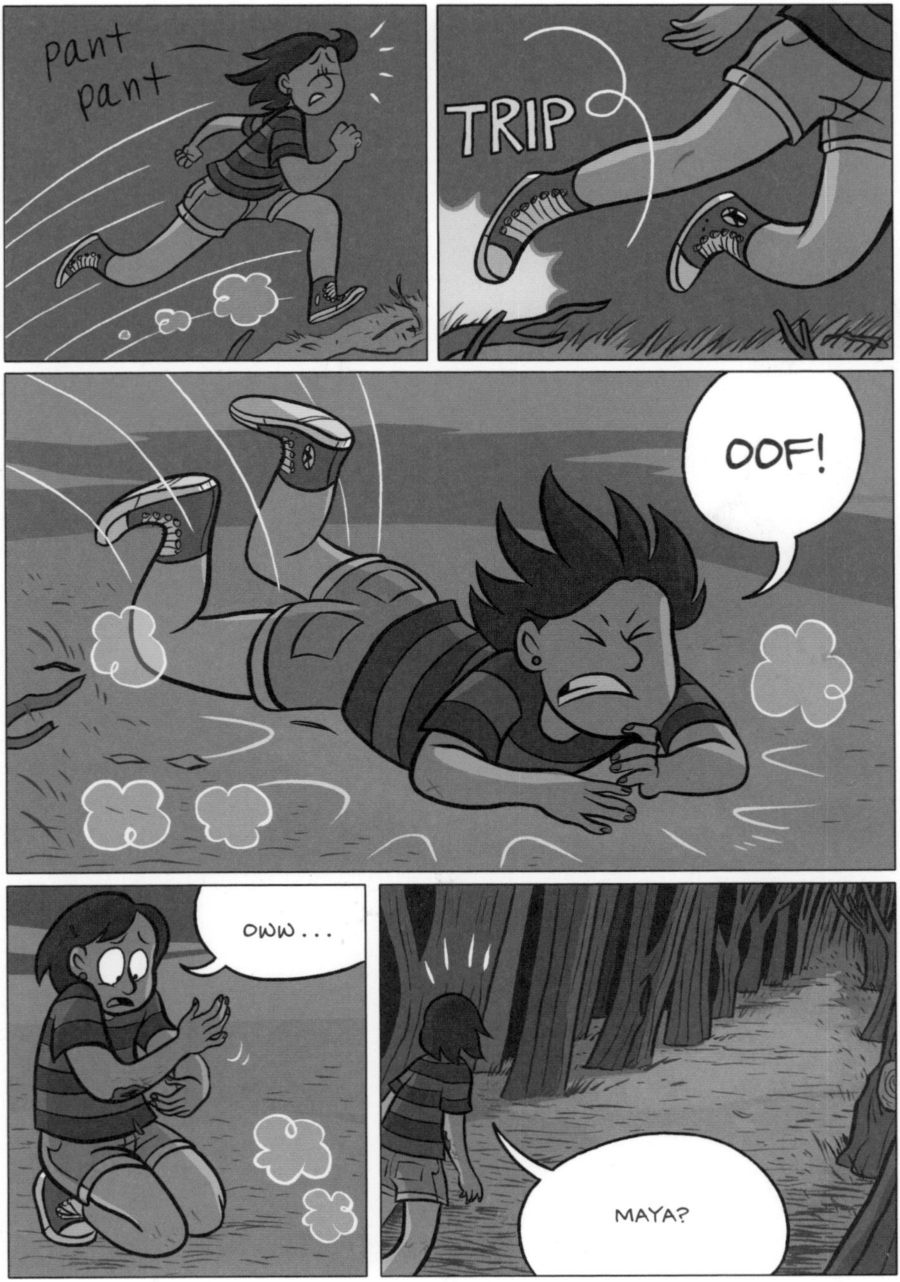
pant
pant
TRIP
OOF!
OWW . . .
MAYA?

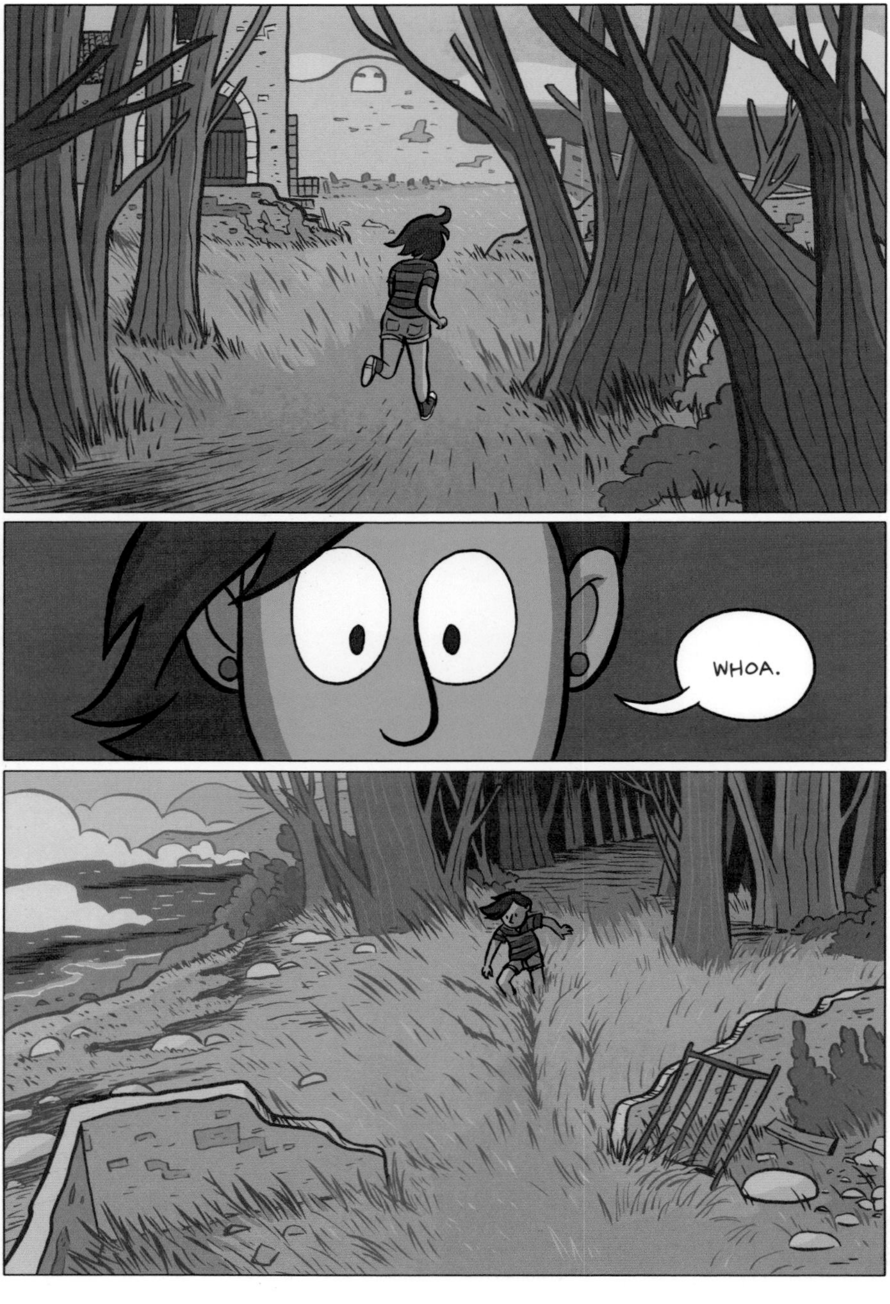
WHOA.

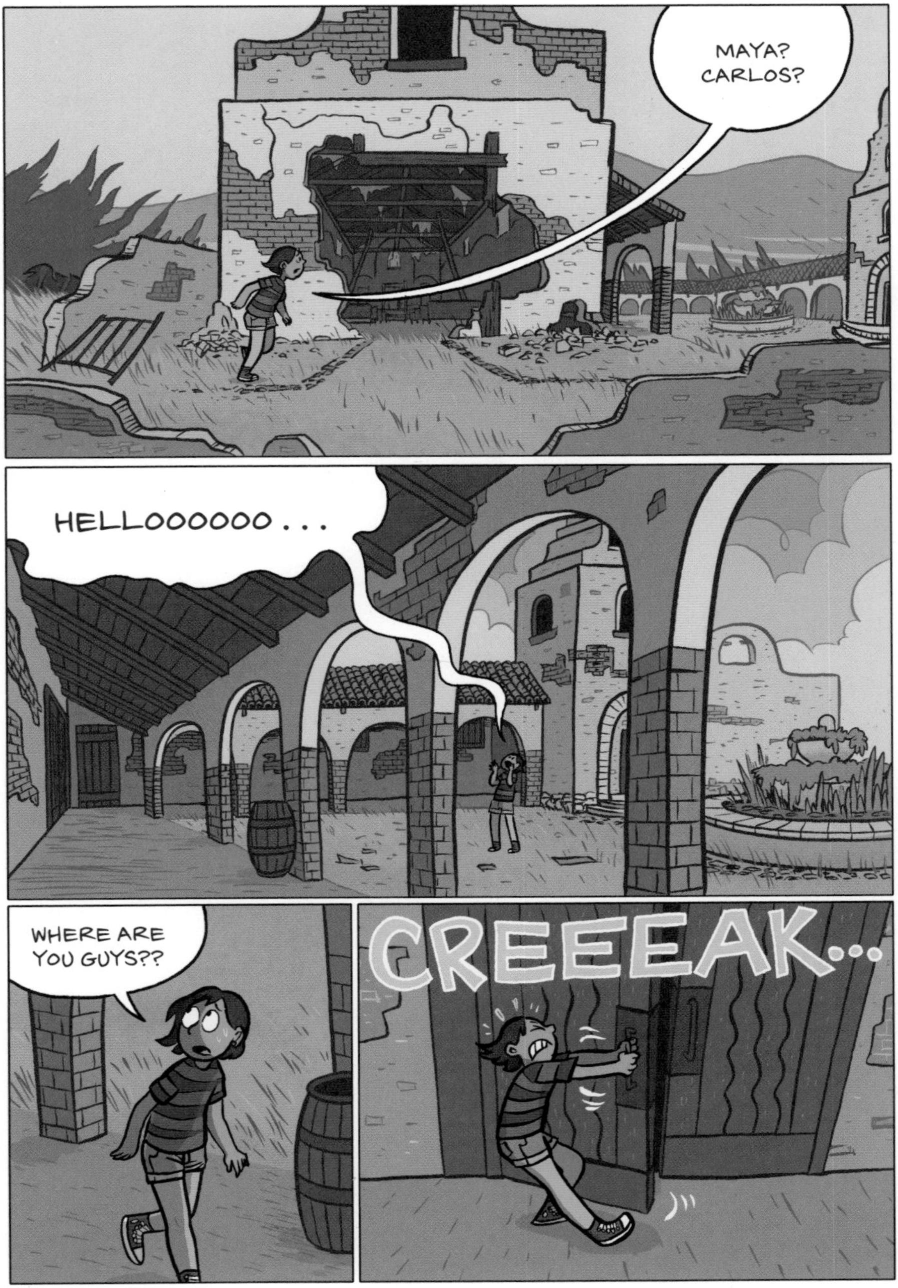
MAYA? CARLOS?
HELLOOOOOO . . .
WHERE ARE YOU GUYS??
CREEEAK...

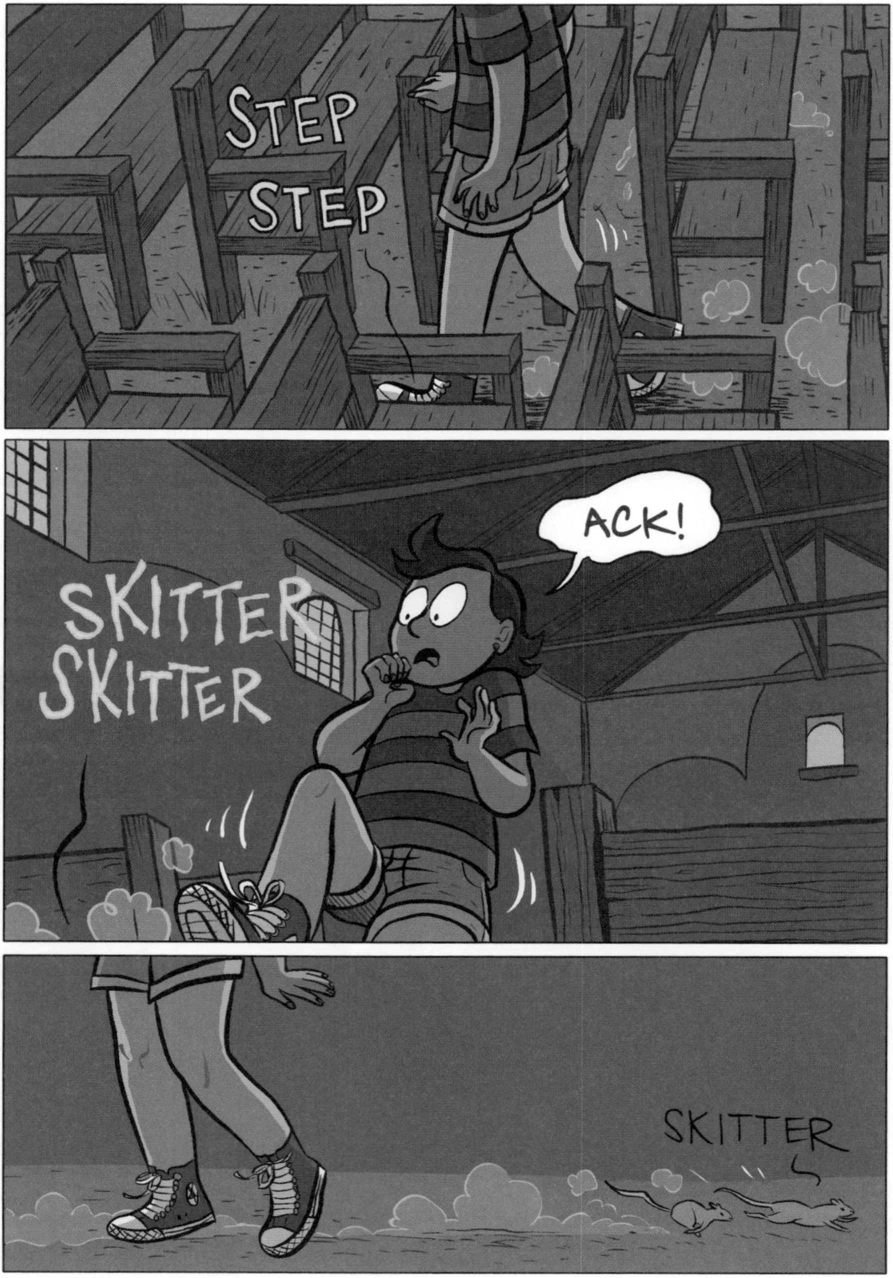
STEP
STEP
SKITTER
SKITTER
ACK!
SKITTER

whew.

WHHHHHHHHHHSSSSSSS

Peek

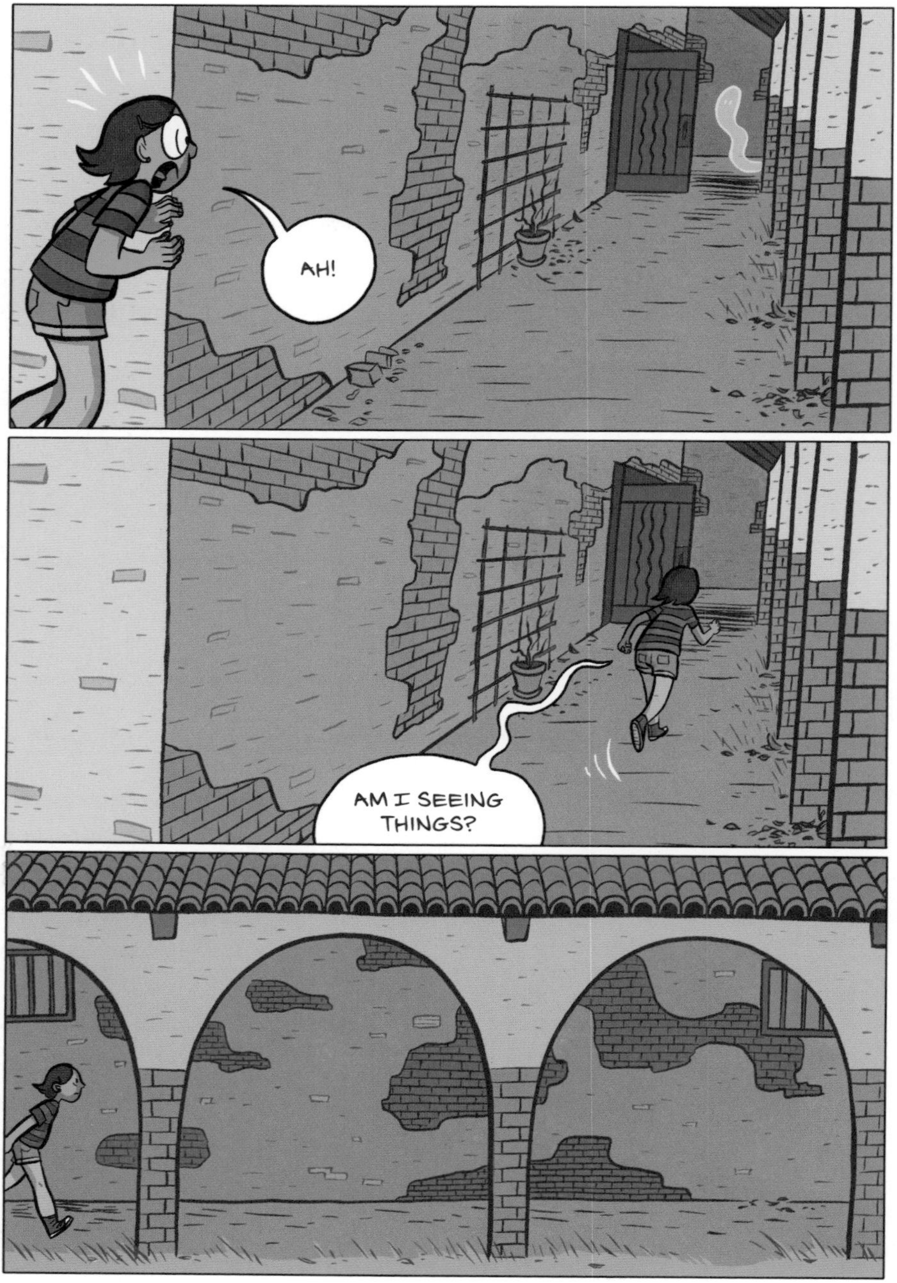
AH!
AM I SEEING THINGS?

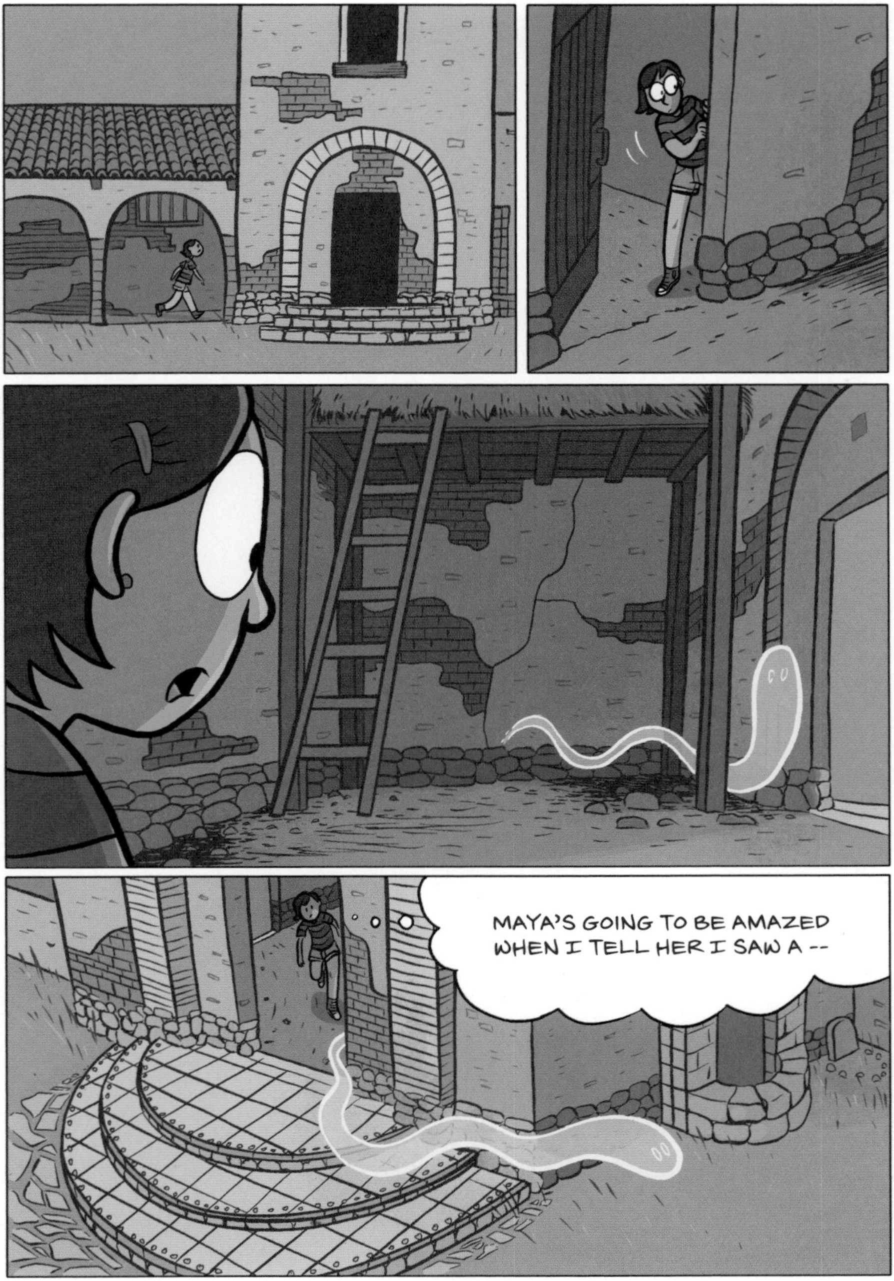
MAYA'S GOING TO BE AMAZED WHEN I TELL HER I SAW A --

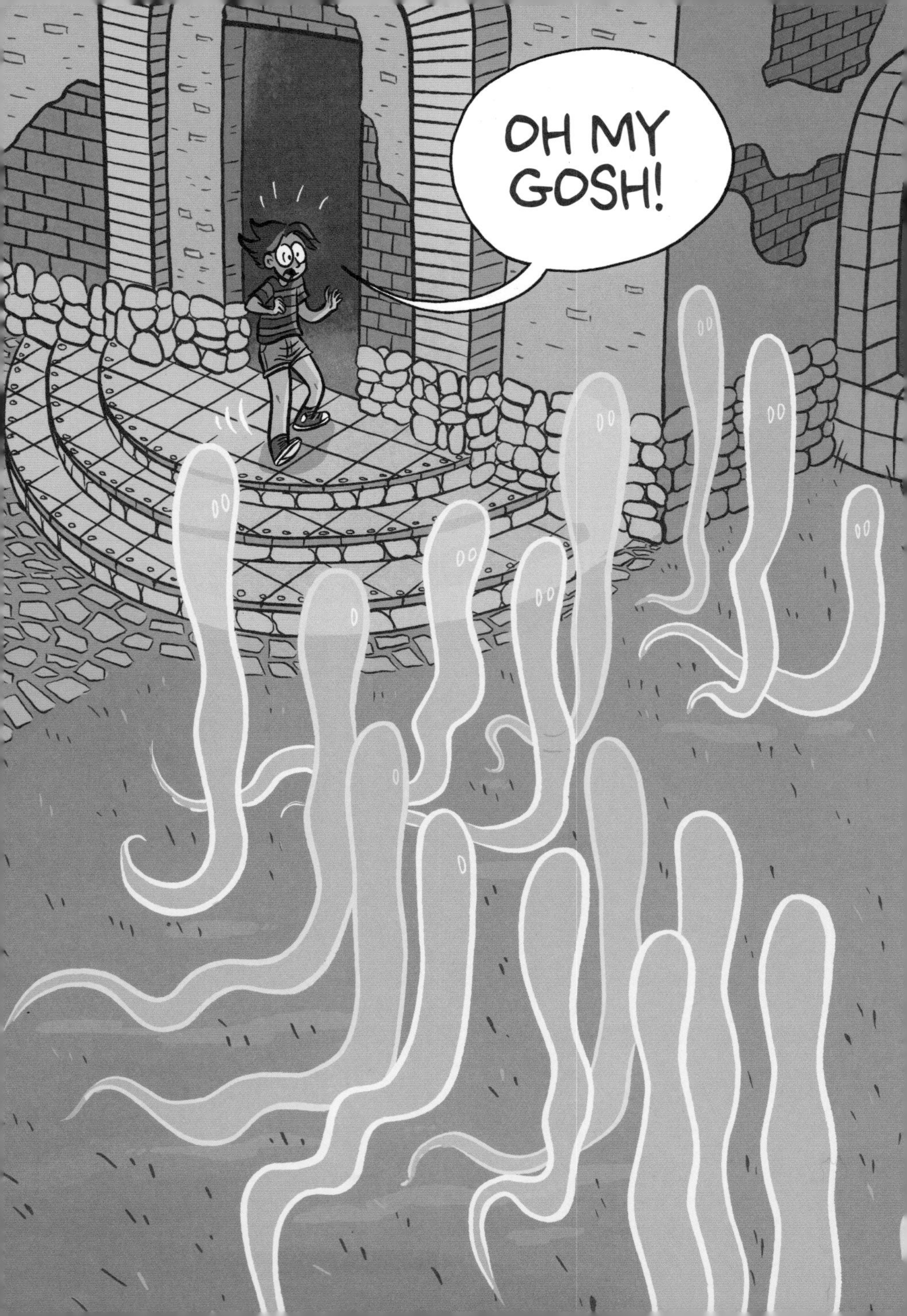
OH MY GOSH!

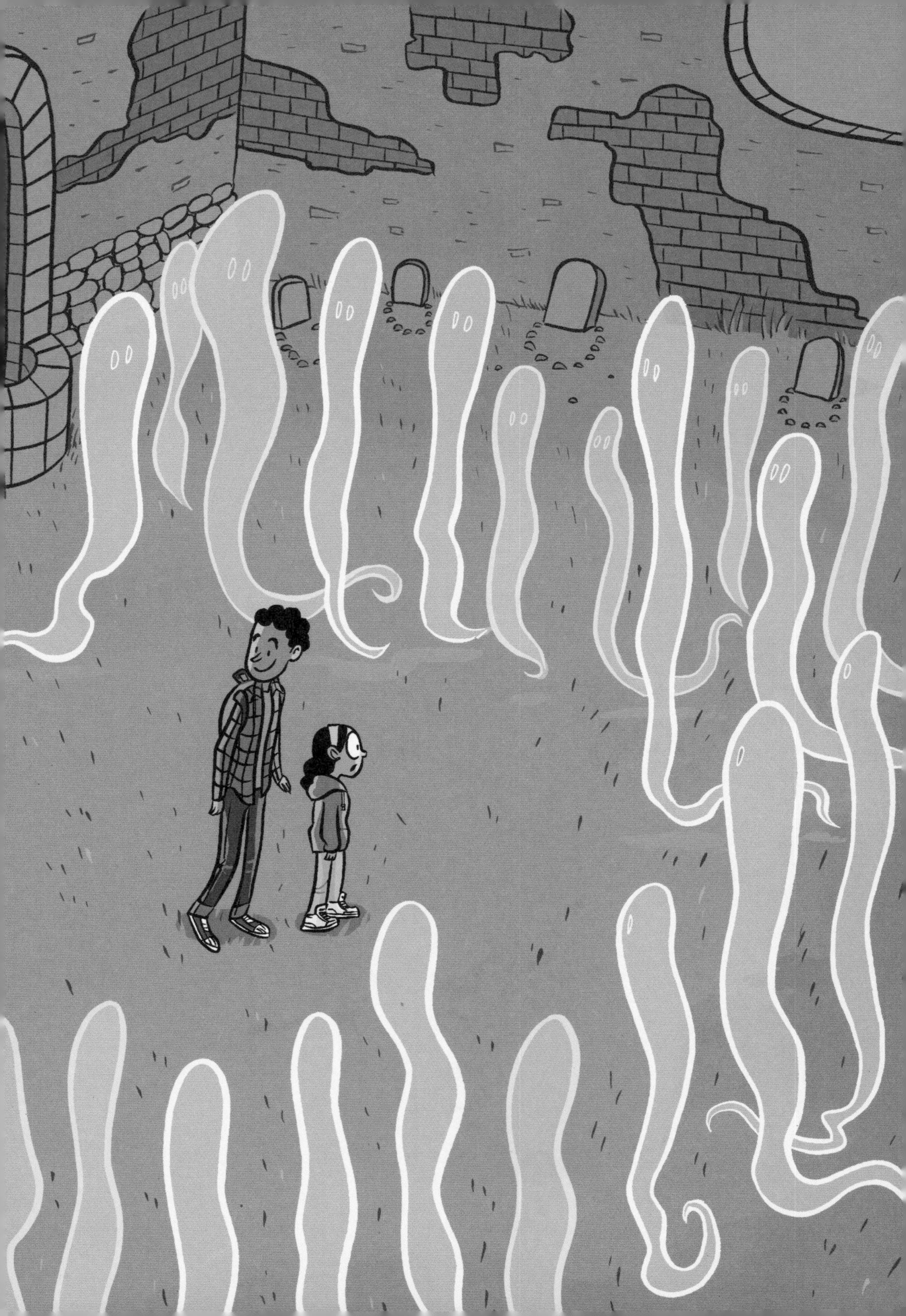

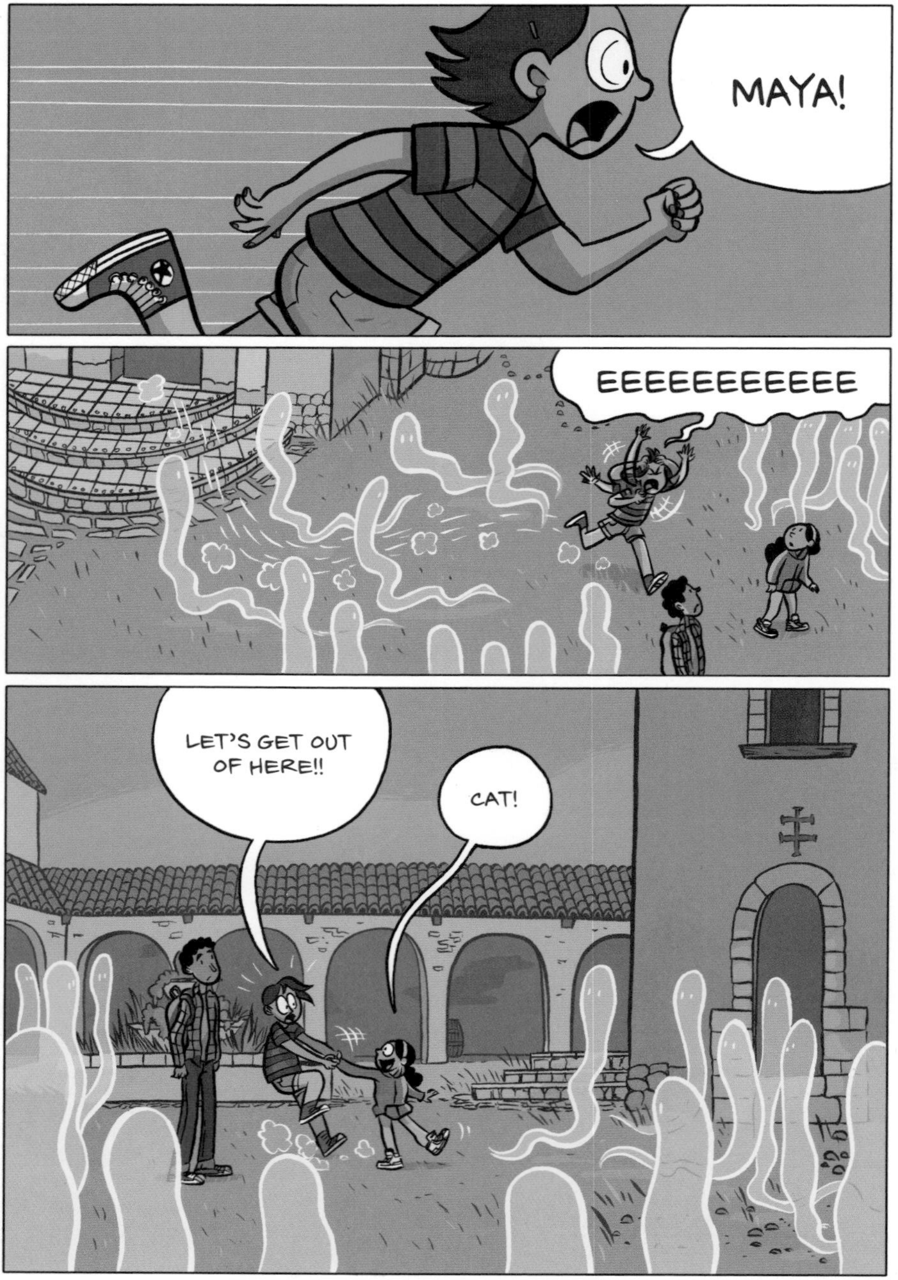
MAYA!
EEEEEEEEEEEE
LET'S GET OUT OF HERE!!
CAT!

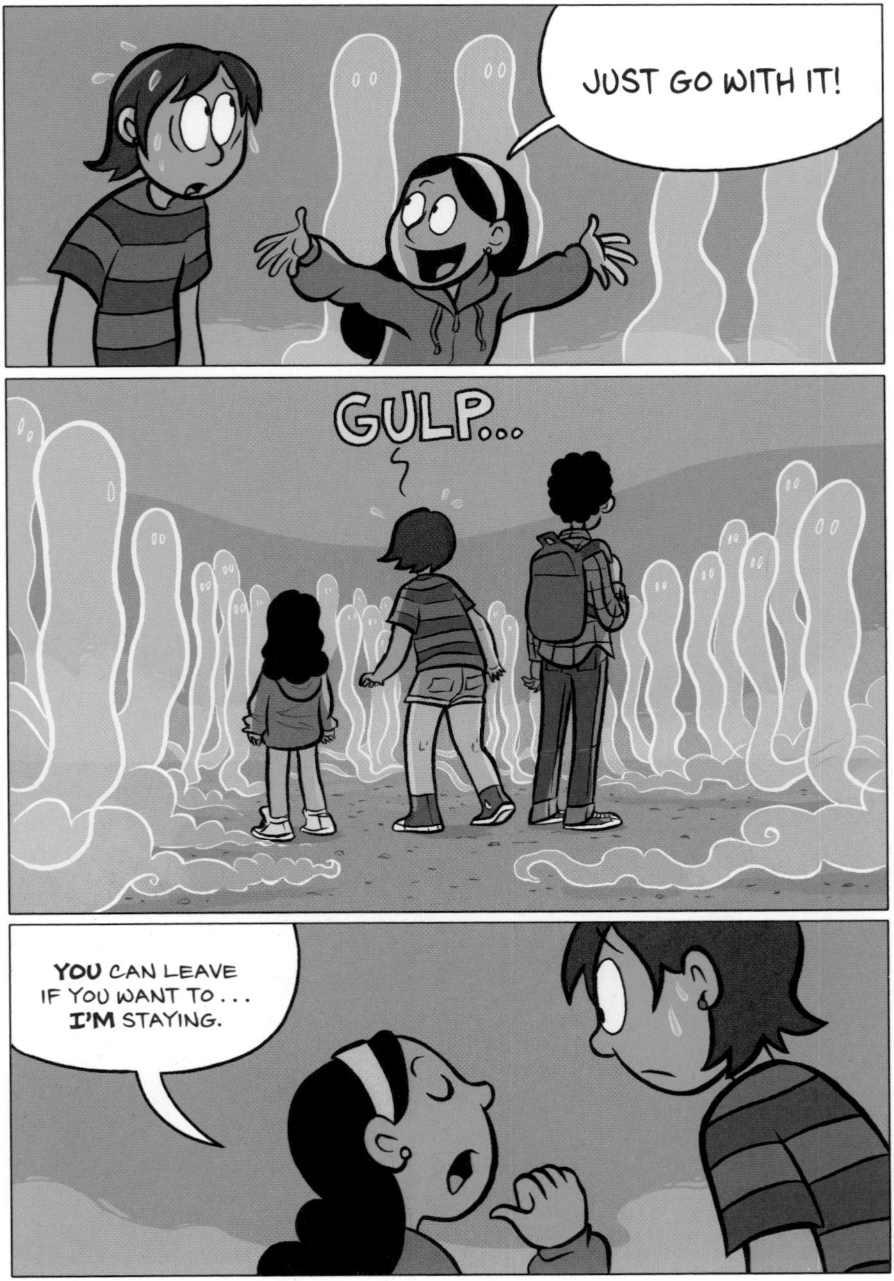
JUST GO WITH IT!
GULP...
YOU CAN LEAVE IF YOU WANT TO . . . I'M STAYING.

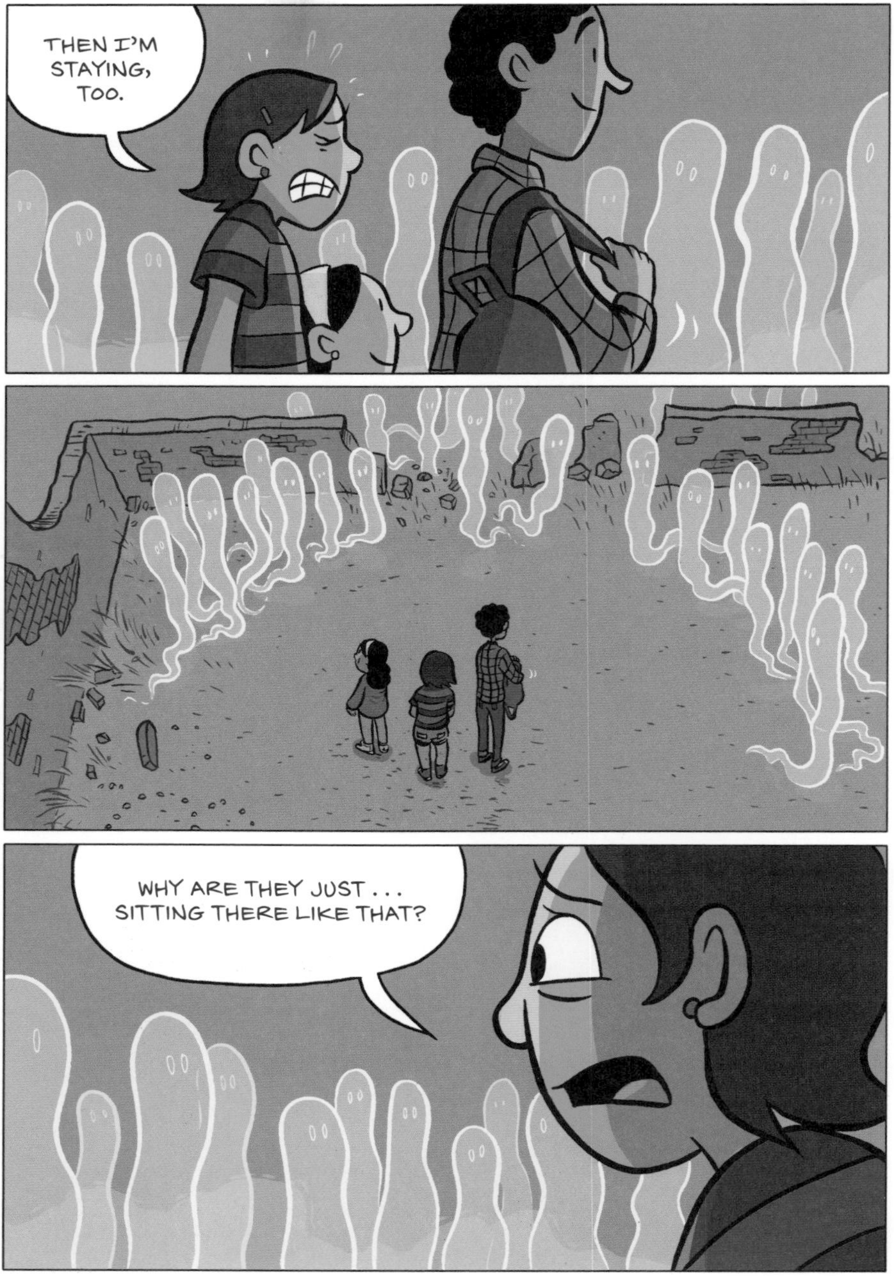
THEN I'M STAYING, TOO.
WHY ARE THEY JUST . . . SITTING THERE LIKE THAT?

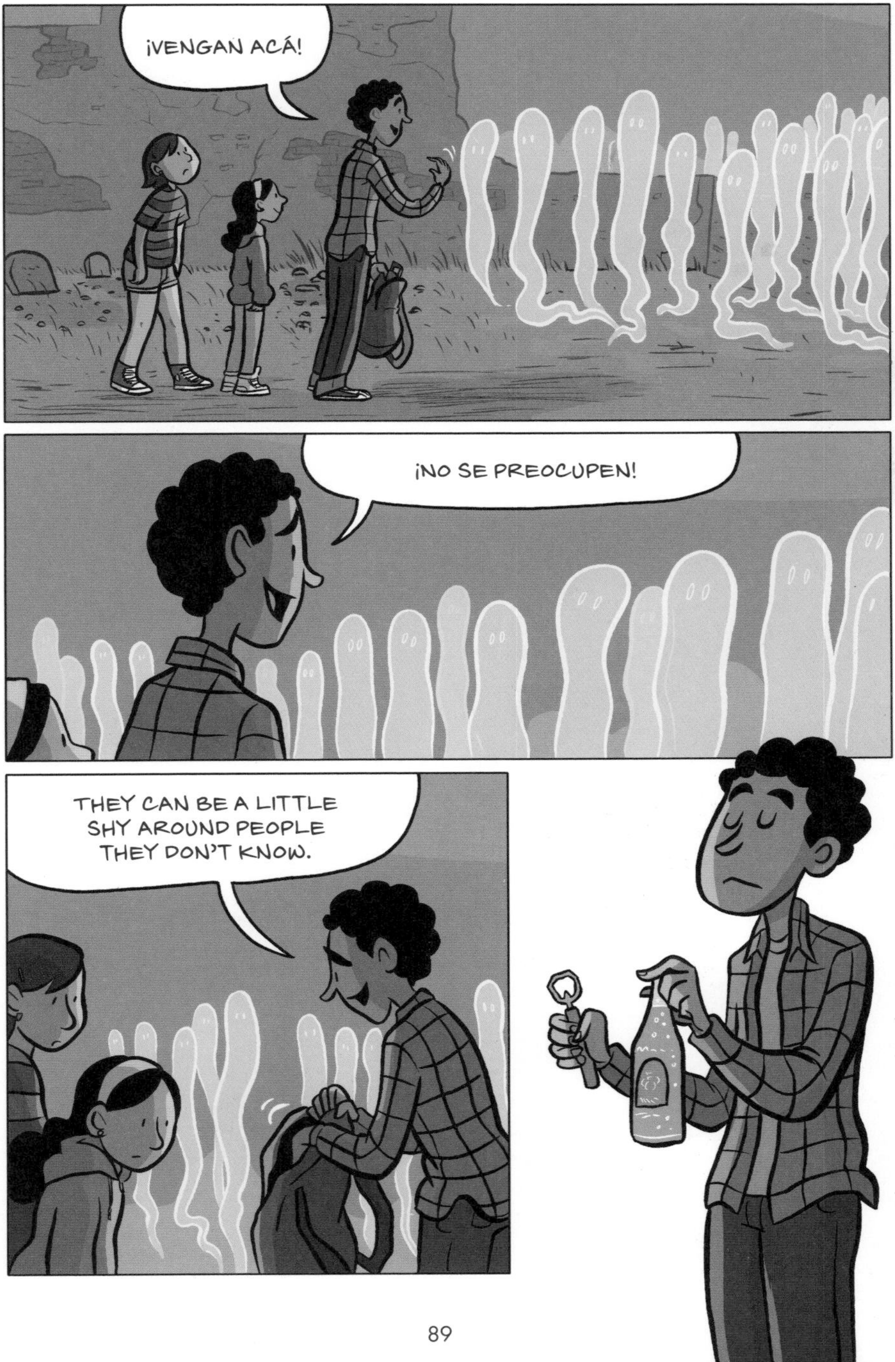
¡VENGAN ACÁ!
¡NO SE PREOCUPEN!
THEY CAN BE A LITTLE SHY AROUND PEOPLE THEY DON'T KNOW.

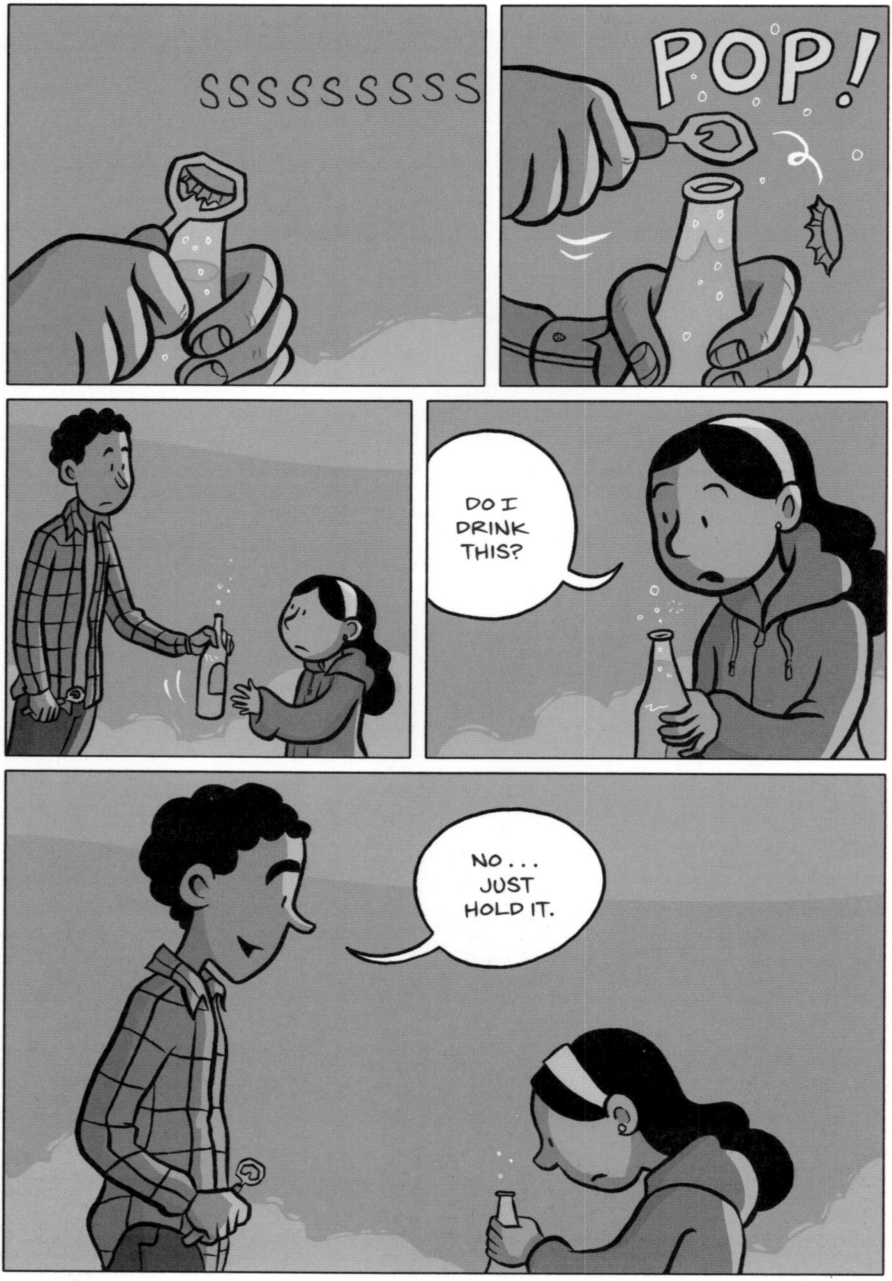
SSSSSSSSSS
POP!
DO I DRINK THIS?
NO . . . JUST HOLD IT.

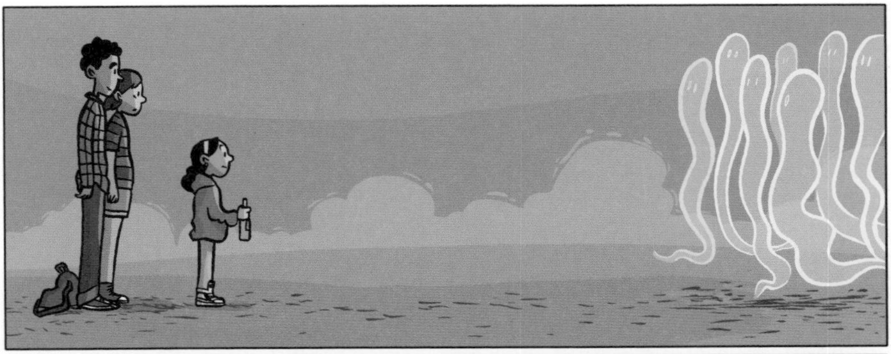
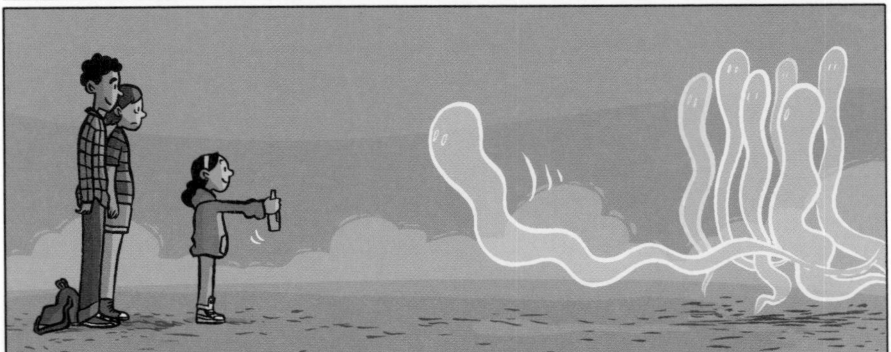
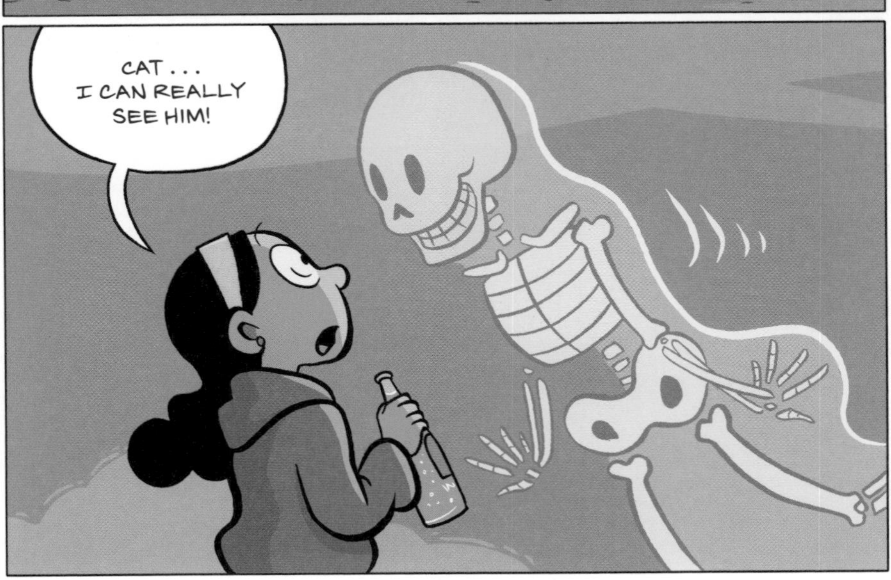
CAT . . . I CAN REALLY SEE HIM!

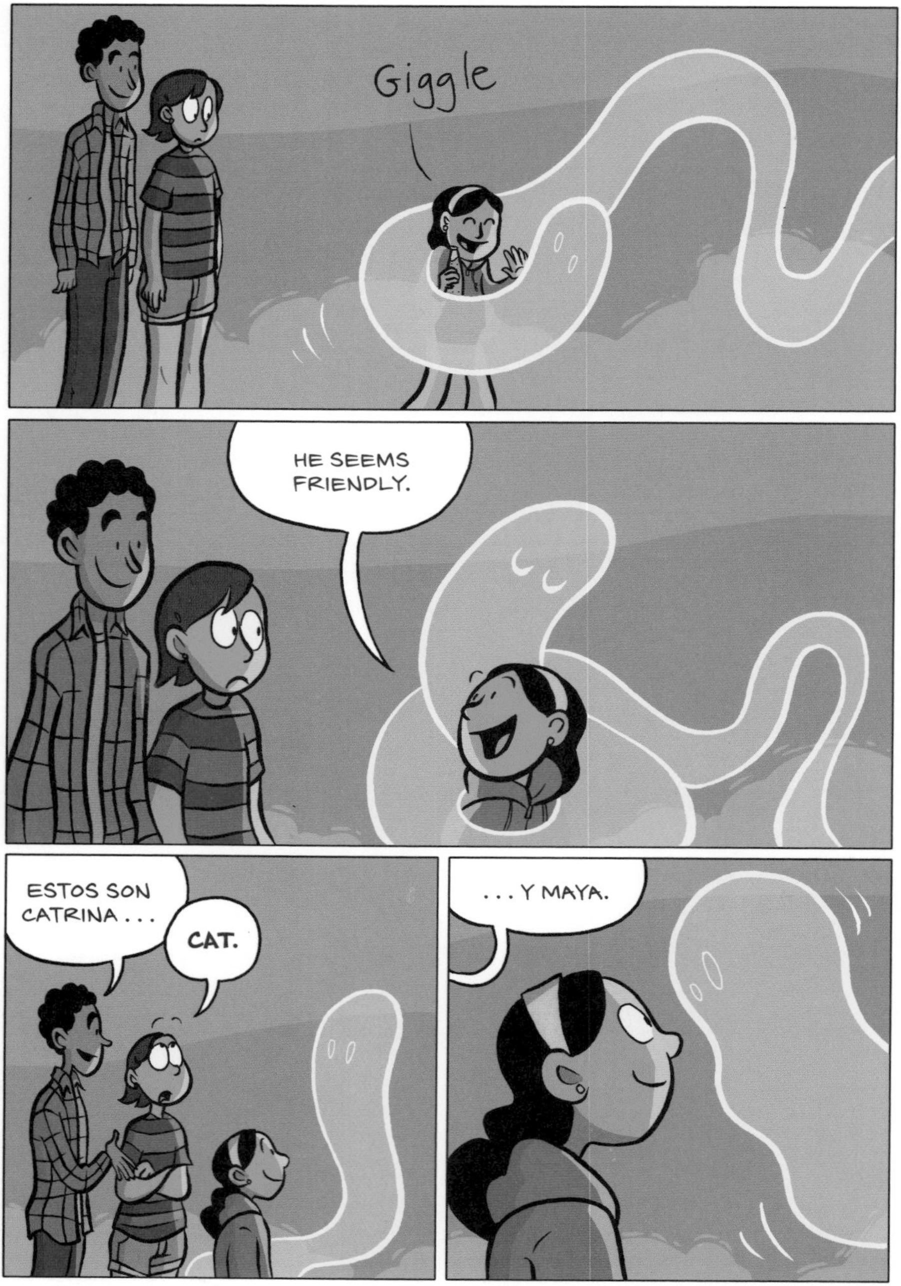
Giggle
HE SEEMS FRIENDLY.
ESTOS SON CATRINA . . .
CAT.
. . . Y MAYA.

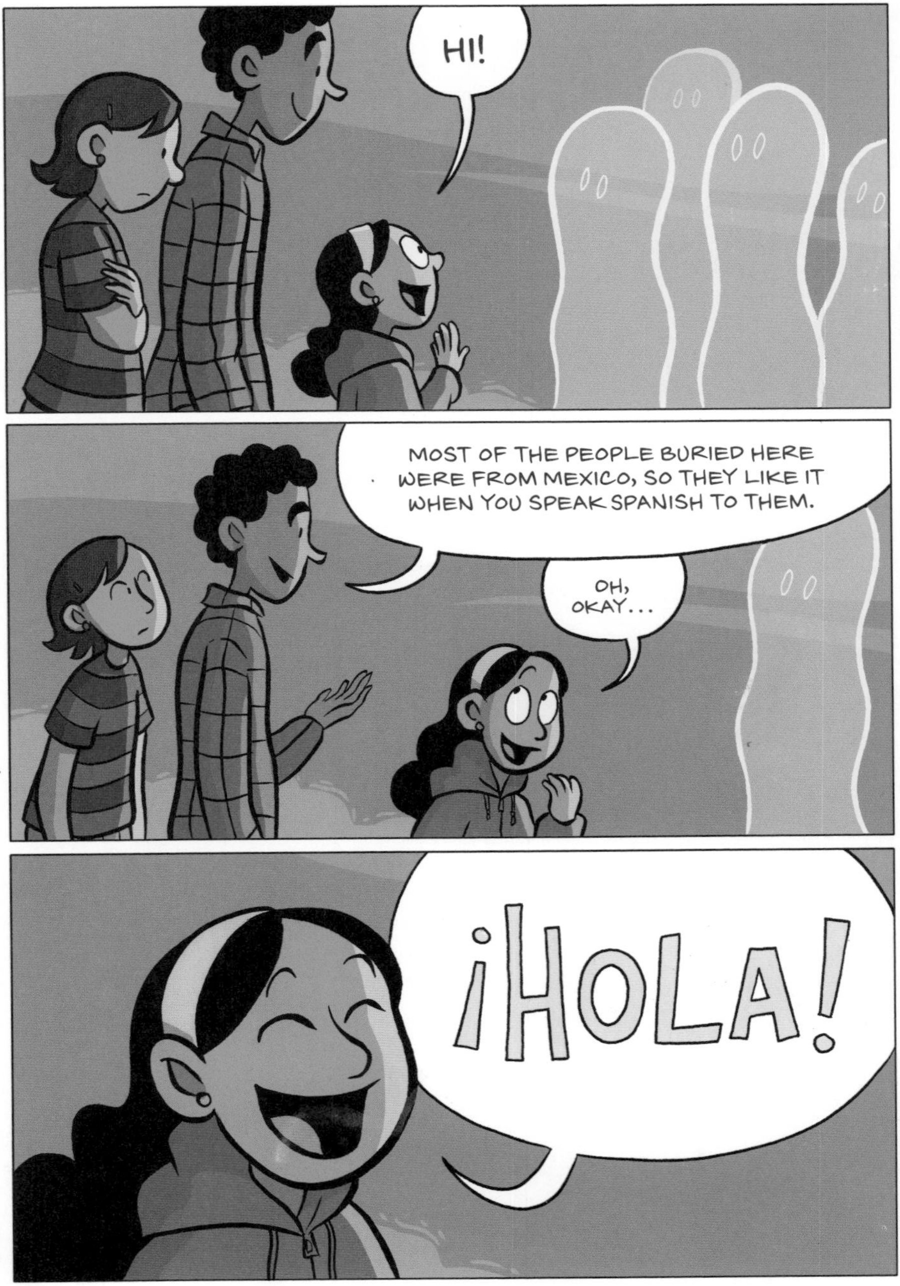
HI!
MOST OF THE PEOPLE BURIED HERE WERE FROM MEXICO, SO THEY LIKE IT WHEN YOU SPEAK SPANISH TO THEM.
OH, OKAY...
¡HOLA!

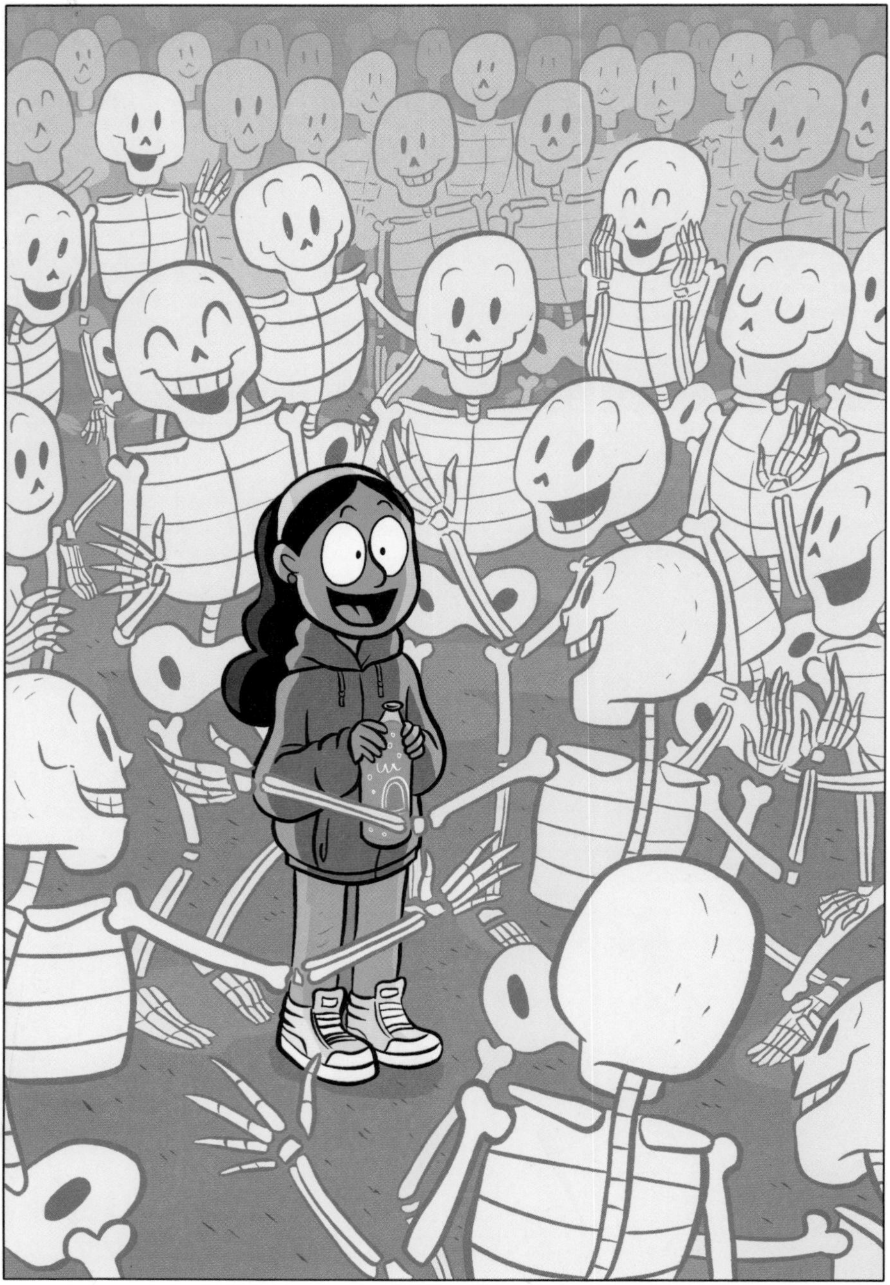

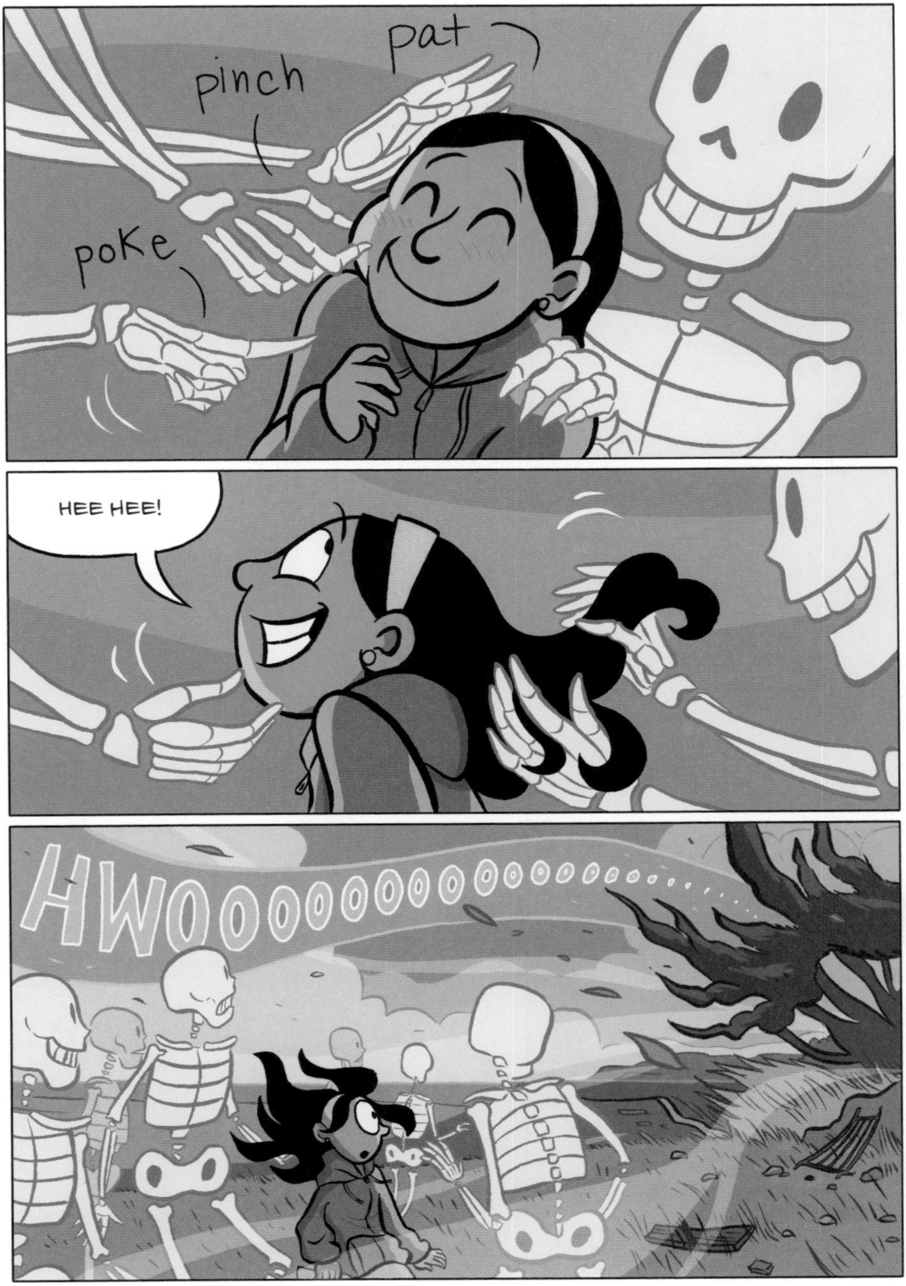
pinch
pat
poke
HEE HEE!
HWOOOOOOOOOOOOOOOOOOOO

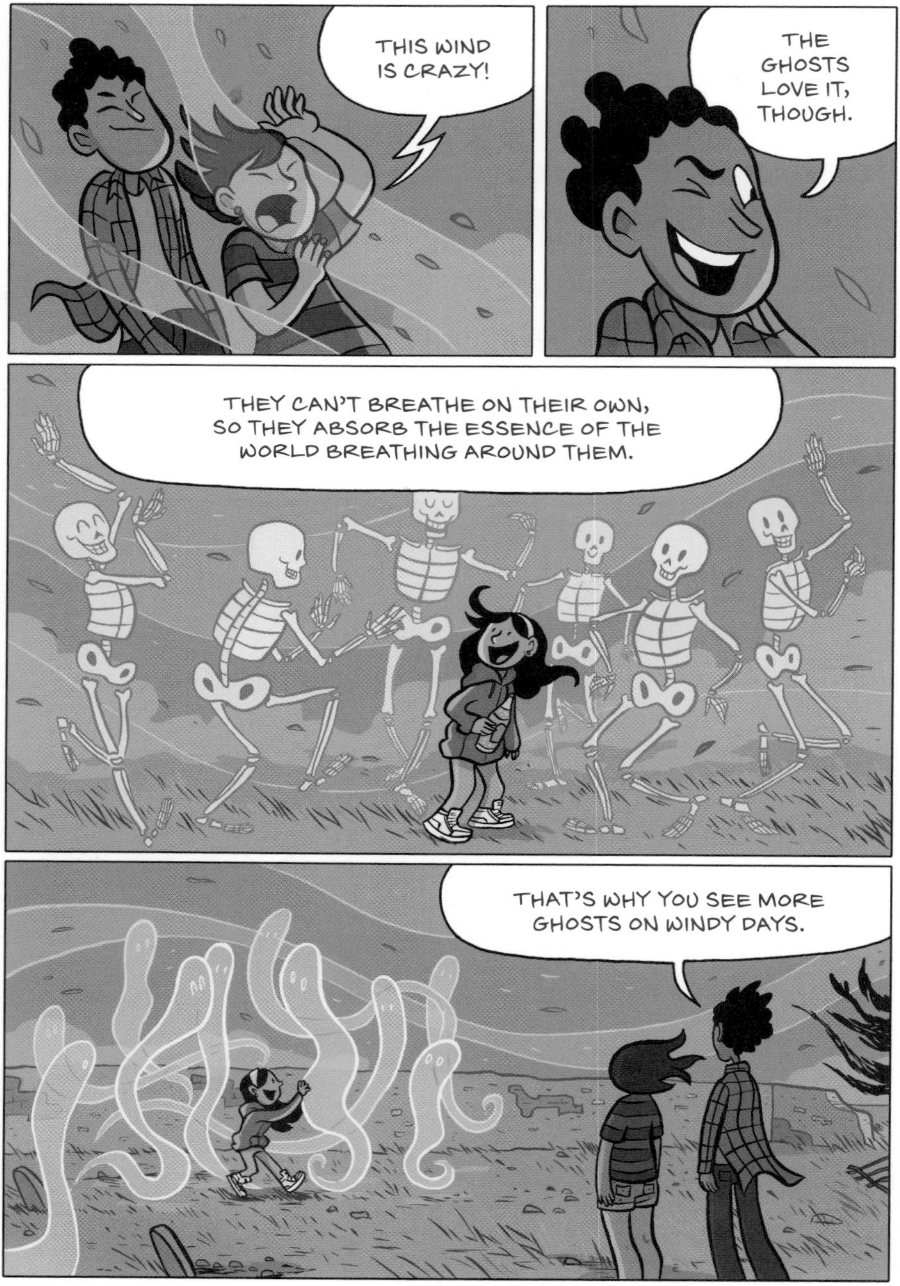
THIS WIND IS CRAZY!
THE GHOSTS LOVE IT, THOUGH.
THEY CAN'T BREATHE ON THEIR OWN, SO THEY ABSORB THE ESSENCE OF THE WORLD BREATHING AROUND THEM.
THAT'S WHY YOU SEE MORE GHOSTS ON WINDY DAYS.

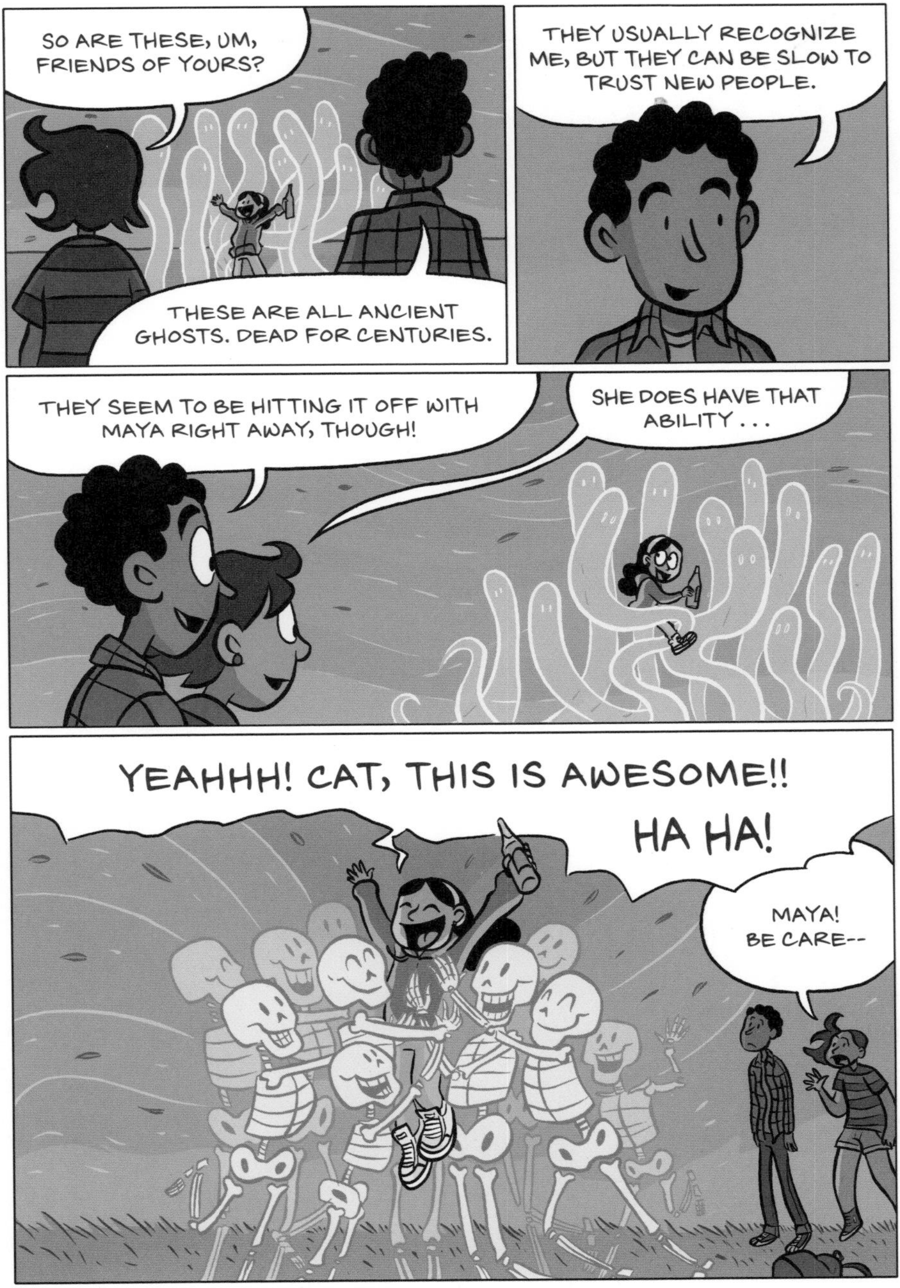
SO ARE THESE, UM, FRIENDS OF YOURS?
THESE ARE ALL ANCIENT GHOSTS. DEAD FOR CENTURIES.
THEY USUALLY RECOGNIZE ME, BUT THEY CAN BE SLOW TO TRUST NEW PEOPLE.
THEY SEEM TO BE HITTING IT OFF WITH MAYA RIGHT AWAY, THOUGH!
SHE DOES HAVE THAT ABILITY . . .
YEAHHH! CAT, THIS IS AWESOME!!
HA HA!
MAYA! BE CARE--

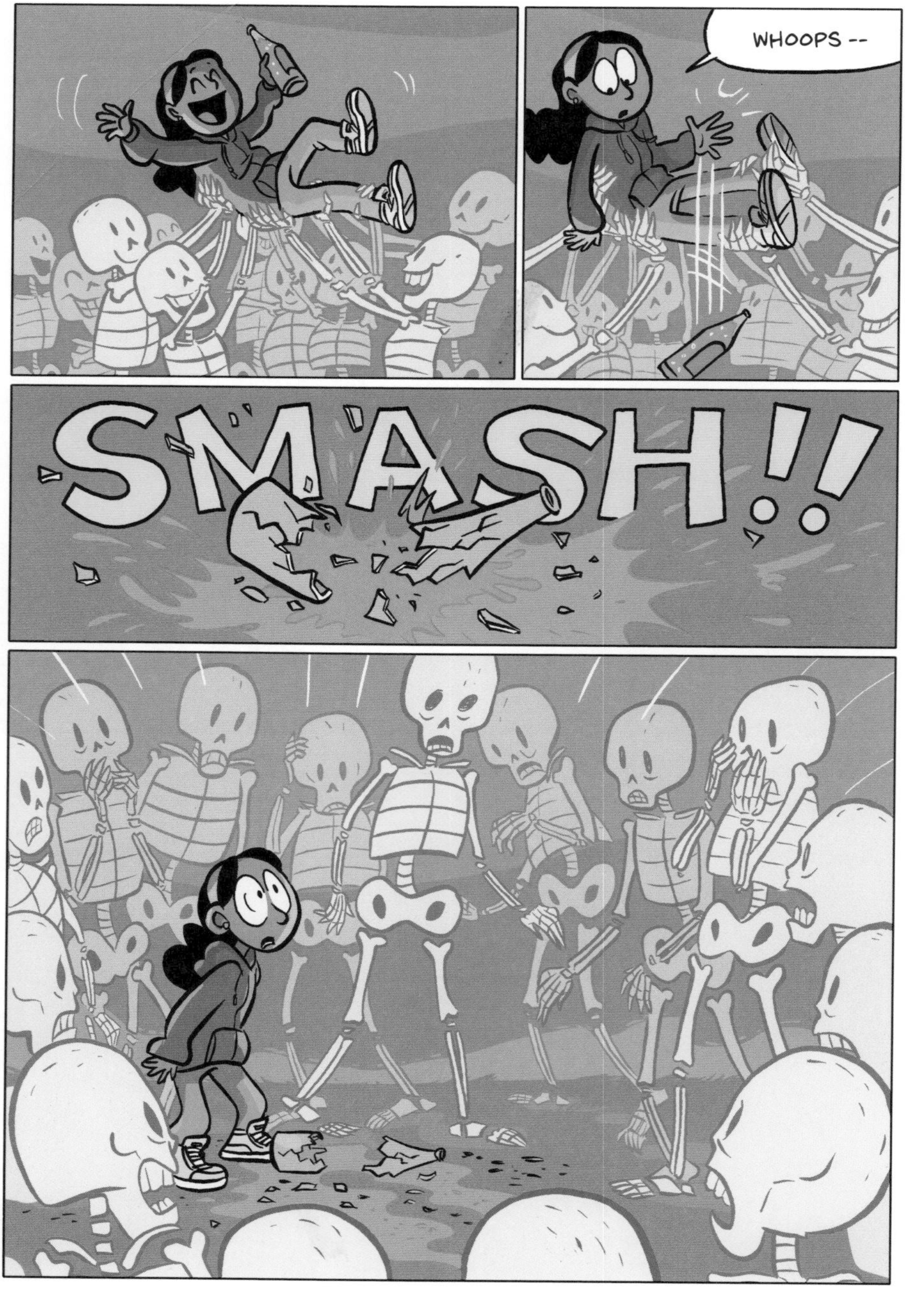
WHOOPS --
SMASH!!

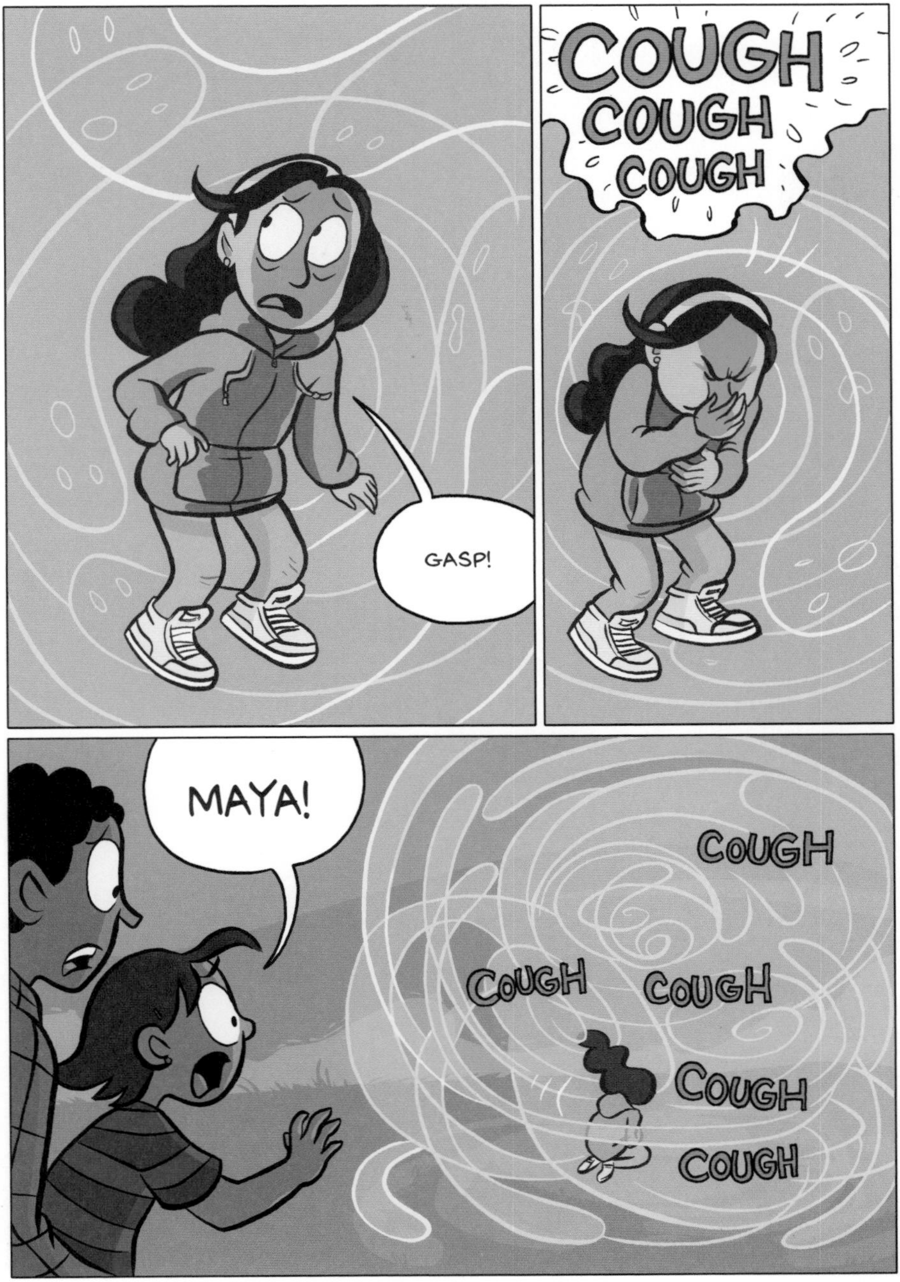
GASP!
COUGH
COUGH
COUGH
MAYA!
COUGH
COUGH
COUGH
COUGH
COUGH

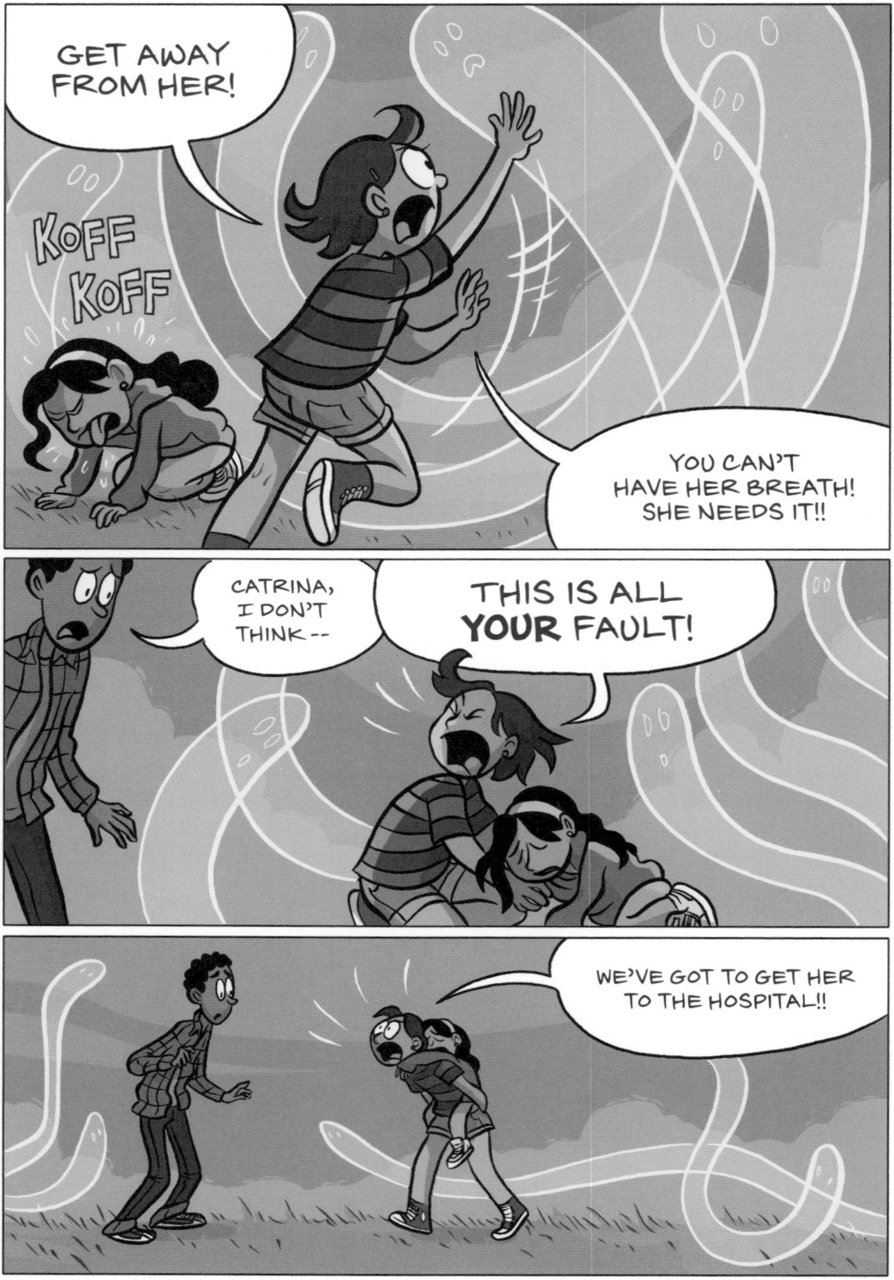
GET AWAY FROM HER!
KOFF KOFF
YOU CAN'T HAVE HER BREATH! SHE NEEDS IT!!
CATRINA, I DON'T THINK--
THIS IS ALL **YOUR** FAULT!
WE'VE GOT TO GET HER TO THE HOSPITAL!!

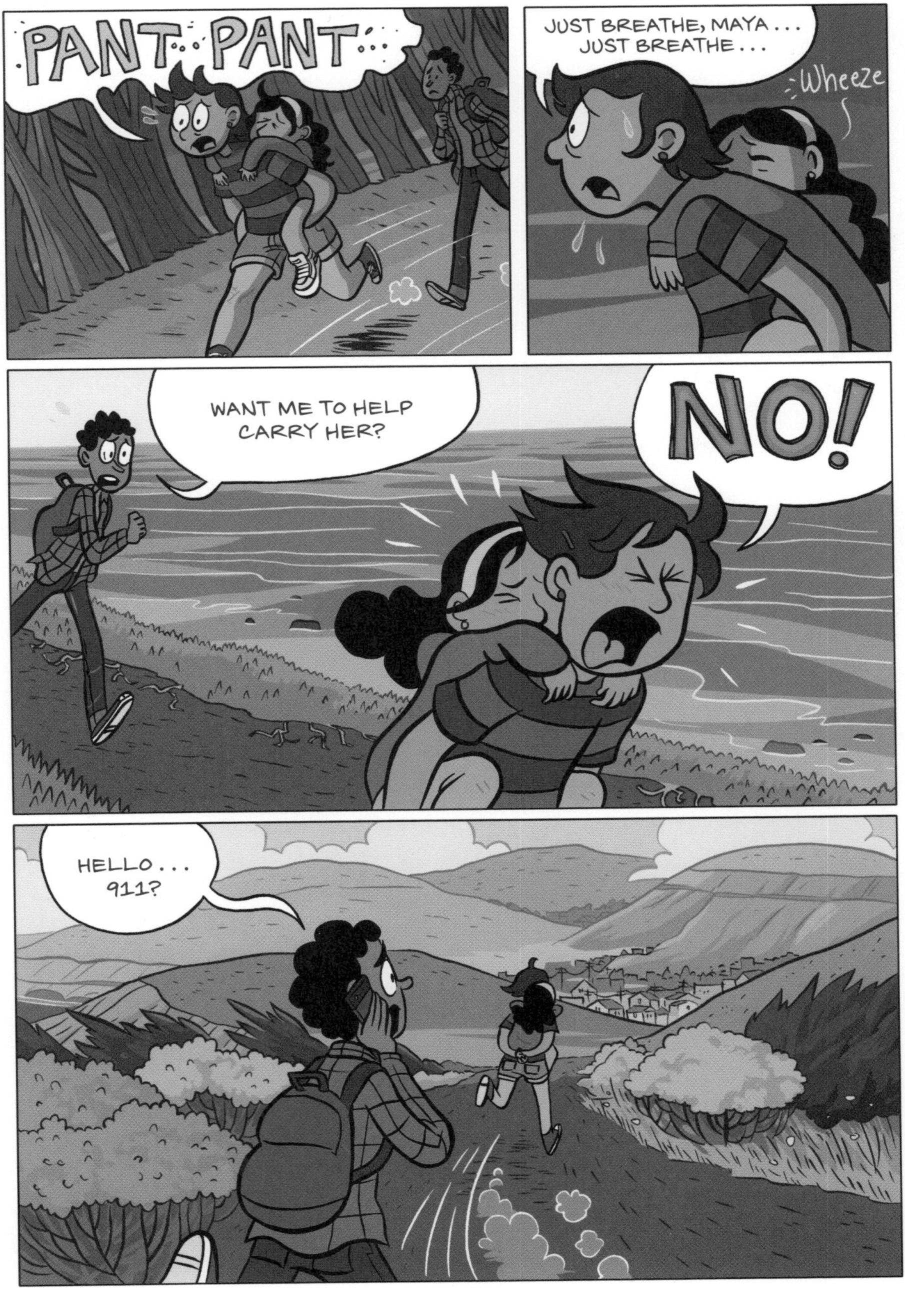
PANT PANT
JUST BREATHE, MAYA . . . JUST BREATHE . . .
Wheeze
WANT ME TO HELP CARRY HER?
NO!
HELLO . . . 911?

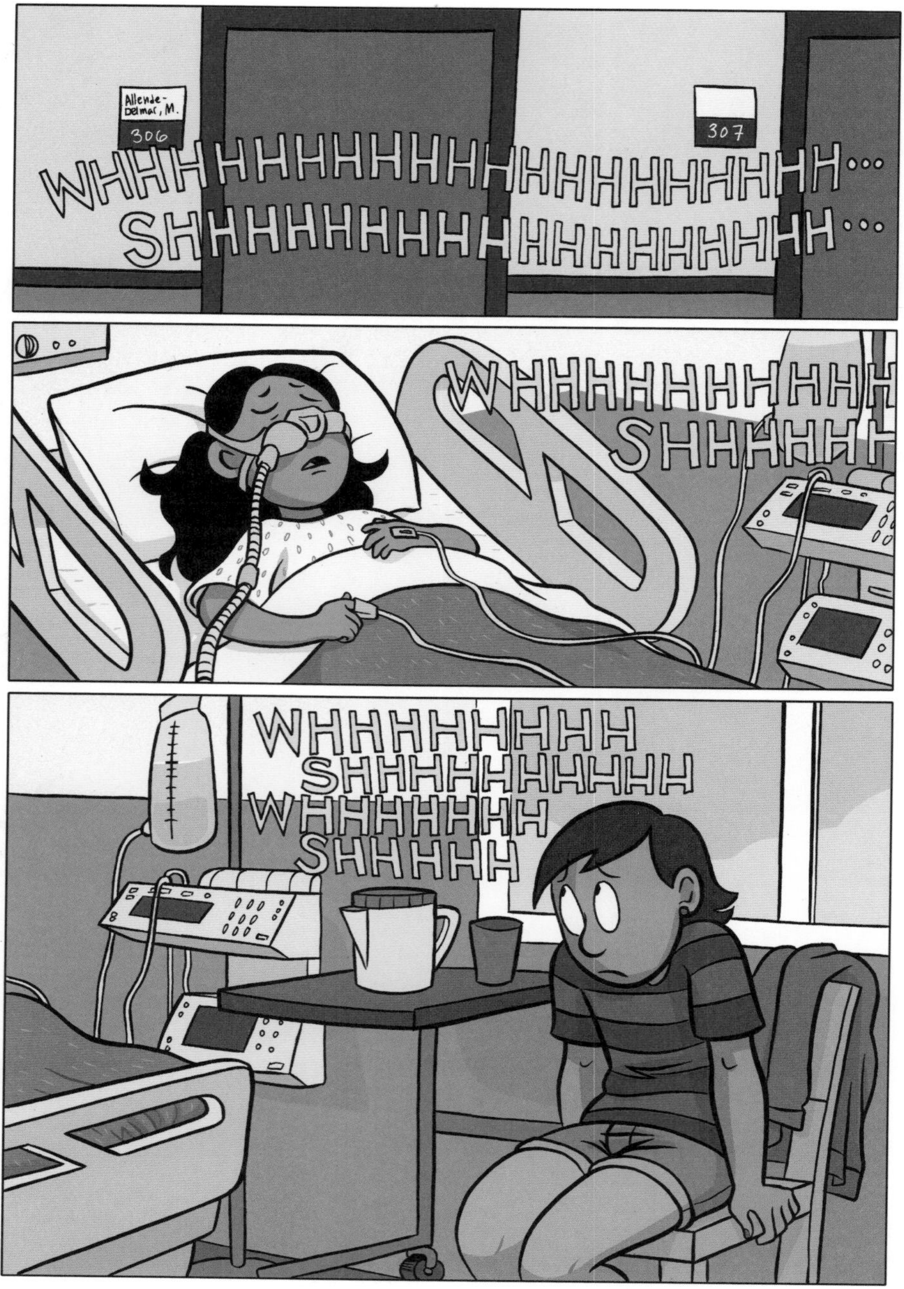
Allende-Delmar, M.
306
307
WHHHHHHHHHHHHHHHHHHHHH...
SHHHHHHHHHHHHHHHHHHH...
WHHHHHHHHHH
SHHHHHH
WHHHHHHHH
SHHHHHHHHHH
WHHHHHHH
SHHHHH

IT'S MOST LIKELY HER ATTACK WAS BROUGHT ON BY THE COLD. THAT, AND OVEREXERTING HERSELF.

WHHHHHH
SHHHHHH
WHHHHHH

CATRINA, WHAT WERE YOU THINKING, TAKING MAYA **HIKING** WITHOUT BRINGING HER MEDICATION?

WHHHHH HHH
SHHH HHH

I'M SORRY! SHE JUST . . . REALLY WANTED TO GO RIGHT THEN, AND I THOUGHT . . .

WHHHHH
SHHHHH

WE EXPECT MORE FROM YOU, CAT.

I KNOW.

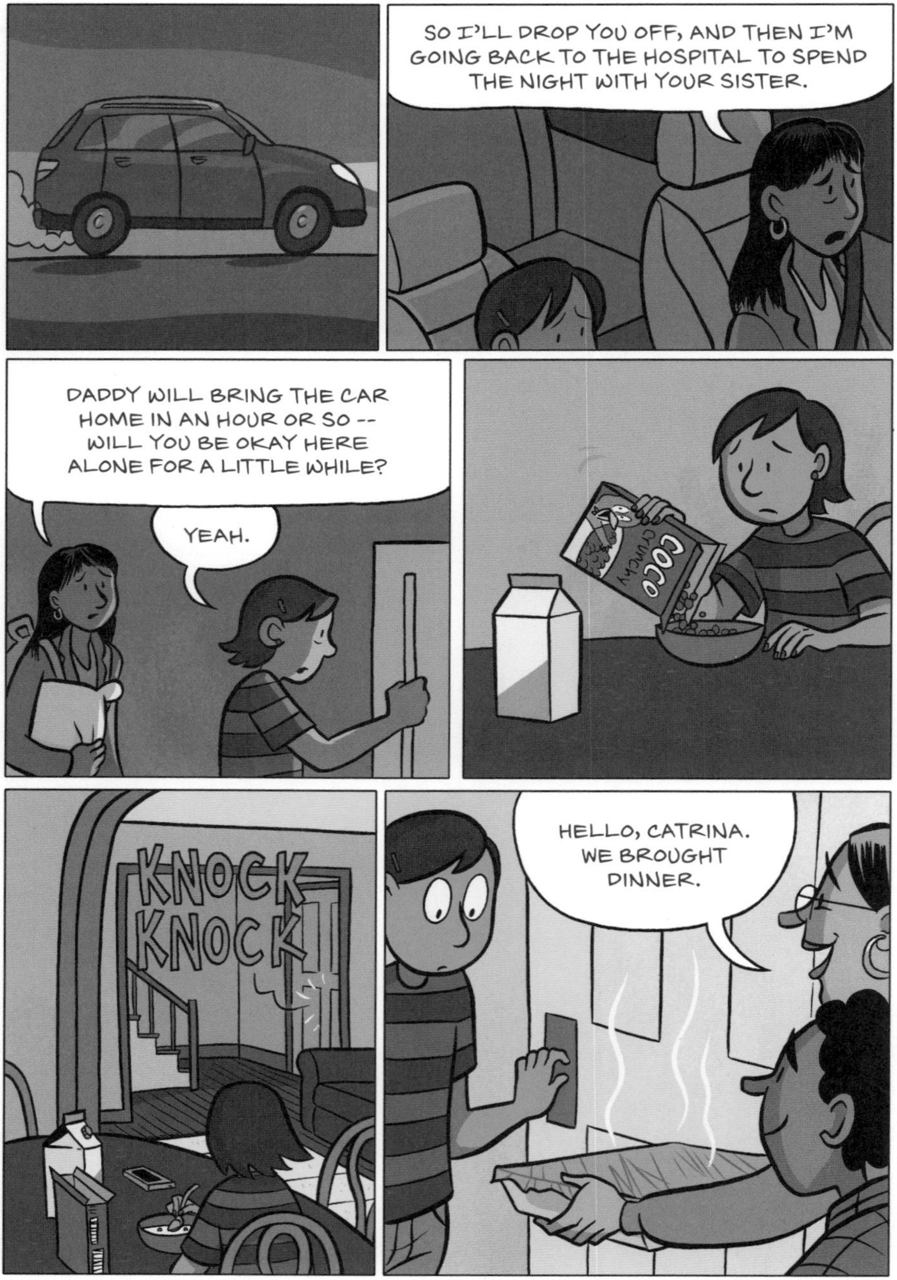
SO I'LL DROP YOU OFF, AND THEN I'M GOING BACK TO THE HOSPITAL TO SPEND THE NIGHT WITH YOUR SISTER.
DADDY WILL BRING THE CAR HOME IN AN HOUR OR SO -- WILL YOU BE OKAY HERE ALONE FOR A LITTLE WHILE?
YEAH.
COCO Crunchy
KNOCK KNOCK
HELLO, CATRINA. WE BROUGHT DINNER.

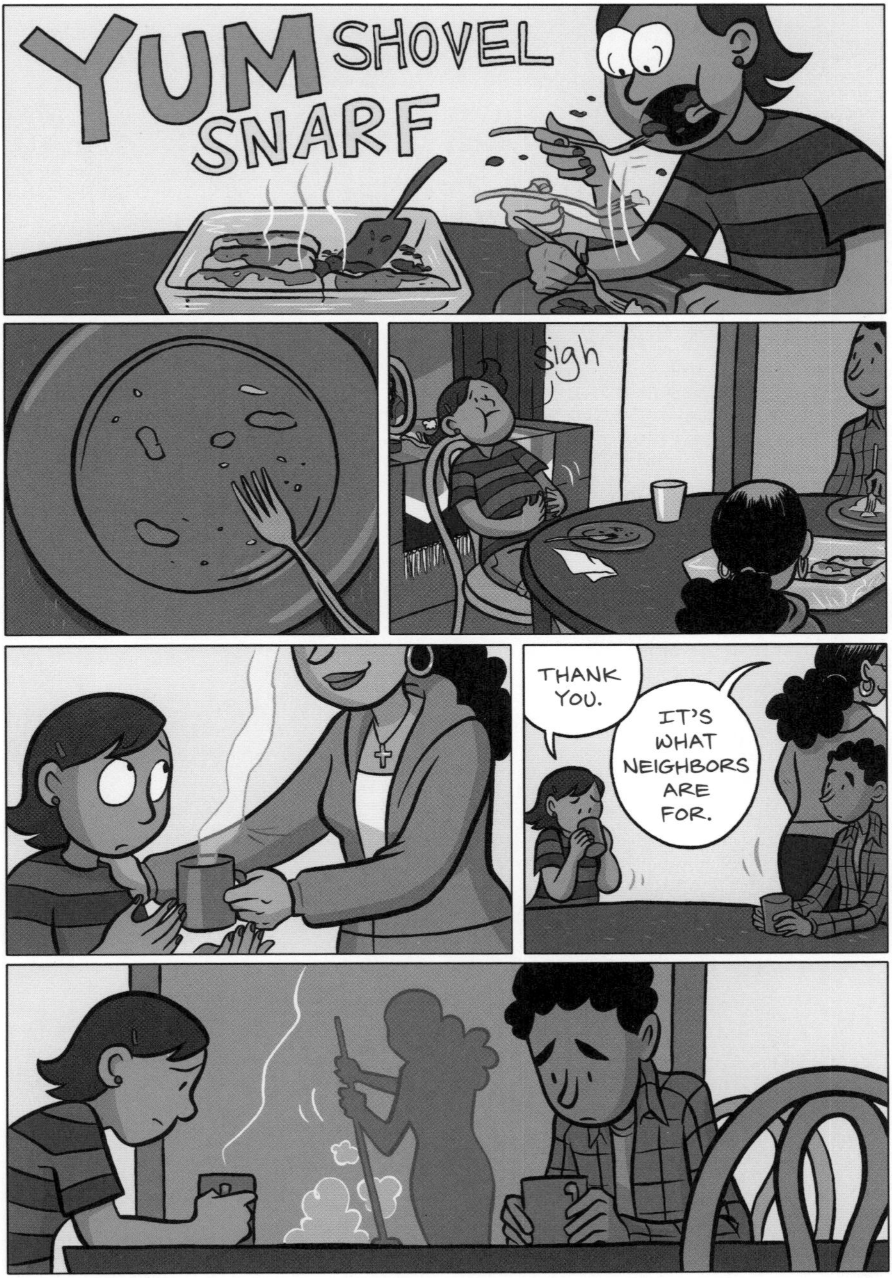
YUM
SHOVEL
SNARF
sigh
THANK YOU.
IT'S WHAT NEIGHBORS ARE FOR.

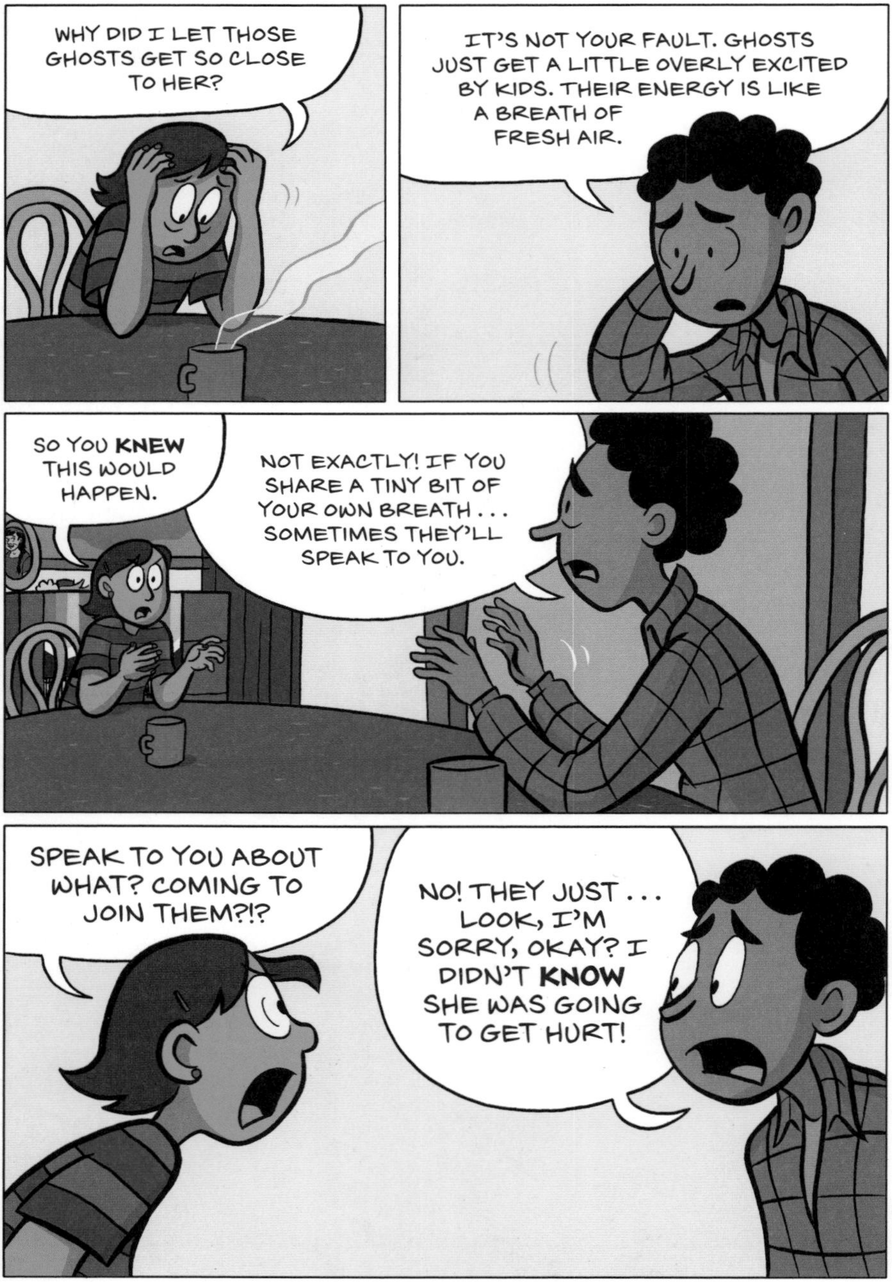
WHY DID I LET THOSE GHOSTS GET SO CLOSE TO HER?
IT'S NOT YOUR FAULT. GHOSTS JUST GET A LITTLE OVERLY EXCITED BY KIDS. THEIR ENERGY IS LIKE A BREATH OF FRESH AIR.
SO YOU **KNEW** THIS WOULD HAPPEN.
NOT EXACTLY! IF YOU SHARE A TINY BIT OF YOUR OWN BREATH . . . SOMETIMES THEY'LL SPEAK TO YOU.
SPEAK TO YOU ABOUT WHAT? COMING TO JOIN THEM?!?
NO! THEY JUST . . . LOOK, I'M SORRY, OKAY? I DIDN'T **KNOW** SHE WAS GOING TO GET HURT!

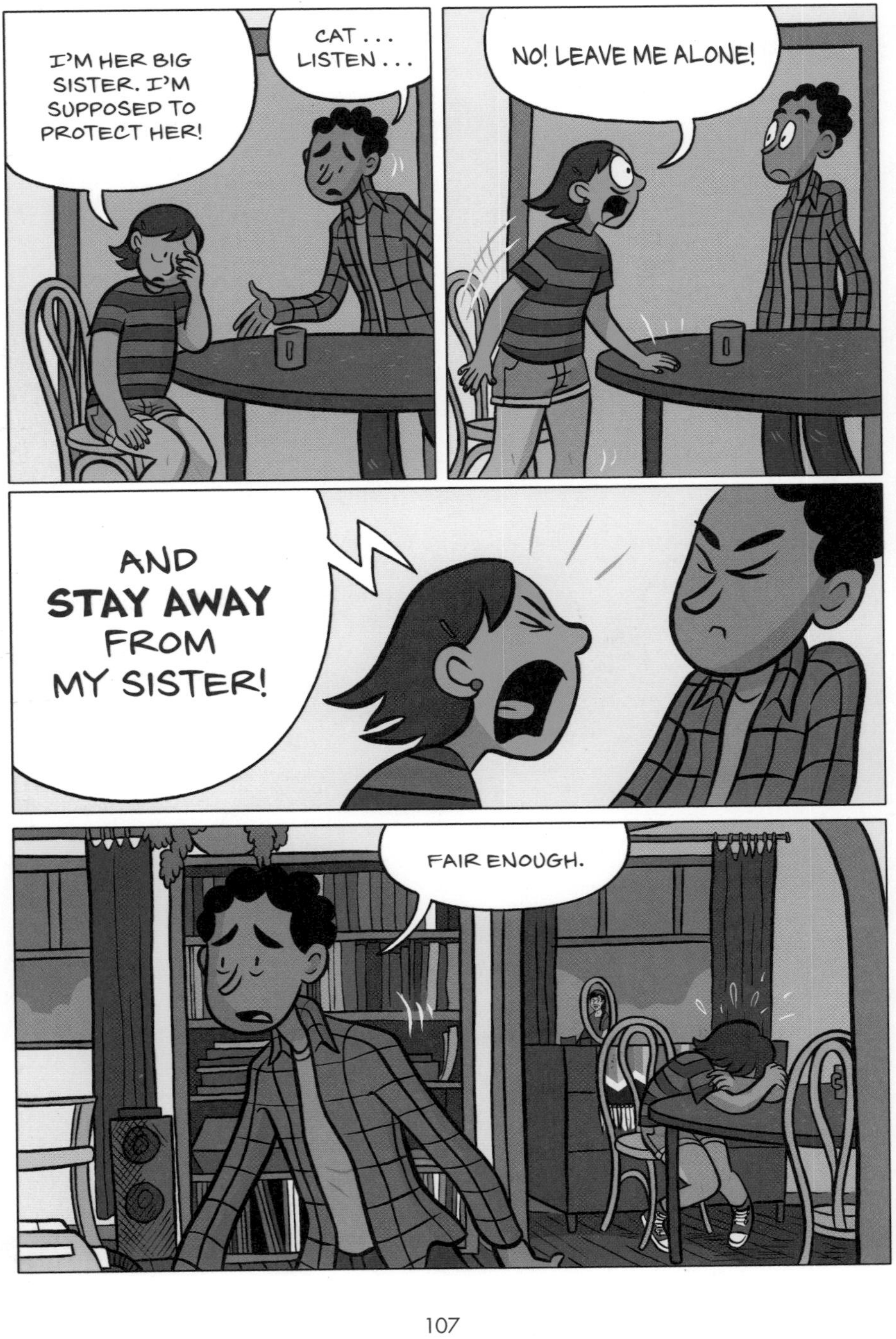
I'M HER BIG SISTER. I'M SUPPOSED TO PROTECT HER!
CAT . . . LISTEN . . .
NO! LEAVE ME ALONE!
AND **STAY AWAY** FROM MY SISTER!
FAIR ENOUGH.

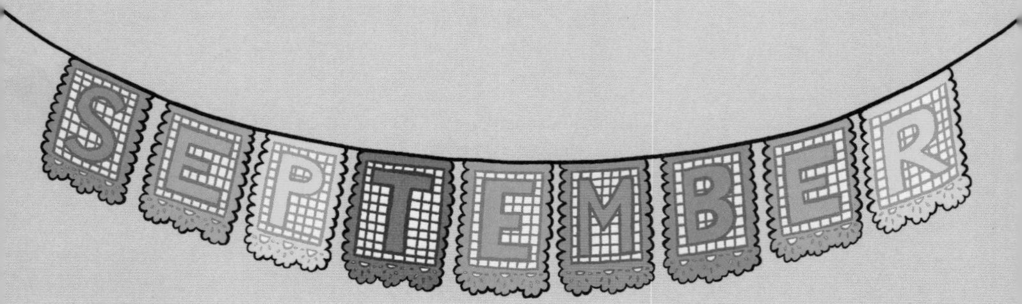
SEPTEMBER

Name: Allende-Delmar, Catrina
Grade: 6
Student ID: 637792

Per.	Room	Course	Instructor
0	119	Hmrm	Vasquez, J.
1	312	21E2 Eng	Mitchell, M.
2	111	21H1 His	Nakazawa, K.
3	30	21M5 Ma2	Theodus, T.
4	R	Lunch	
	305	21SP Span.	Diaz
	205	G6 Gym	Lee, J.
	121	21SC Sci	Garcin, V.

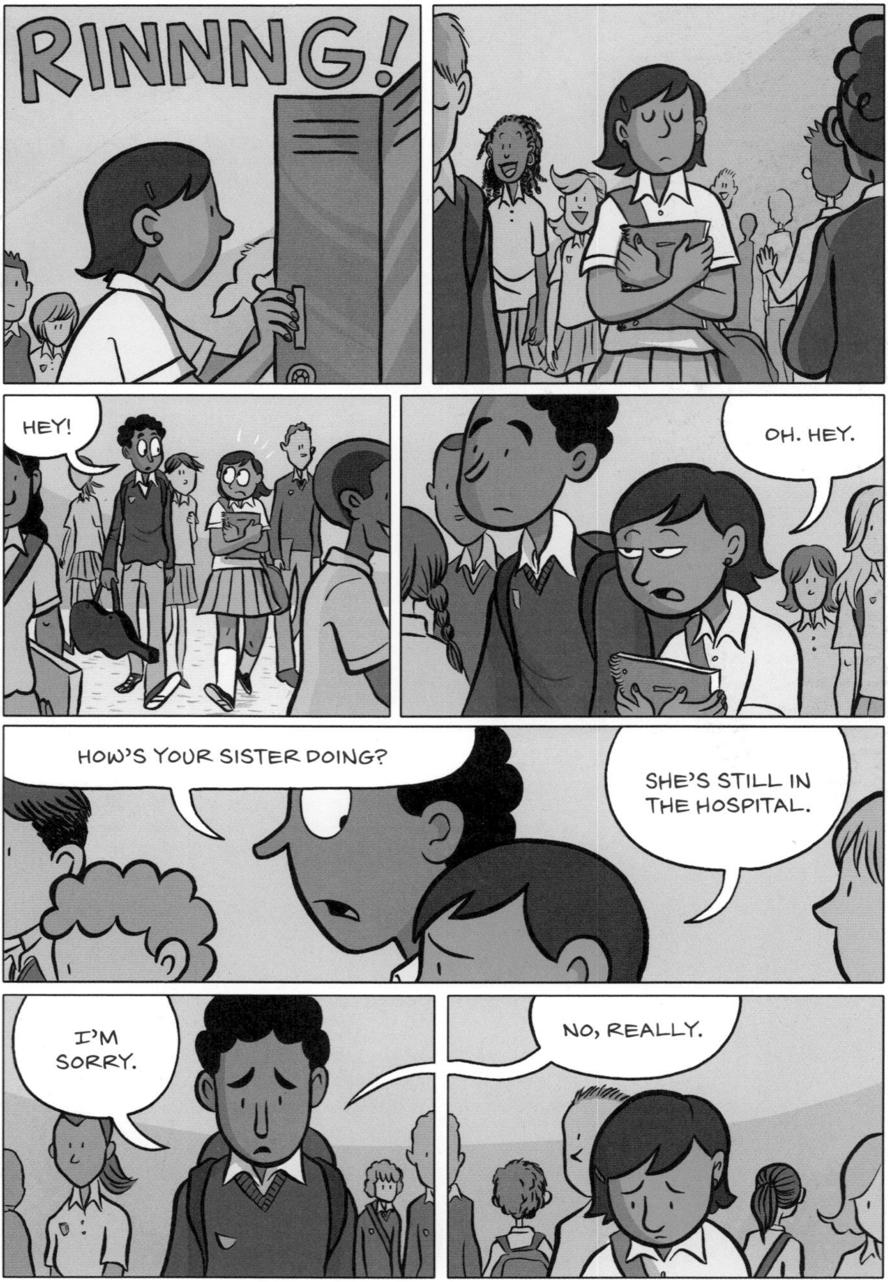
RINNNG!
HEY!
OH. HEY.
HOW'S YOUR SISTER DOING?
SHE'S STILL IN THE HOSPITAL.
I'M SORRY.
NO, REALLY.

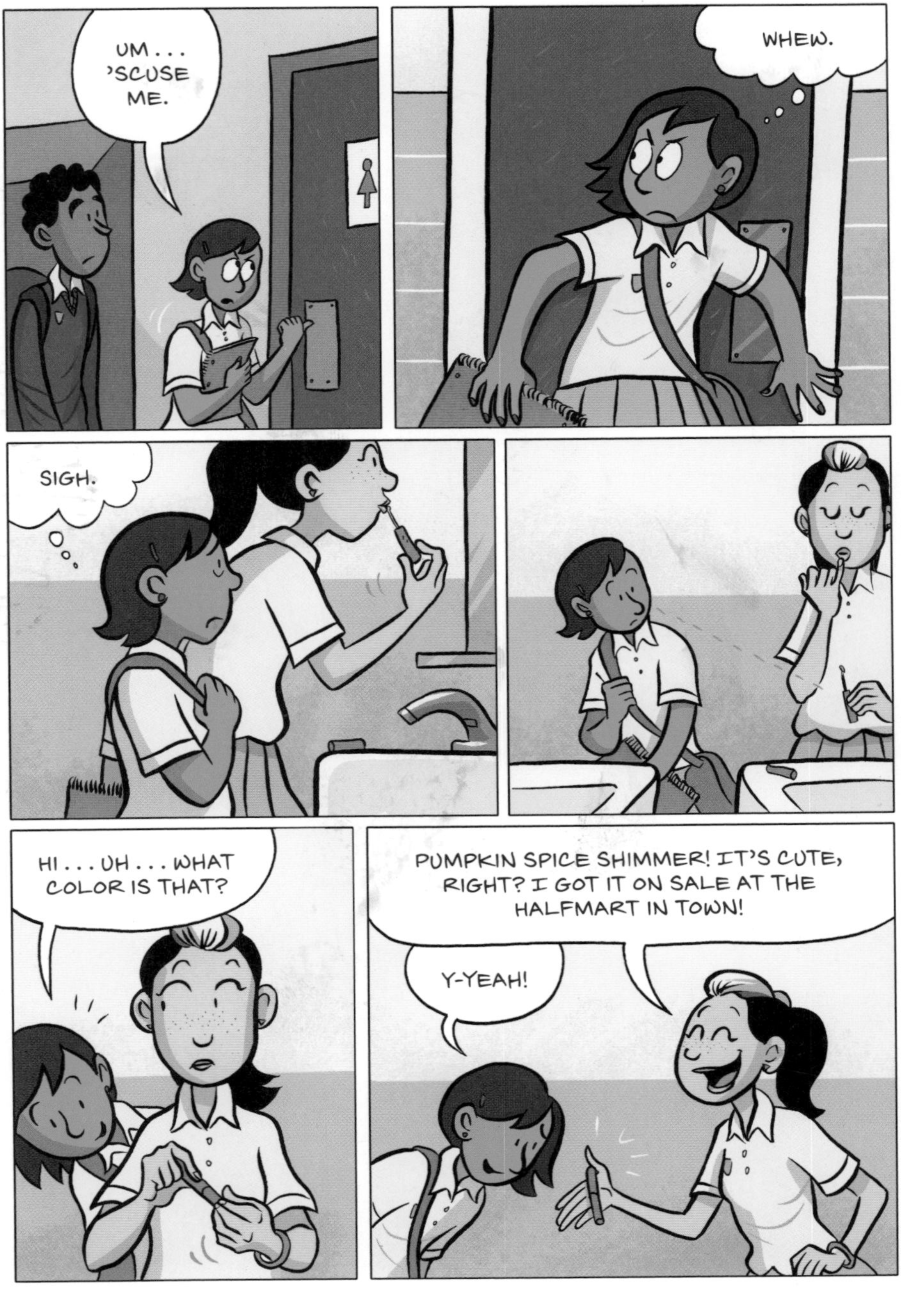
UM . . . 'SCUSE ME.
WHEW.
SIGH.
HI . . . UH . . . WHAT COLOR IS THAT?
PUMPKIN SPICE SHIMMER! IT'S CUTE, RIGHT? I GOT IT ON SALE AT THE HALFMART IN TOWN!
Y-YEAH!

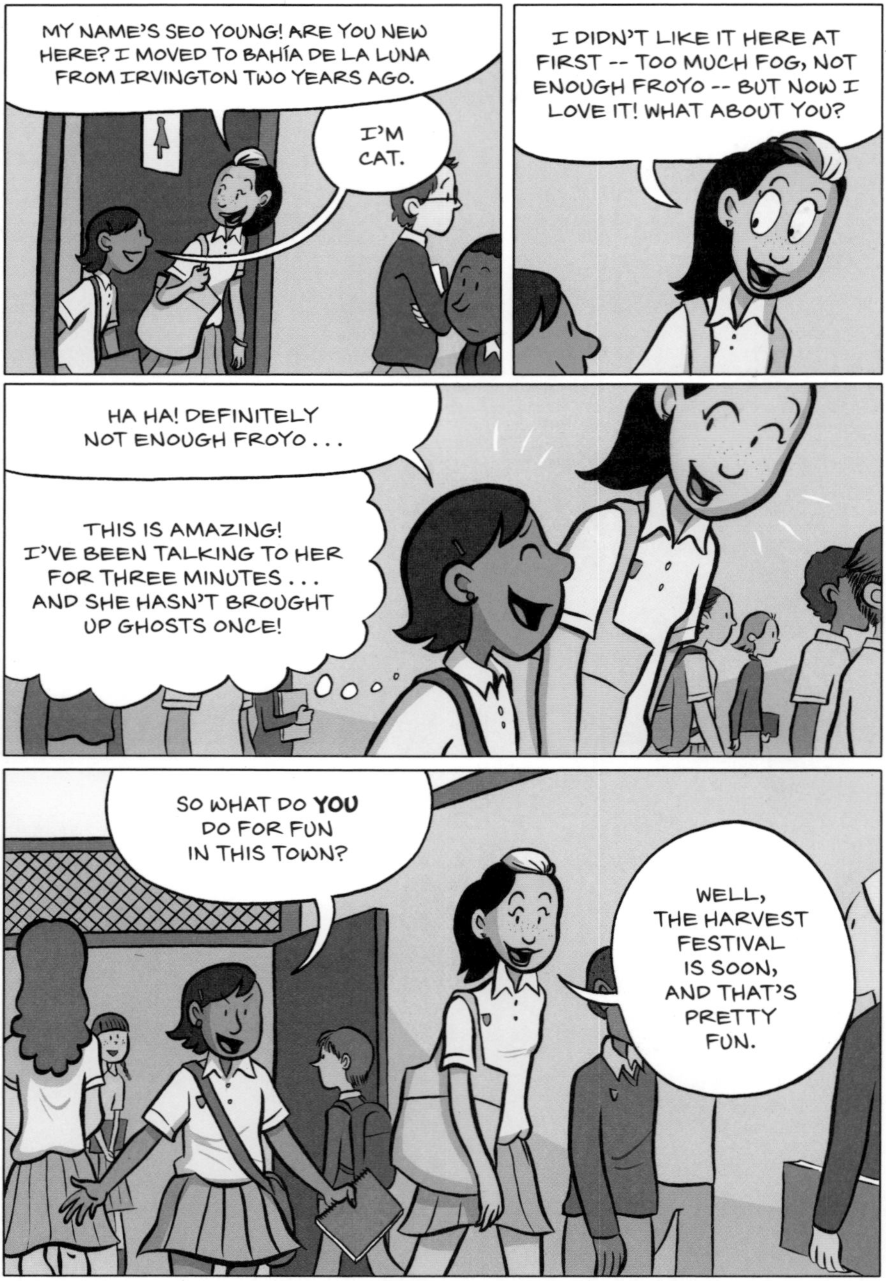

MY NAME'S SEO YOUNG! ARE YOU NEW HERE? I MOVED TO BAHÍA DE LA LUNA FROM IRVINGTON TWO YEARS AGO.
I'M CAT.
I DIDN'T LIKE IT HERE AT FIRST -- TOO MUCH FOG, NOT ENOUGH FROYO -- BUT NOW I LOVE IT! WHAT ABOUT YOU?
HA HA! DEFINITELY NOT ENOUGH FROYO . . .
THIS IS AMAZING! I'VE BEEN TALKING TO HER FOR THREE MINUTES . . . AND SHE HASN'T BROUGHT UP GHOSTS ONCE!
SO WHAT DO **YOU** DO FOR FUN IN THIS TOWN?
WELL, THE HARVEST FESTIVAL IS SOON, AND THAT'S PRETTY FUN.

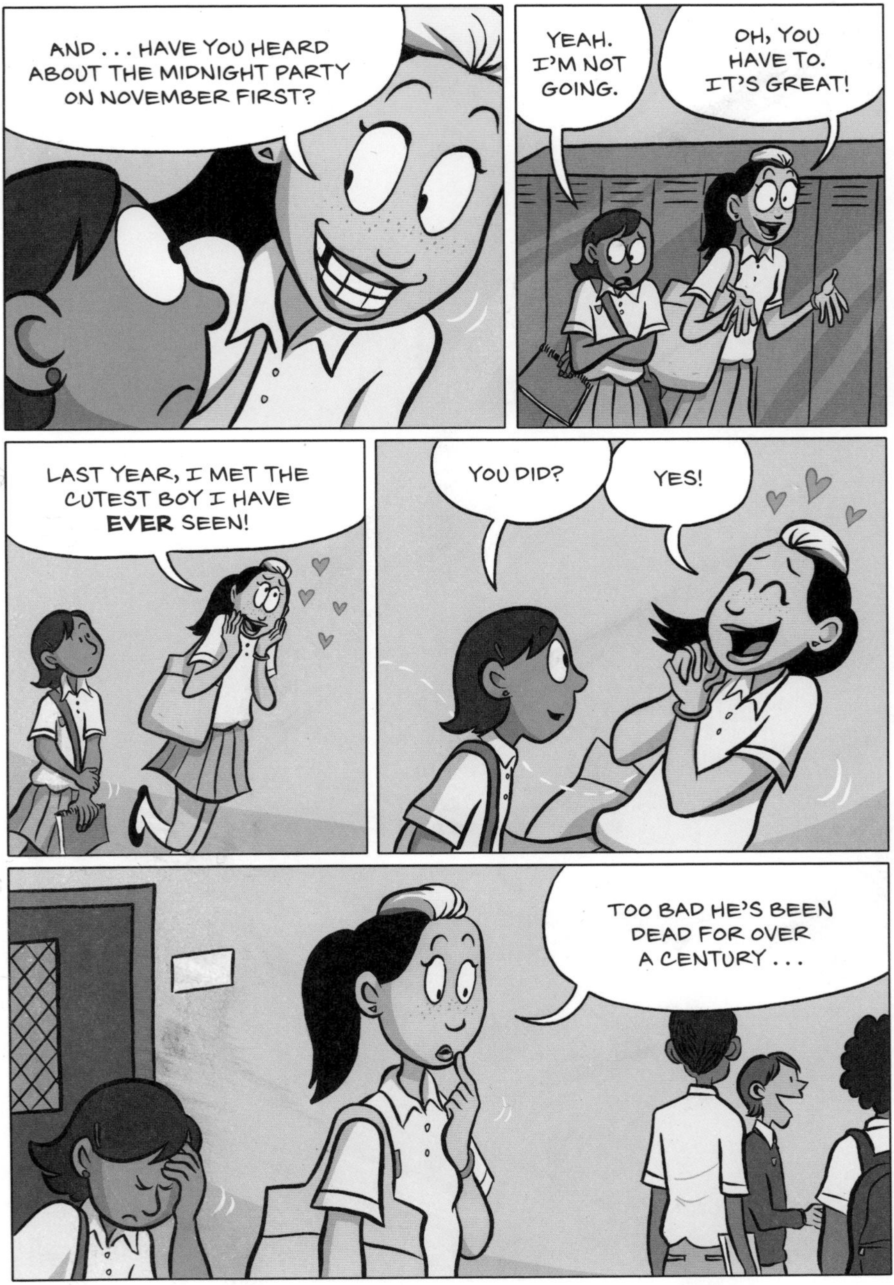
AND . . . HAVE YOU HEARD ABOUT THE MIDNIGHT PARTY ON NOVEMBER FIRST?
YEAH. I'M NOT GOING.
OH, YOU HAVE TO. IT'S GREAT!
LAST YEAR, I MET THE CUTEST BOY I HAVE **EVER** SEEN!
YOU DID?
YES!
TOO BAD HE'S BEEN DEAD FOR OVER A CENTURY . . .

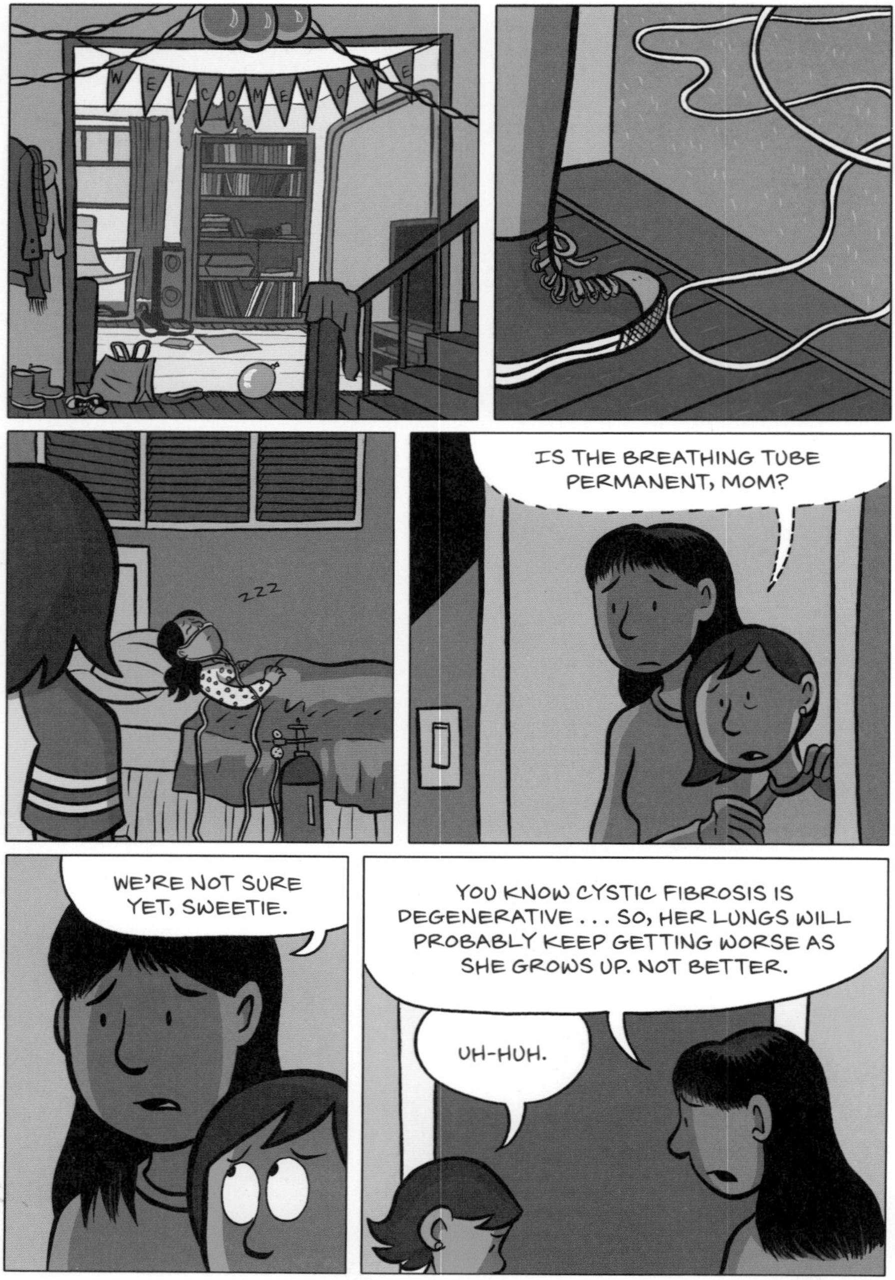
WELCOME HOME
ZZZ
IS THE BREATHING TUBE PERMANENT, MOM?
WE'RE NOT SURE YET, SWEETIE.
YOU KNOW CYSTIC FIBROSIS IS DEGENERATIVE . . . SO, HER LUNGS WILL PROBABLY KEEP GETTING WORSE AS SHE GROWS UP. NOT BETTER.
UH-HUH.

HOWEVER . . . THIS IS MAYA WE'RE TALKING ABOUT.

EVERY TIME SHE HAS A SETBACK, SHE SEEMS TO REBOUND WITH TWICE THE POSITIVE ATTITUDE.

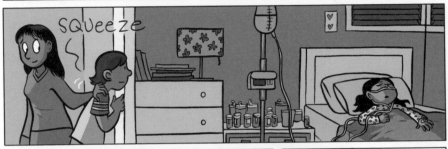

SQUEEZE

IT'S TOO QUIET WHEN YOU'RE SICK.

Tap Tap

115

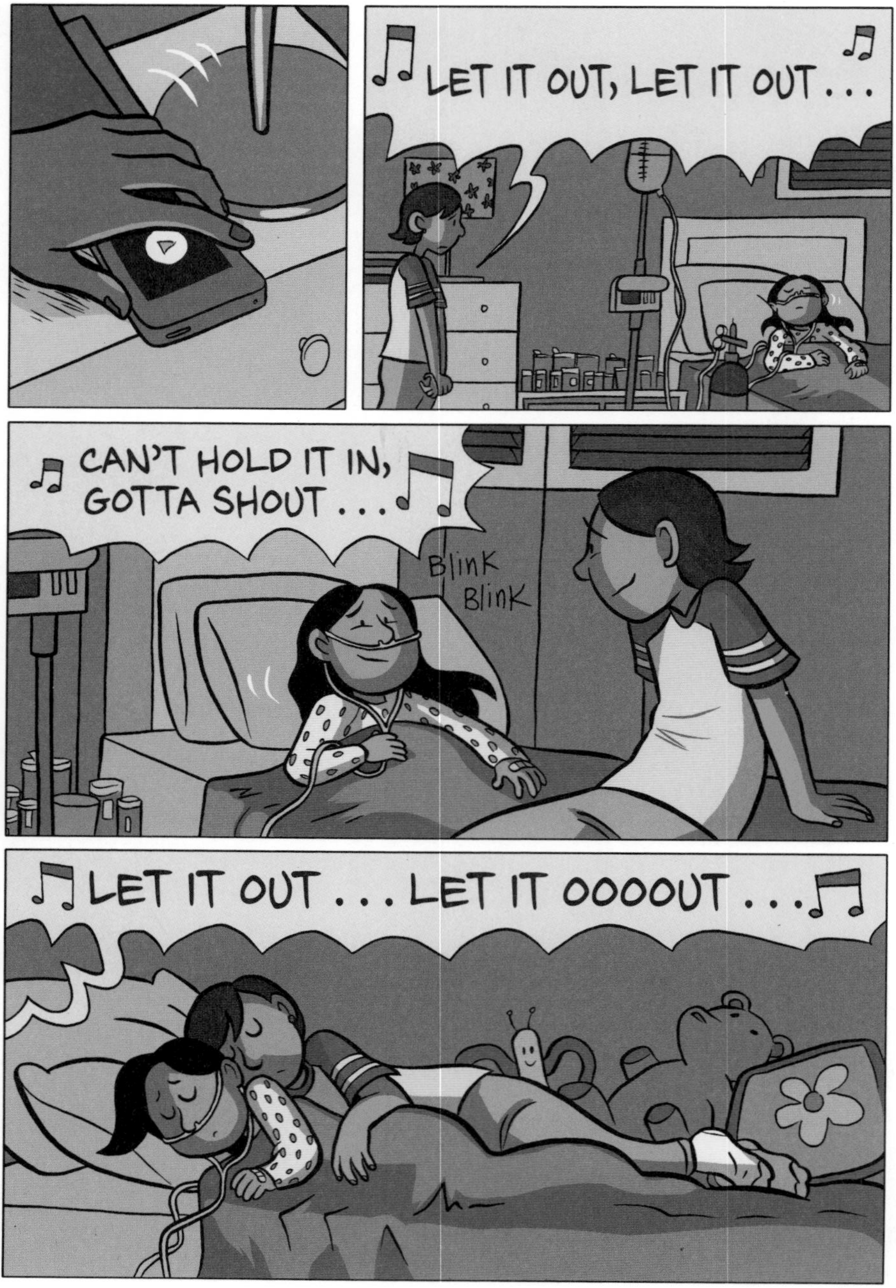
LET IT OUT, LET IT OUT . . .
CAN'T HOLD IT IN, GOTTA SHOUT . . .
BLINK BLINK
LET IT OUT . . . LET IT OOOOUT . . .

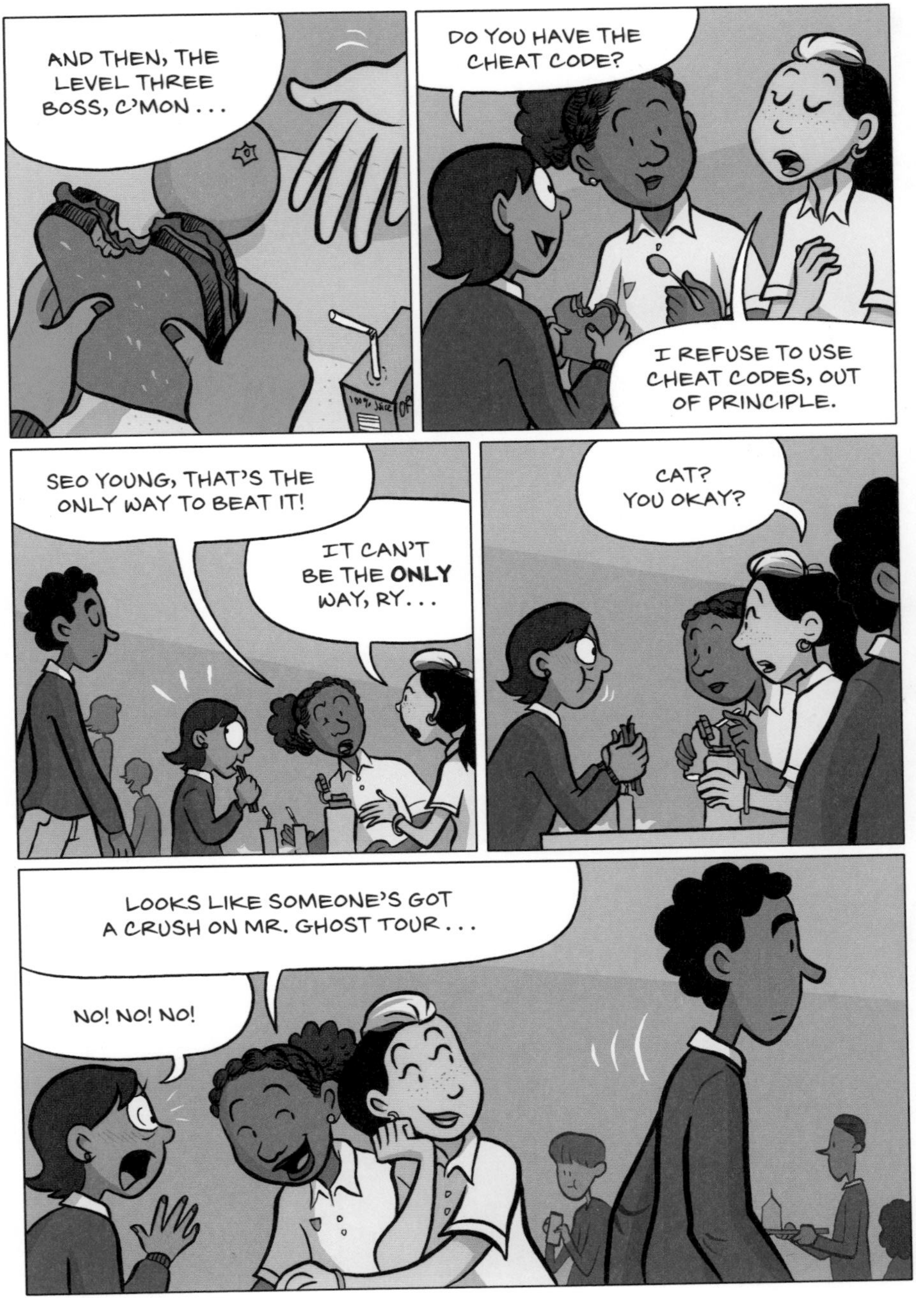
AND THEN, THE LEVEL THREE BOSS, C'MON . . .
DO YOU HAVE THE CHEAT CODE?
I REFUSE TO USE CHEAT CODES, OUT OF PRINCIPLE.
SEO YOUNG, THAT'S THE ONLY WAY TO BEAT IT!
IT CAN'T BE THE **ONLY** WAY, RY . . .
CAT? YOU OKAY?
LOOKS LIKE SOMEONE'S GOT A CRUSH ON MR. GHOST TOUR . . .
NO! NO! NO!

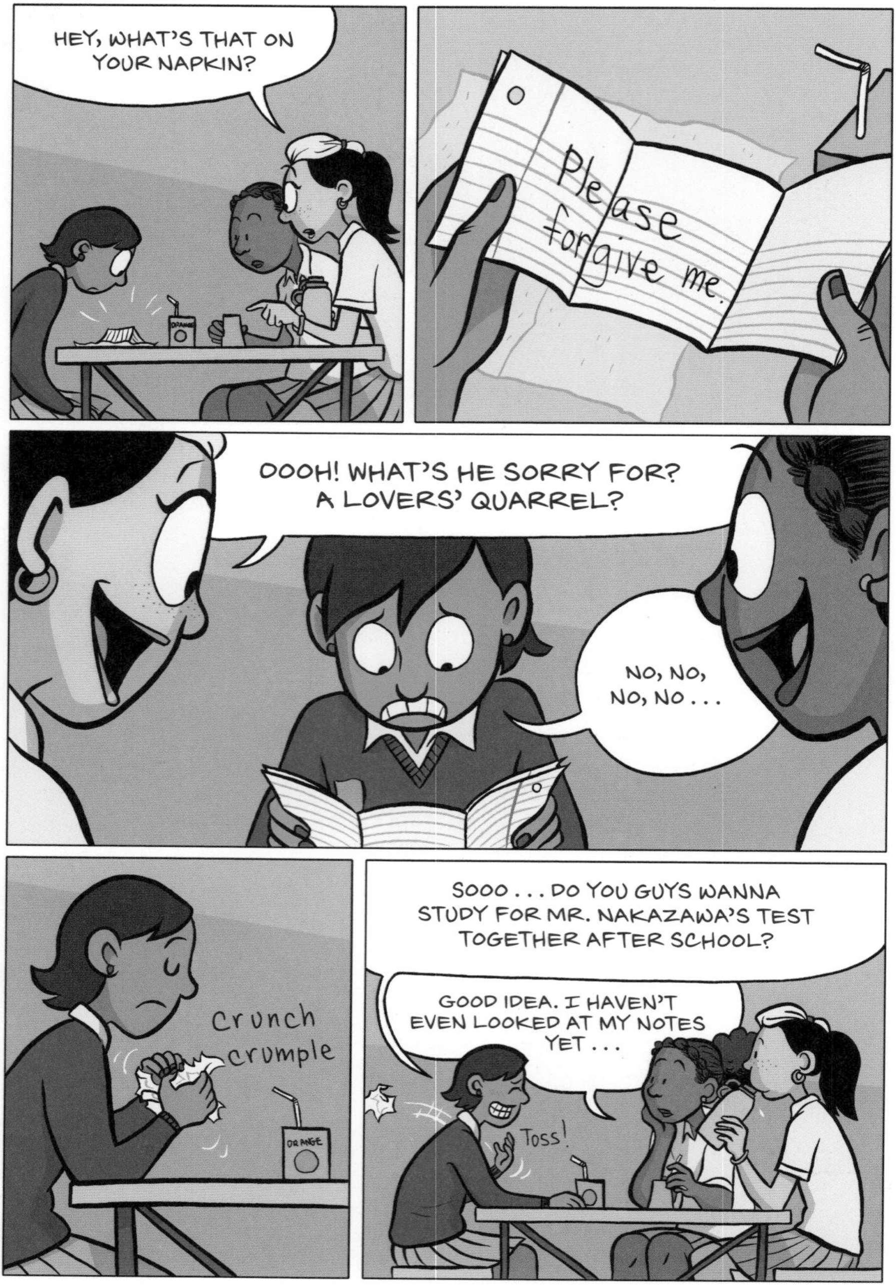
HEY, WHAT'S THAT ON YOUR NAPKIN?
Please forgive me.
OOOH! WHAT'S HE SORRY FOR? A LOVERS' QUARREL?
NO, NO, NO, NO . . .
crunch crumple
SOOO . . . DO YOU GUYS WANNA STUDY FOR MR. NAKAZAWA'S TEST TOGETHER AFTER SCHOOL?
GOOD IDEA. I HAVEN'T EVEN LOOKED AT MY NOTES YET . . .
Toss!

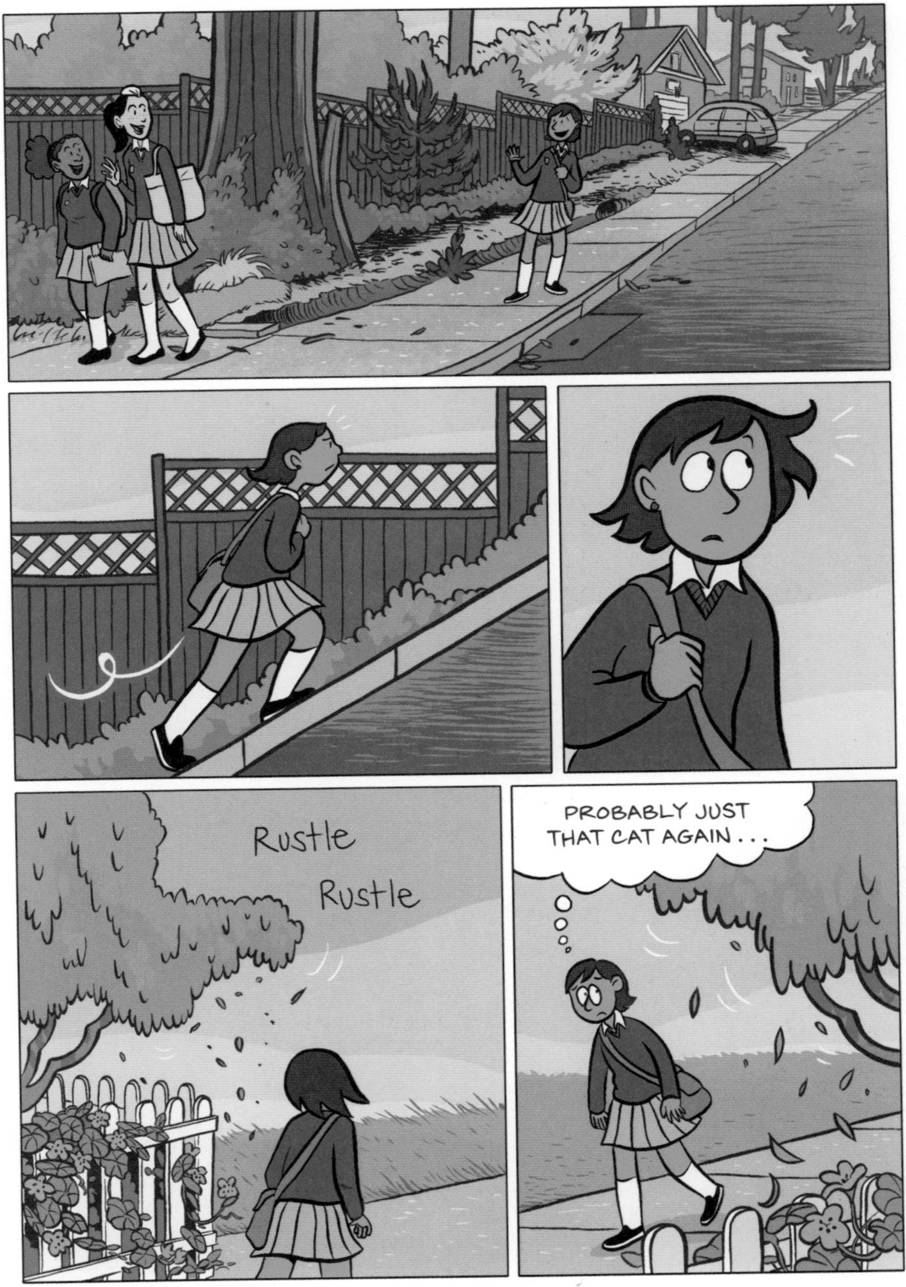
Rustle
Rustle
PROBABLY JUST THAT CAT AGAIN . . .

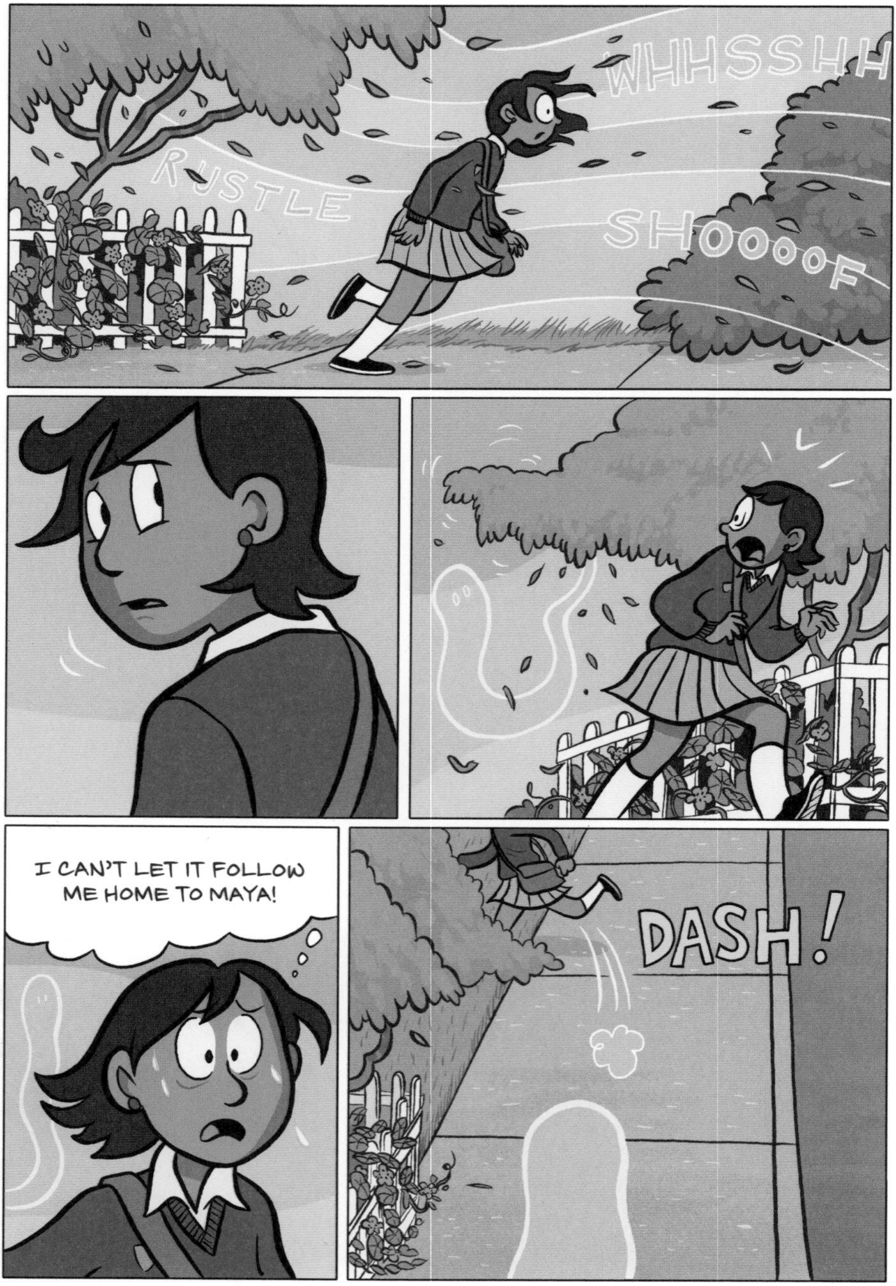
WHHSSHH
RUSTLE
SHOOOOF
I CAN'T LET IT FOLLOW ME HOME TO MAYA!
DASH!

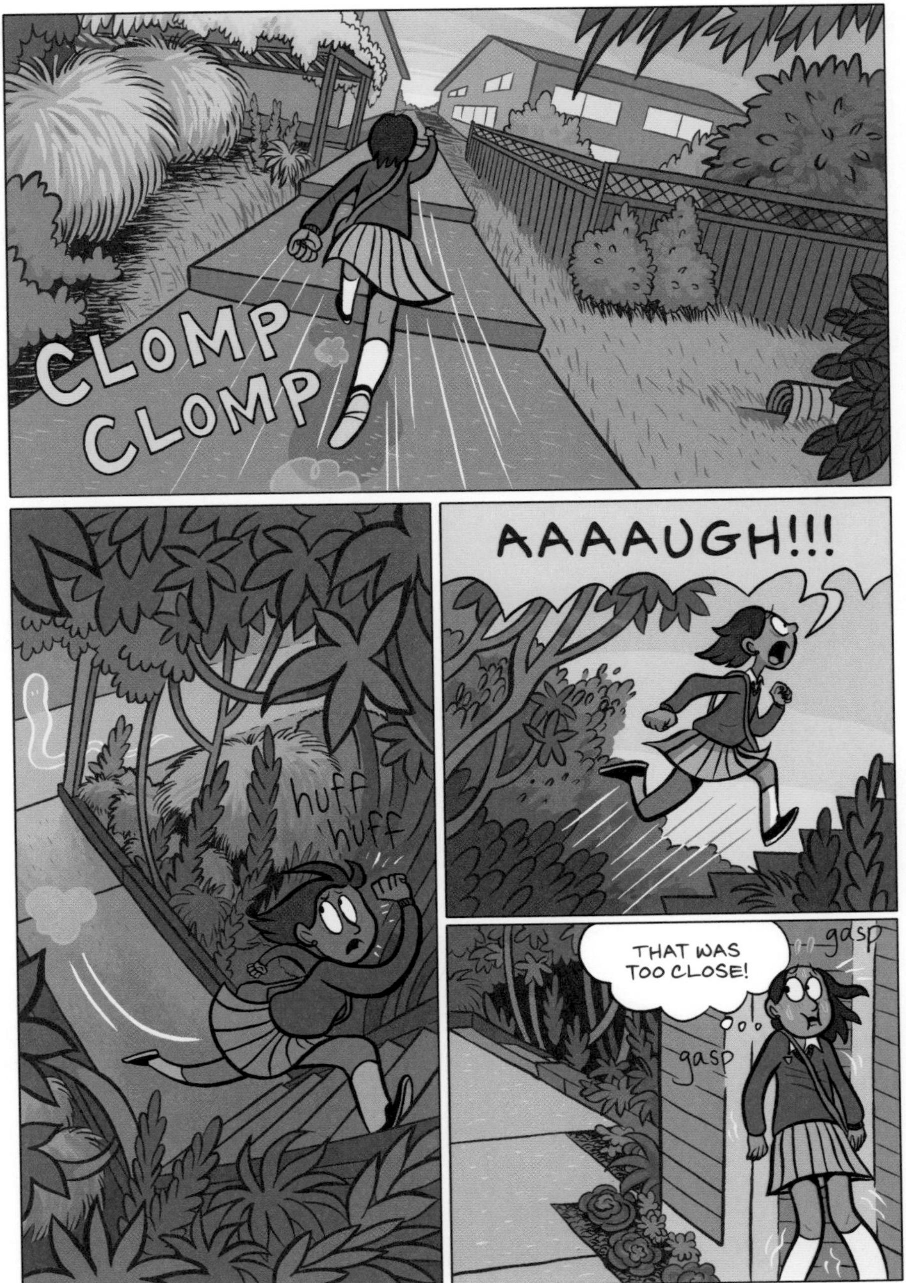
CLOMP
CLOMP
huff
huff
AAAAUGH!!!
gasp
THAT WAS TOO CLOSE!
gasp

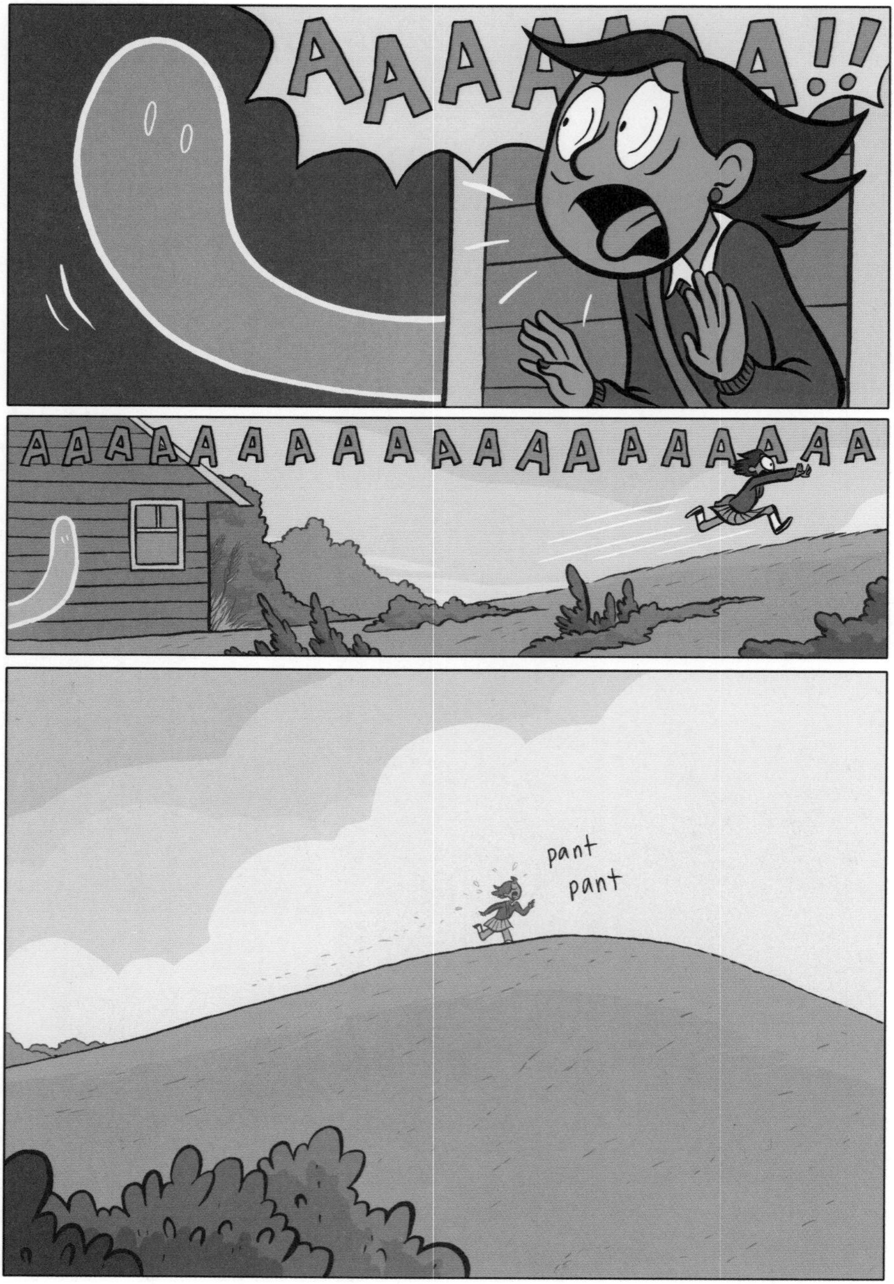
AAAAA!!
AAAAAAAAAAAAAAAAAAA
pant pant

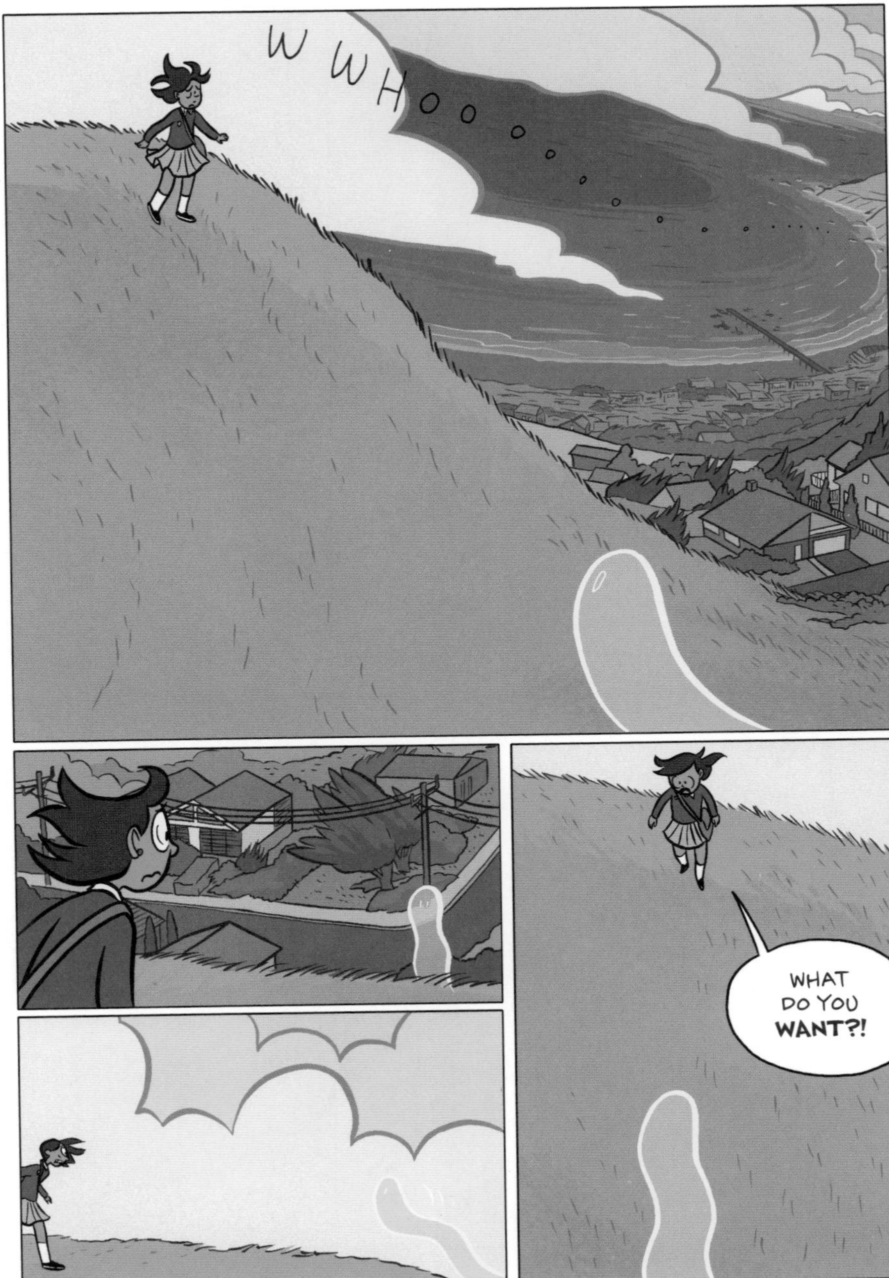
WWHOOOOOOO......
WHAT DO YOU WANT?!

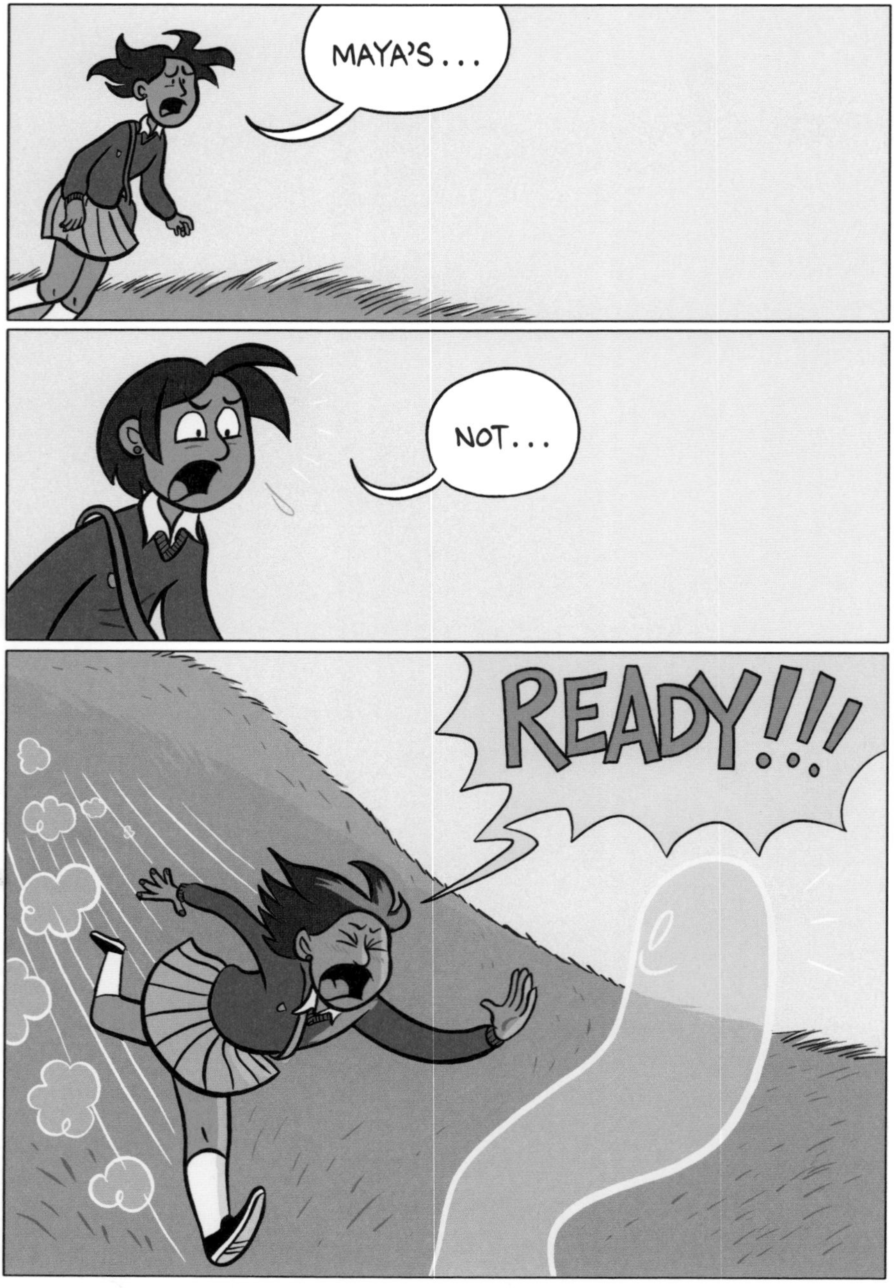
MAYA'S...
NOT...
READY!!!

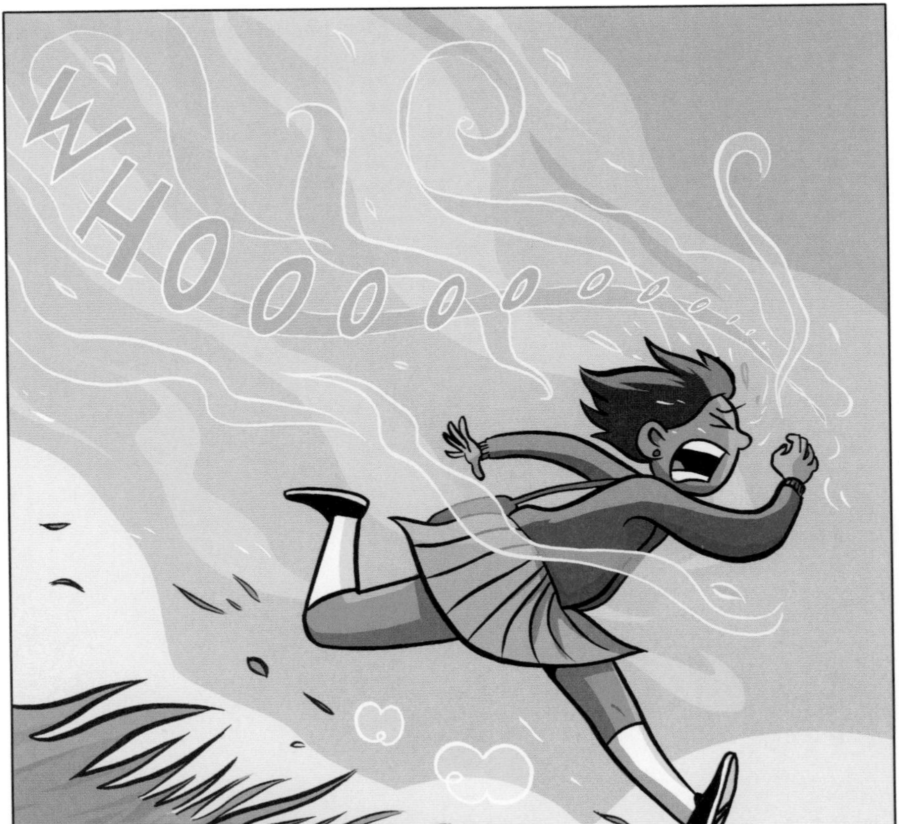
WHOOOOOOOOOOO

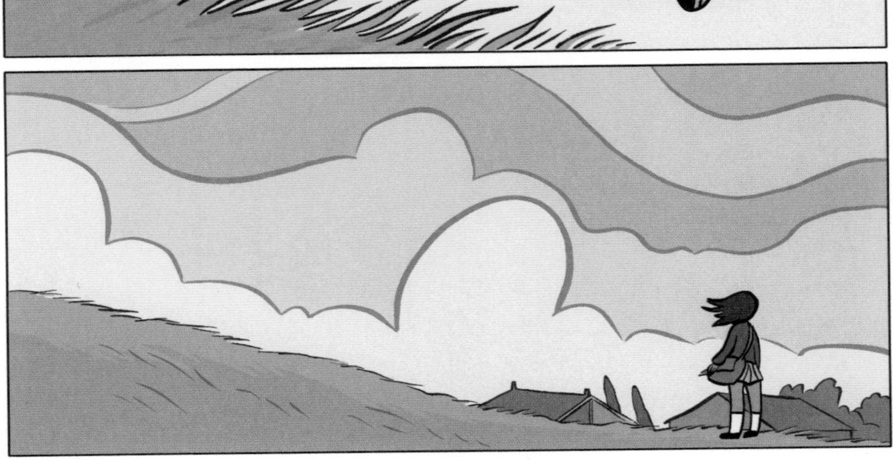

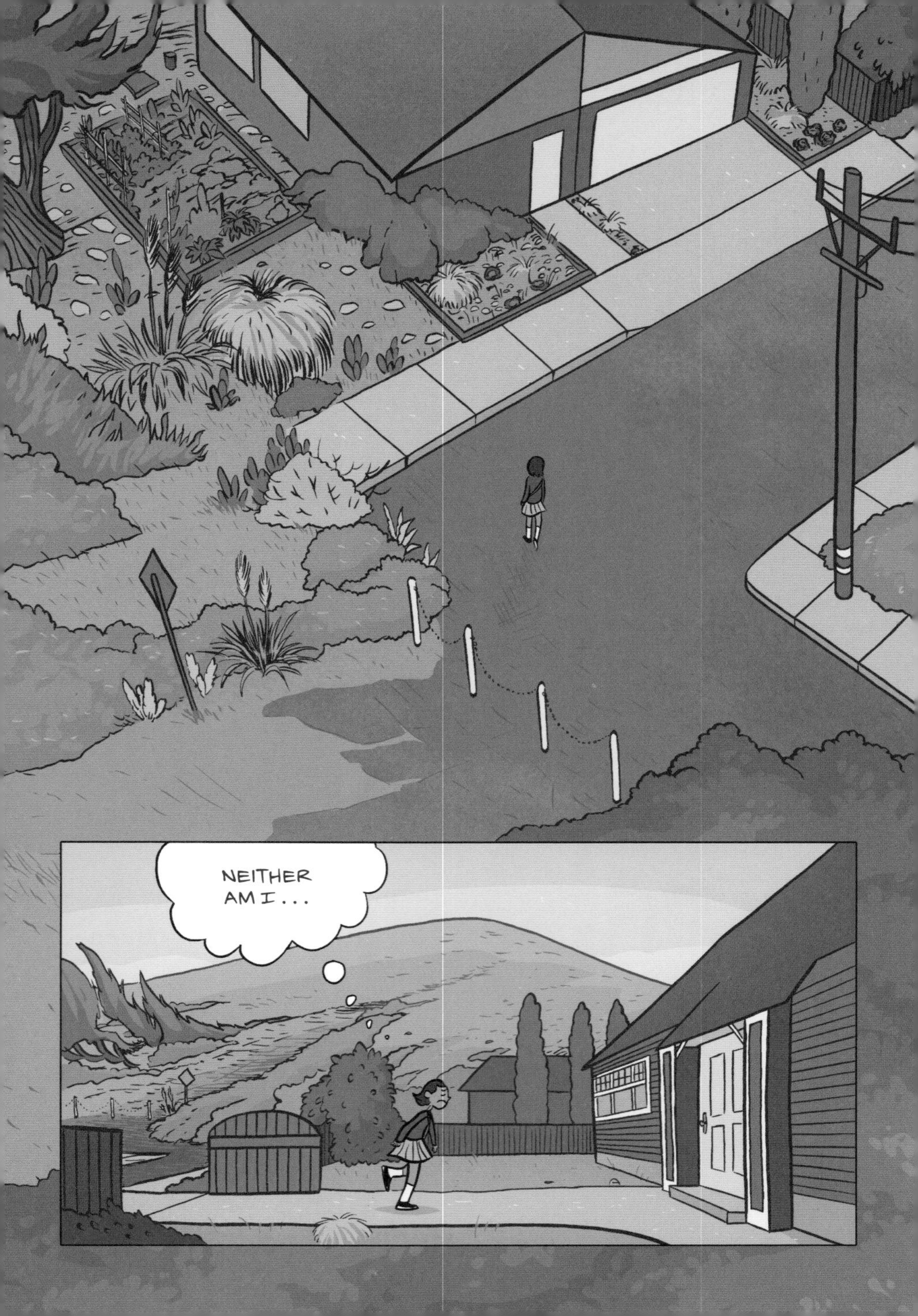
NEITHER AM I . . .

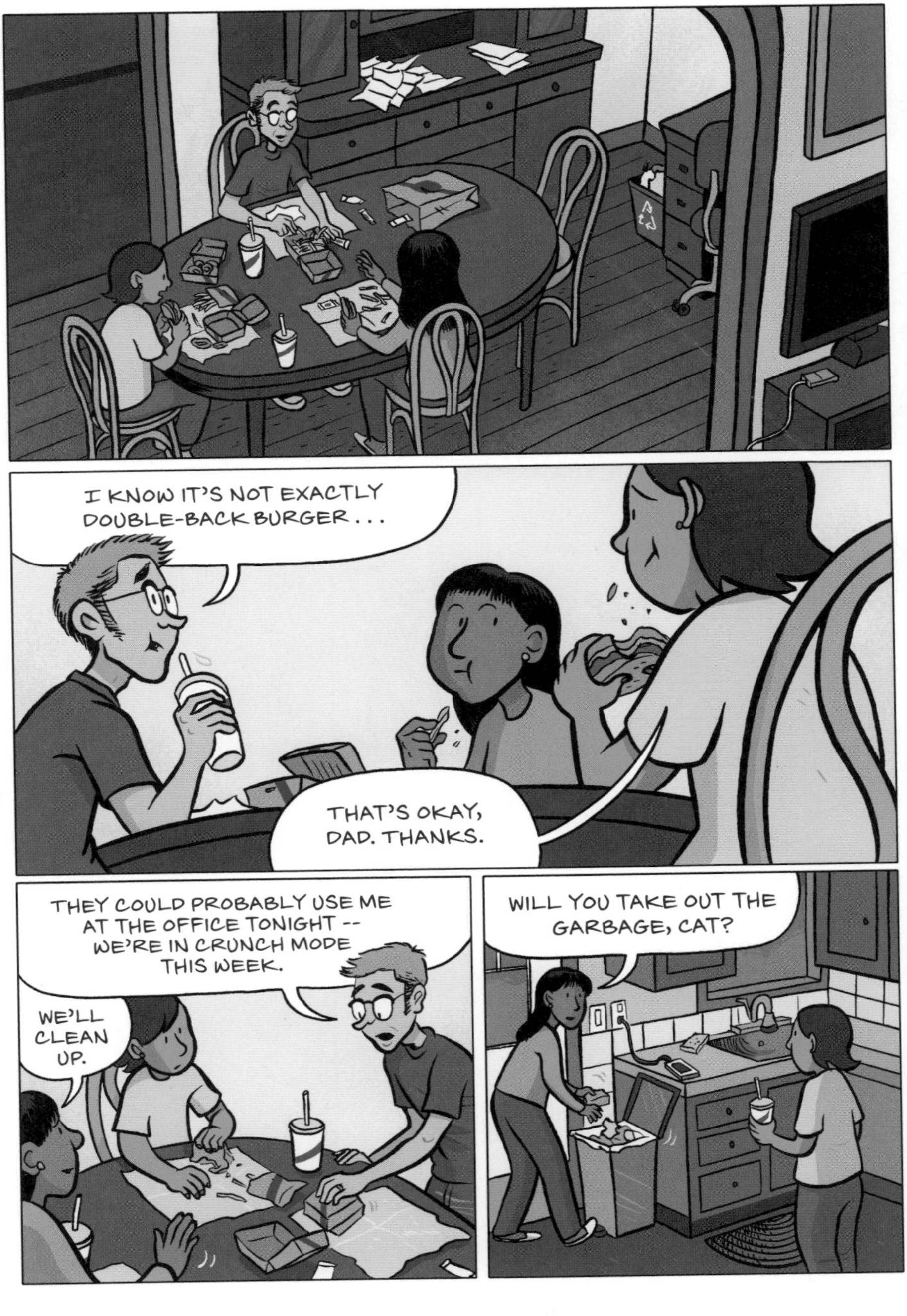
I KNOW IT'S NOT EXACTLY DOUBLE-BACK BURGER . . .
THAT'S OKAY, DAD. THANKS.
THEY COULD PROBABLY USE ME AT THE OFFICE TONIGHT -- WE'RE IN CRUNCH MODE THIS WEEK.
WE'LL CLEAN UP.
WILL YOU TAKE OUT THE GARBAGE, CAT?

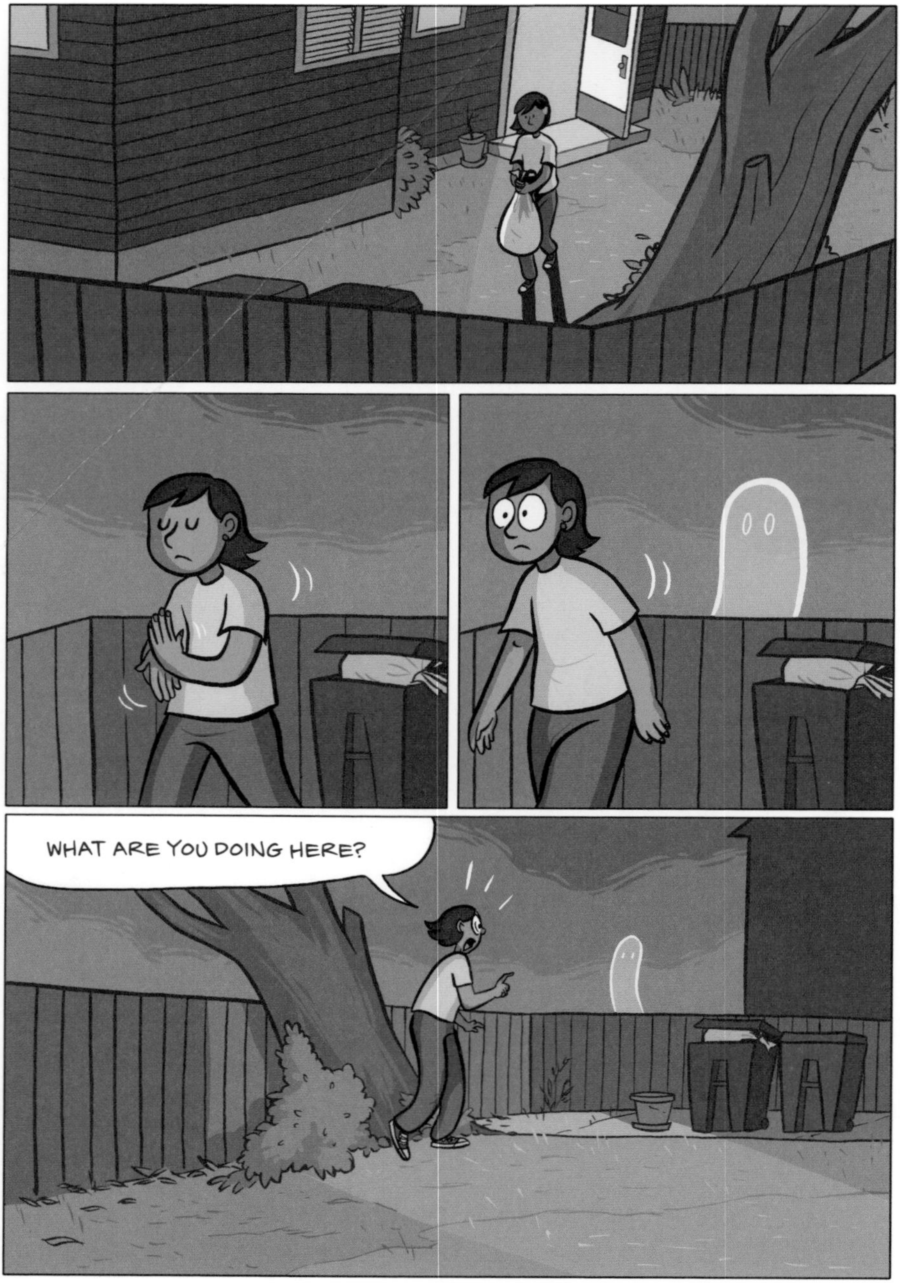
WHAT ARE YOU DOING HERE?

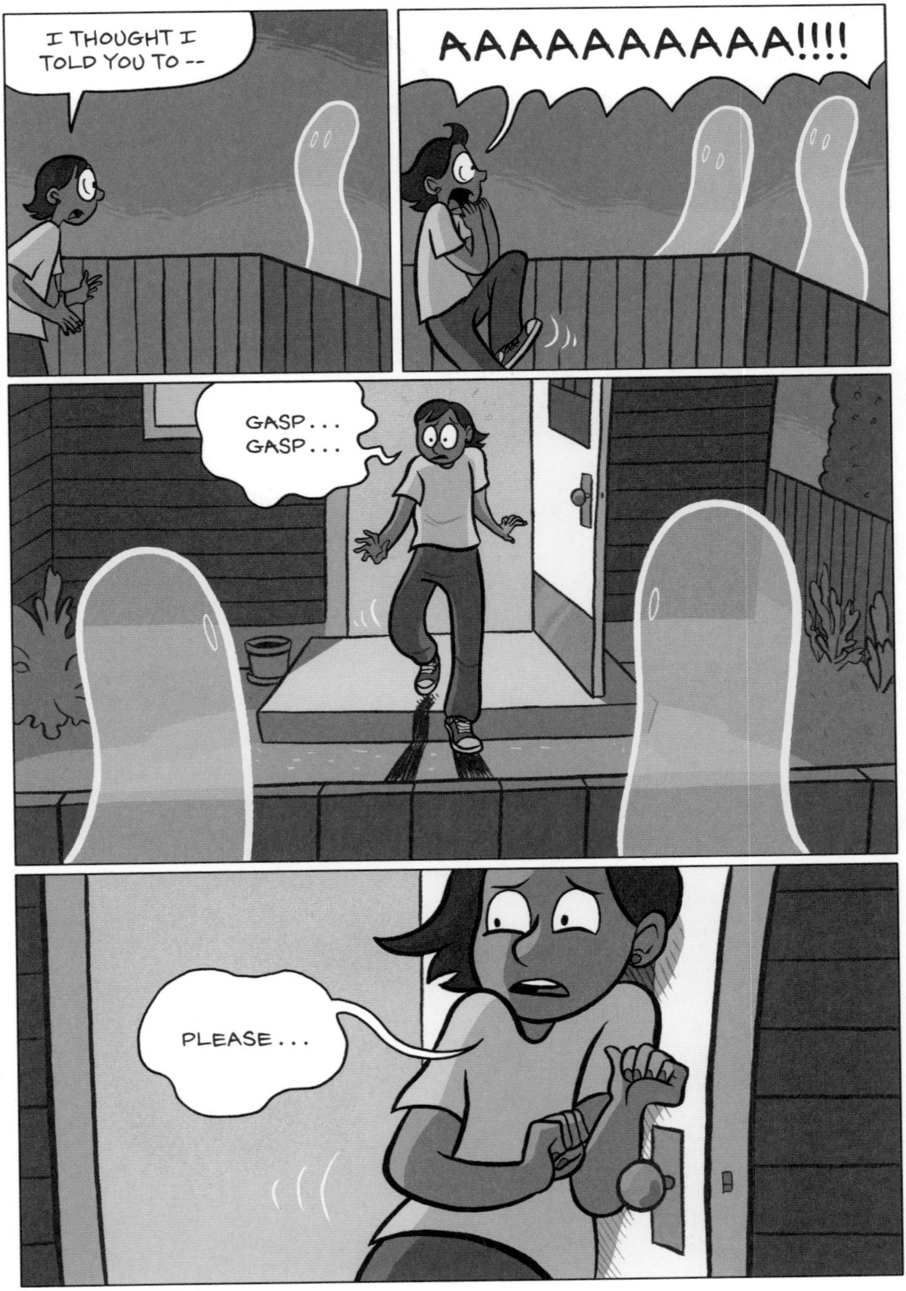
I THOUGHT I TOLD YOU TO --
AAAAAAAAAAA!!!!
GASP... GASP...
PLEASE...

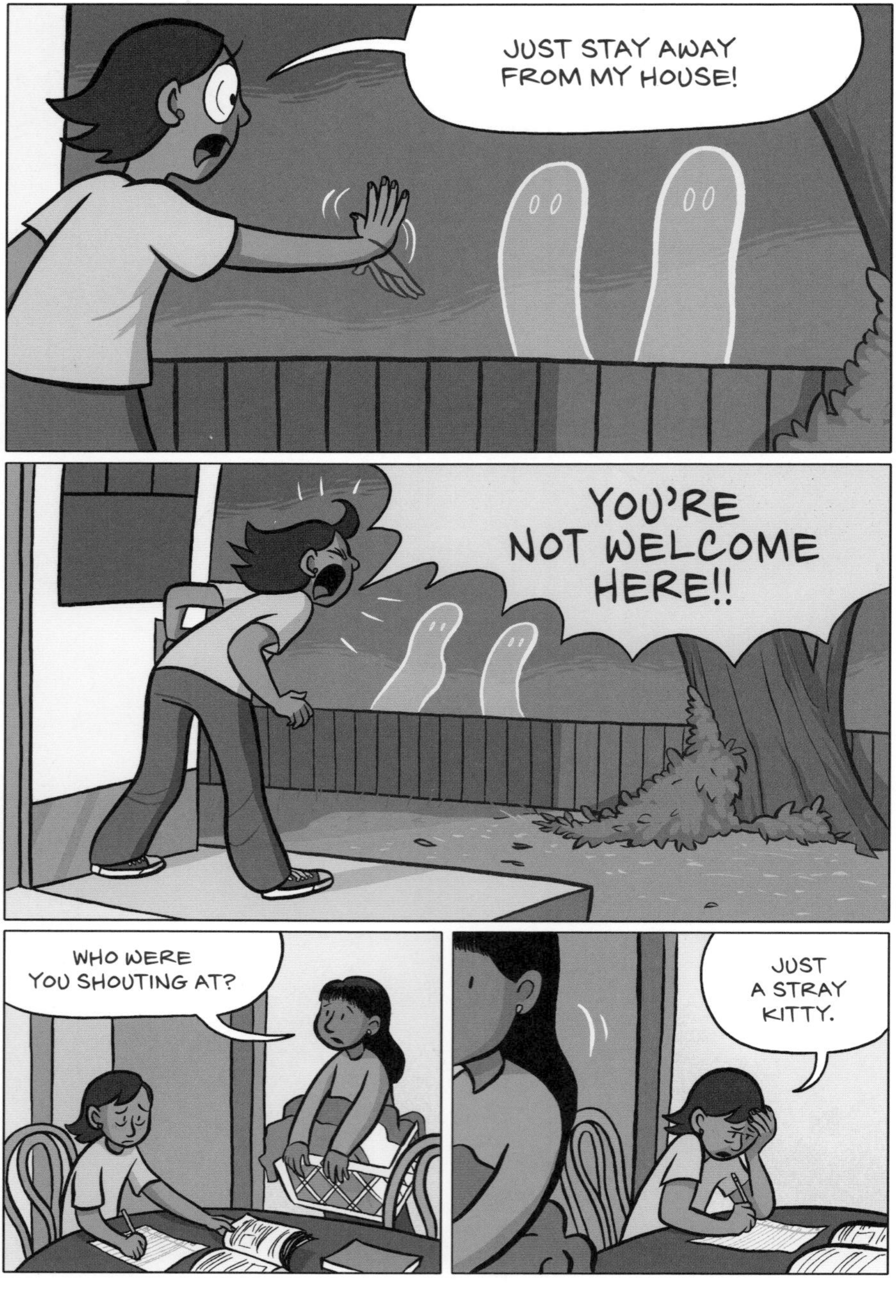
JUST STAY AWAY FROM MY HOUSE!
YOU'RE NOT WELCOME HERE!!
WHO WERE YOU SHOUTING AT?
JUST A STRAY KITTY.

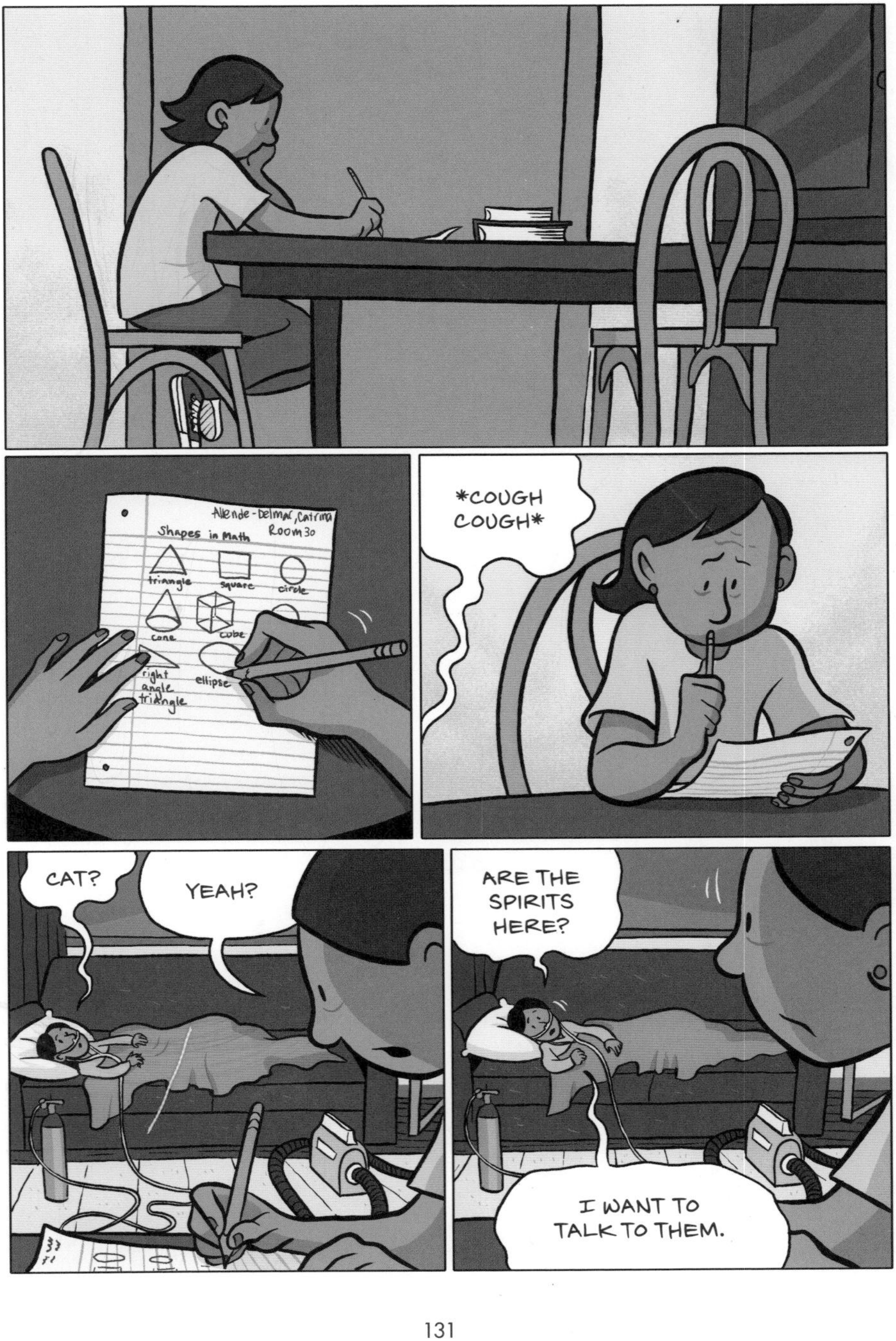
Allende-Delmar, Catrina
Room 30
Shapes in Math
triangle
square
circle
cone
cube
right angle triangle
ellipse
COUGH COUGH
CAT?
YEAH?
ARE THE SPIRITS HERE?
I WANT TO TALK TO THEM.

SQUINT

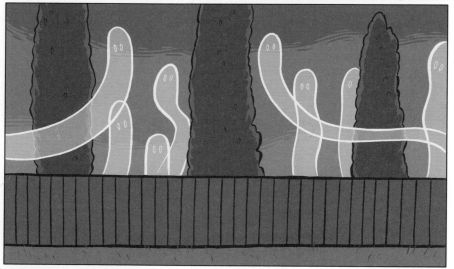

SHOOF!!

NOBODY HERE.

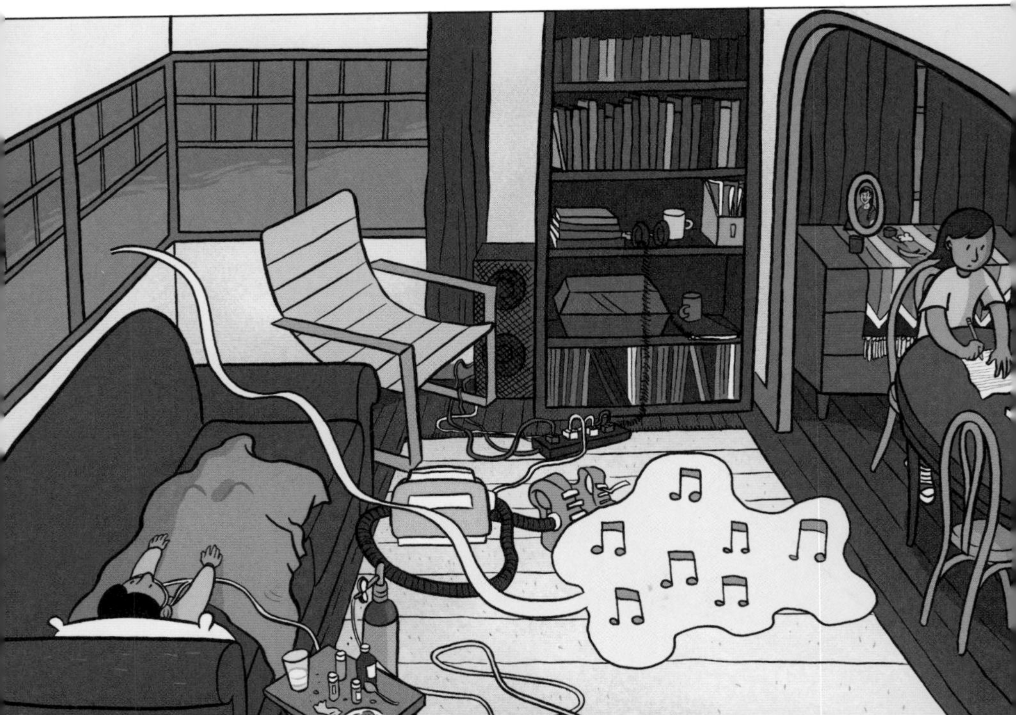

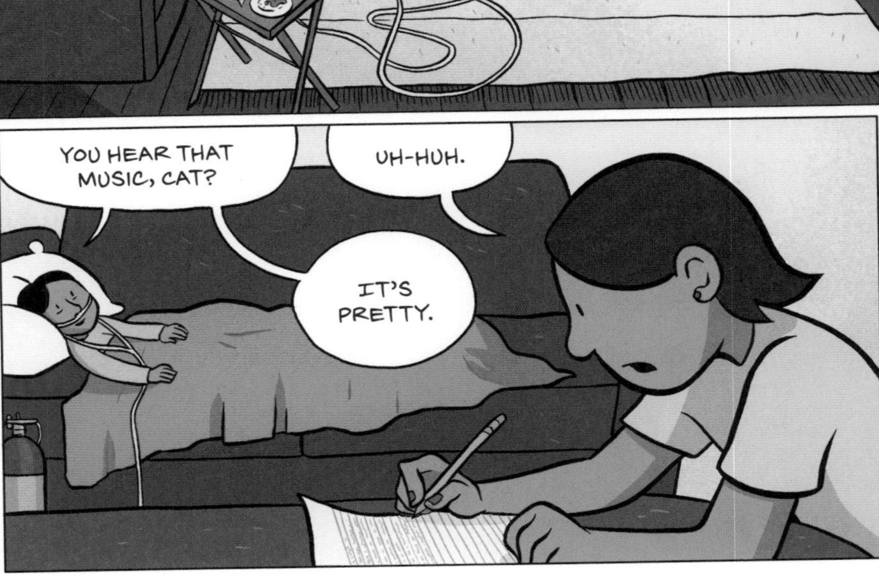
YOU HEAR THAT MUSIC, CAT?
UH-HUH.
IT'S PRETTY.

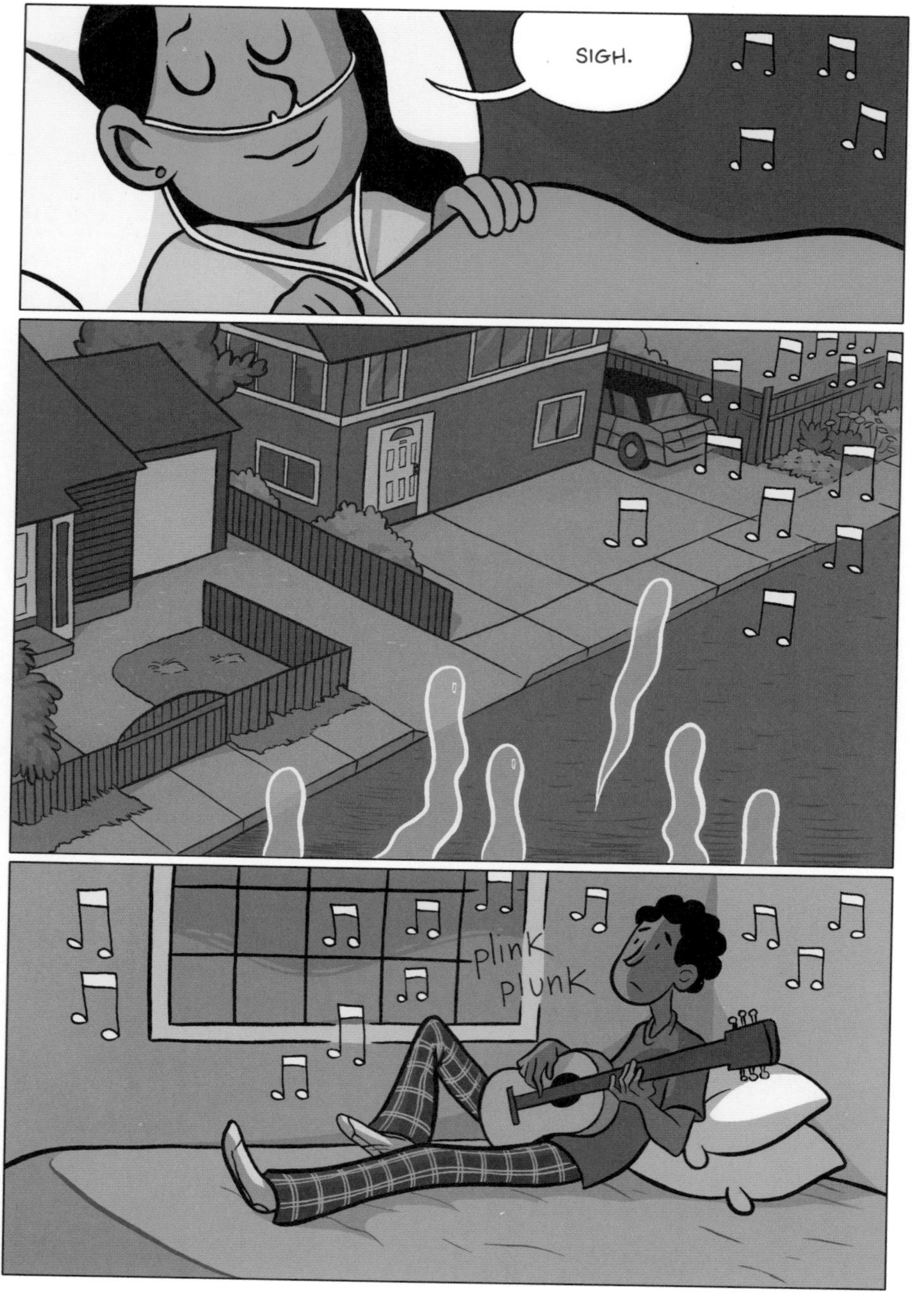
SIGH.
plink
plunk

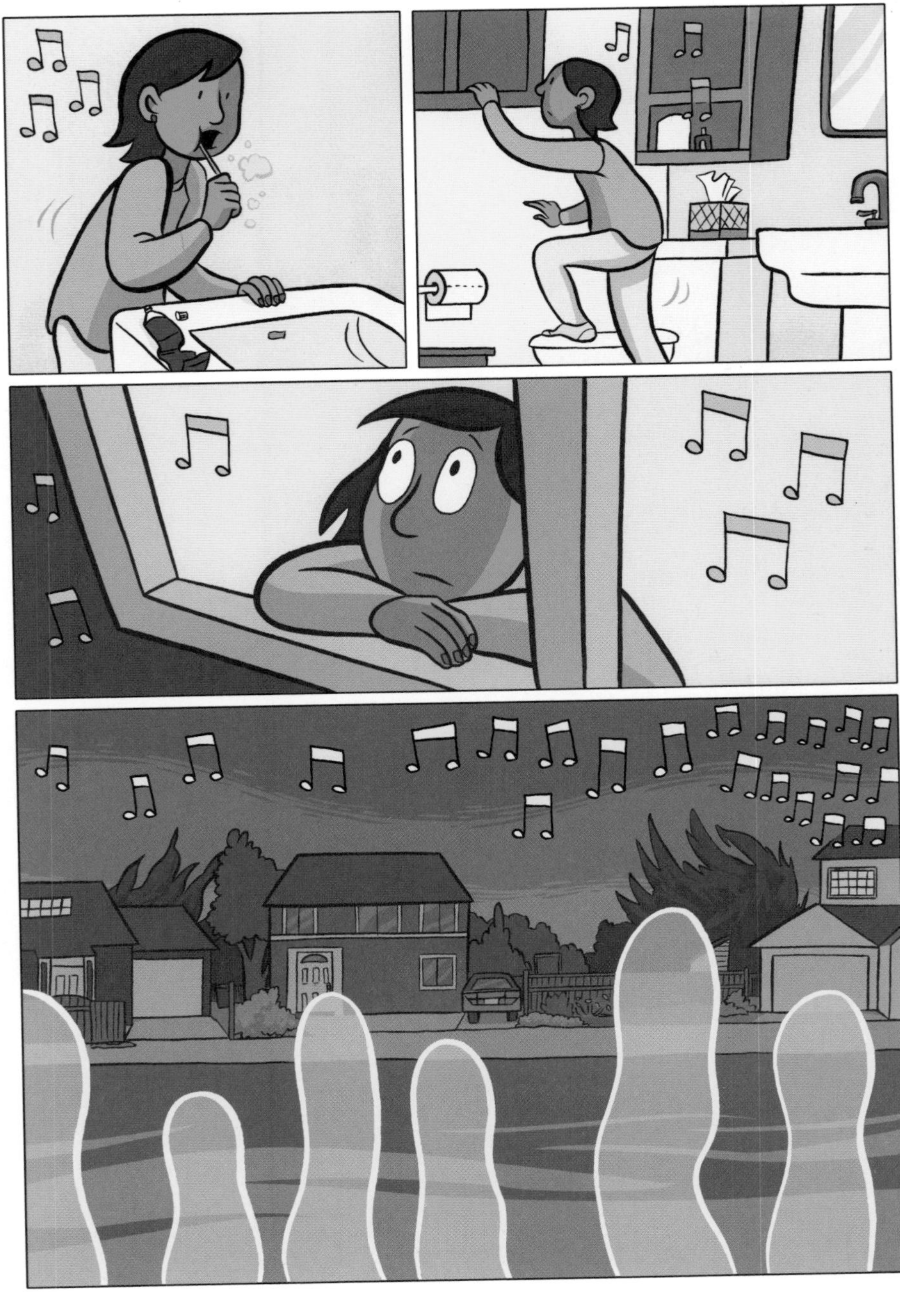

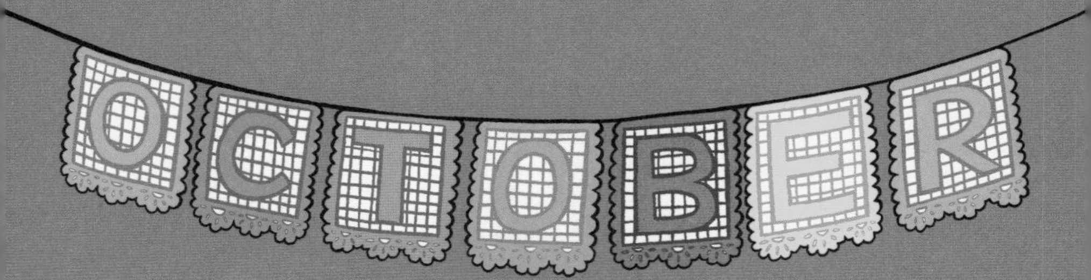
OCTOBER

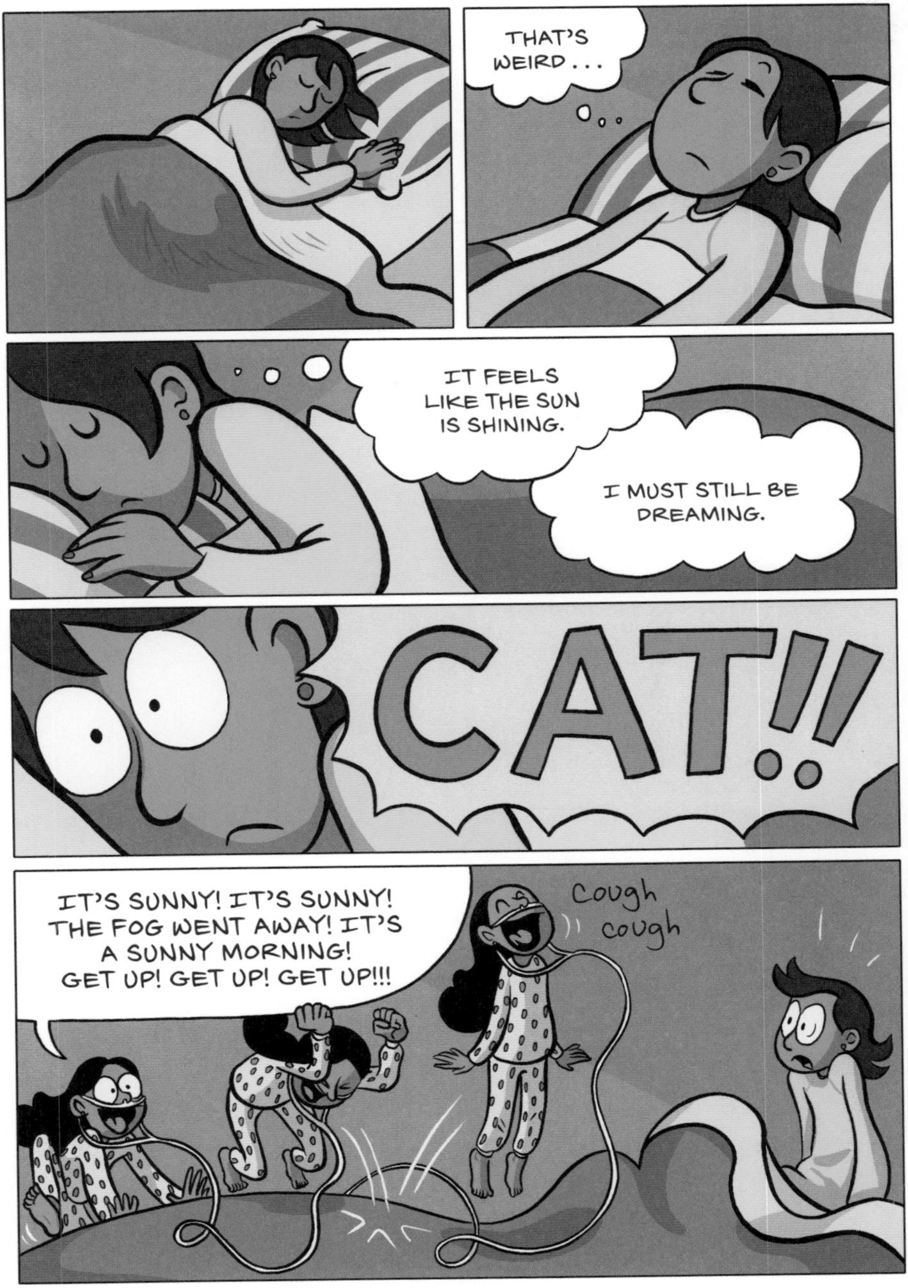
THAT'S WEIRD . . .
IT FEELS LIKE THE SUN IS SHINING.
I MUST STILL BE DREAMING.
CAT!!
IT'S SUNNY! IT'S SUNNY! THE FOG WENT AWAY! IT'S A SUNNY MORNING! GET UP! GET UP! GET UP!!!
cough cough

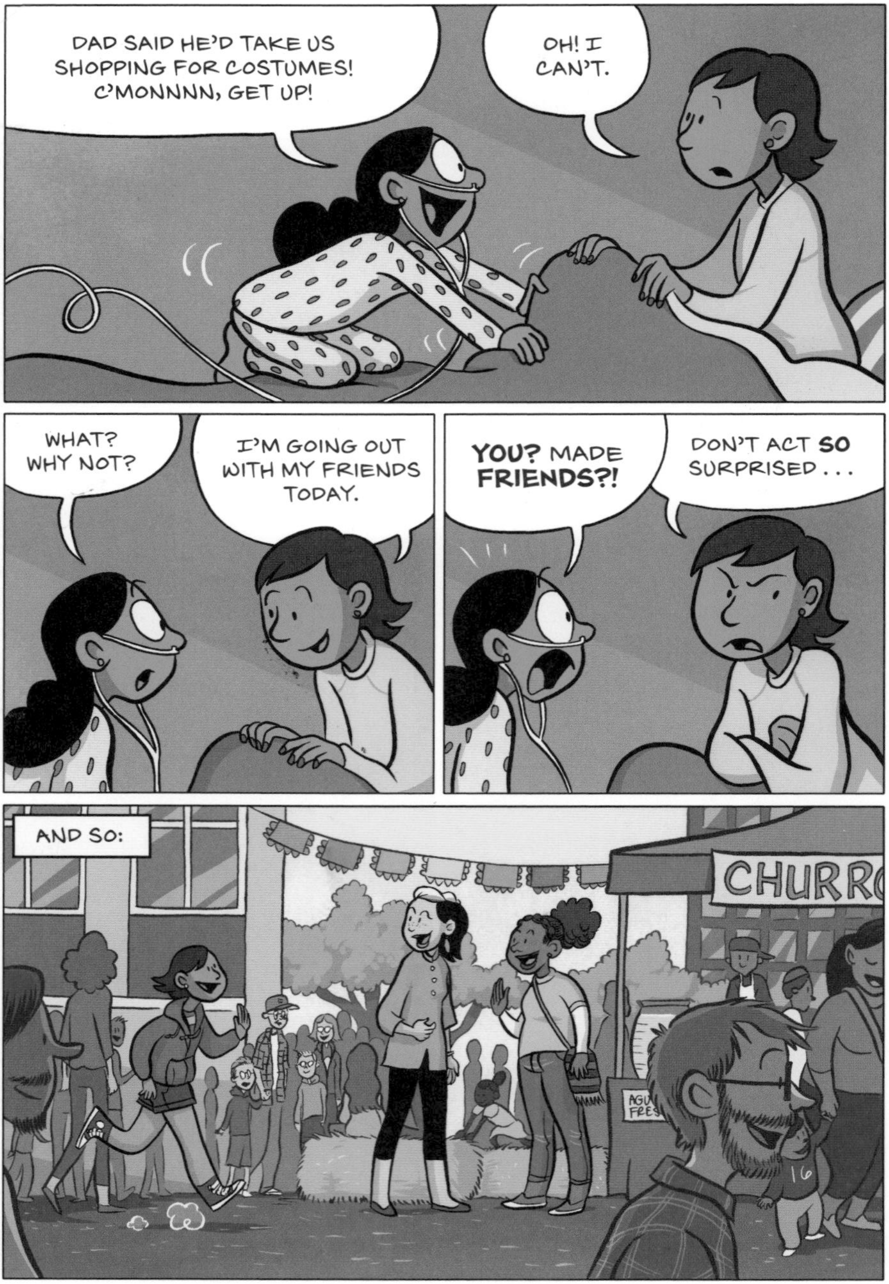
DAD SAID HE'D TAKE US SHOPPING FOR COSTUMES! C'MONNNN, GET UP!
OH! I CAN'T.
WHAT? WHY NOT?
I'M GOING OUT WITH MY FRIENDS TODAY.
YOU? MADE **FRIENDS?!**
DON'T ACT **SO** SURPRISED . . .
AND SO:
CHURRO

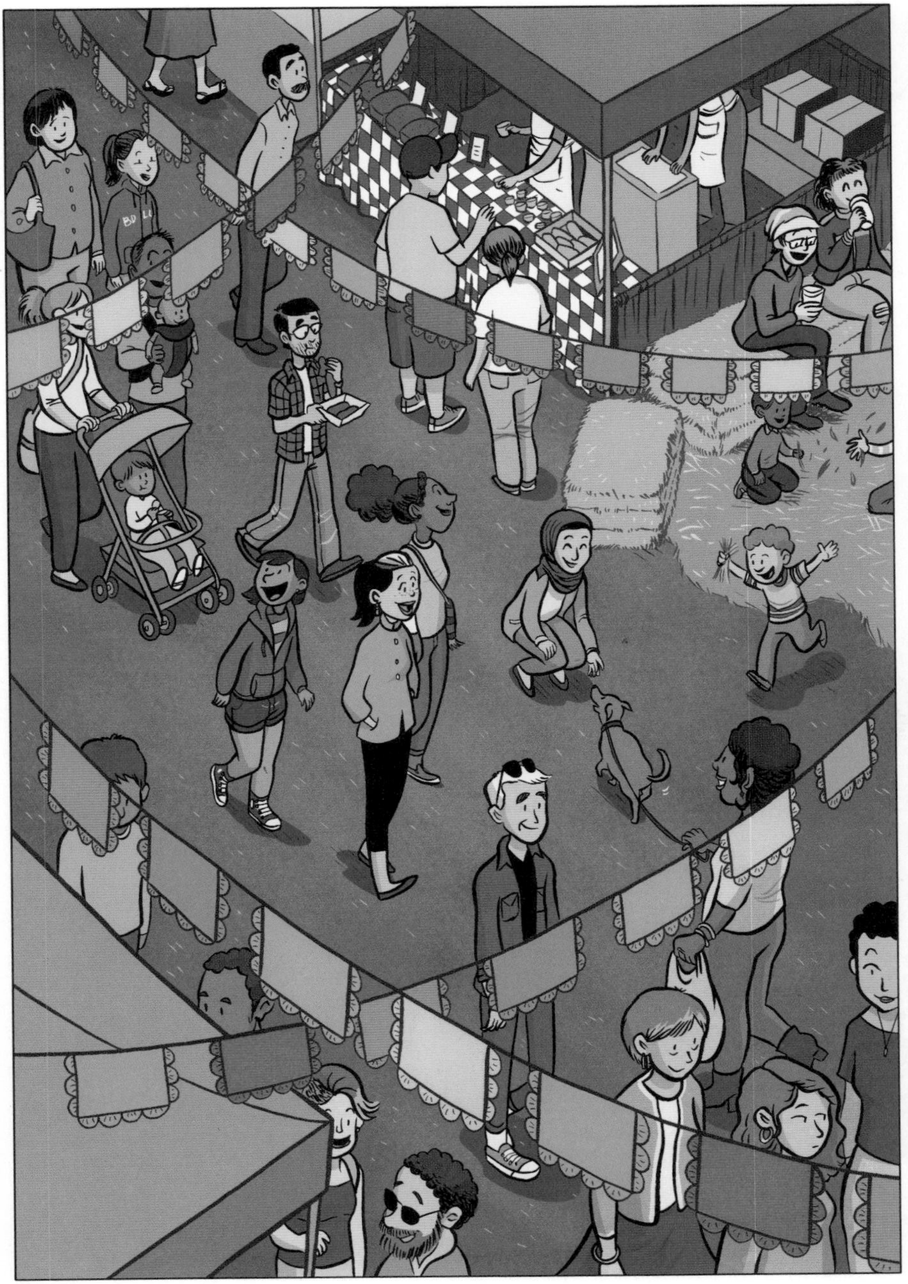

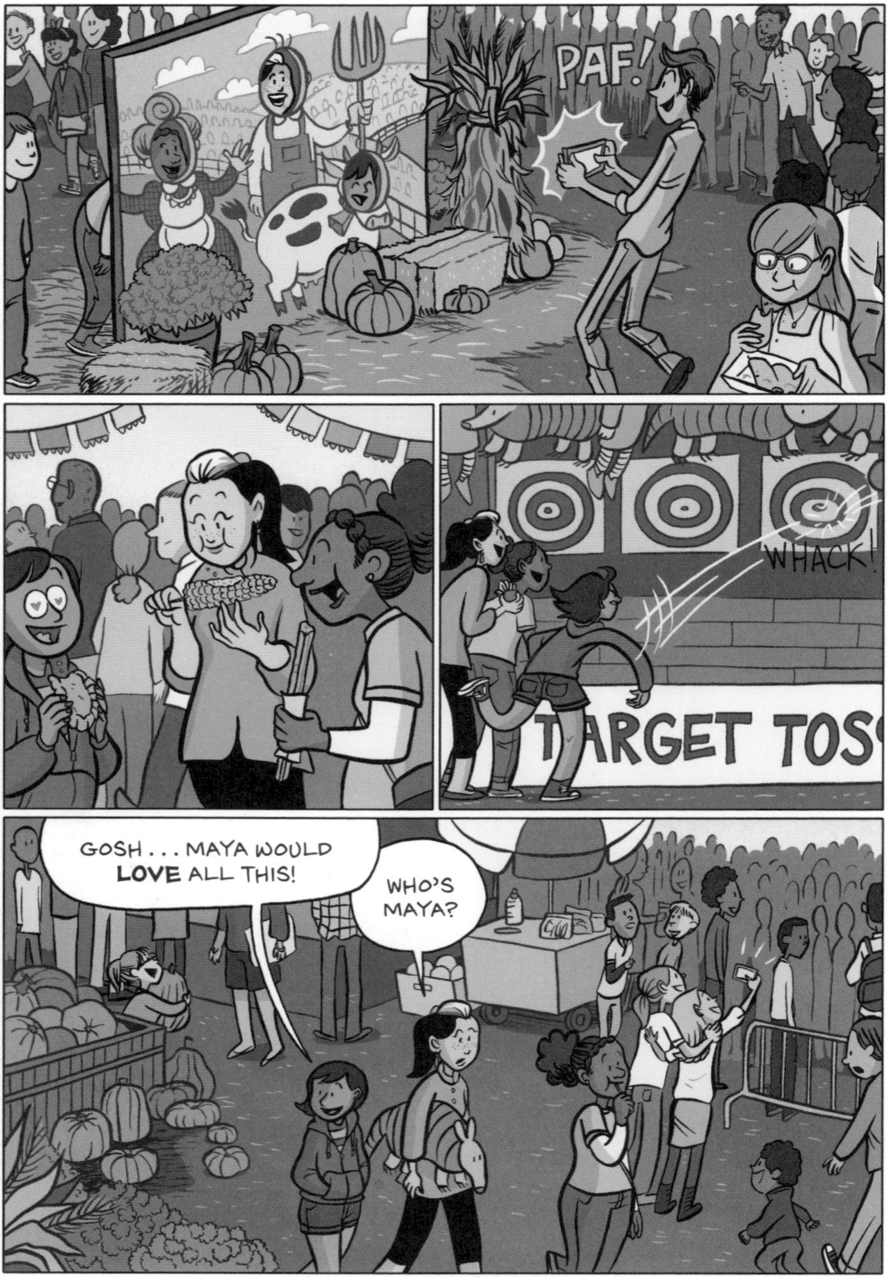
PAF!
WHACK!
TARGET TOS
GOSH . . . MAYA WOULD LOVE ALL THIS!
WHO'S MAYA?

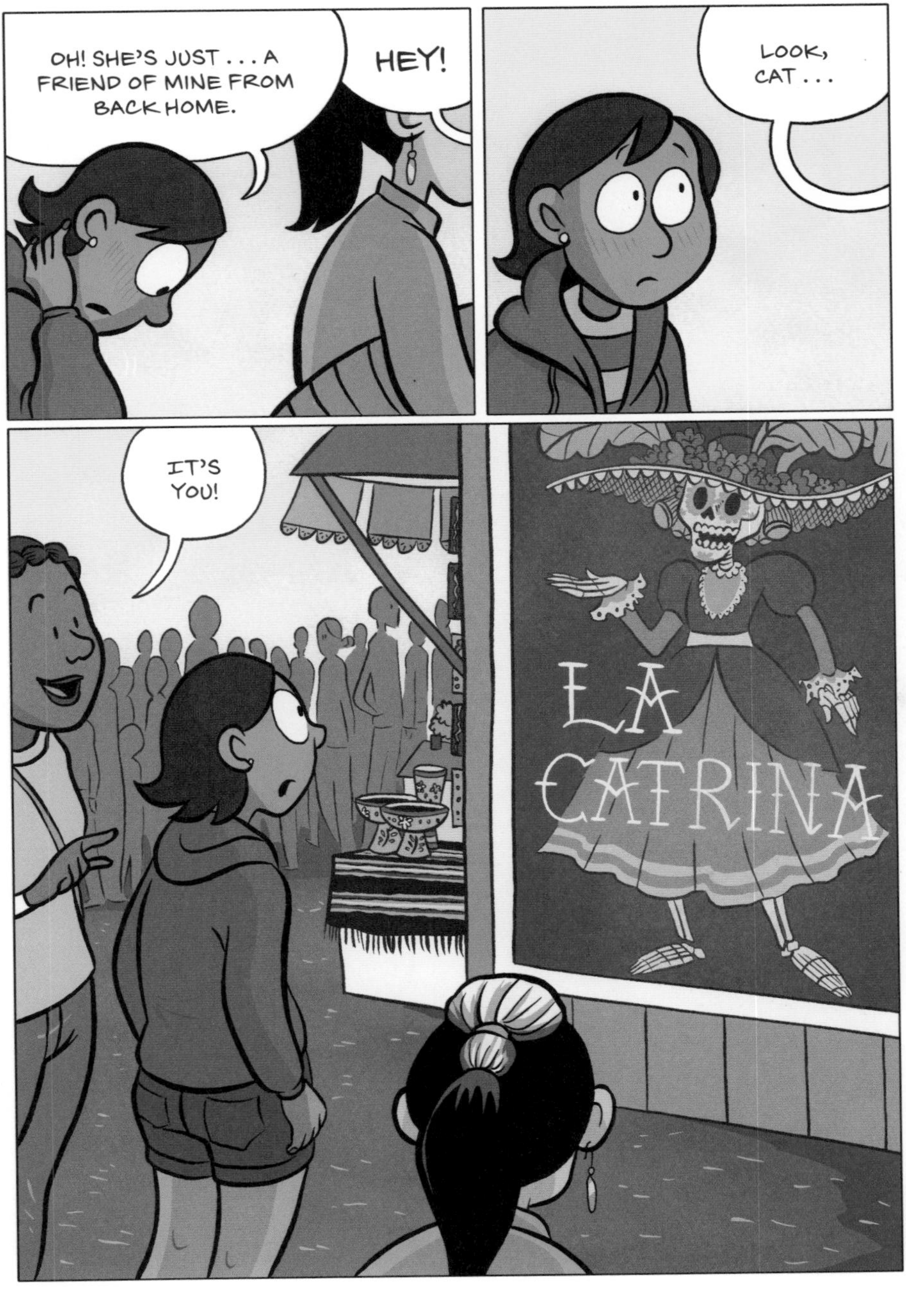
OH! SHE'S JUST . . . A FRIEND OF MINE FROM BACK HOME.
HEY!
LOOK, CAT . . .
IT'S YOU!
LA CATRINA

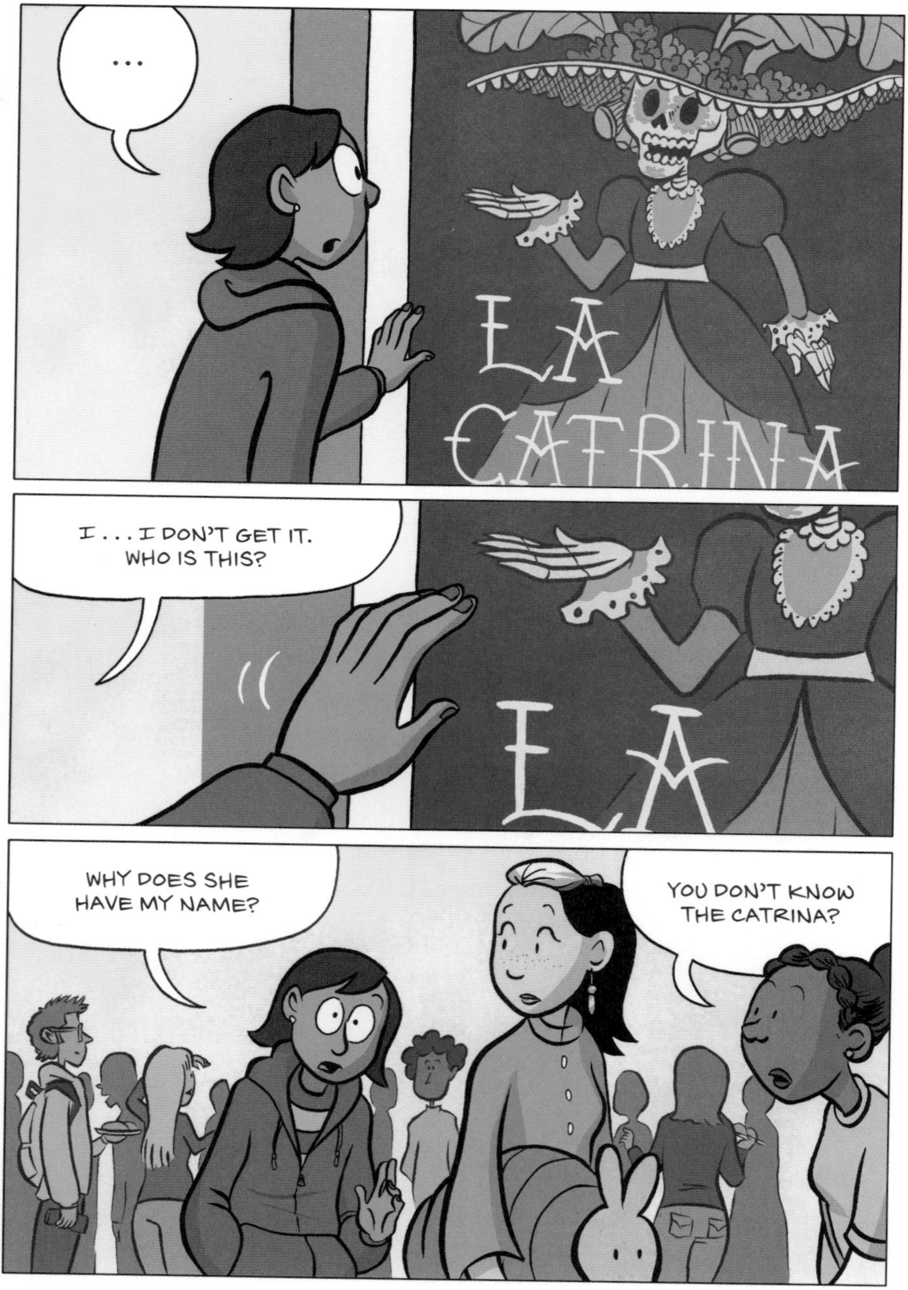
...
LA CATRINA
I . . . I DON'T GET IT. WHO IS THIS?
LA
WHY DOES SHE HAVE MY NAME?
YOU DON'T KNOW THE CATRINA?

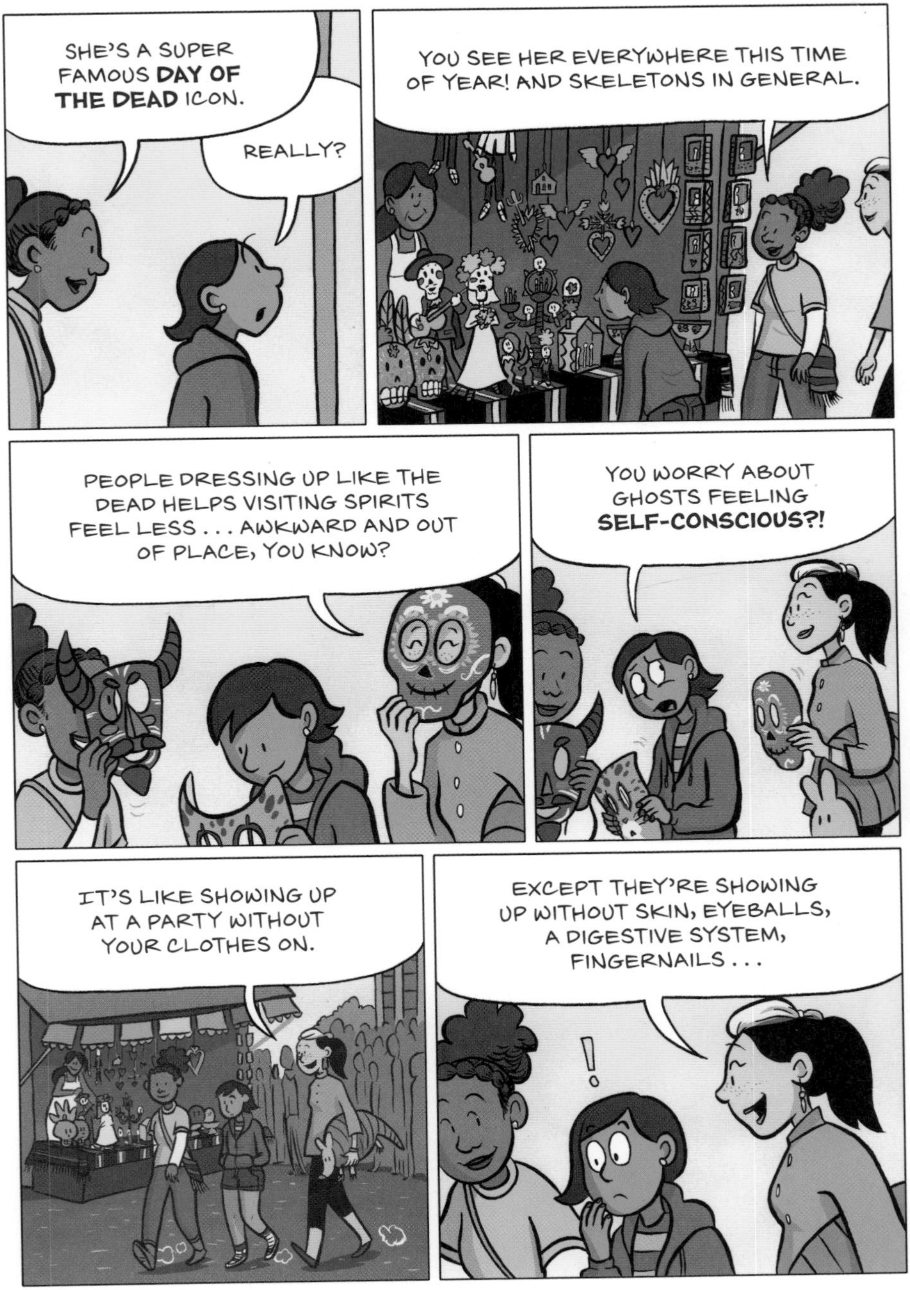

SHE'S A SUPER FAMOUS **DAY OF THE DEAD** ICON.
REALLY?
YOU SEE HER EVERYWHERE THIS TIME OF YEAR! AND SKELETONS IN GENERAL.
PEOPLE DRESSING UP LIKE THE DEAD HELPS VISITING SPIRITS FEEL LESS . . . AWKWARD AND OUT OF PLACE, YOU KNOW?
YOU WORRY ABOUT GHOSTS FEELING **SELF-CONSCIOUS?!**
IT'S LIKE SHOWING UP AT A PARTY WITHOUT YOUR CLOTHES ON.
EXCEPT THEY'RE SHOWING UP WITHOUT SKIN, EYEBALLS, A DIGESTIVE SYSTEM, FINGERNAILS . . .
!

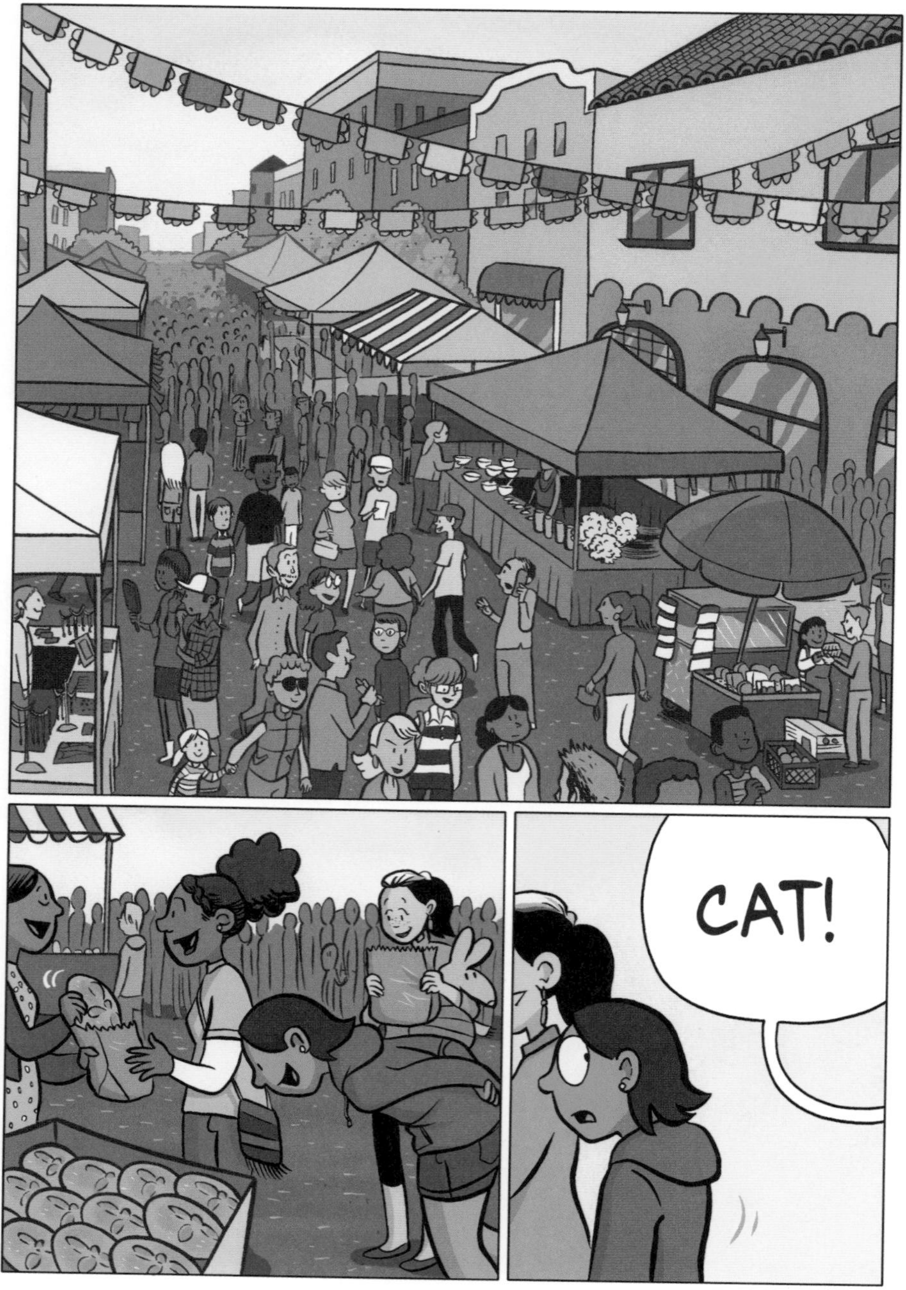
CAT!

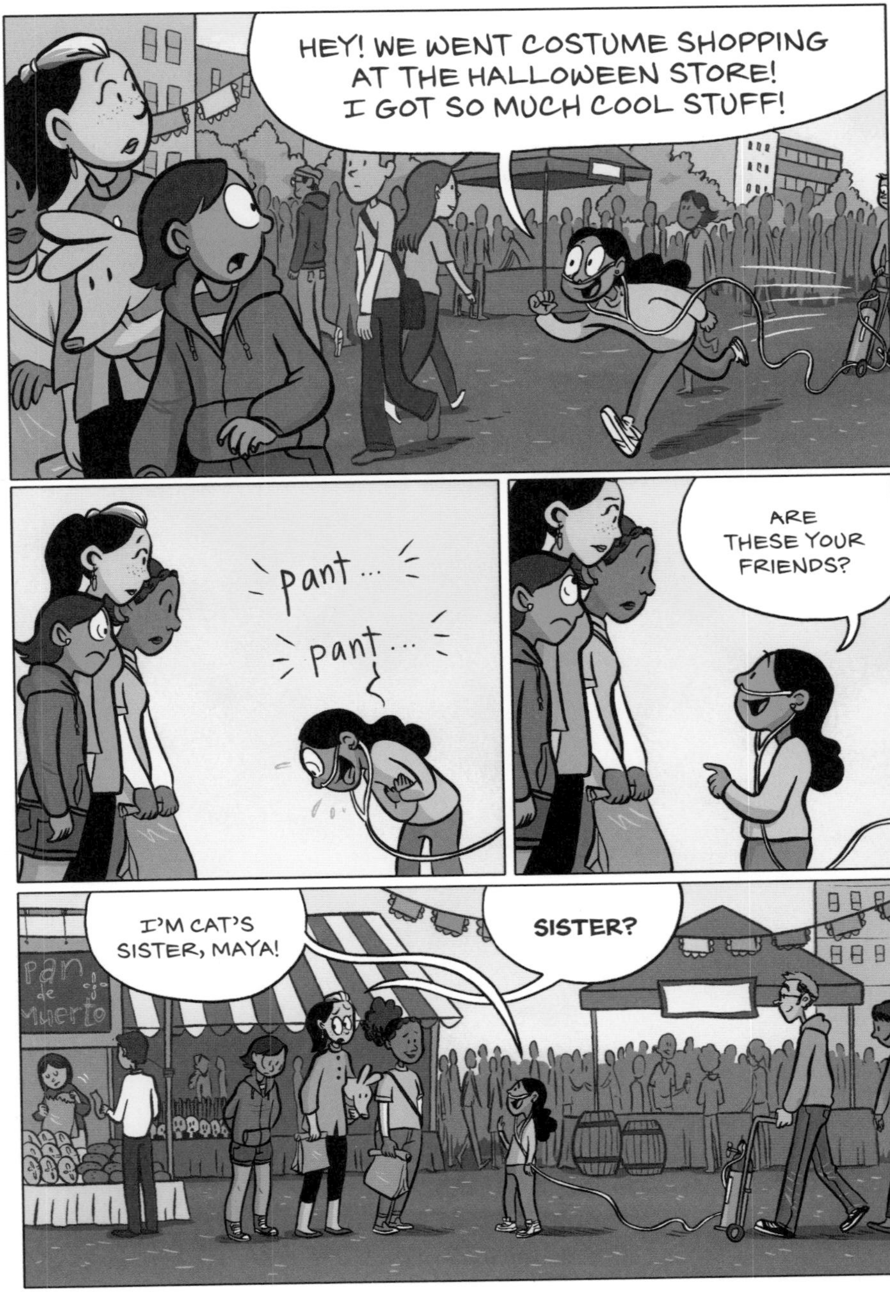
HEY! WE WENT COSTUME SHOPPING AT THE HALLOWEEN STORE! I GOT SO MUCH COOL STUFF!
pant...
pant...
ARE THESE YOUR FRIENDS?
Pan de Muerto
I'M CAT'S SISTER, MAYA!
SISTER?

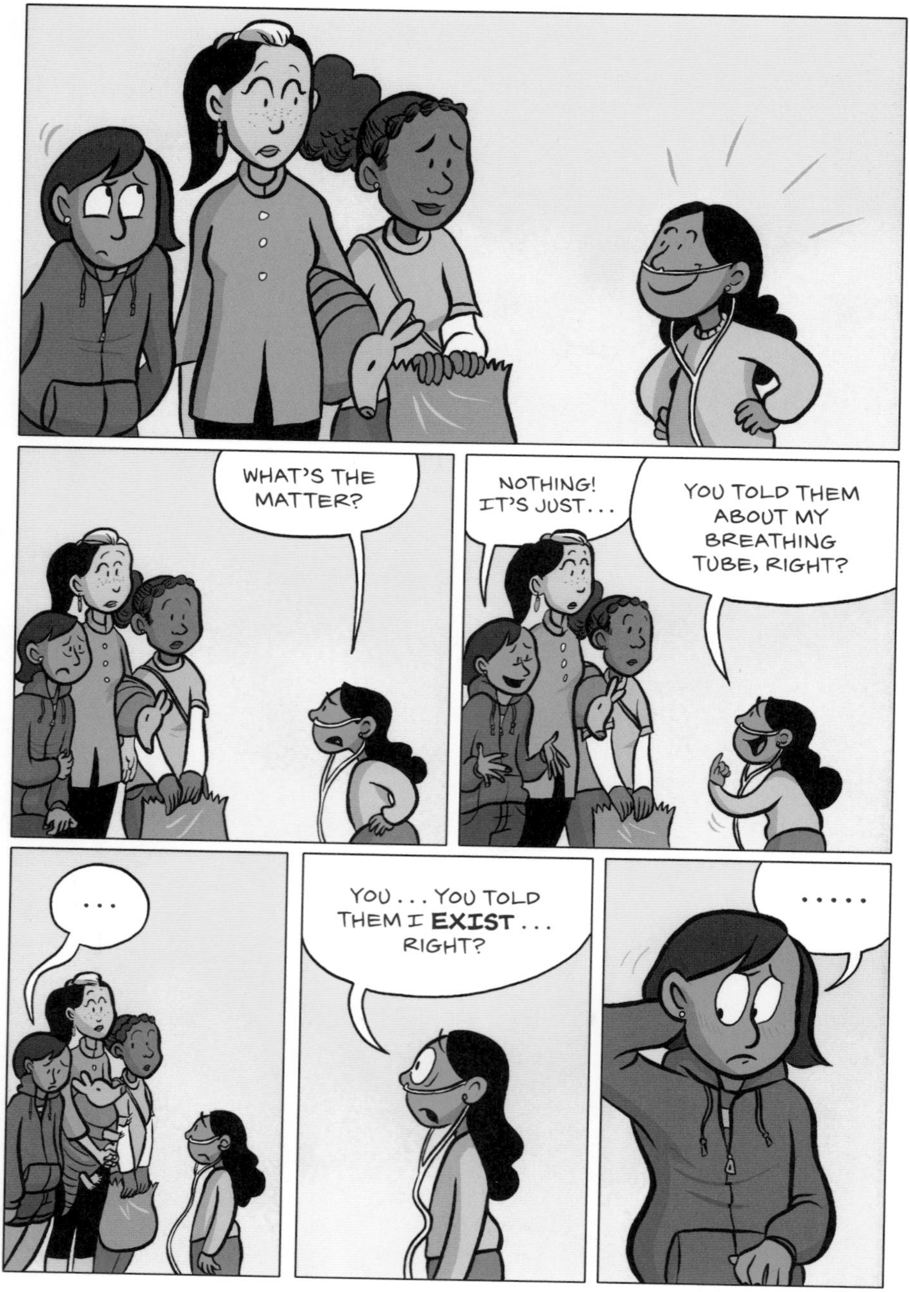
WHAT'S THE MATTER?
NOTHING! IT'S JUST...
YOU TOLD THEM ABOUT MY BREATHING TUBE, RIGHT?
...
YOU... YOU TOLD THEM I **EXIST**... RIGHT?
.....

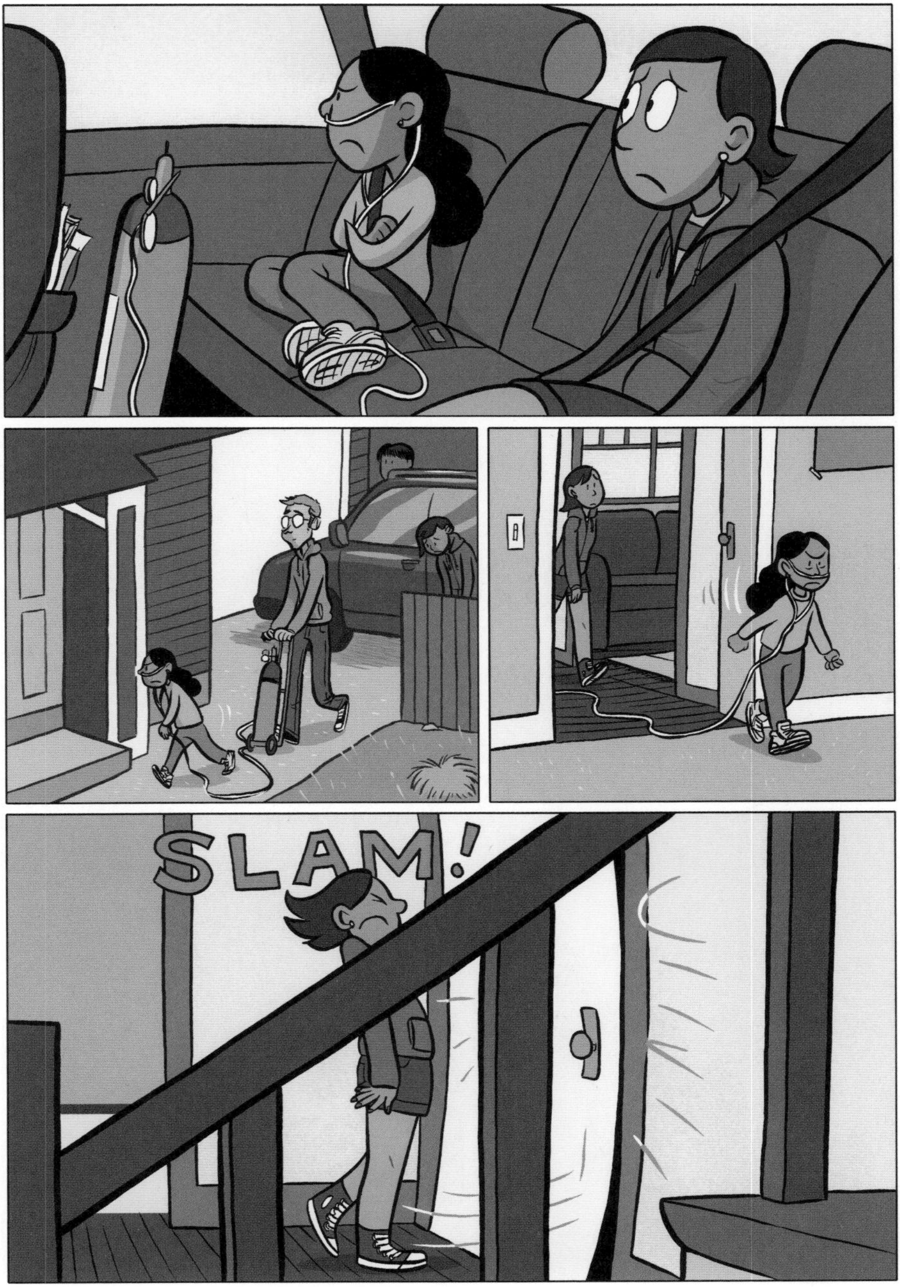
SLAM!

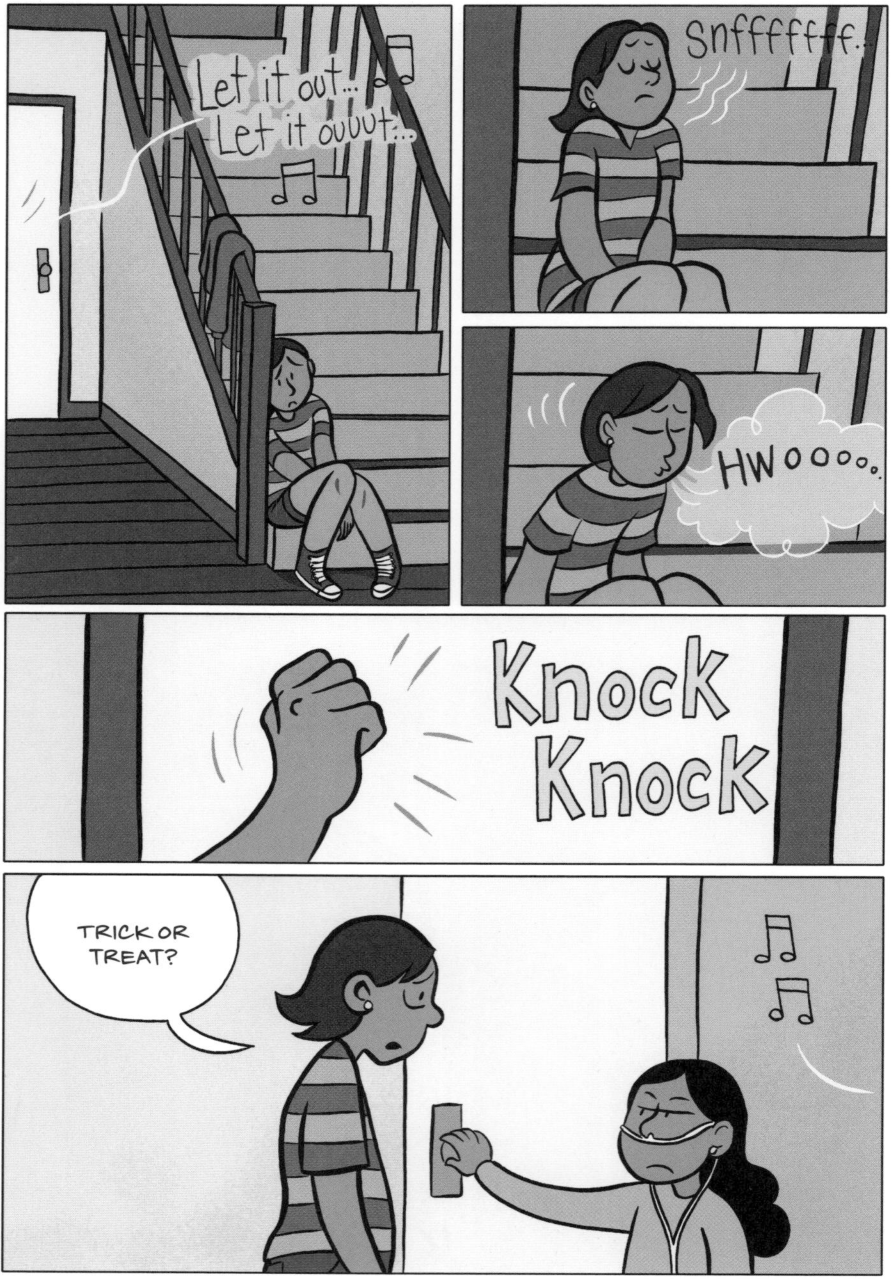
Let it out...
Let it ouuut...
Snffffff...
HWooooo.
Knock
Knock
TRICK OR TREAT?

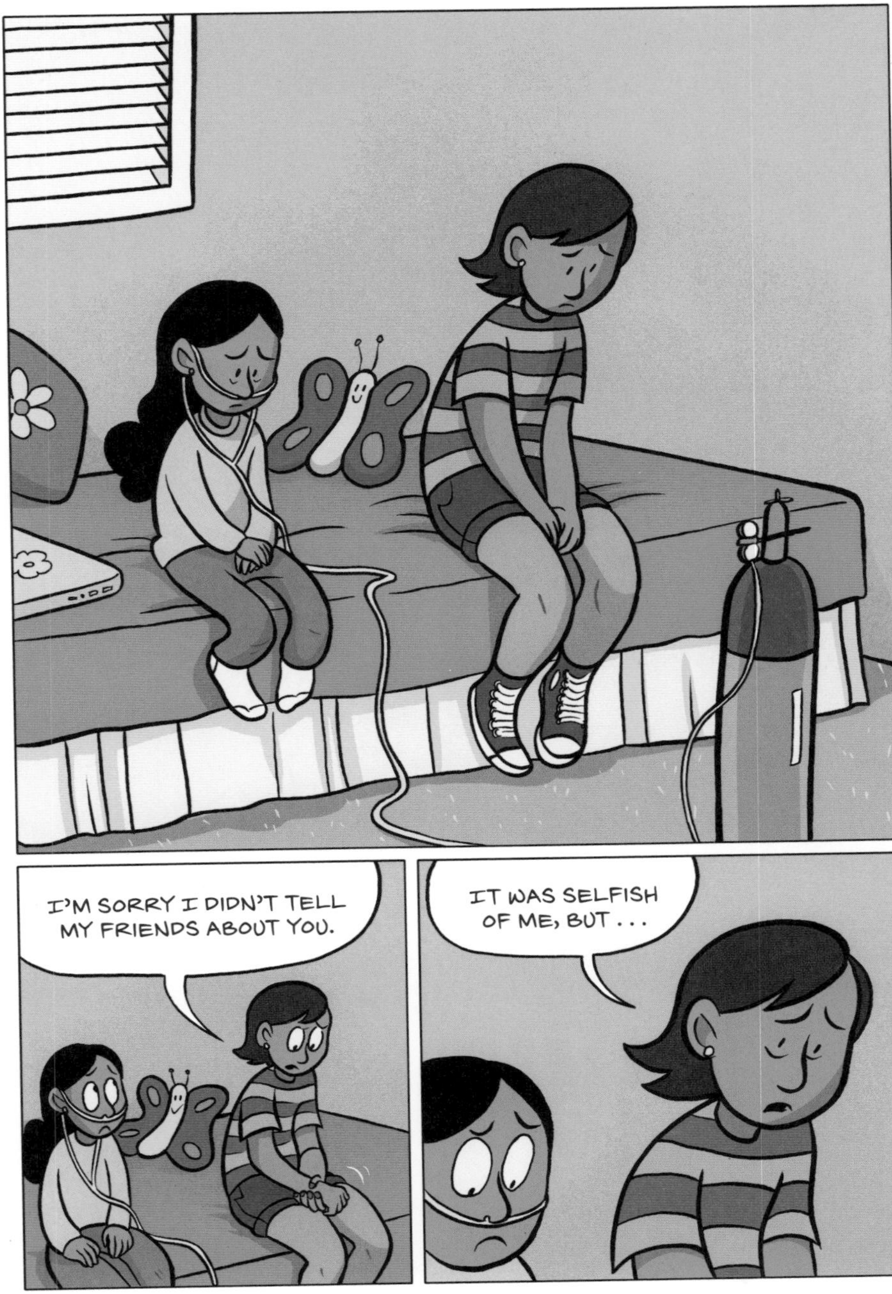
I'M SORRY I DIDN'T TELL MY FRIENDS ABOUT YOU.
IT WAS SELFISH OF ME, BUT . . .

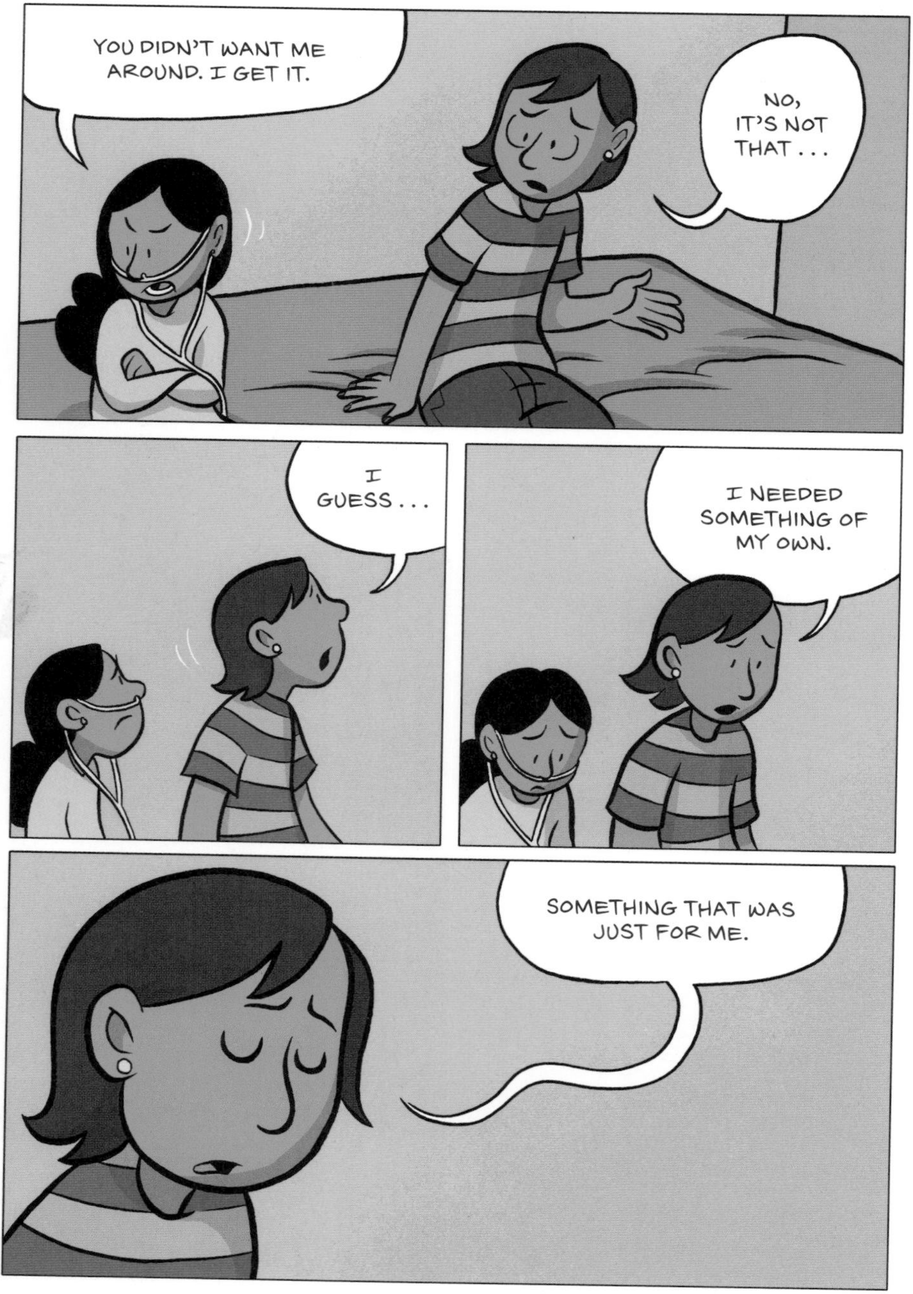
YOU DIDN'T WANT ME AROUND. I GET IT.
NO, IT'S NOT THAT . . .
I GUESS . . .
I NEEDED SOMETHING OF MY OWN.
SOMETHING THAT WAS JUST FOR ME.

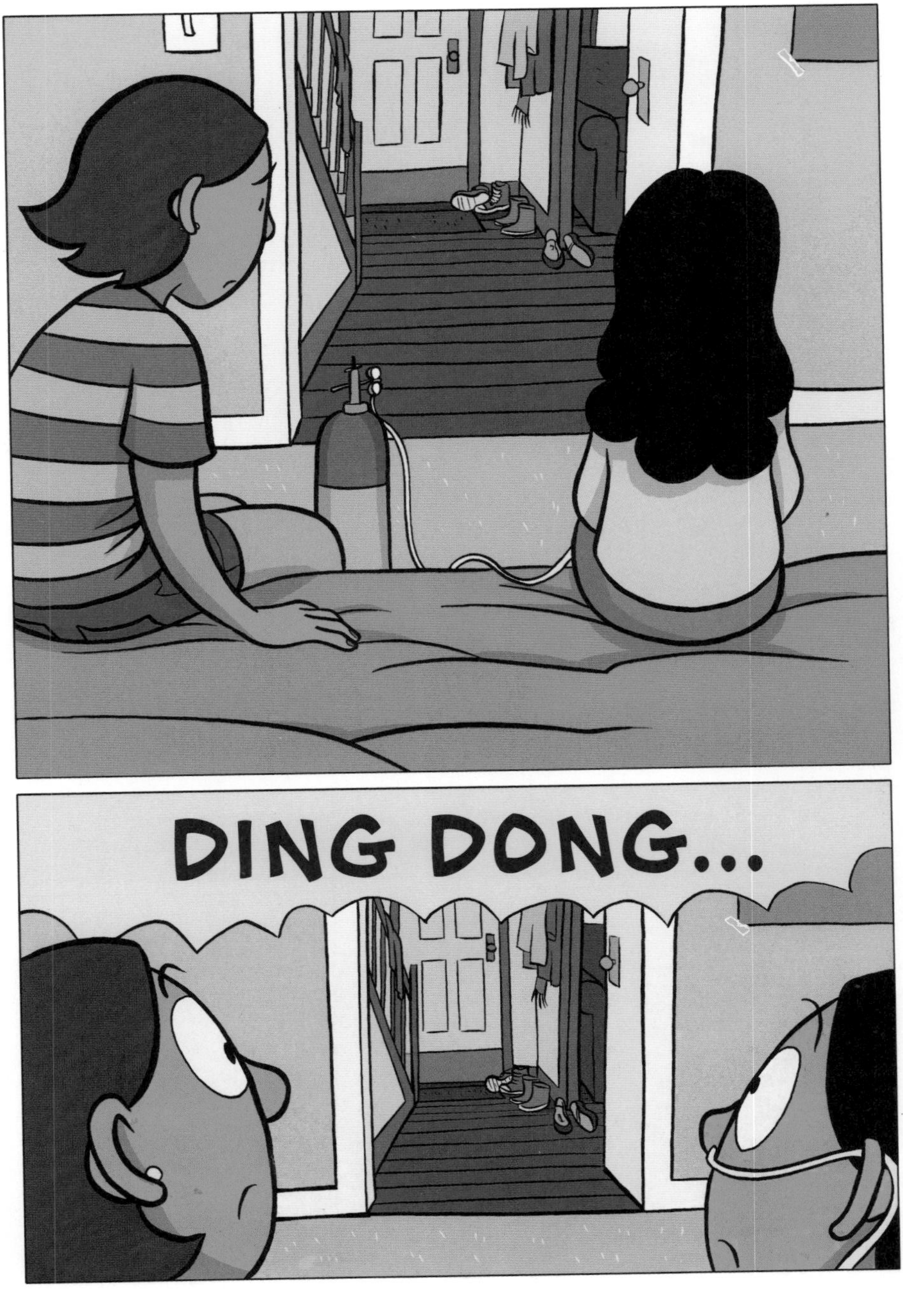
DING DONG...

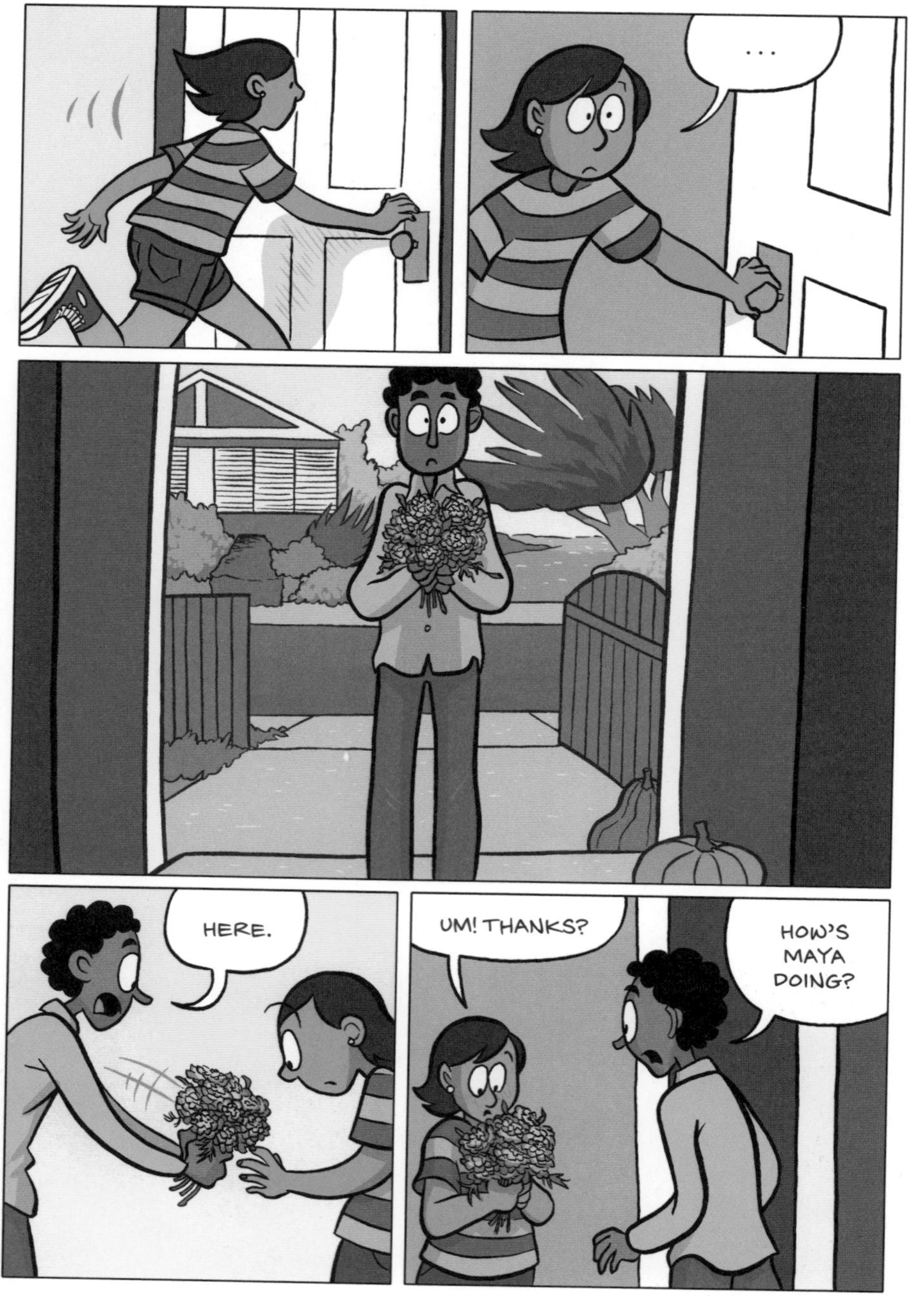
...
HERE.
UM! THANKS?
HOW'S MAYA DOING?

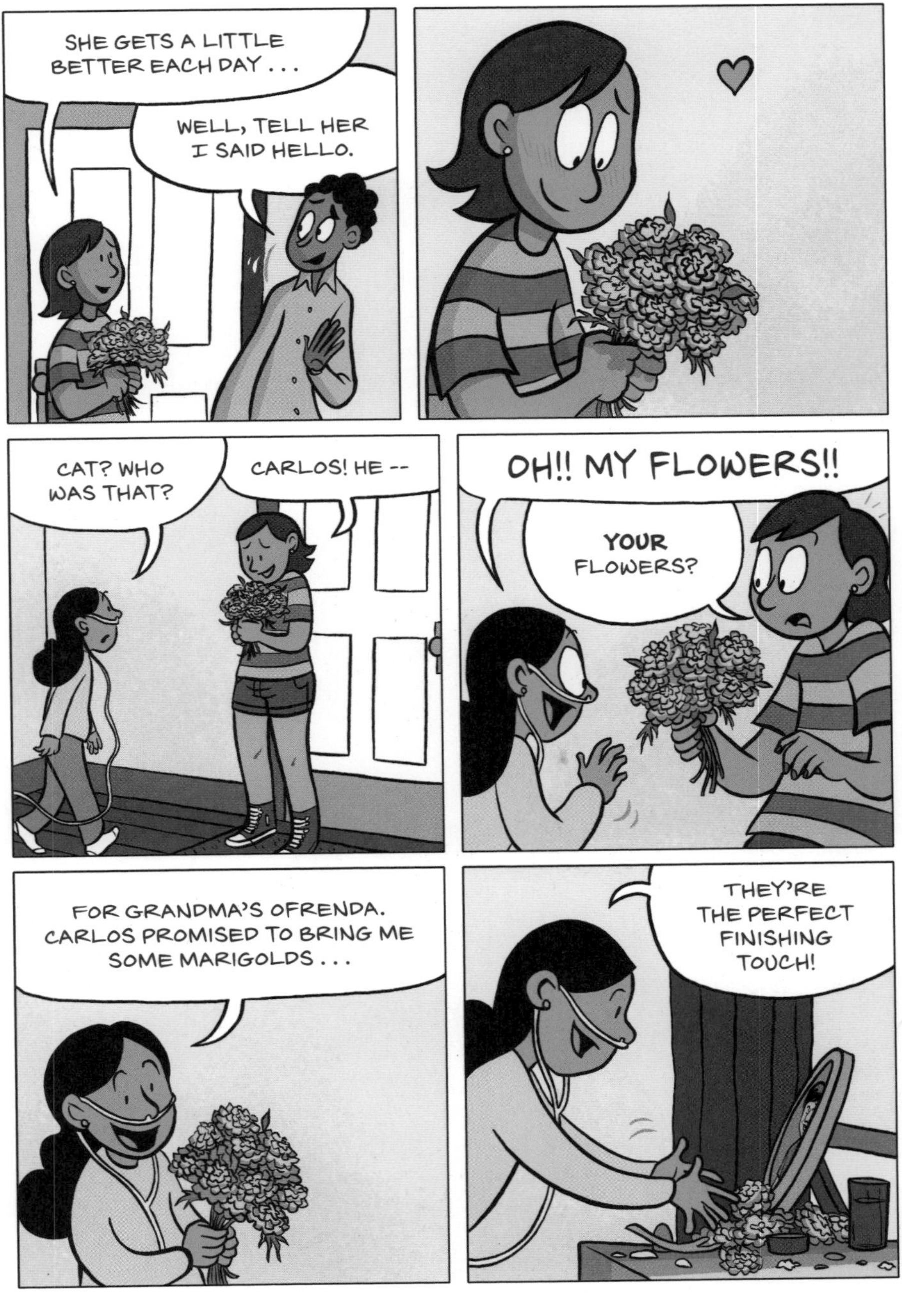

SHE GETS A LITTLE BETTER EACH DAY . . .
WELL, TELL HER I SAID HELLO.
CAT? WHO WAS THAT?
CARLOS! HE --
OH!! MY FLOWERS!!
YOUR FLOWERS?
FOR GRANDMA'S OFRENDA. CARLOS PROMISED TO BRING ME SOME MARIGOLDS . . .
THEY'RE THE PERFECT FINISHING TOUCH!

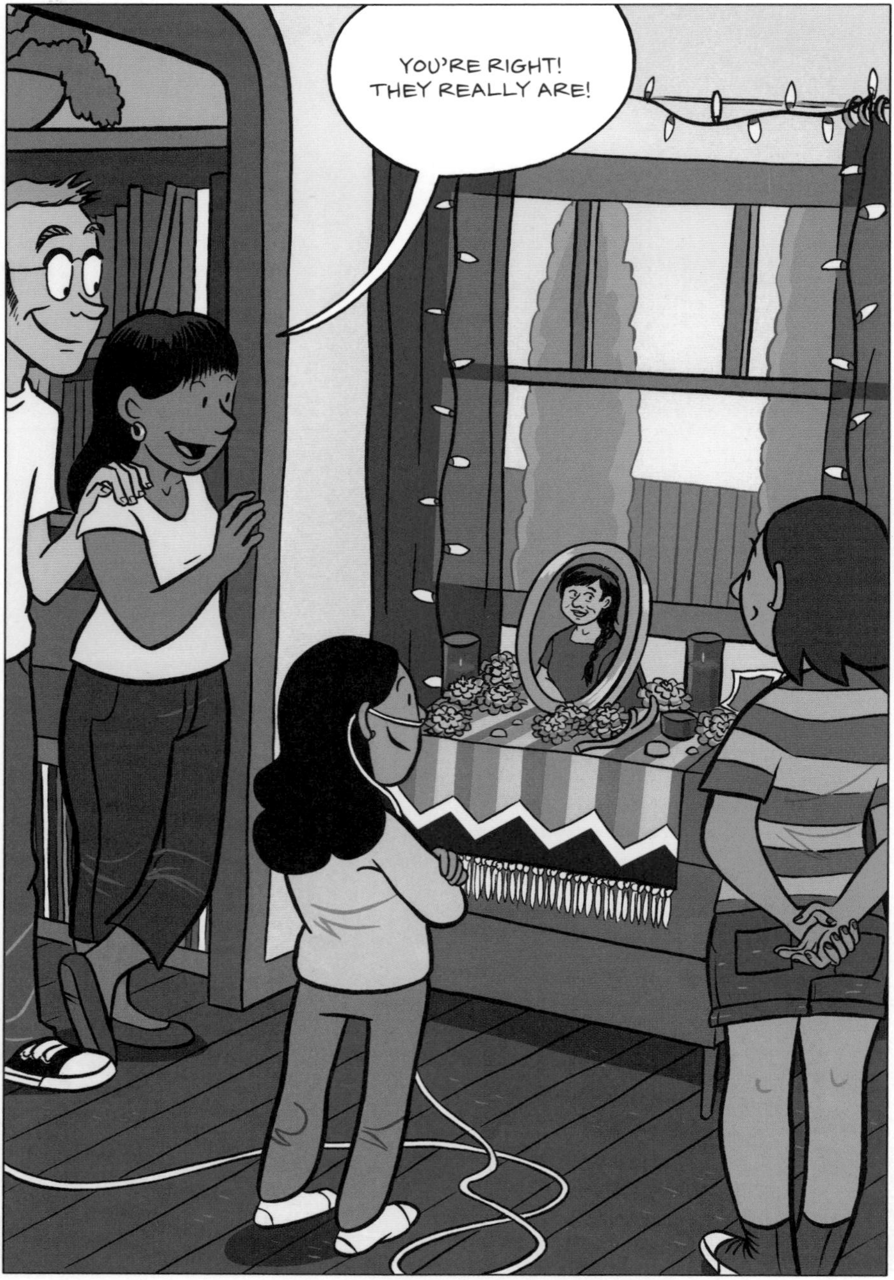
YOU'RE RIGHT!
THEY REALLY ARE!

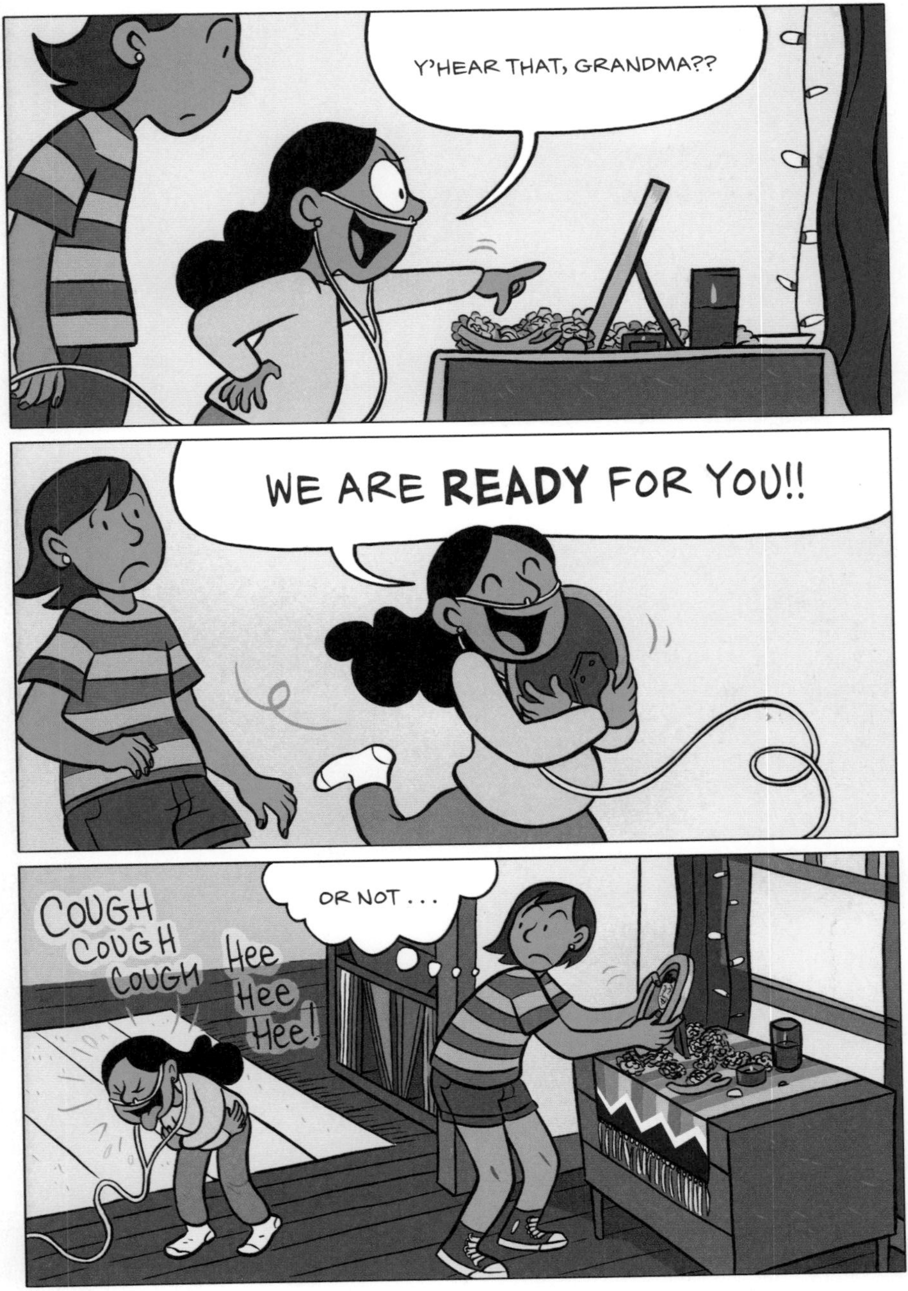
Y'HEAR THAT, GRANDMA??
WE ARE **READY** FOR YOU!!
COUGH
COUGH
COUGH
Hee
Hee
Hee!
OR NOT . . .

LATE OCTOBER

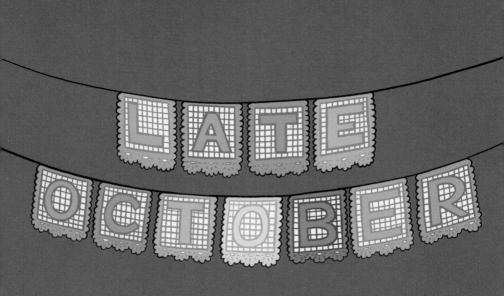

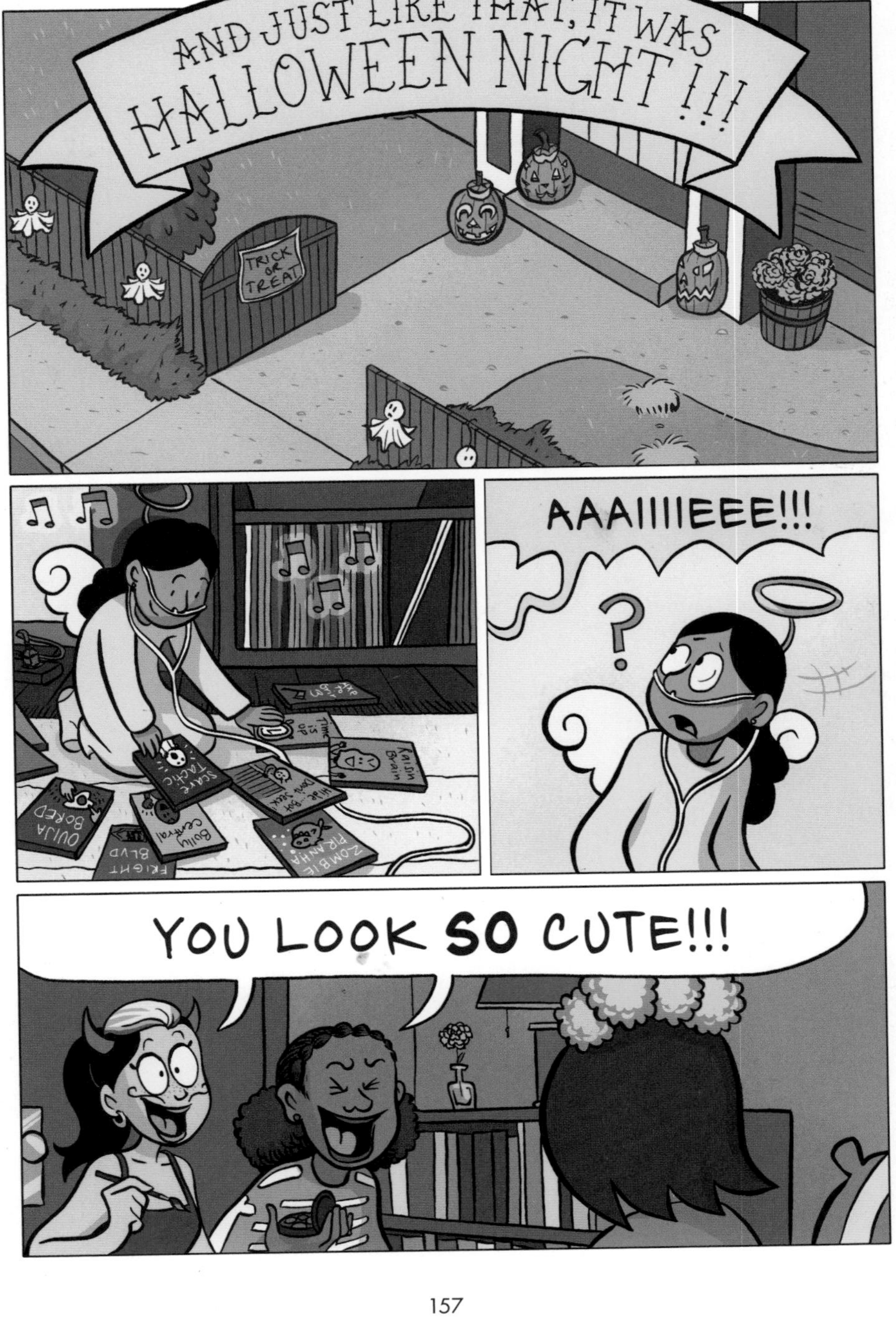
AND JUST LIKE THAT, IT WAS HALLOWEEN NIGHT!!!
TRICK OR TREAT
SCARE TACTIC
OUIJA BORED
Raisin Brain
Time is up
Bully Central
ZOMBIE PIRANHA
FRIGHT BLVD
AAAIIIIEEEE!!!
?
YOU LOOK SO CUTE!!!

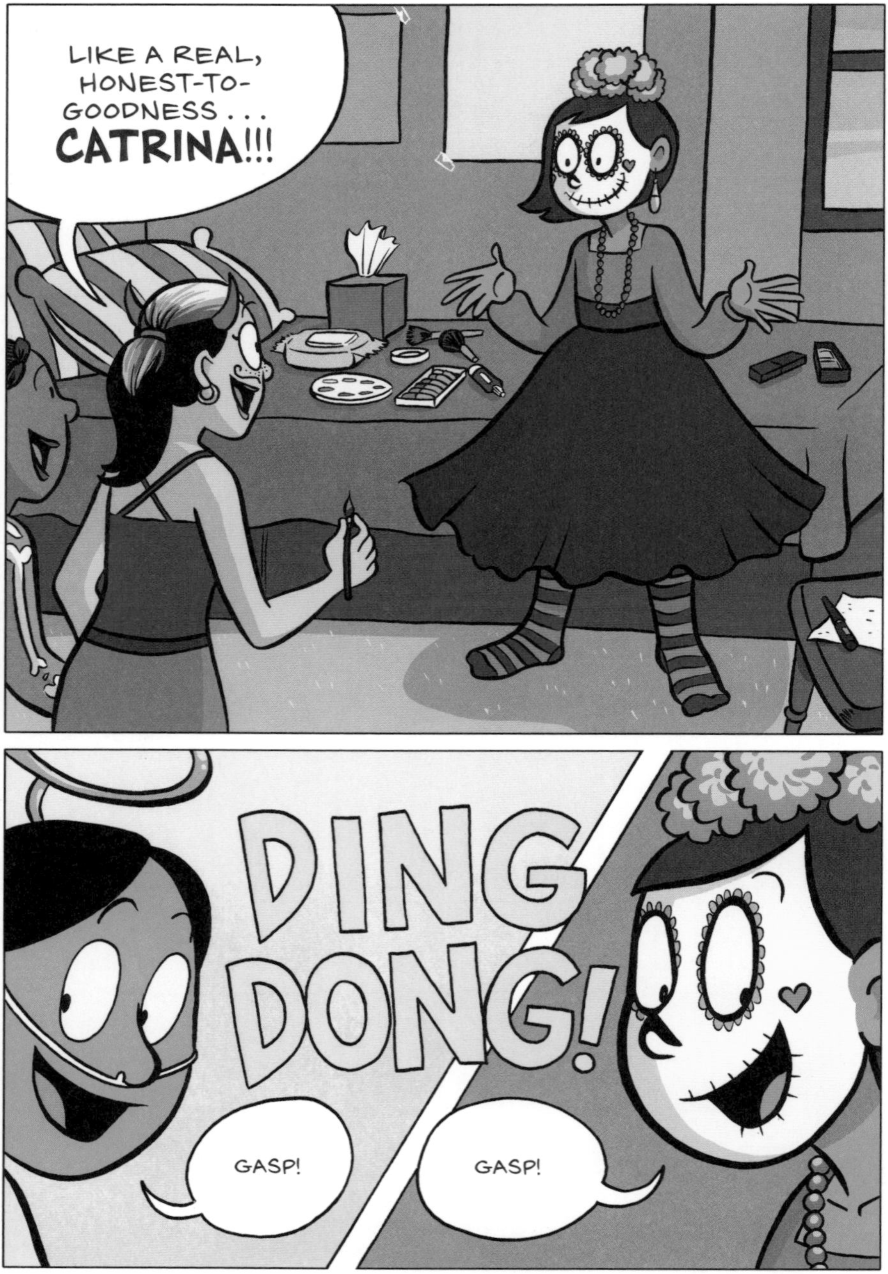
LIKE A REAL, HONEST-TO-GOODNESS . . . CATRINA!!!
DING DONG!
GASP!
GASP!

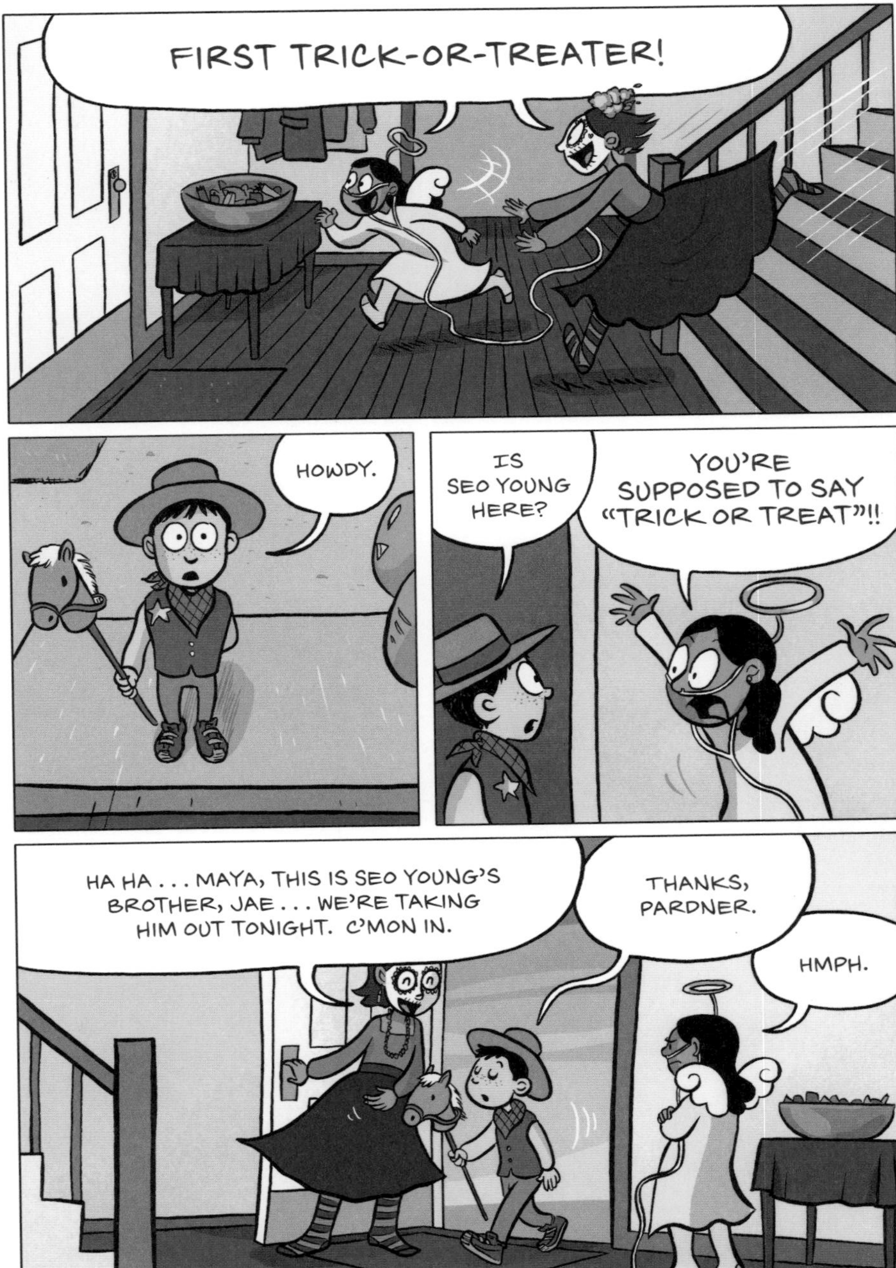
FIRST TRICK-OR-TREATER!
HOWDY.
IS SEO YOUNG HERE?
YOU'RE SUPPOSED TO SAY "TRICK OR TREAT"!!
HA HA . . . MAYA, THIS IS SEO YOUNG'S BROTHER, JAE . . . WE'RE TAKING HIM OUT TONIGHT. C'MON IN.
THANKS, PARDNER.
HMPH.

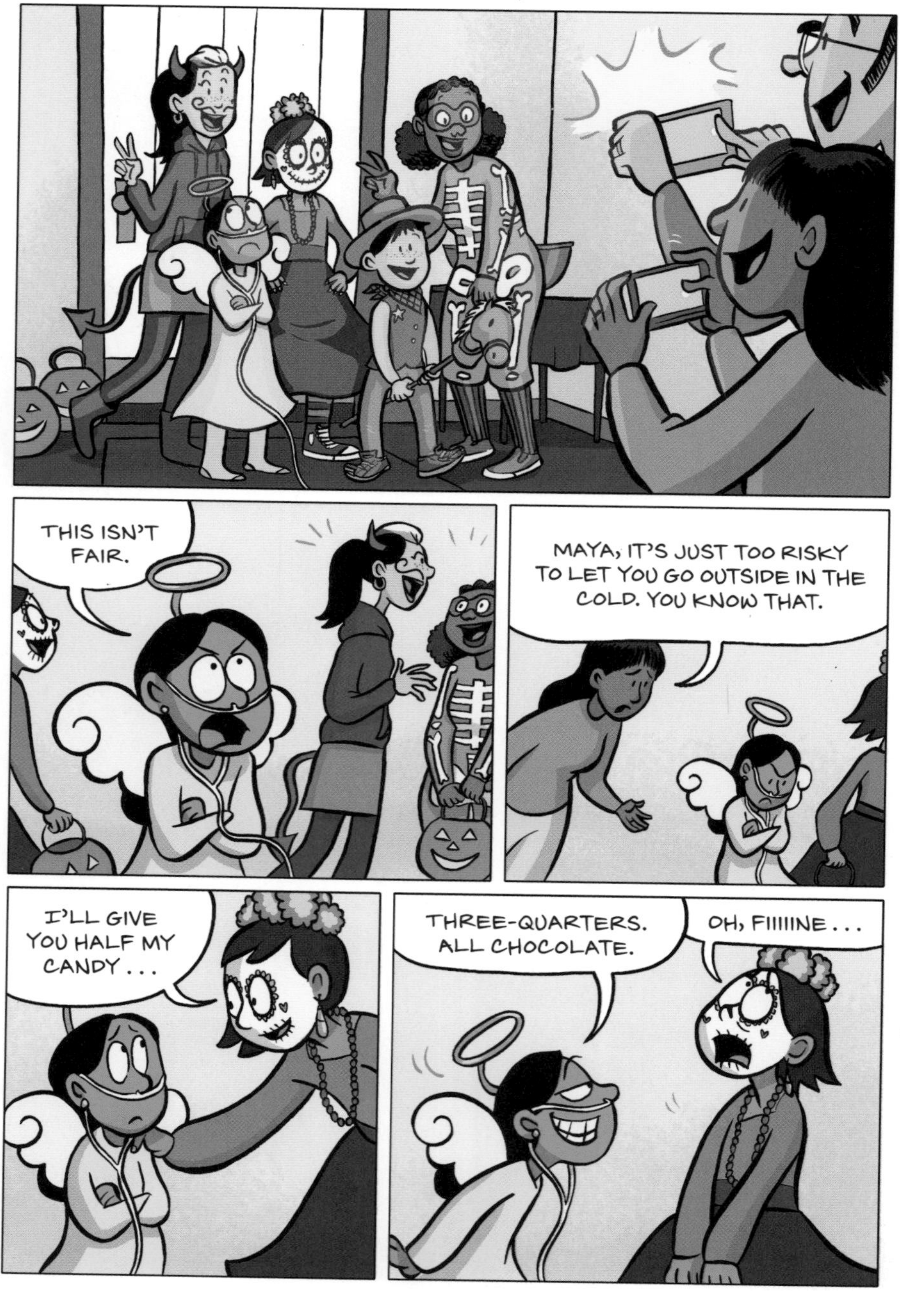
THIS ISN'T FAIR.
MAYA, IT'S JUST TOO RISKY TO LET YOU GO OUTSIDE IN THE COLD. YOU KNOW THAT.
I'LL GIVE YOU HALF MY CANDY . . .
THREE-QUARTERS. ALL CHOCOLATE.
OH, FIIIIINE . . .

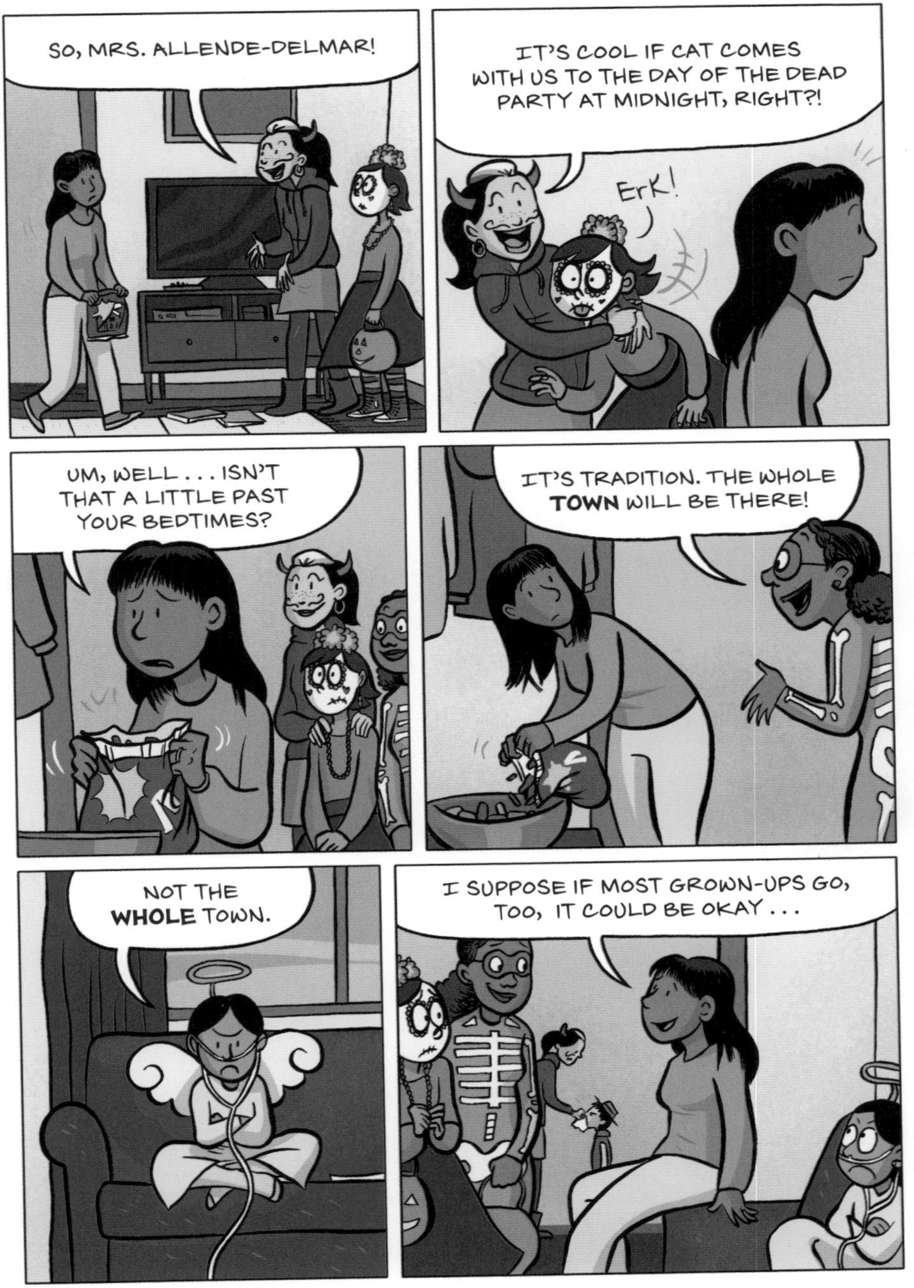
SO, MRS. ALLENDE-DELMAR!
IT'S COOL IF CAT COMES WITH US TO THE DAY OF THE DEAD PARTY AT MIDNIGHT, RIGHT?!
ErK!
UM, WELL . . . ISN'T THAT A LITTLE PAST YOUR BEDTIMES?
IT'S TRADITION. THE WHOLE **TOWN** WILL BE THERE!
NOT THE **WHOLE** TOWN.
I SUPPOSE IF MOST GROWN-UPS GO, TOO, IT COULD BE OKAY . . .

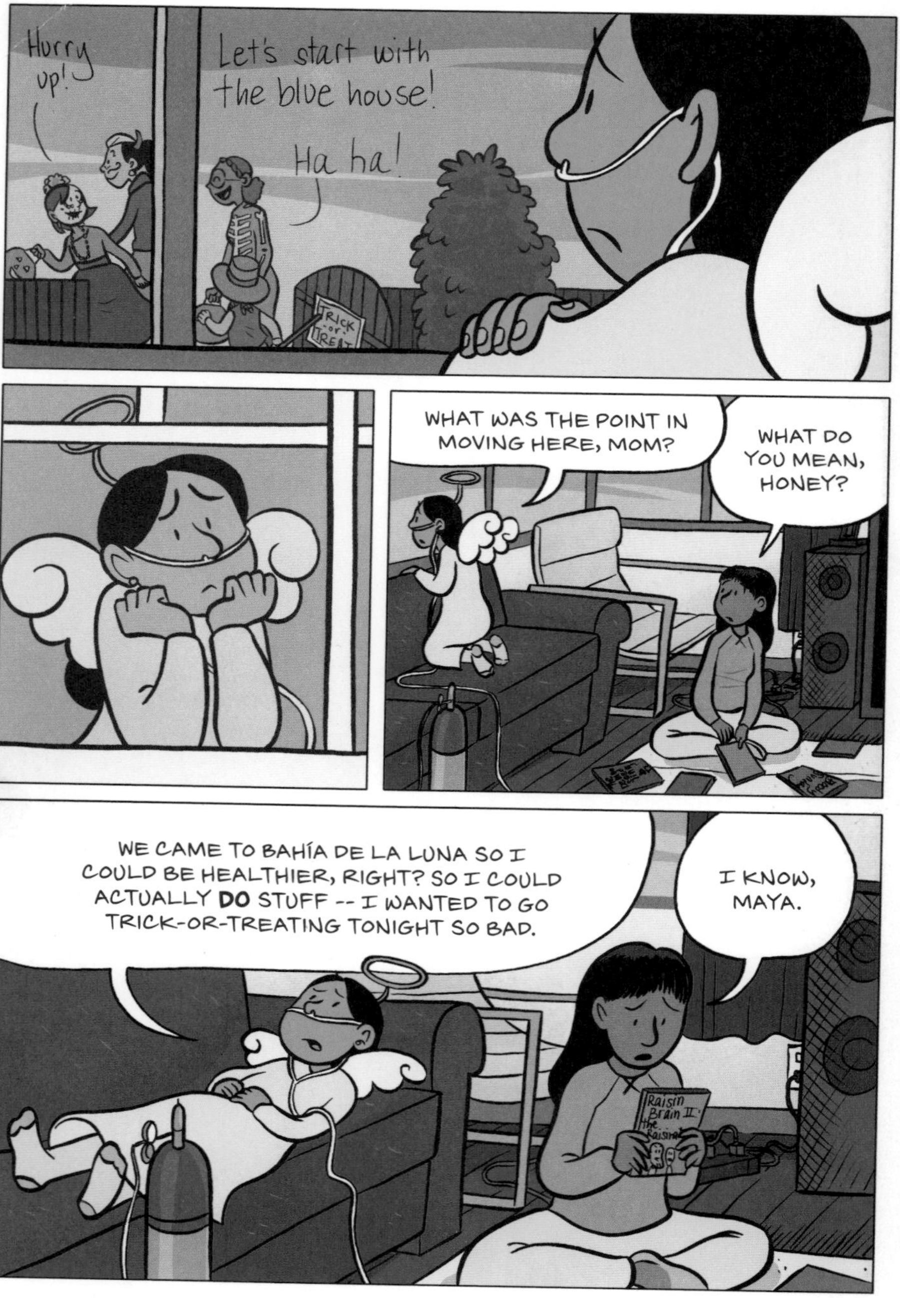
Hurry up!
Let's start with the blue house!
Ha ha!
TRICK -or- TREAT
WHAT WAS THE POINT IN MOVING HERE, MOM?
WHAT DO YOU MEAN, HONEY?
WE CAME TO BAHÍA DE LA LUNA SO I COULD BE HEALTHIER, RIGHT? SO I COULD ACTUALLY **DO** STUFF -- I WANTED TO GO TRICK-OR-TREATING TONIGHT SO BAD.
I KNOW, MAYA.
Raisin Brain II

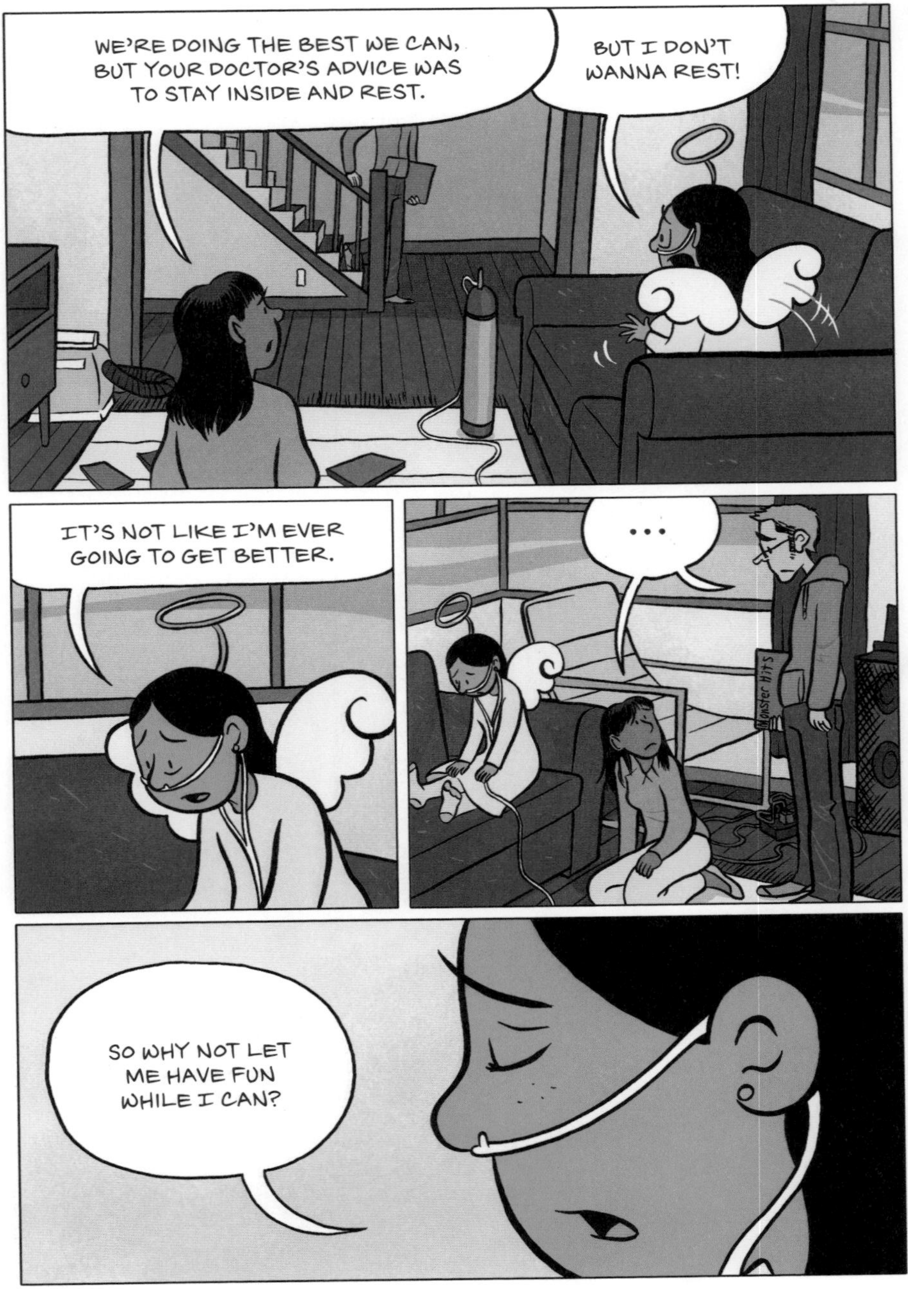
WE'RE DOING THE BEST WE CAN, BUT YOUR DOCTOR'S ADVICE WAS TO STAY INSIDE AND REST.
BUT I DON'T WANNA REST!
IT'S NOT LIKE I'M EVER GOING TO GET BETTER.
...
Monster Hits
SO WHY NOT LET ME HAVE FUN WHILE I CAN?

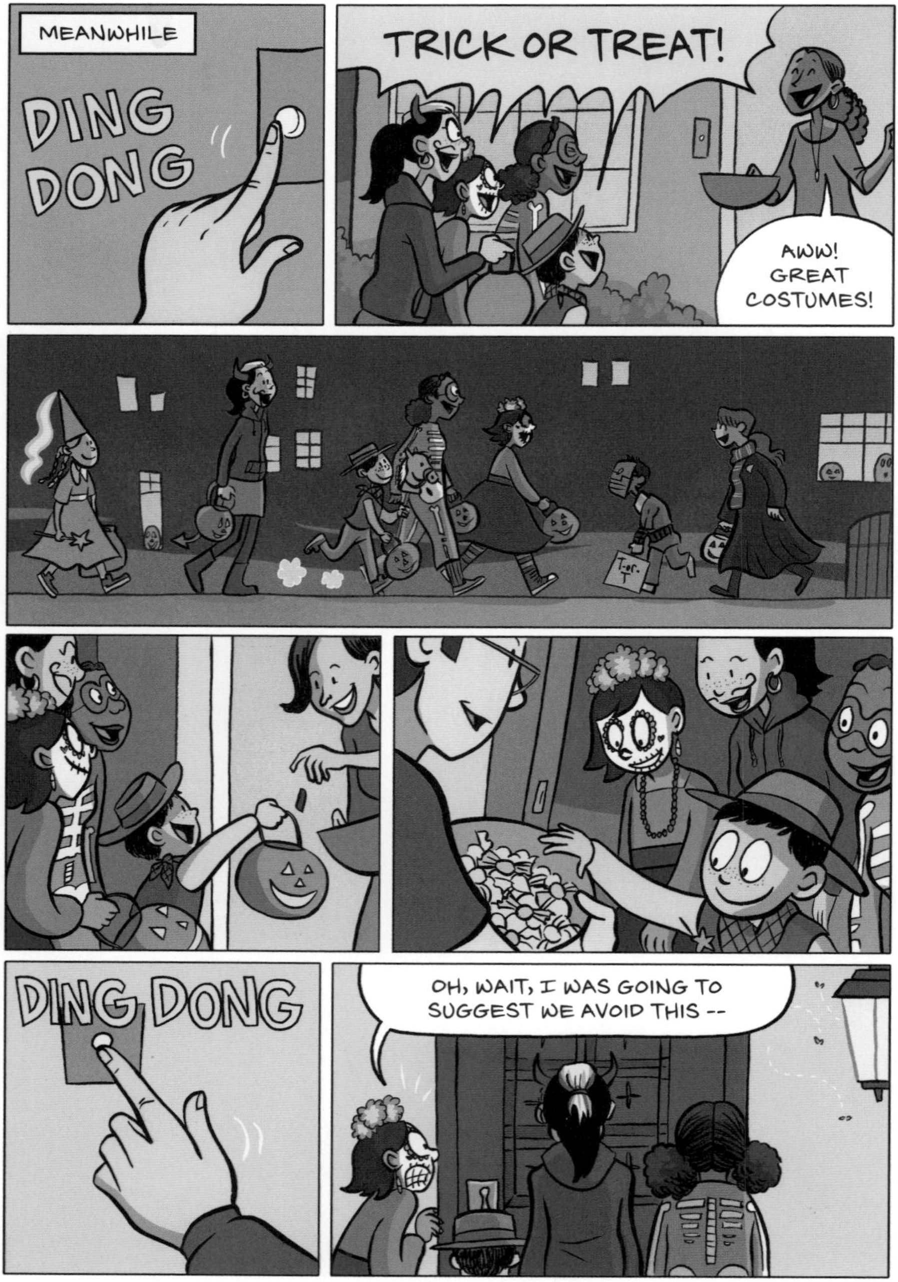
MEANWHILE
DING DONG
TRICK OR TREAT!
AWW! GREAT COSTUMES!
T-or-T
DING DONG
OH, WAIT, I WAS GOING TO SUGGEST WE AVOID THIS --

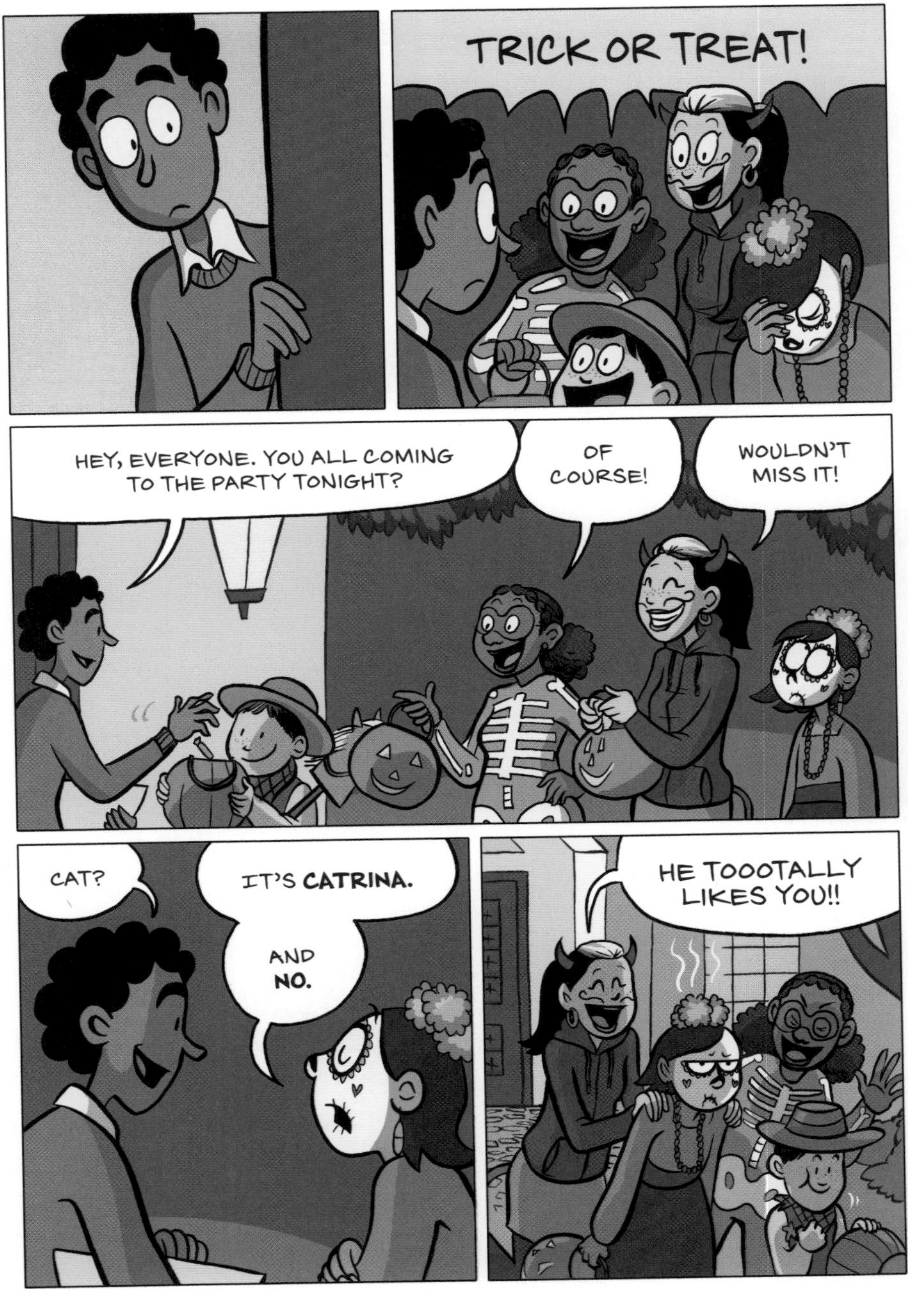
TRICK OR TREAT!
HEY, EVERYONE. YOU ALL COMING TO THE PARTY TONIGHT?
OF COURSE!
WOULDN'T MISS IT!
CAT?
IT'S **CATRINA.**
AND **NO.**
HE TOOOTALLY LIKES YOU!!

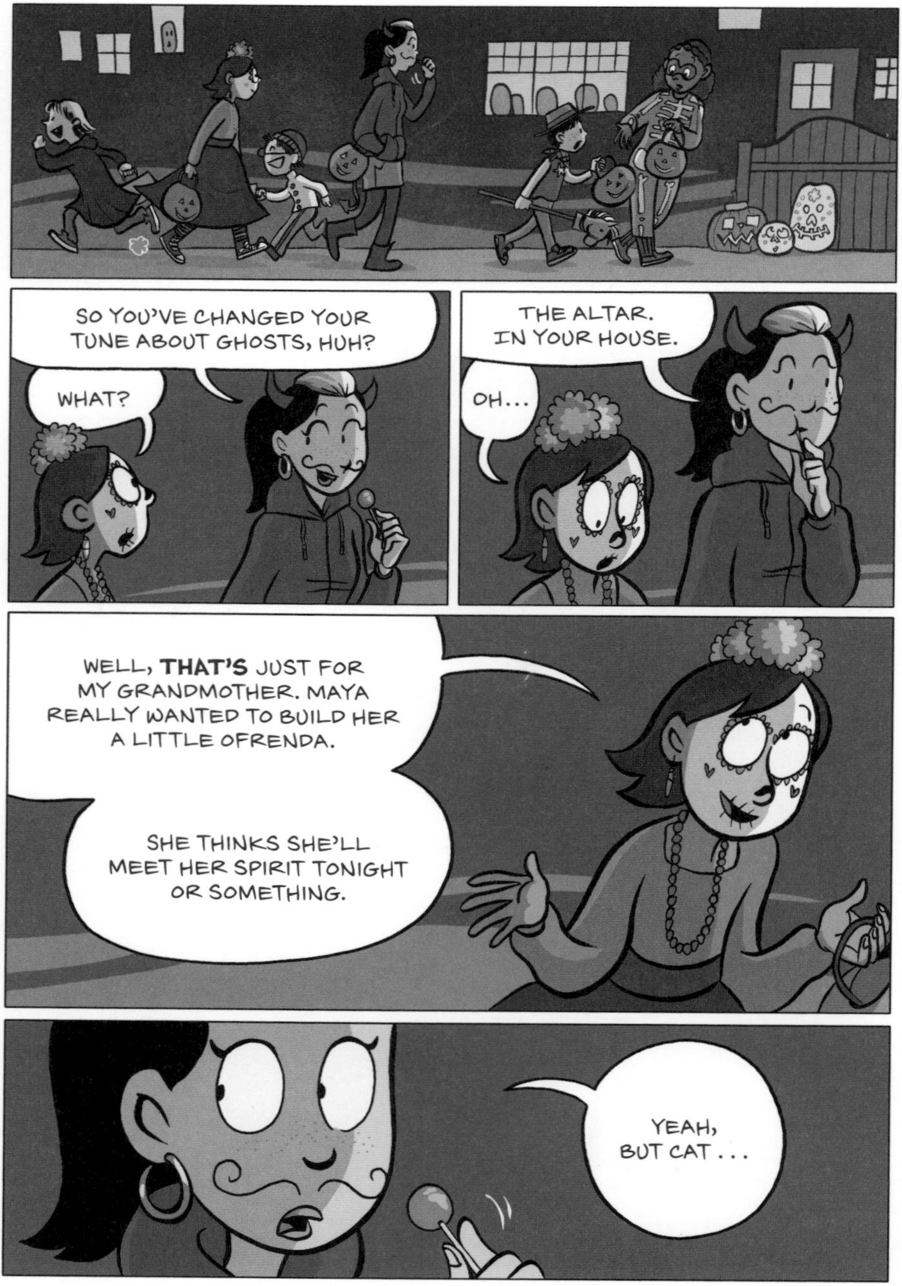
SO YOU'VE CHANGED YOUR TUNE ABOUT GHOSTS, HUH?
WHAT?
THE ALTAR. IN YOUR HOUSE.
OH...
WELL, **THAT'S** JUST FOR MY GRANDMOTHER. MAYA REALLY WANTED TO BUILD HER A LITTLE OFRENDA.
SHE THINKS SHE'LL MEET HER SPIRIT TONIGHT OR SOMETHING.
YEAH, BUT CAT . . .

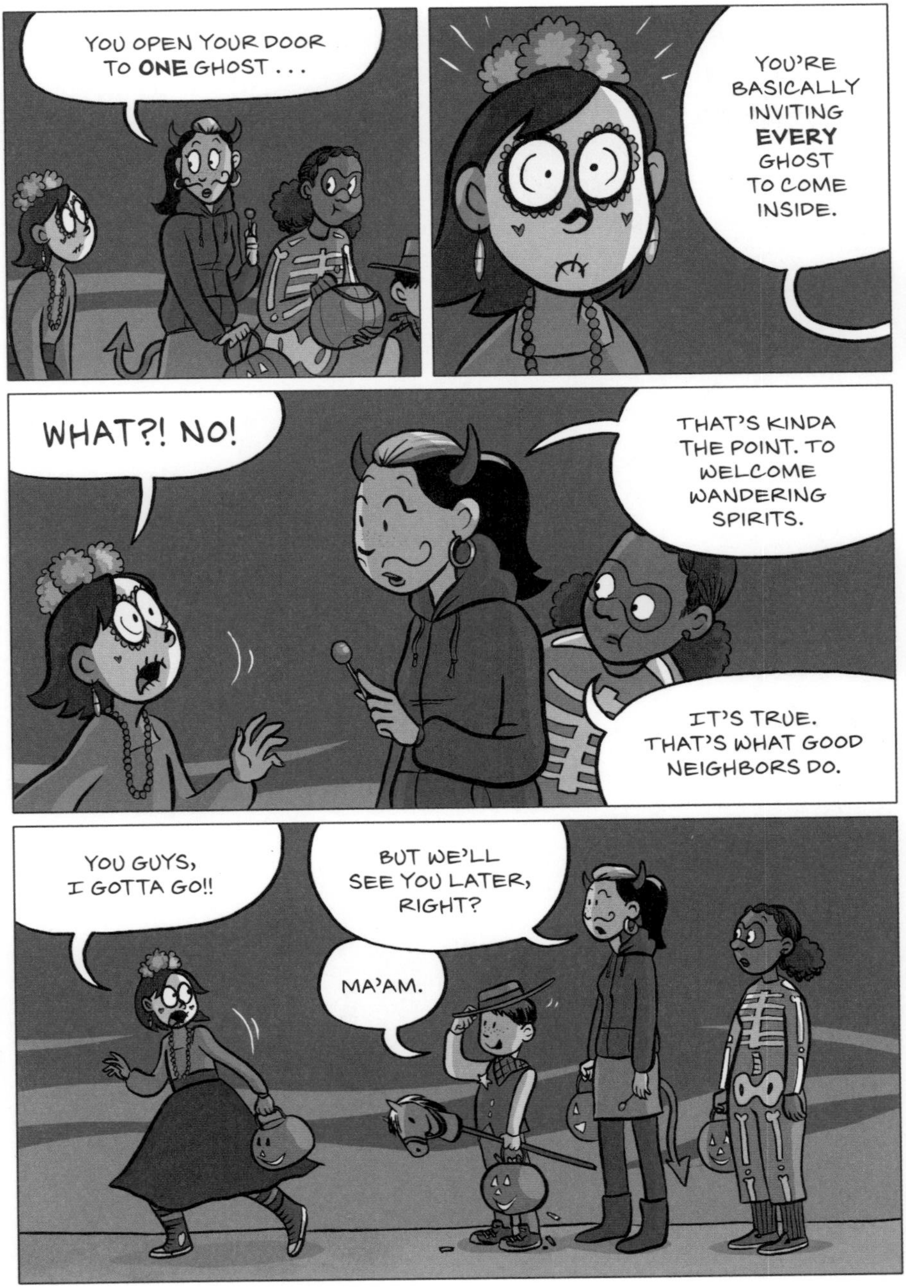
YOU OPEN YOUR DOOR TO **ONE** GHOST . . .
YOU'RE BASICALLY INVITING **EVERY** GHOST TO COME INSIDE.
WHAT?! NO!
THAT'S KINDA THE POINT. TO WELCOME WANDERING SPIRITS.
IT'S TRUE. THAT'S WHAT GOOD NEIGHBORS DO.
YOU GUYS, I GOTTA GO!!
BUT WE'LL SEE YOU LATER, RIGHT?
MA'AM.

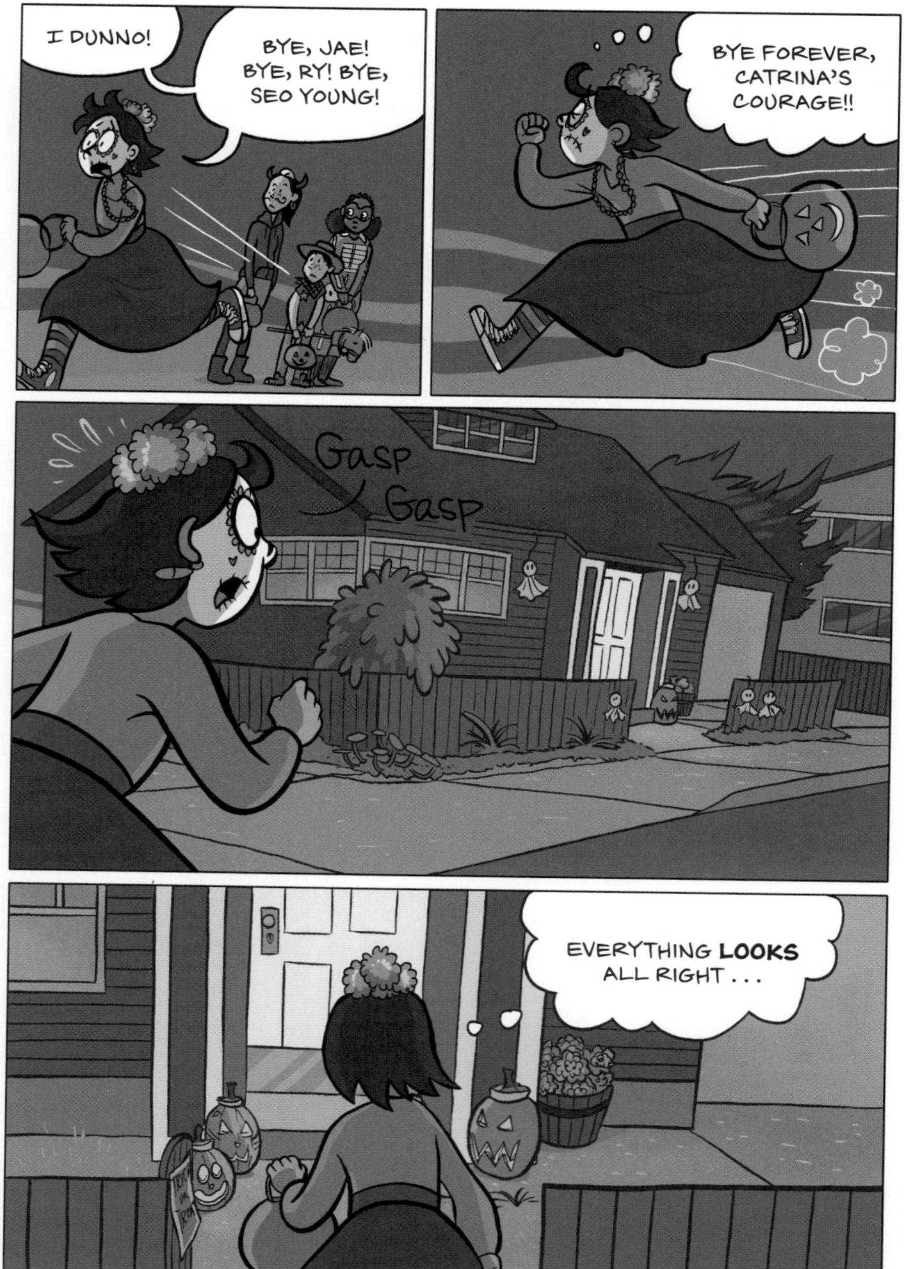
I DUNNO!
BYE, JAE! BYE, RY! BYE, SEO YOUNG!
BYE FOREVER, CATRINA'S COURAGE!!
Gasp
Gasp
EVERYTHING **LOOKS** ALL RIGHT . . .

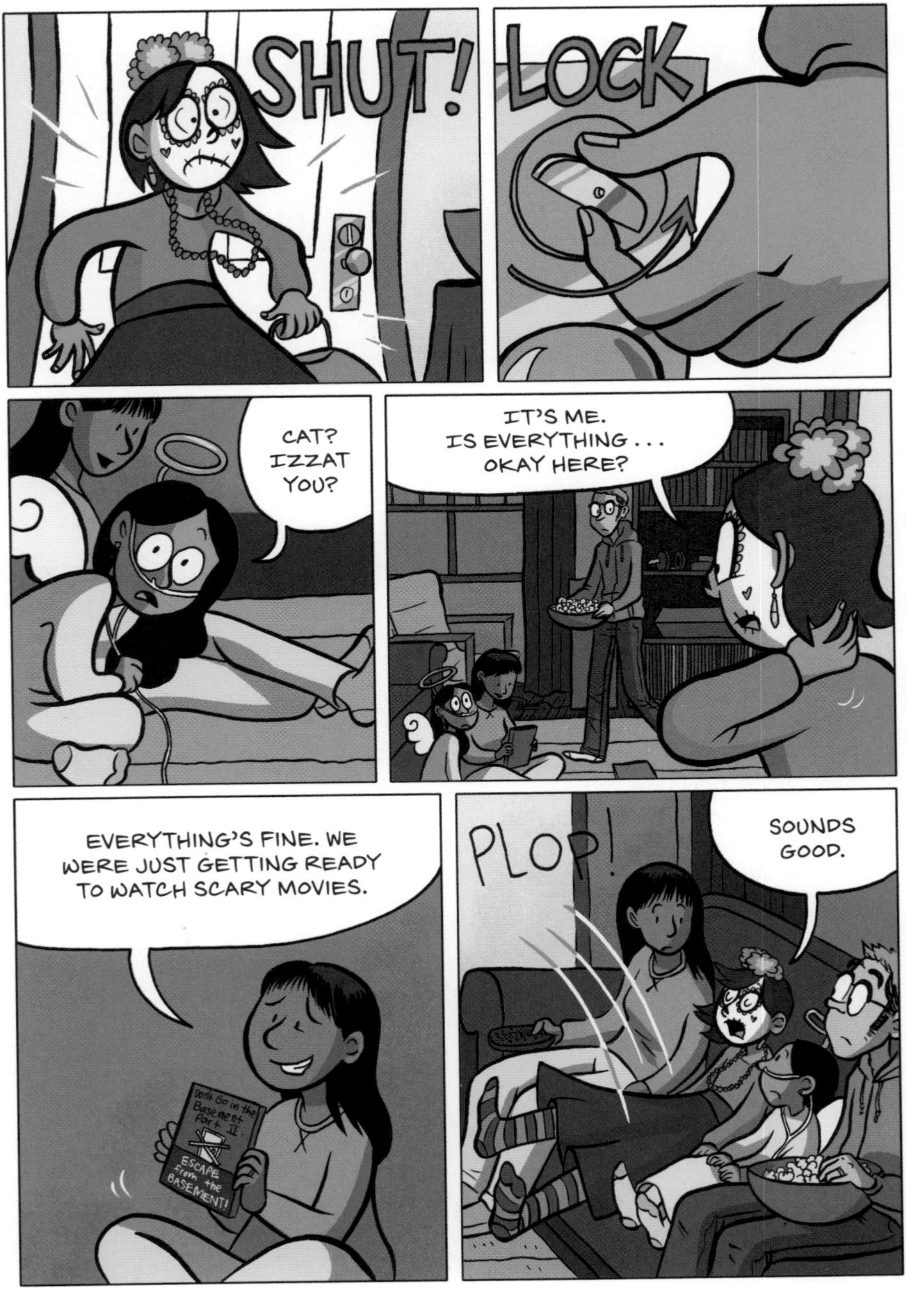
SHUT!
LOCK
CAT? IZZAT YOU?
IT'S ME. IS EVERYTHING . . . OKAY HERE?
EVERYTHING'S FINE. WE WERE JUST GETTING READY TO WATCH SCARY MOVIES.
Don't Go in the Basement Part II: ESCAPE from the BASEMENT!
PLOP!
SOUNDS GOOD.

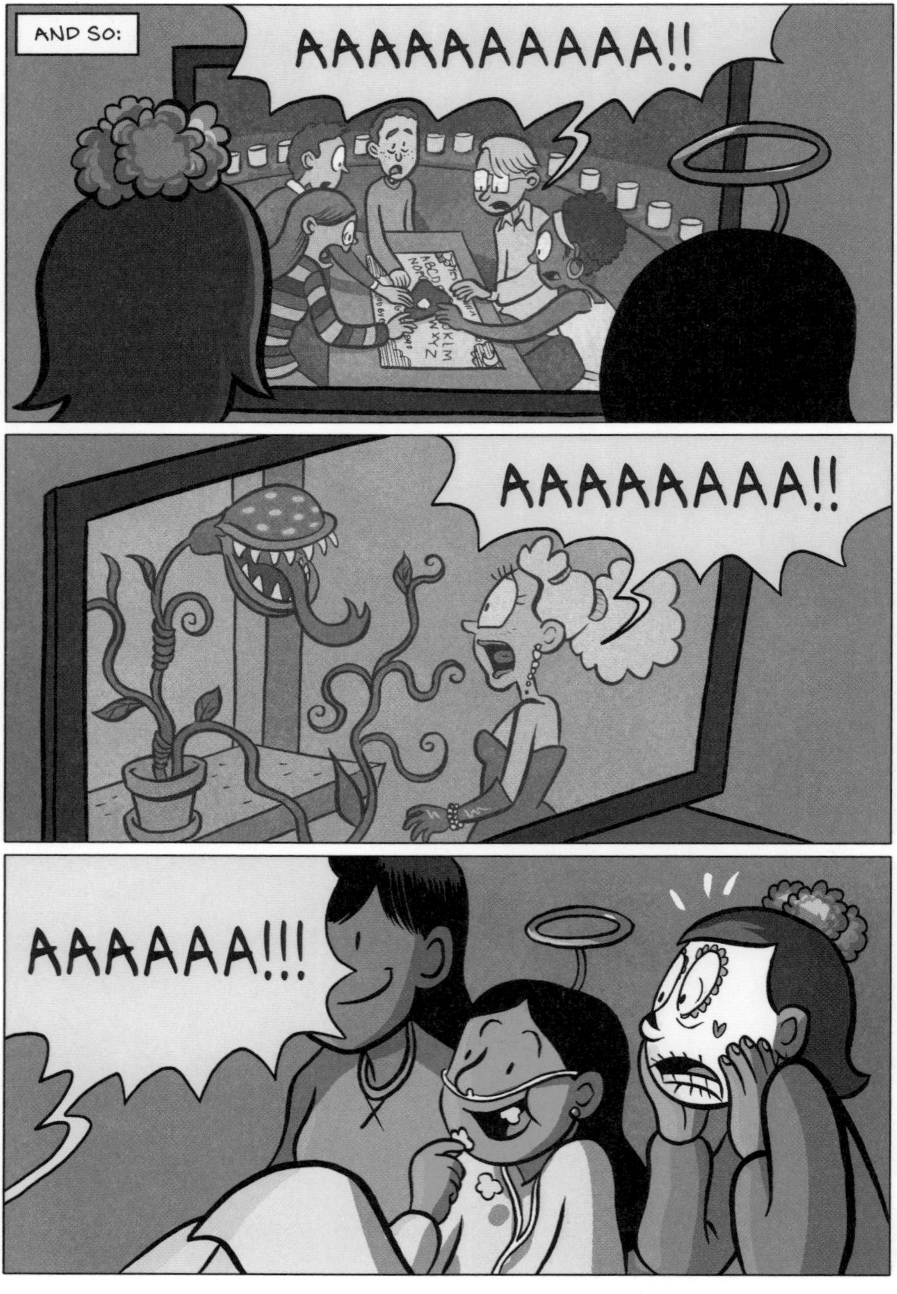
AND SO:
AAAAAAAAAA!!
AAAAAAAA!!
AAAAAA!!!

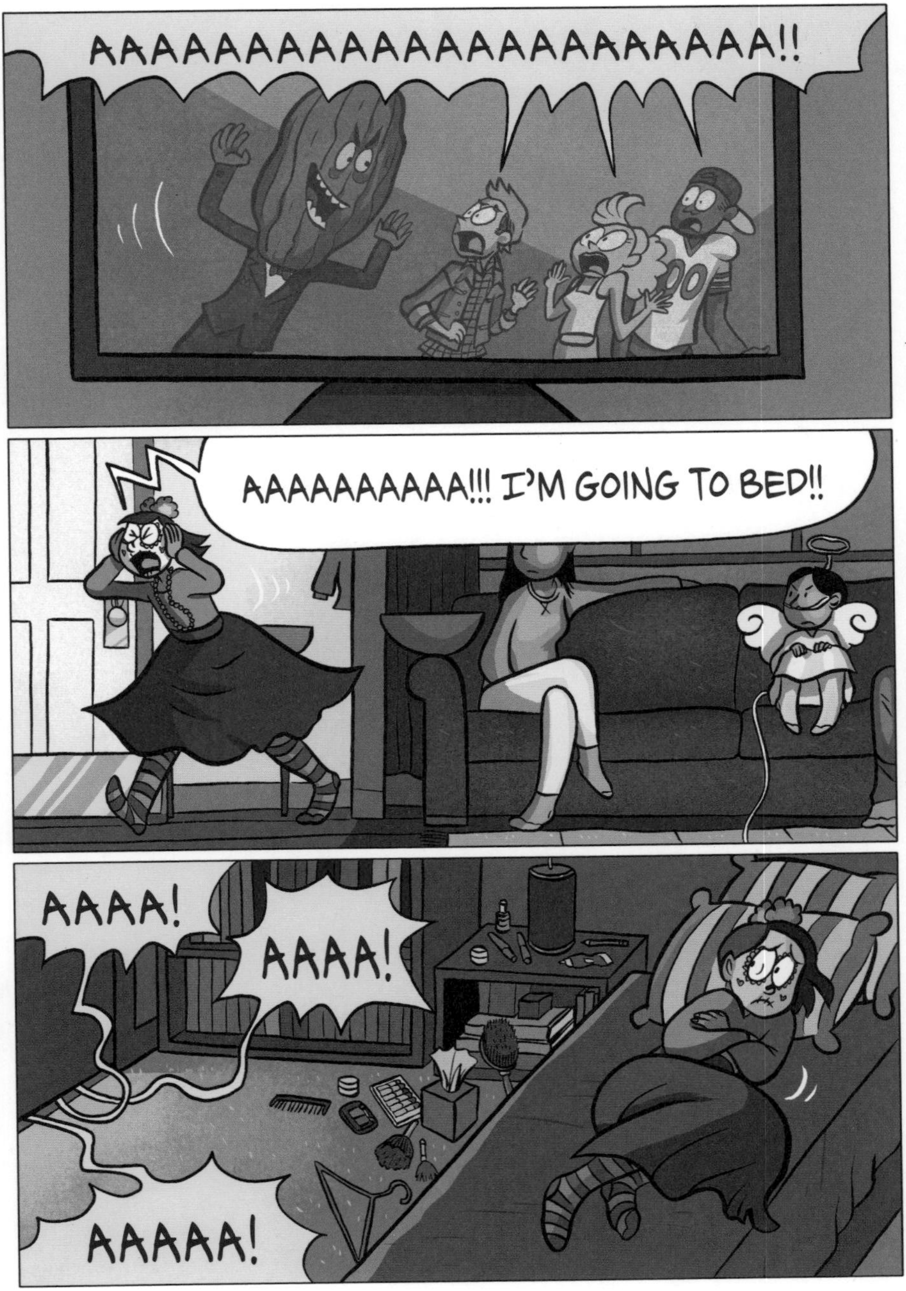
AAAAAAAAAAAAAAAAAAAAAA!!
AAAAAAAAAA!!! I'M GOING TO BED!!
AAAA!
AAAA!
AAAAA!

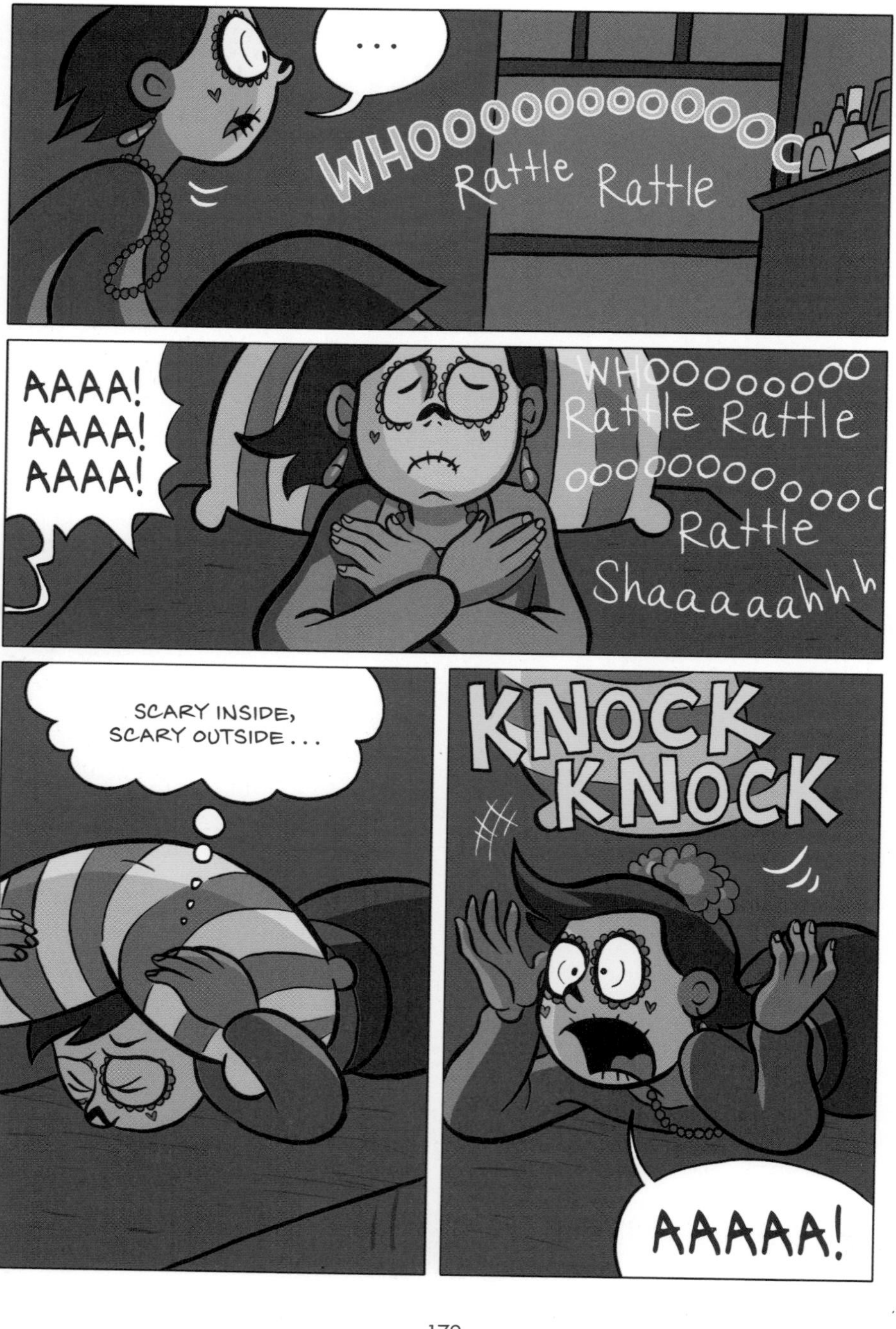
...
WHOOOOOOOOOOOOO
Rattle Rattle
AAAA! AAAA! AAAA!
WHOOOOOOOOOO
Rattle Rattle
OOOOOOOOOOOOOO
Rattle
Shaaaaaahhh
SCARY INSIDE, SCARY OUTSIDE...
KNOCK KNOCK
AAAAA!

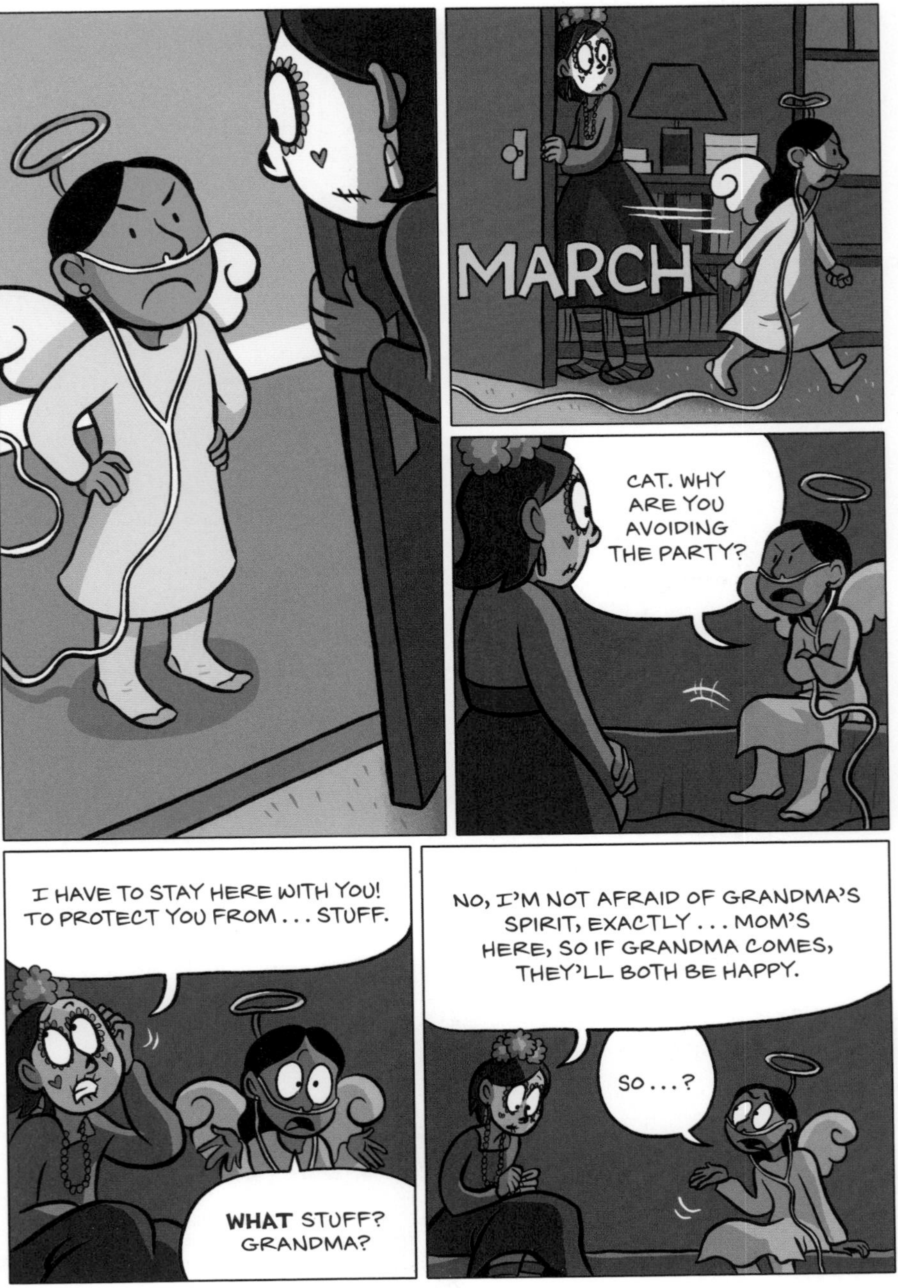
MARCH
CAT. WHY ARE YOU AVOIDING THE PARTY?
I HAVE TO STAY HERE WITH YOU! TO PROTECT YOU FROM . . . STUFF.
WHAT STUFF? GRANDMA?
NO, I'M NOT AFRAID OF GRANDMA'S SPIRIT, EXACTLY . . . MOM'S HERE, SO IF GRANDMA COMES, THEY'LL BOTH BE HAPPY.
SO . . . ?

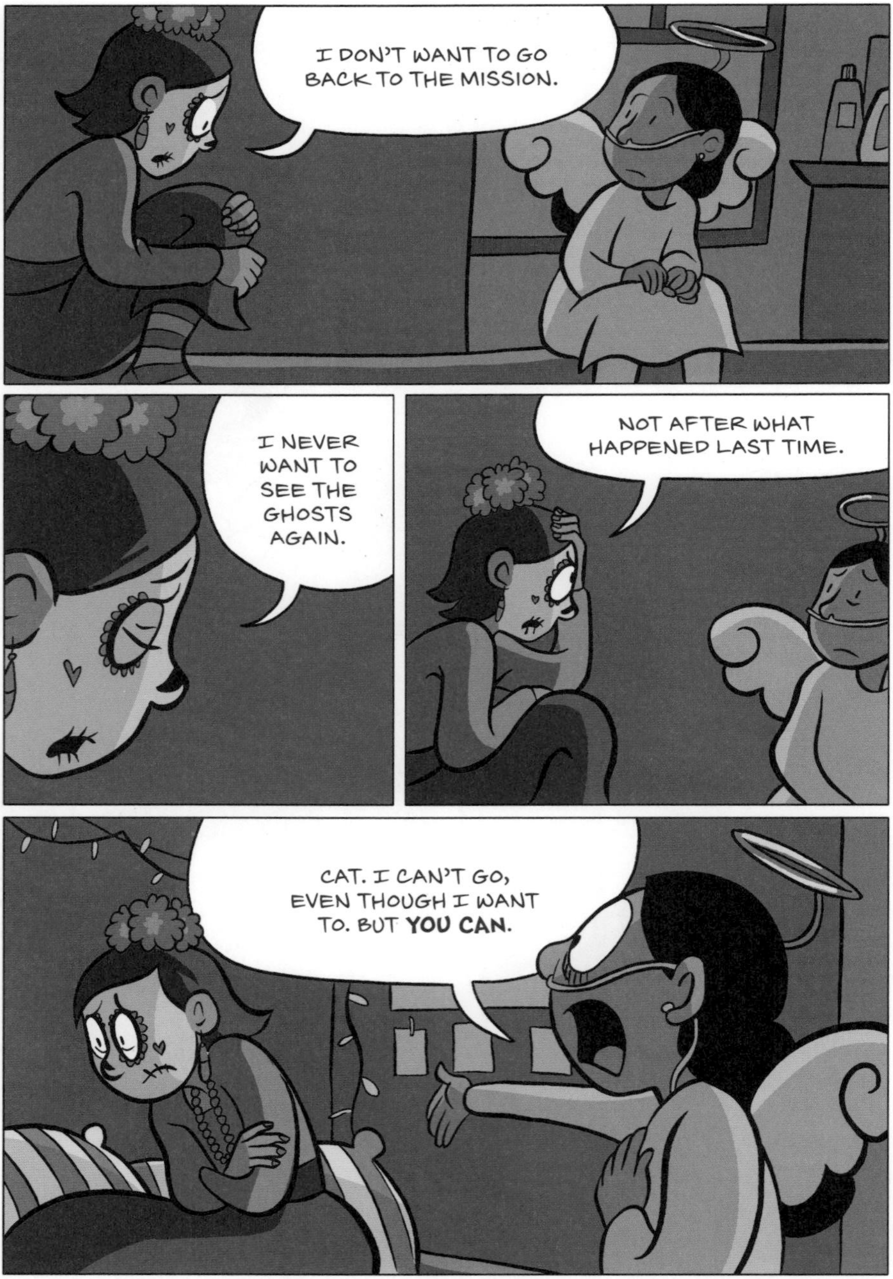
I DON'T WANT TO GO BACK TO THE MISSION.
I NEVER WANT TO SEE THE GHOSTS AGAIN.
NOT AFTER WHAT HAPPENED LAST TIME.
CAT. I CAN'T GO, EVEN THOUGH I WANT TO. BUT **YOU CAN**.

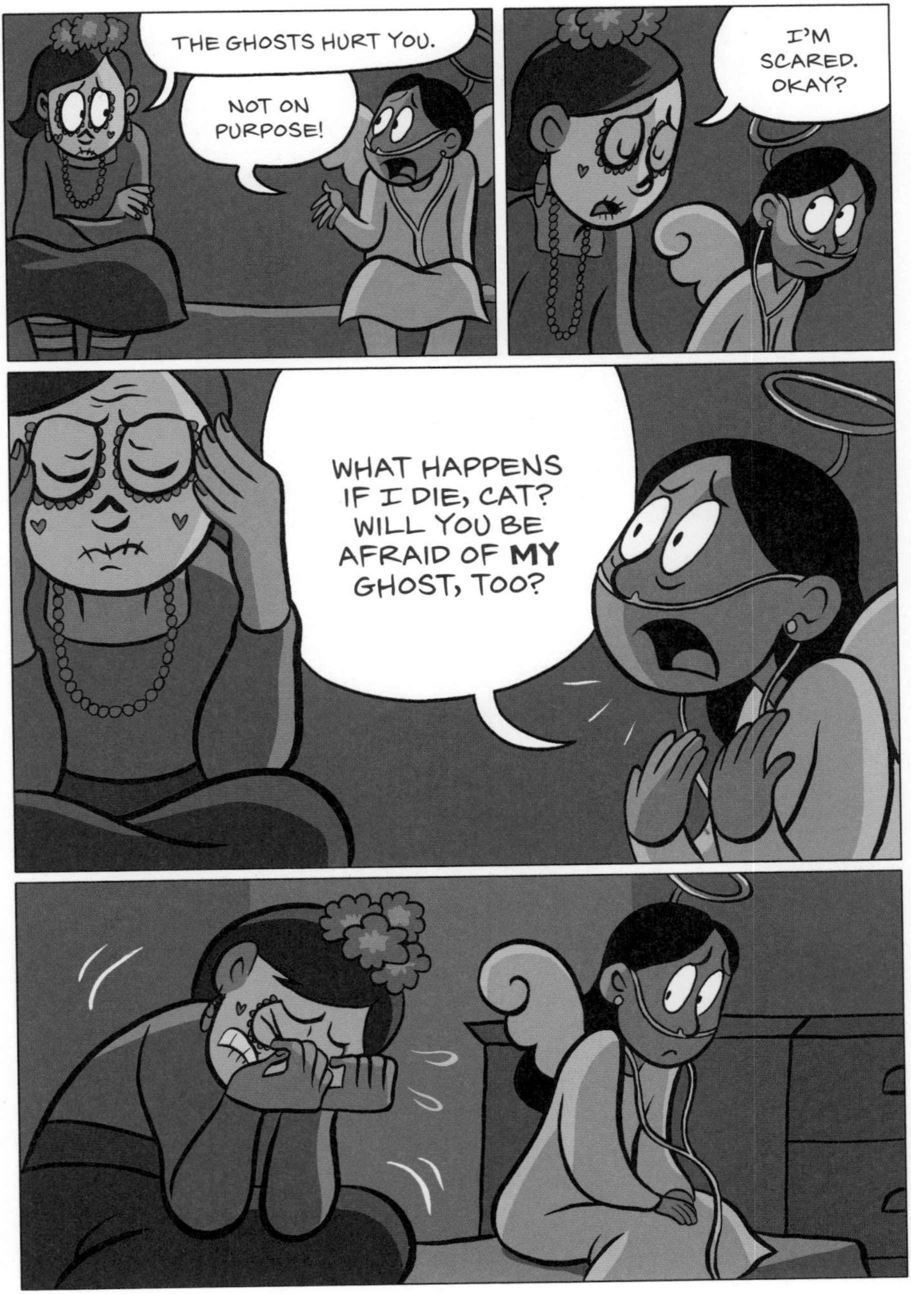
THE GHOSTS HURT YOU.
NOT ON PURPOSE!
I'M SCARED. OKAY?
WHAT HAPPENS IF I DIE, CAT? WILL YOU BE AFRAID OF **MY** GHOST, TOO?

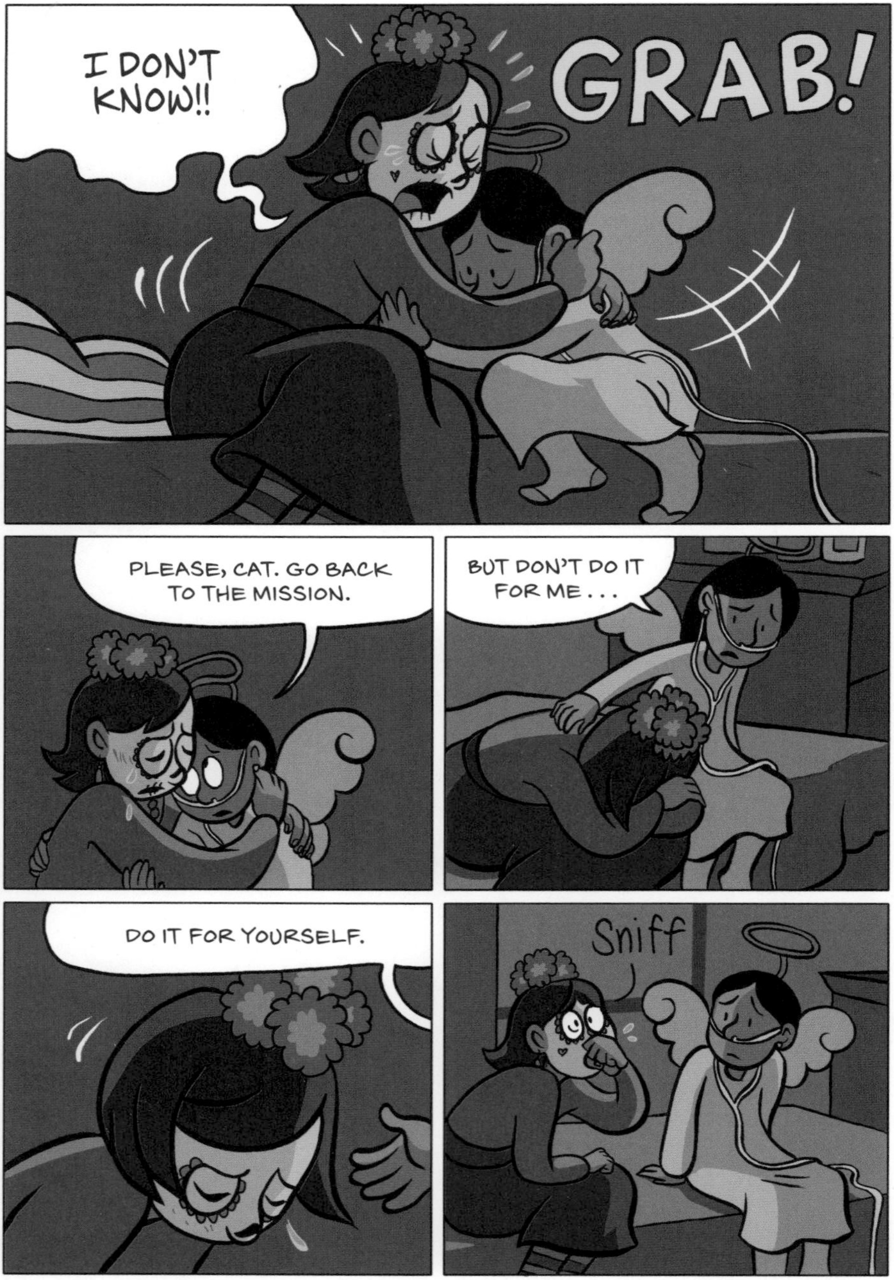
I DON'T KNOW!!
GRAB!
PLEASE, CAT. GO BACK TO THE MISSION.
BUT DON'T DO IT FOR ME . . .
DO IT FOR YOURSELF.
Sniff

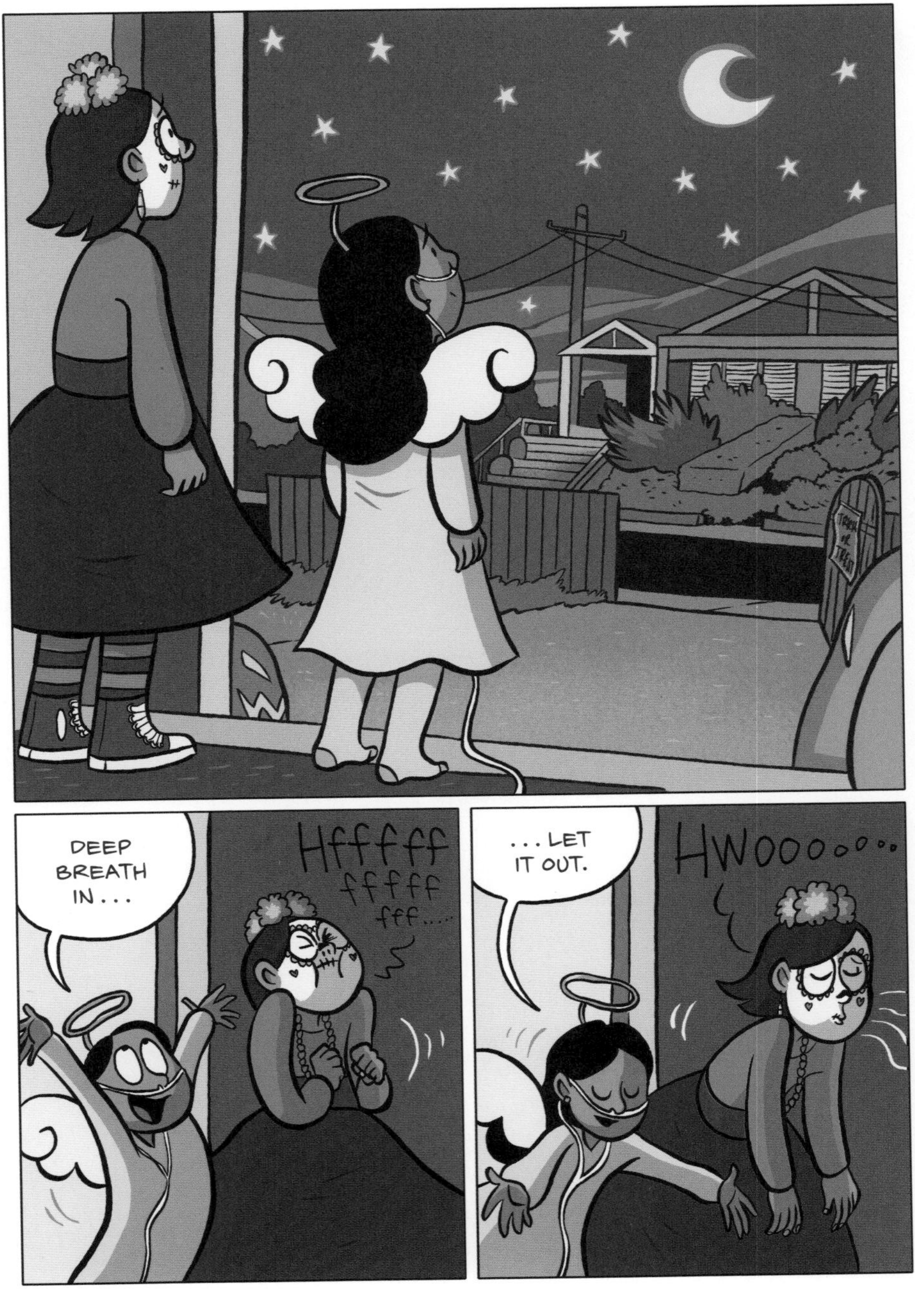
TRICK OR TREAT
DEEP BREATH IN . . .
Hffffff fffff fff.....
. . . LET IT OUT.
HWooooooo..

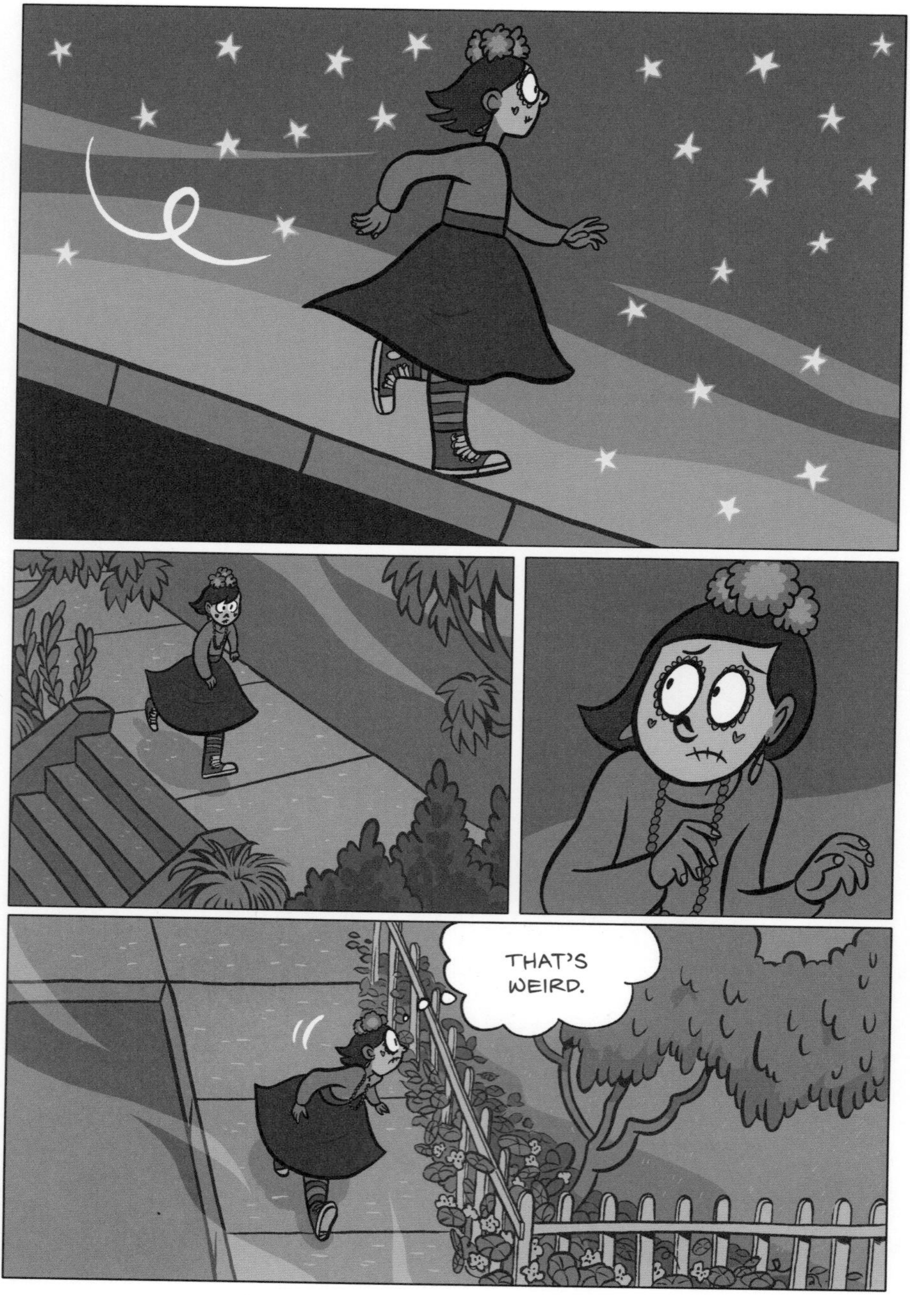
THAT'S WEIRD.

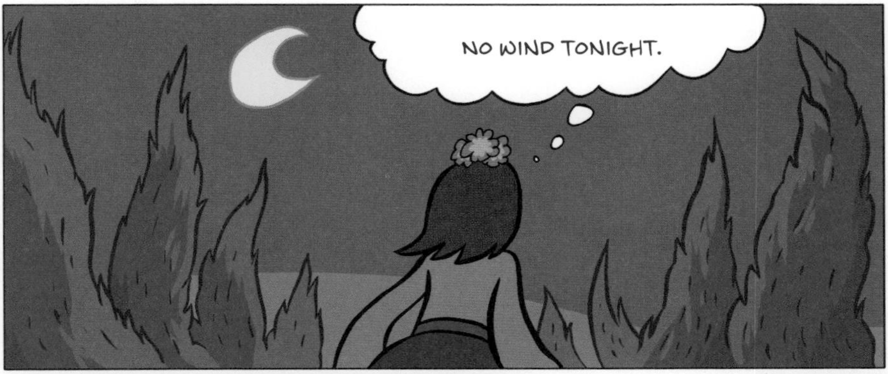
NO WIND TONIGHT.

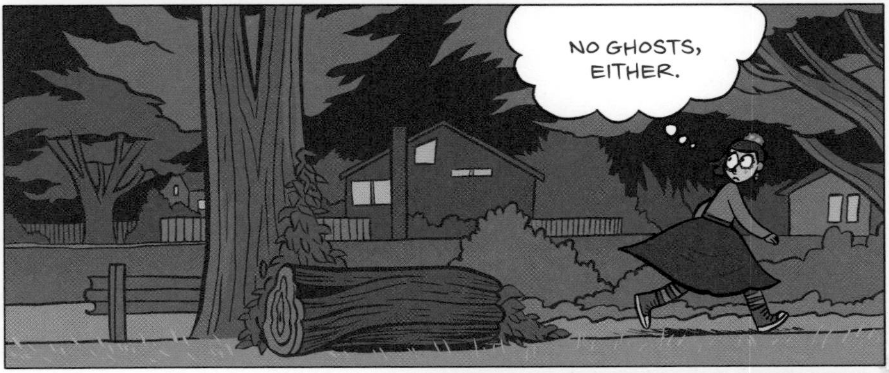
NO GHOSTS, EITHER.

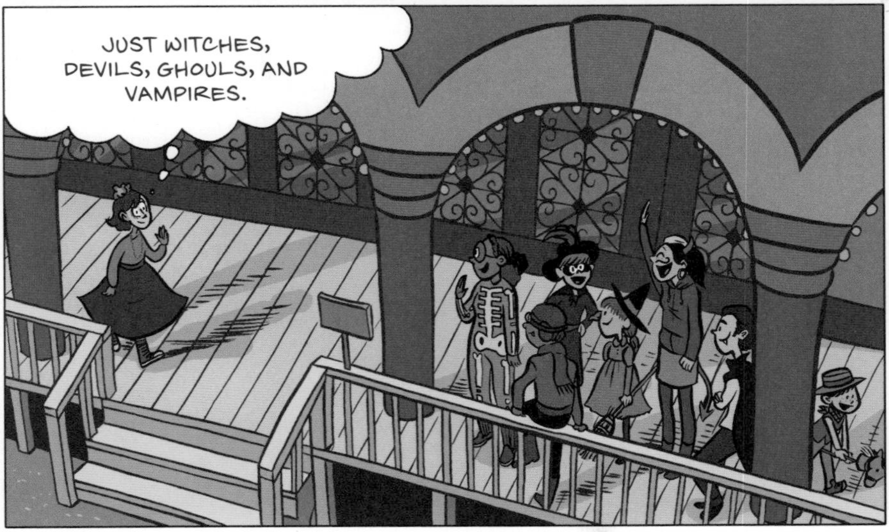
JUST WITCHES, DEVILS, GHOULS, AND VAMPIRES.

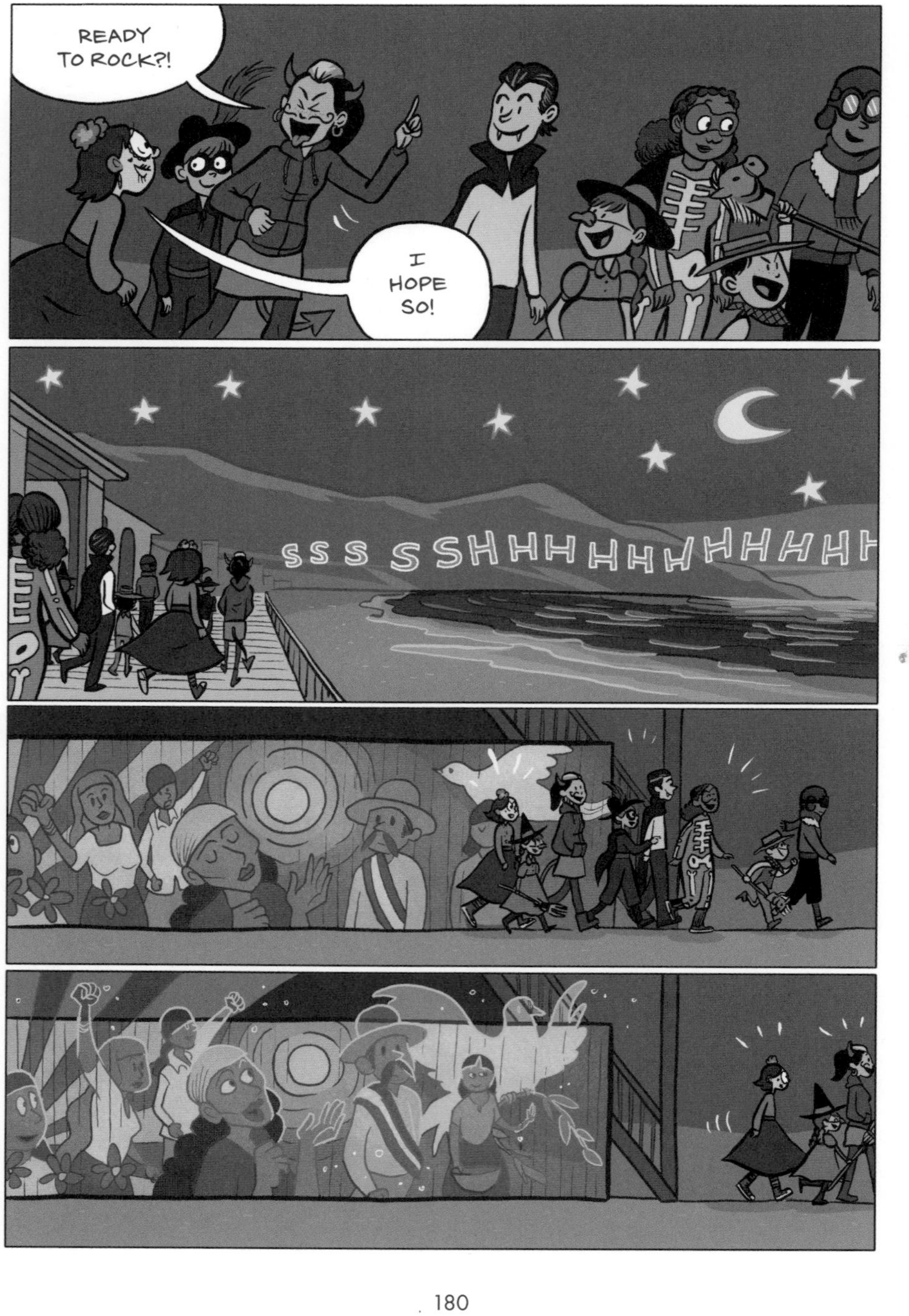
READY TO ROCK?!
I HOPE SO!
SSS SSHHHHHHHHHHHHHH

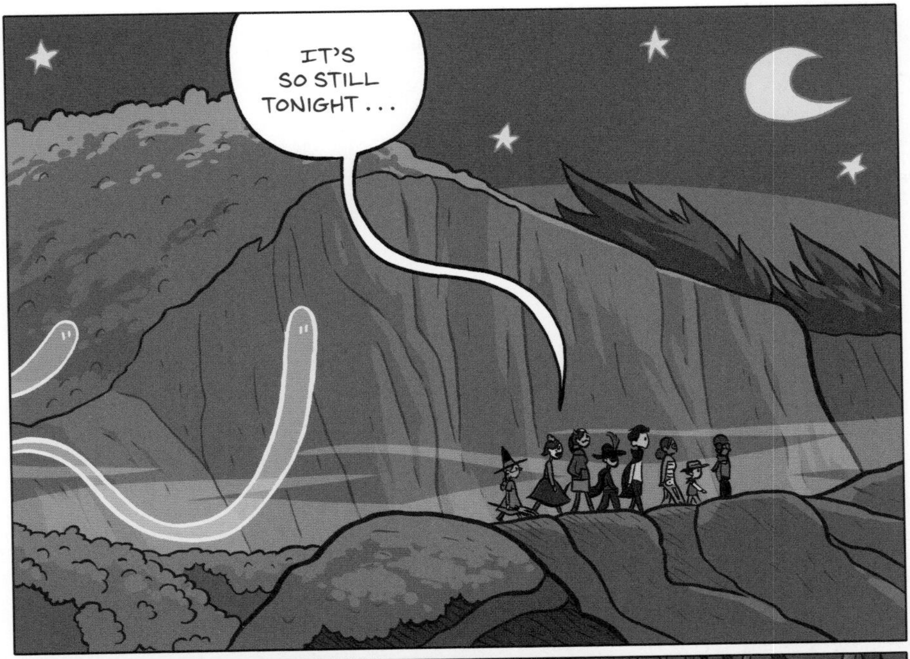
IT'S SO STILL TONIGHT . . .

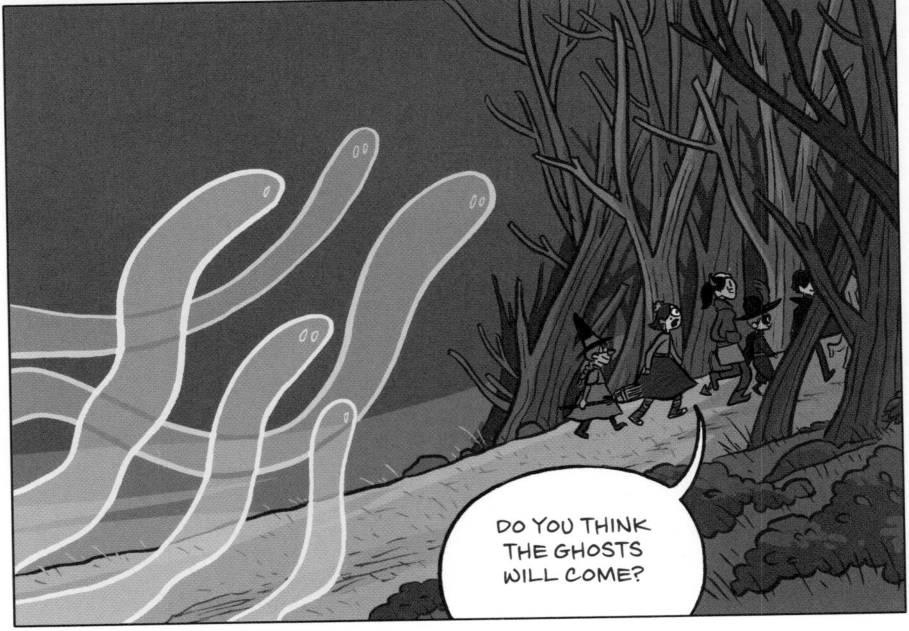
DO YOU THINK THE GHOSTS WILL COME?

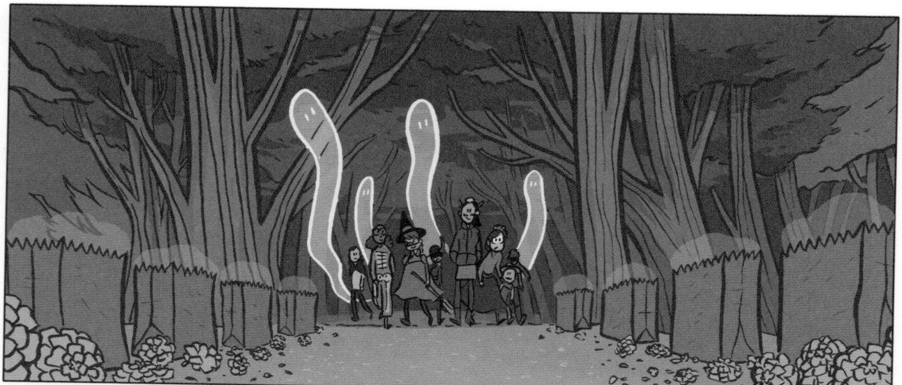

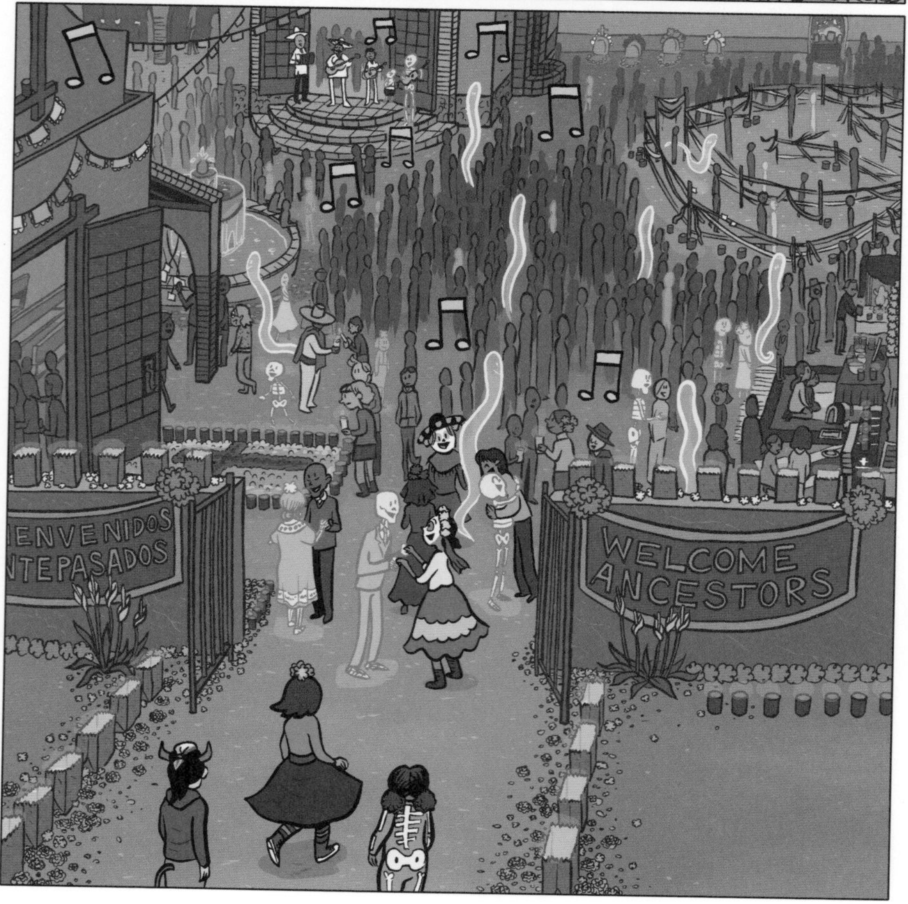
IENVENIDOS
NTEPASADOS
WELCOME
ANCESTORS

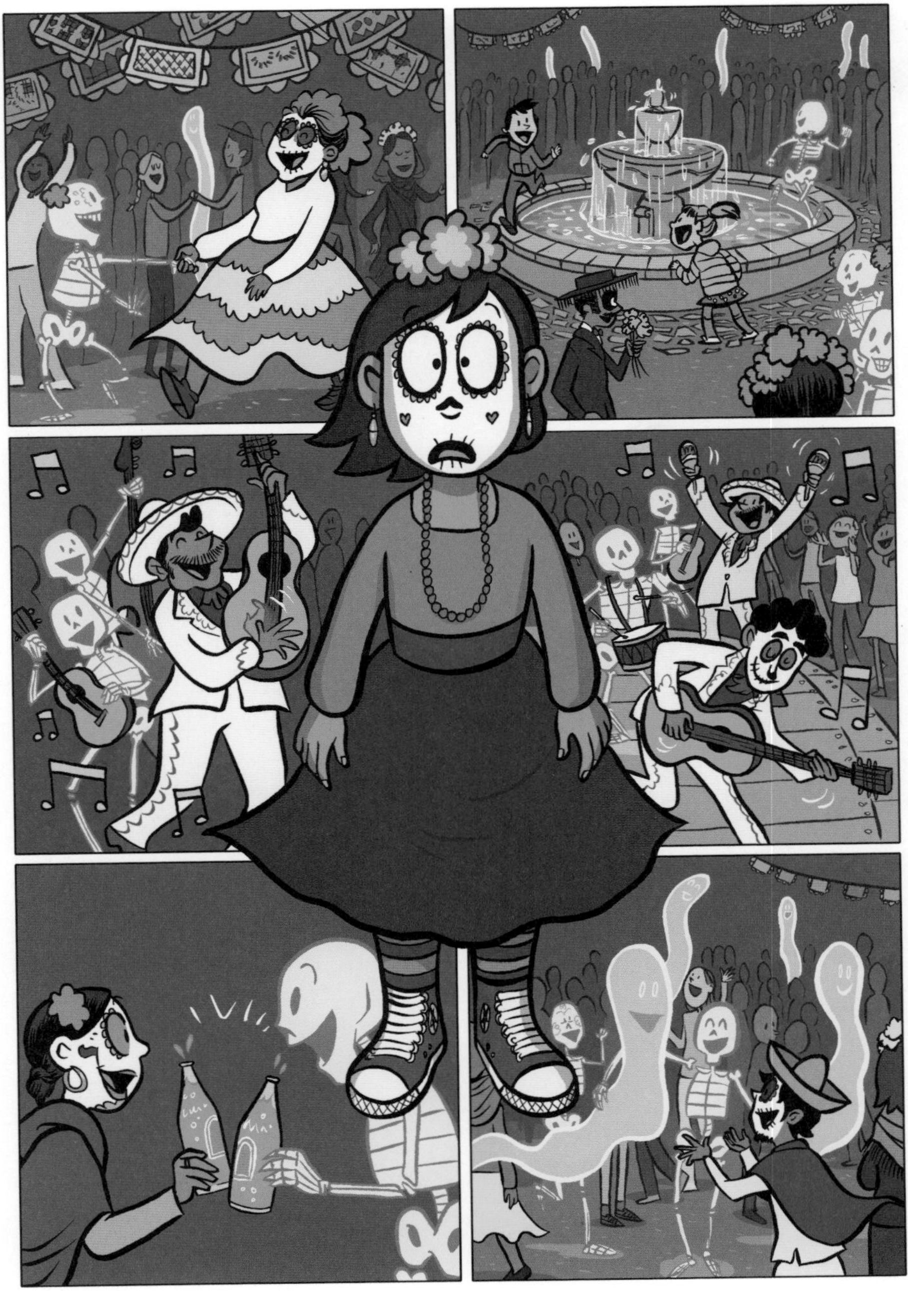

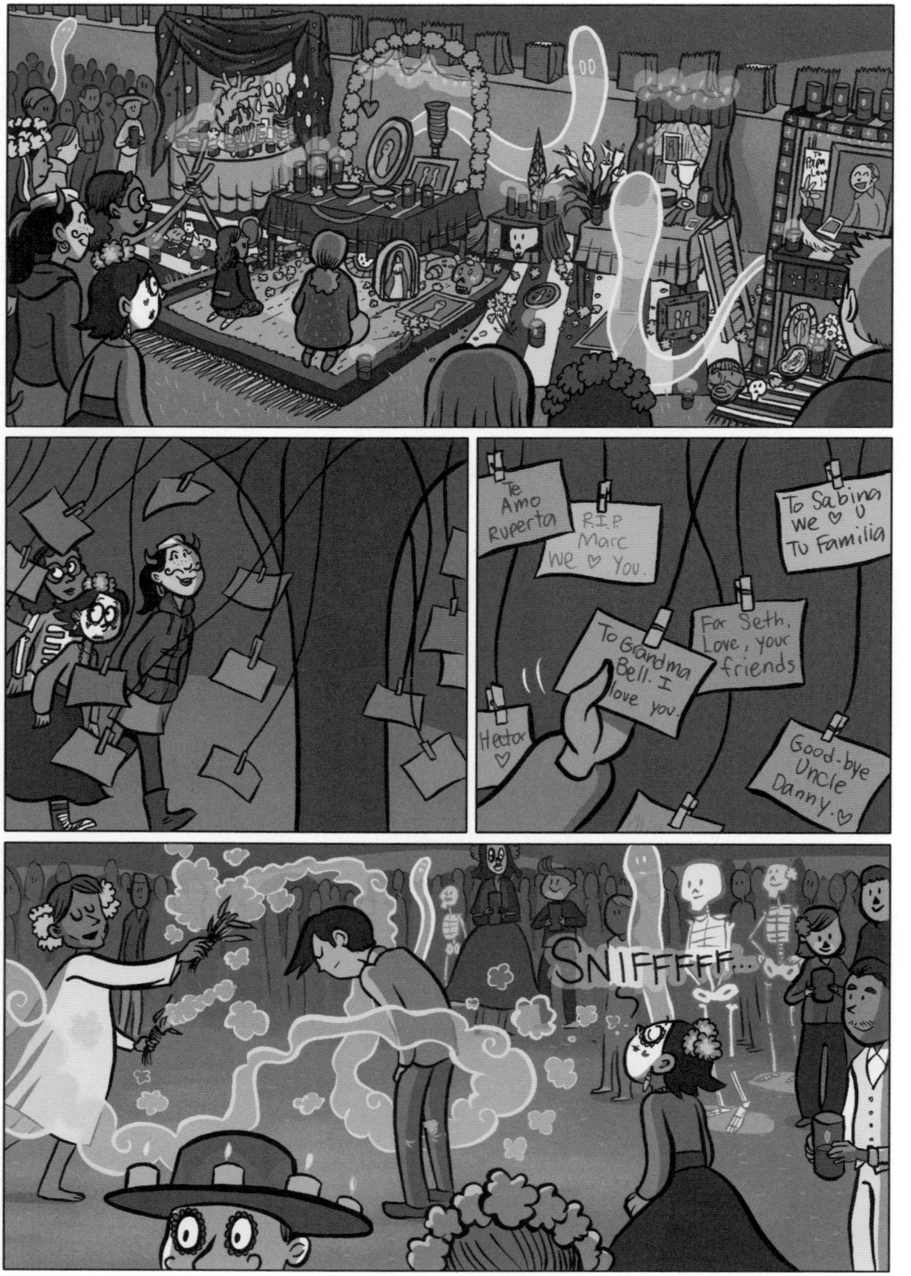
LOVE
Te Amo Ruperta
R.I.P. Marc We ♡ You.
To Sabina We ♡ U To Familia
To Grandma Bell. I love you.
For Seth, Love, your friends
Hector ♡
Good-bye Uncle Danny. ♡
SNIFFFFF...

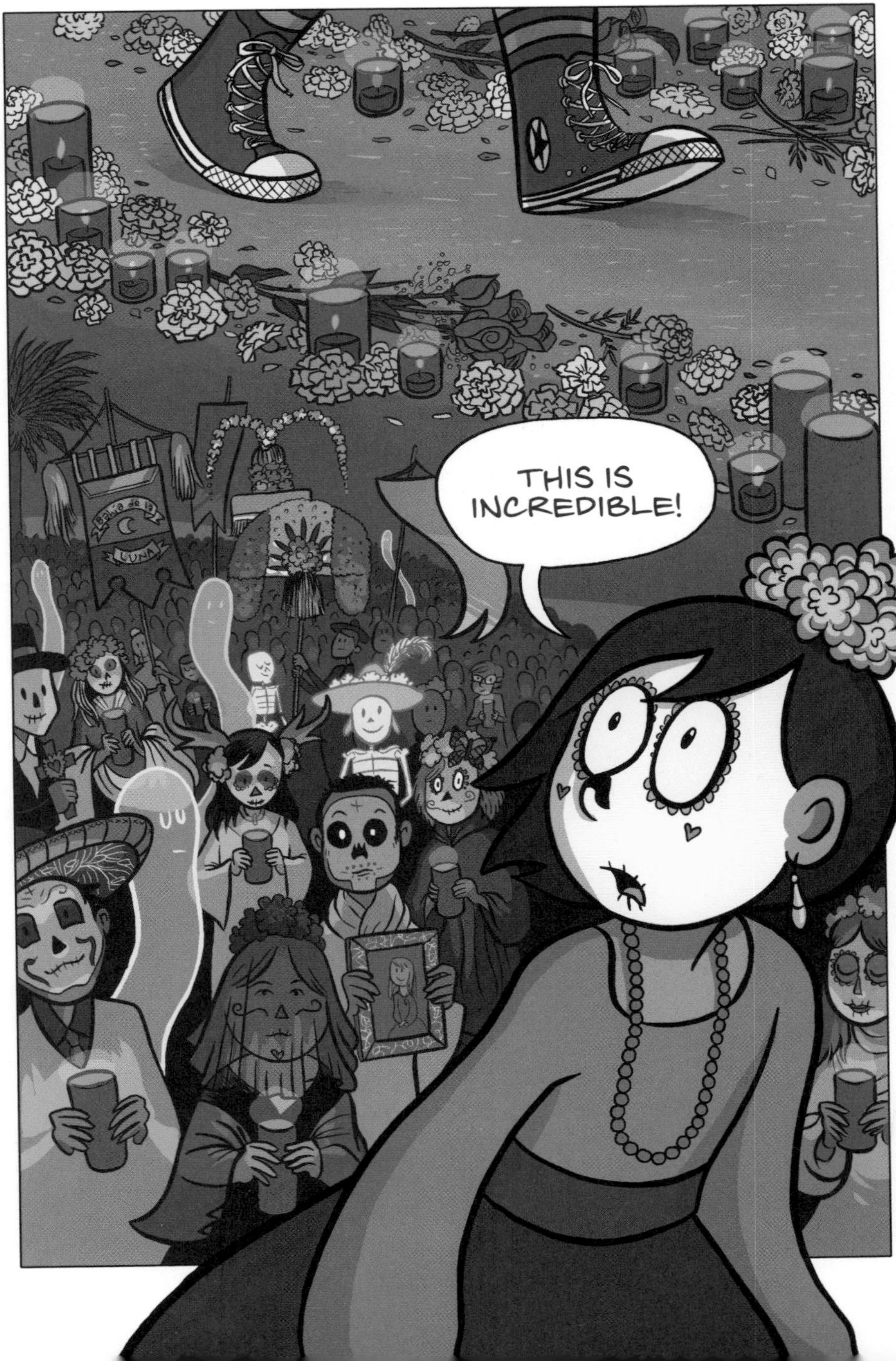
THIS IS INCREDIBLE!

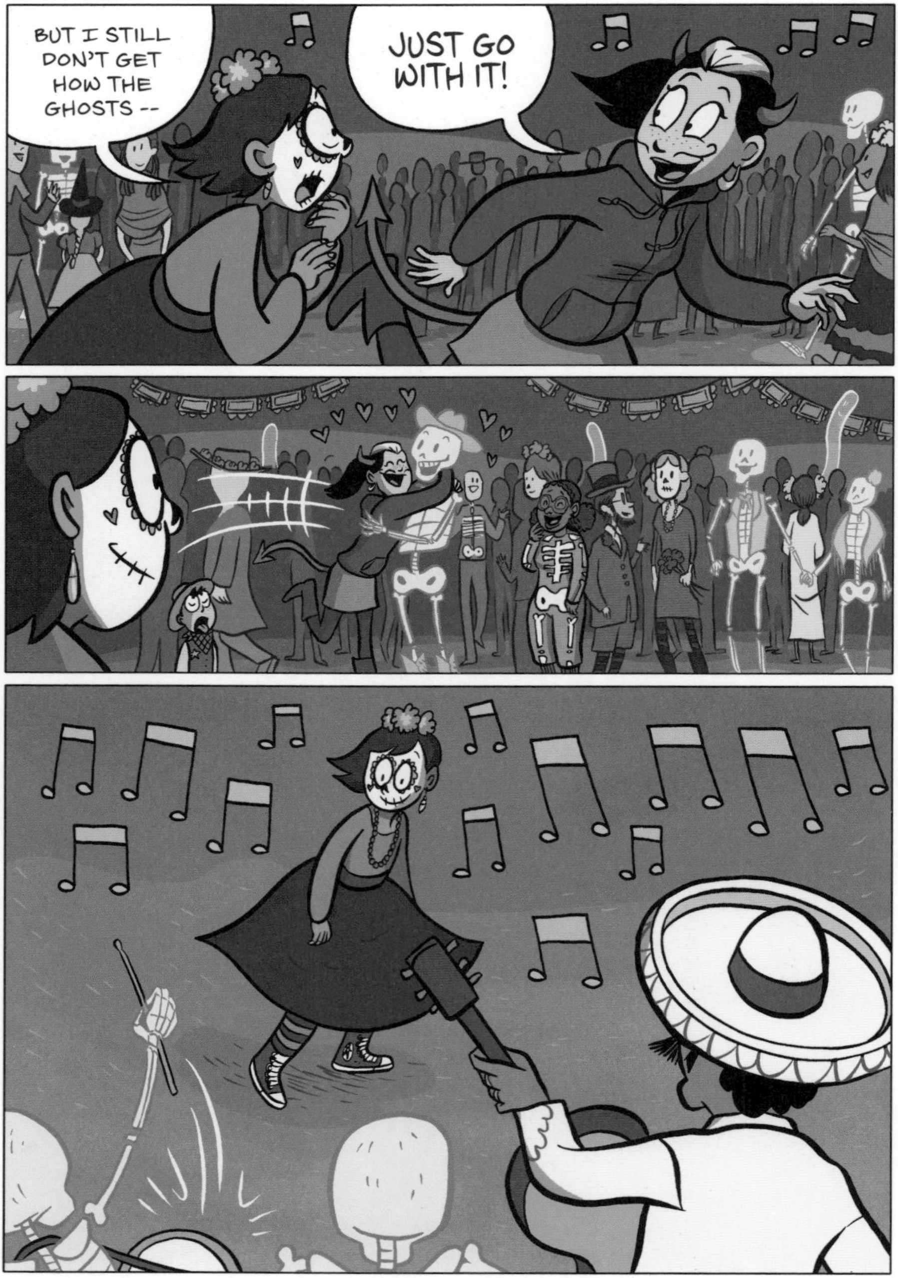
BUT I STILL DON'T GET HOW THE GHOSTS --
JUST GO WITH IT!

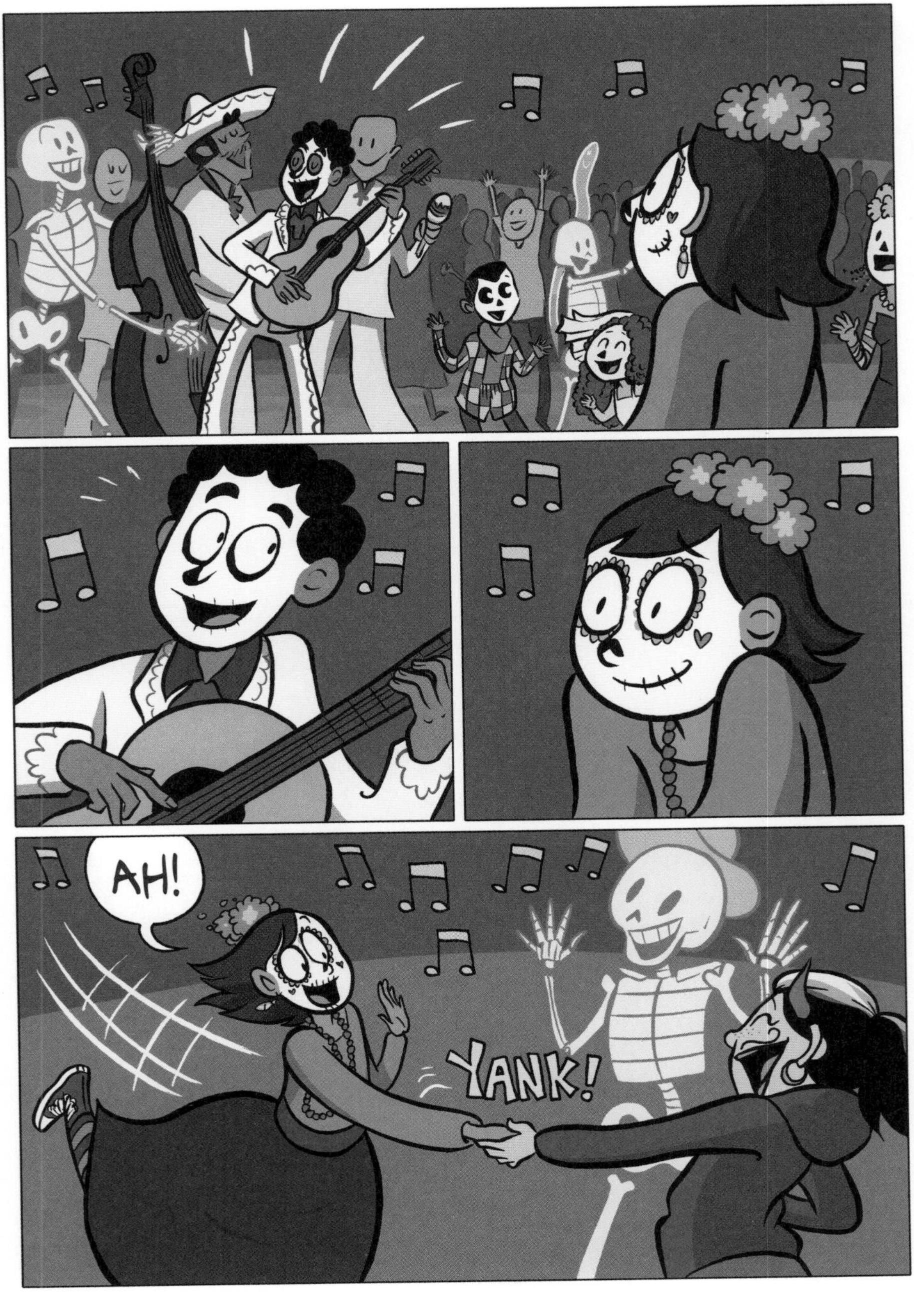
AH!
YANK!

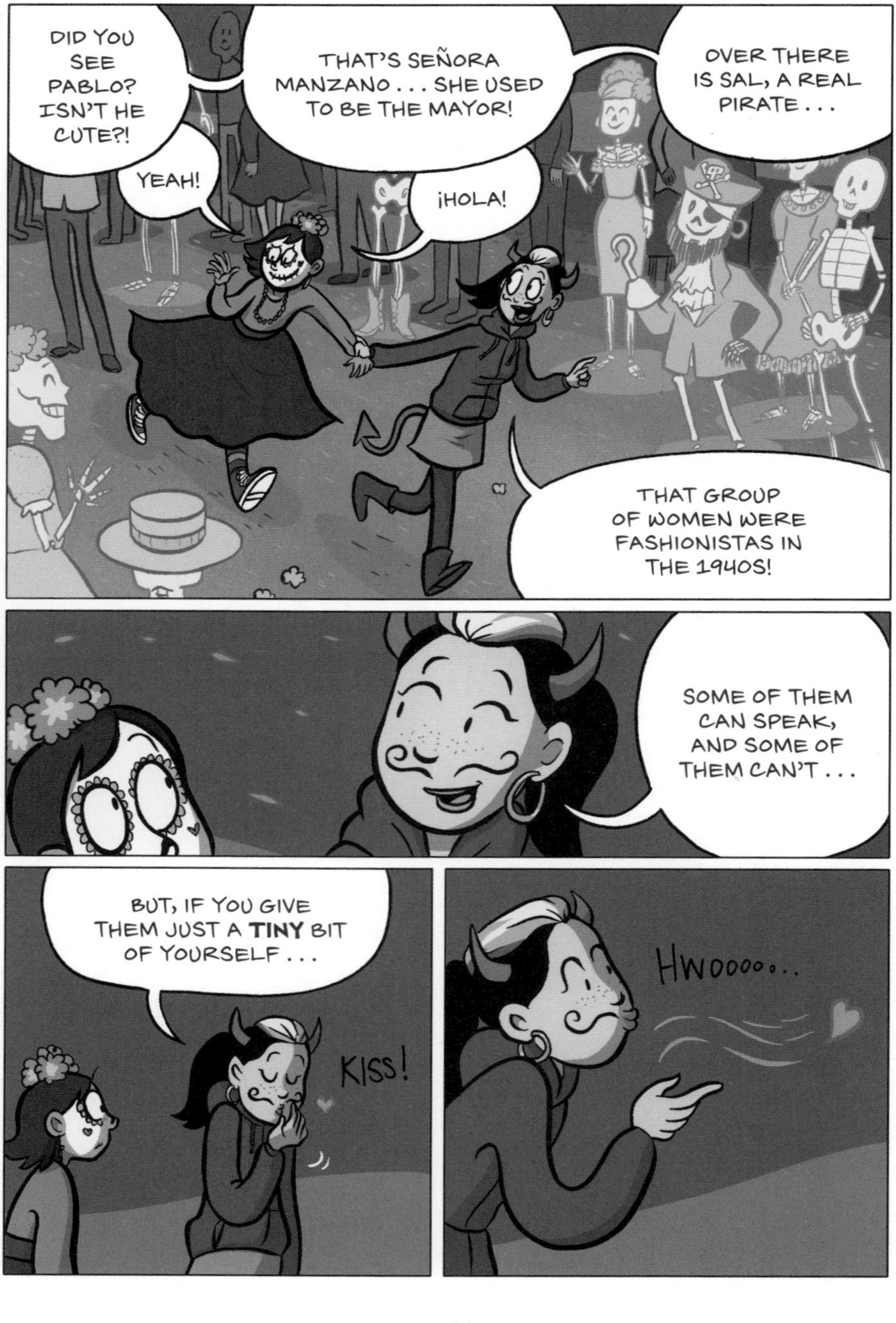
DID YOU SEE PABLO? ISN'T HE CUTE?!
YEAH!
THAT'S SEÑORA MANZANO . . . SHE USED TO BE THE MAYOR!
¡HOLA!
OVER THERE IS SAL, A REAL PIRATE . . .
THAT GROUP OF WOMEN WERE FASHIONISTAS IN THE 1940S!
SOME OF THEM CAN SPEAK, AND SOME OF THEM CAN'T . . .
BUT, IF YOU GIVE THEM JUST A **TINY** BIT OF YOURSELF . . .
KISS!
HWOOOOO . . .

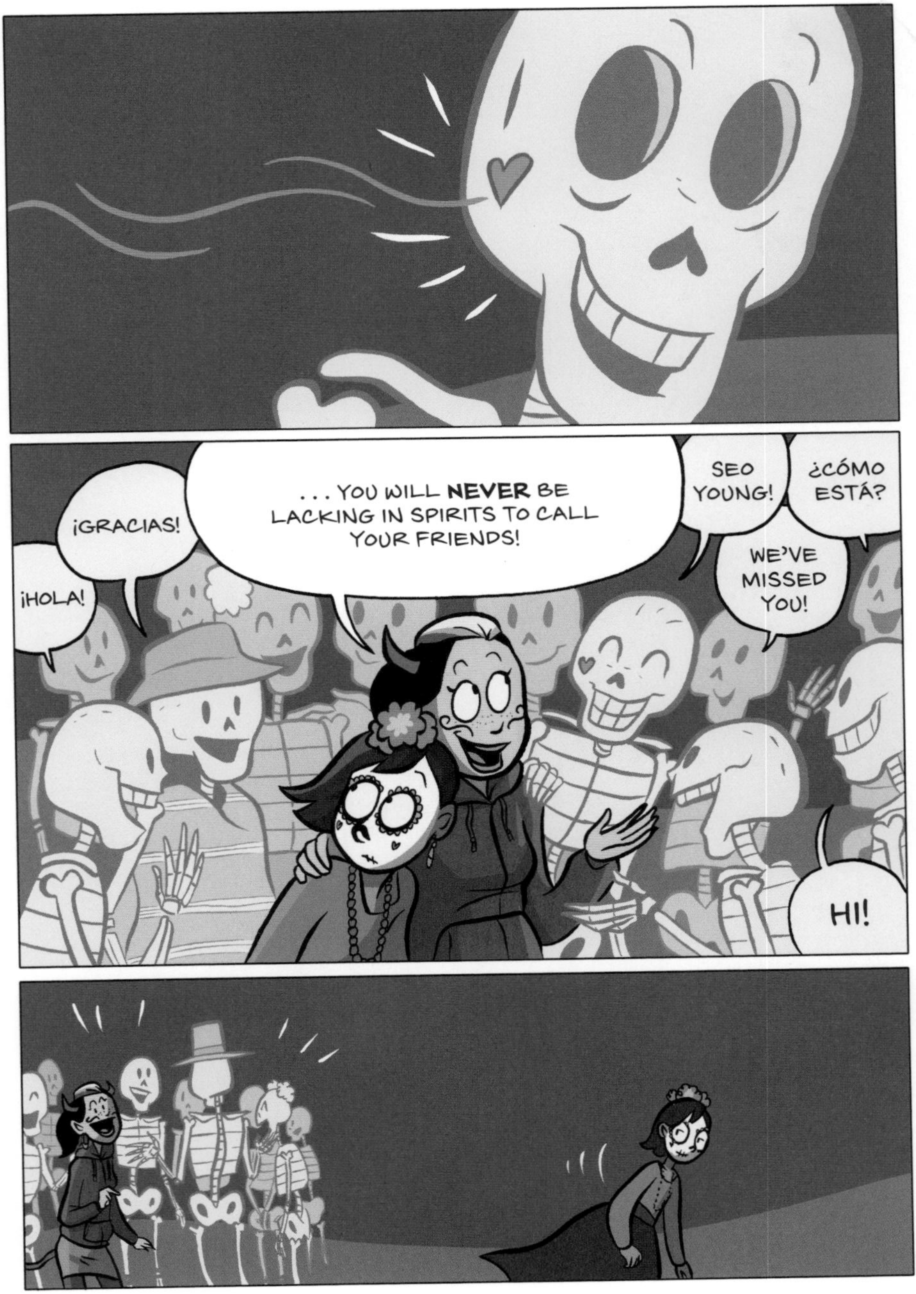

¡HOLA!
¡GRACIAS!
. . . YOU WILL **NEVER** BE LACKING IN SPIRITS TO CALL YOUR FRIENDS!
SEO YOUNG!
¿CÓMO ESTÁ?
WE'VE MISSED YOU!
HI!

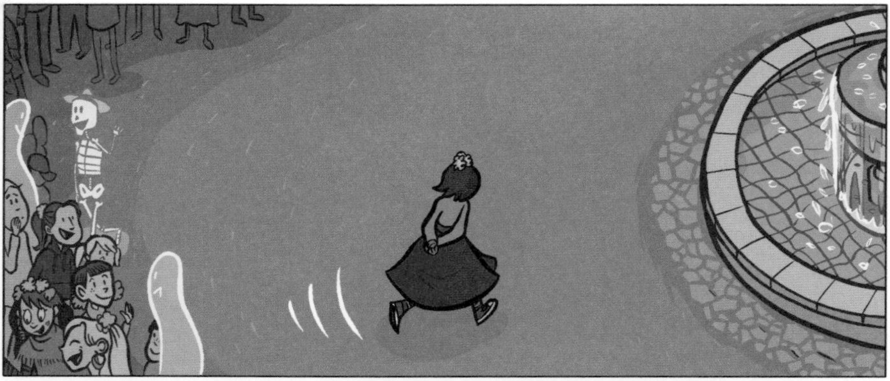

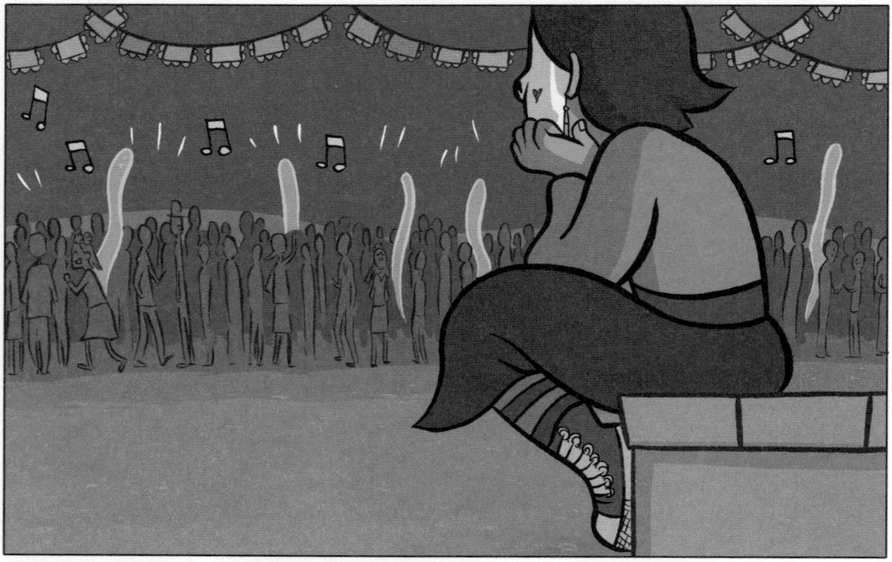

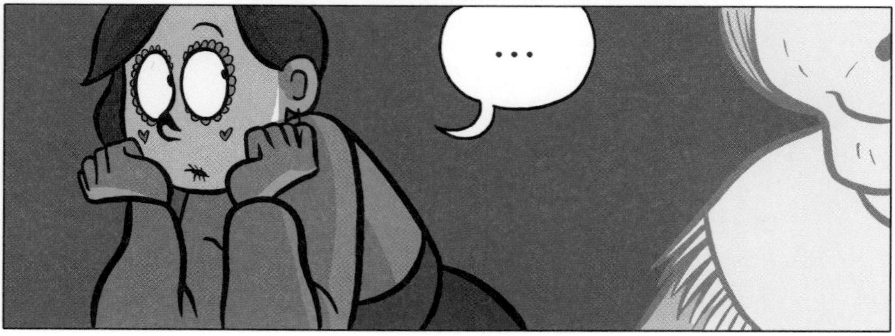
...

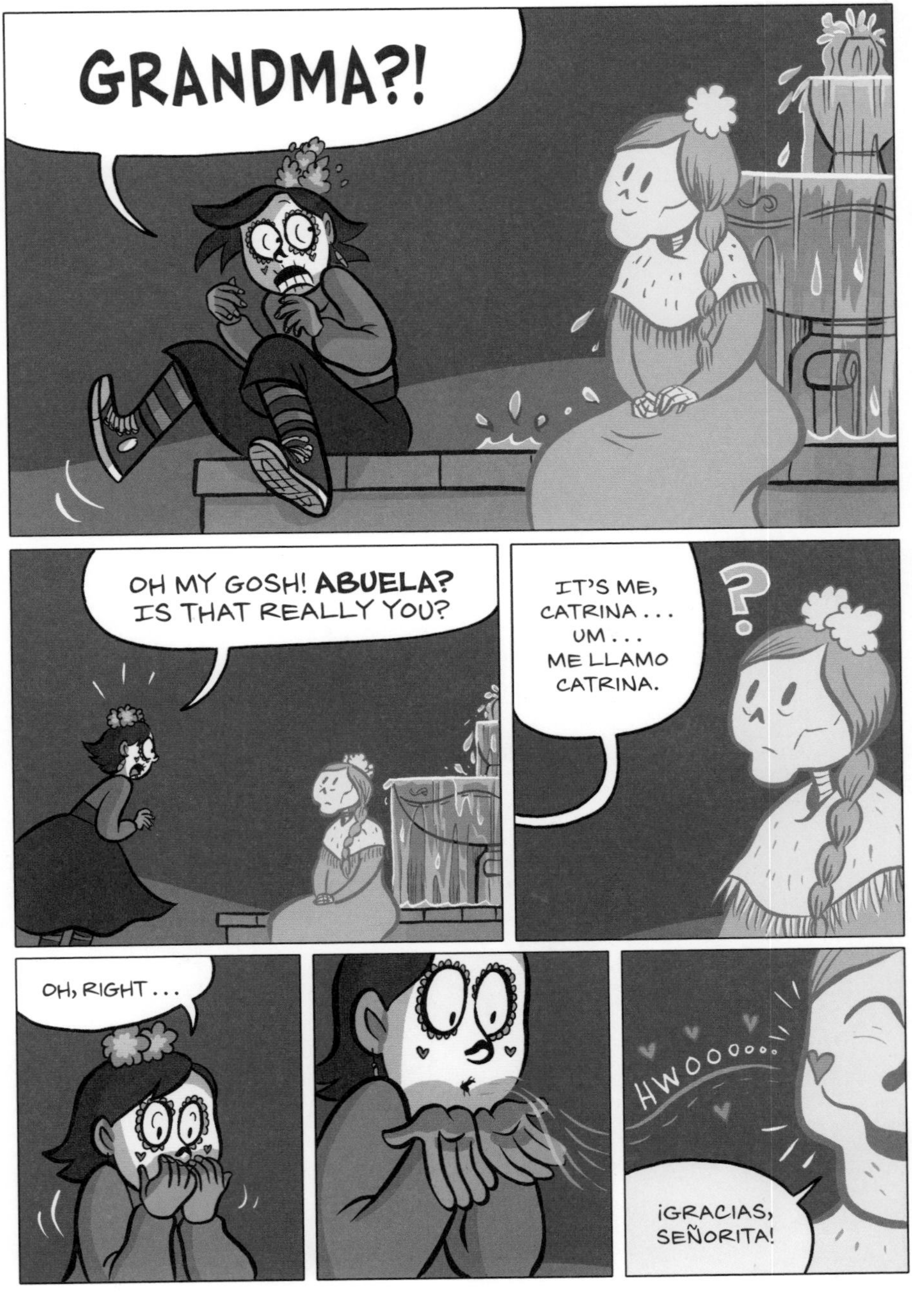
GRANDMA?!
OH MY GOSH! ABUELA? IS THAT REALLY YOU?
IT'S ME, CATRINA . . . UM . . . ME LLAMO CATRINA.
?
OH, RIGHT . . .
HWOOoooo.
¡GRACIAS, SEÑORITA!

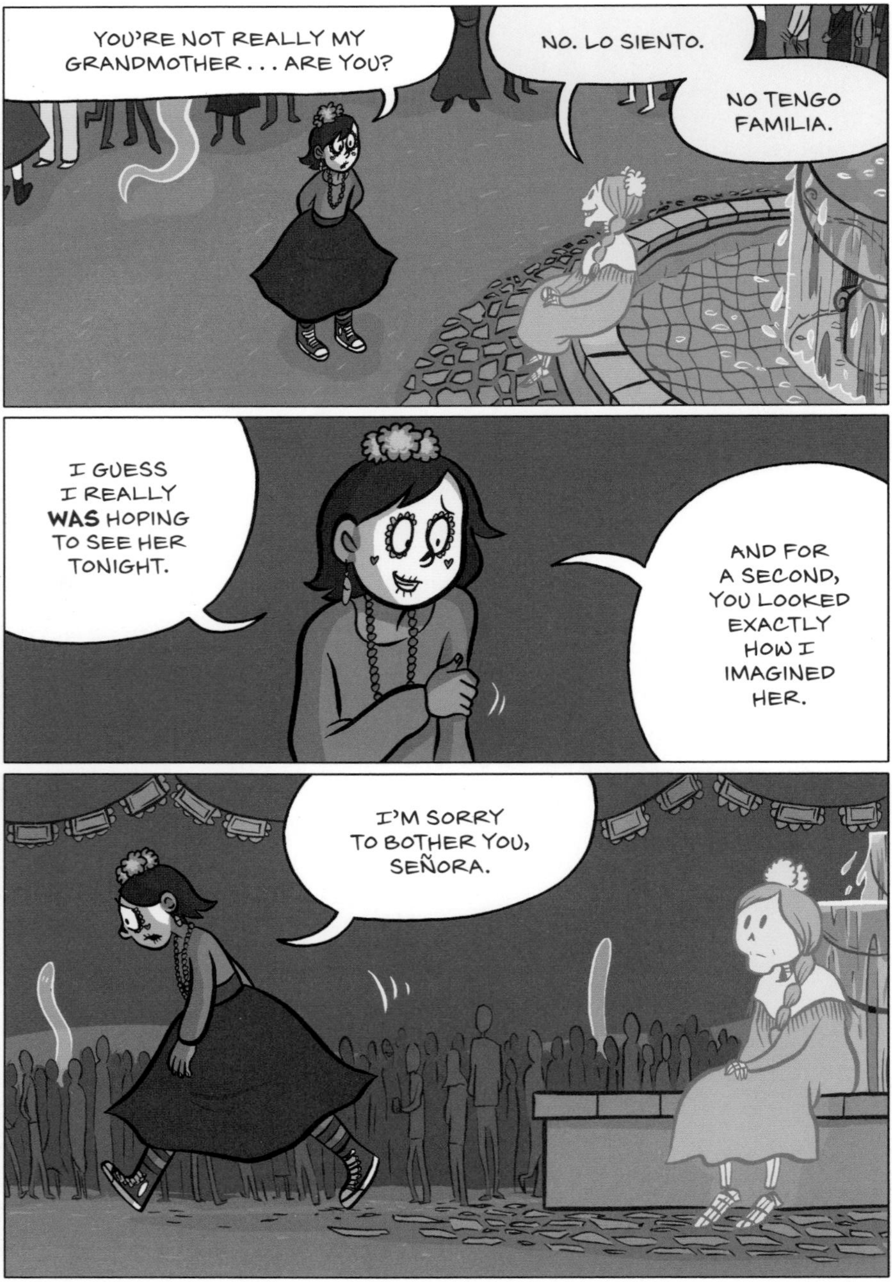
YOU'RE NOT REALLY MY GRANDMOTHER . . . ARE YOU?
NO. LO SIENTO.
NO TENGO FAMILIA.
I GUESS I REALLY **WAS** HOPING TO SEE HER TONIGHT.
AND FOR A SECOND, YOU LOOKED EXACTLY HOW I IMAGINED HER.
I'M SORRY TO BOTHER YOU, SEÑORA.

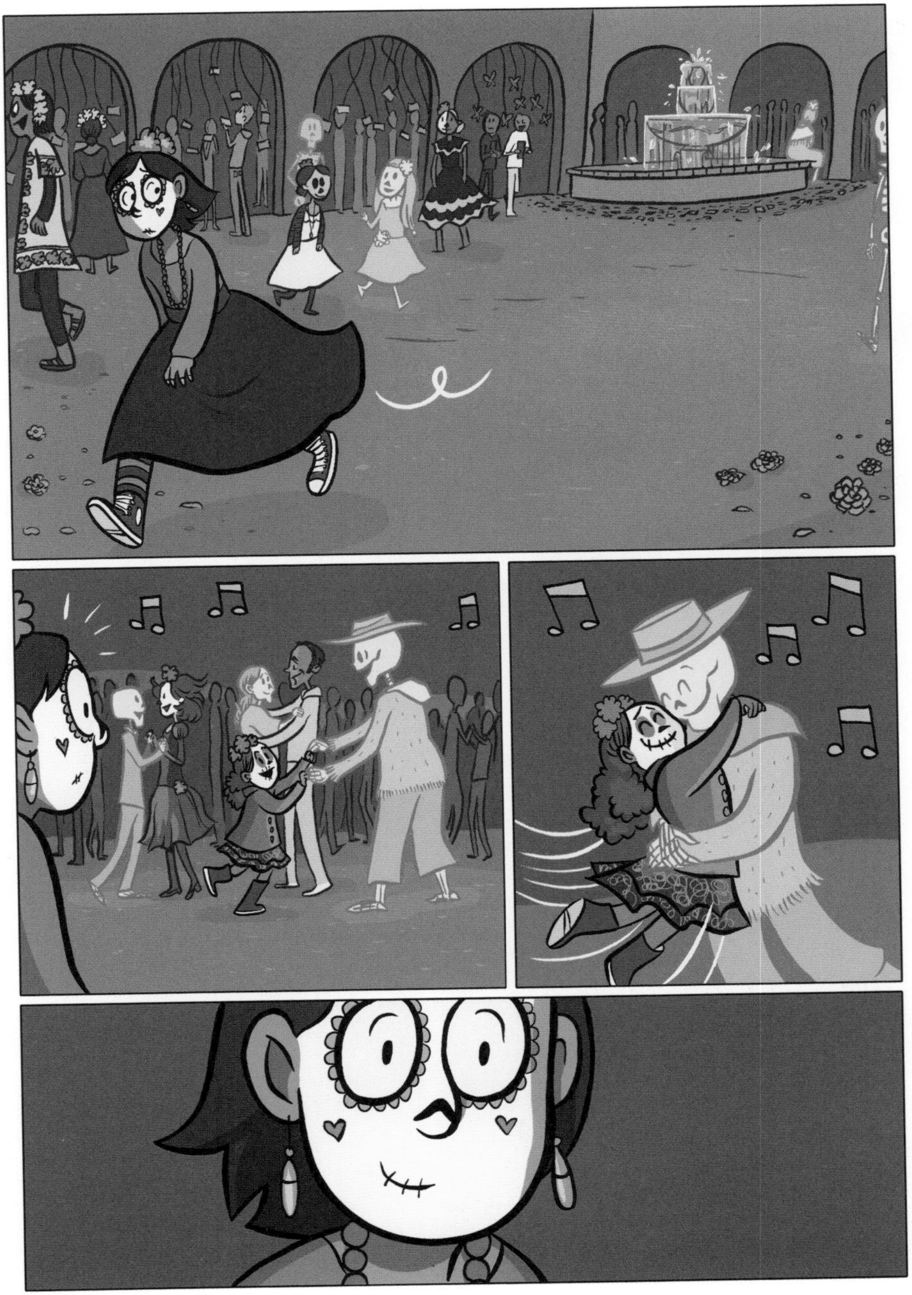

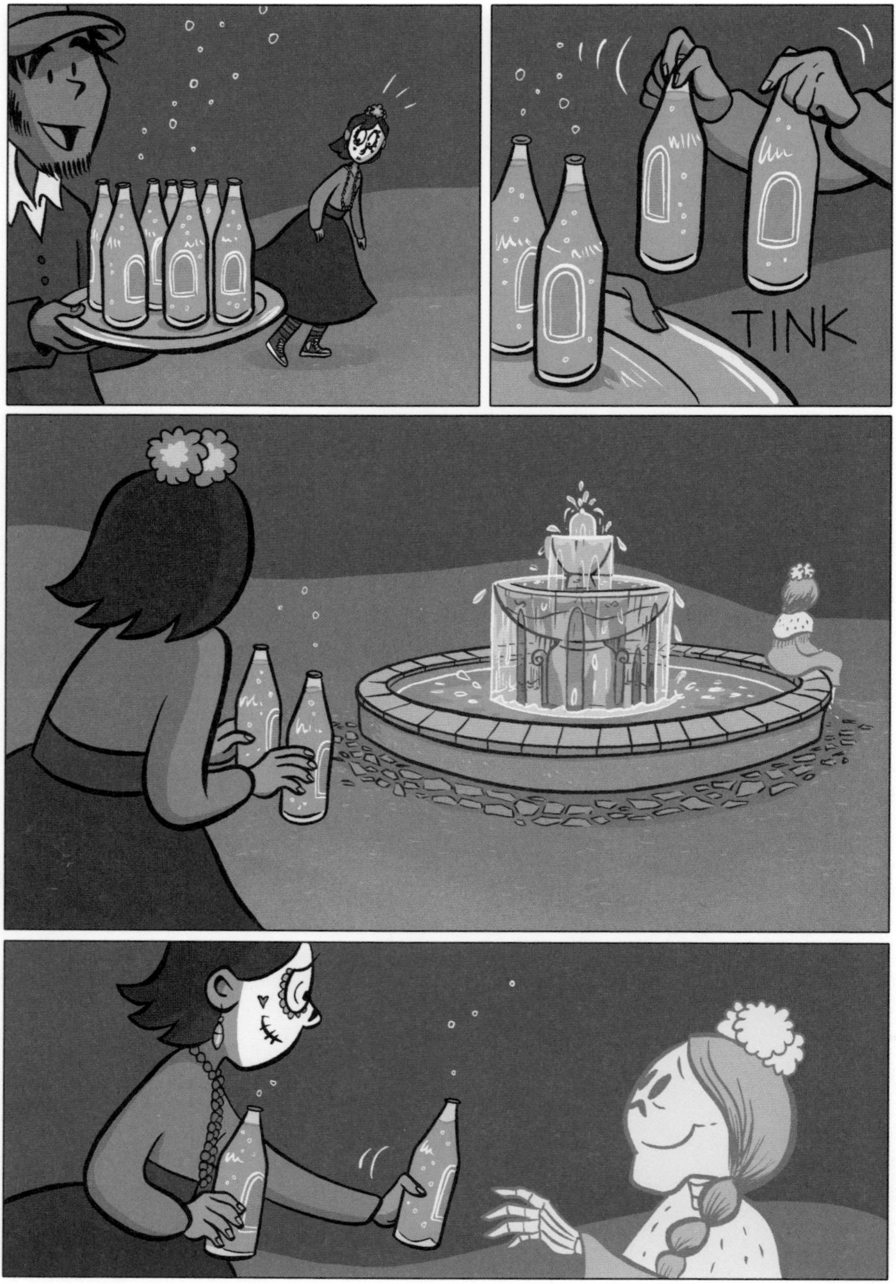
TINK

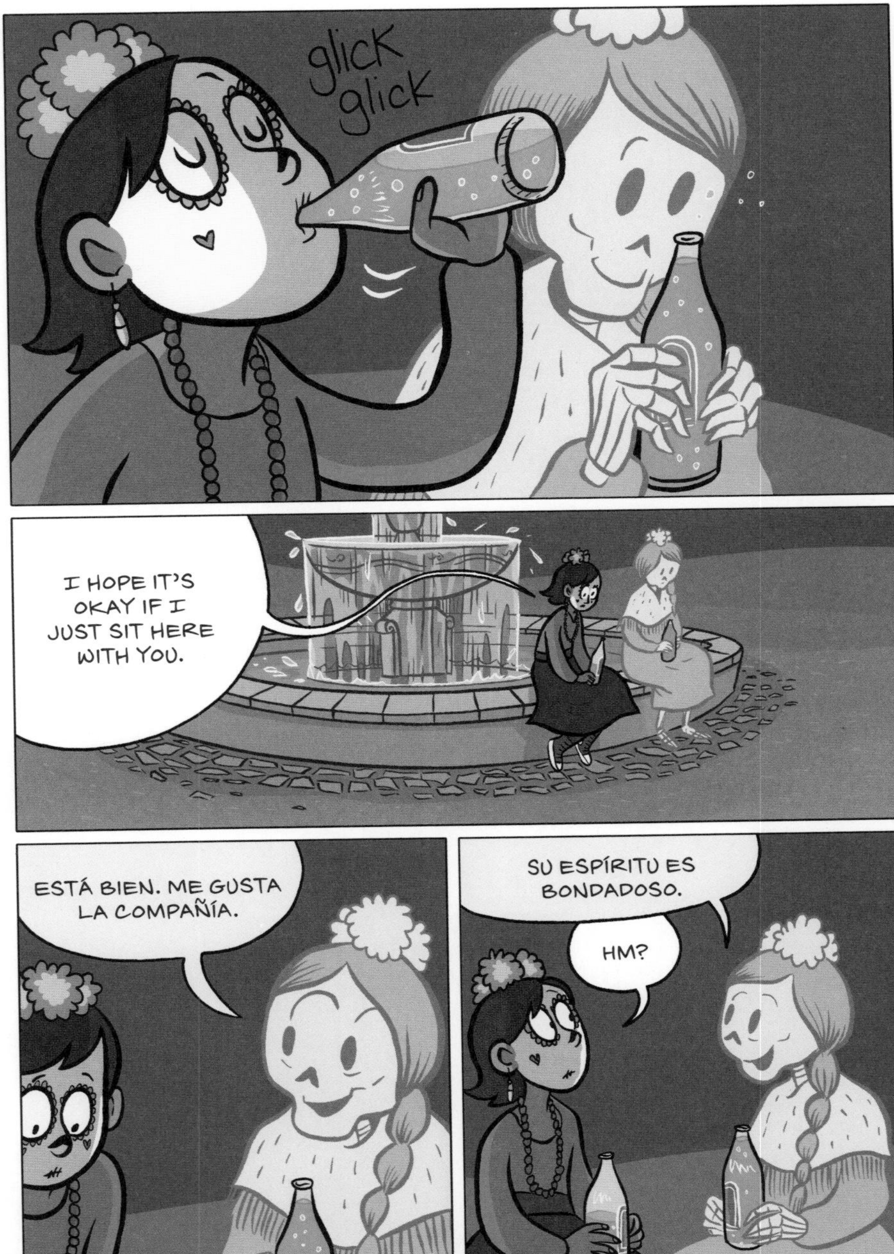
glick glick
I HOPE IT'S OKAY IF I JUST SIT HERE WITH YOU.
ESTÁ BIEN. ME GUSTA LA COMPAÑÍA.
SU ESPÍRITU ES BONDADOSO.
HM?

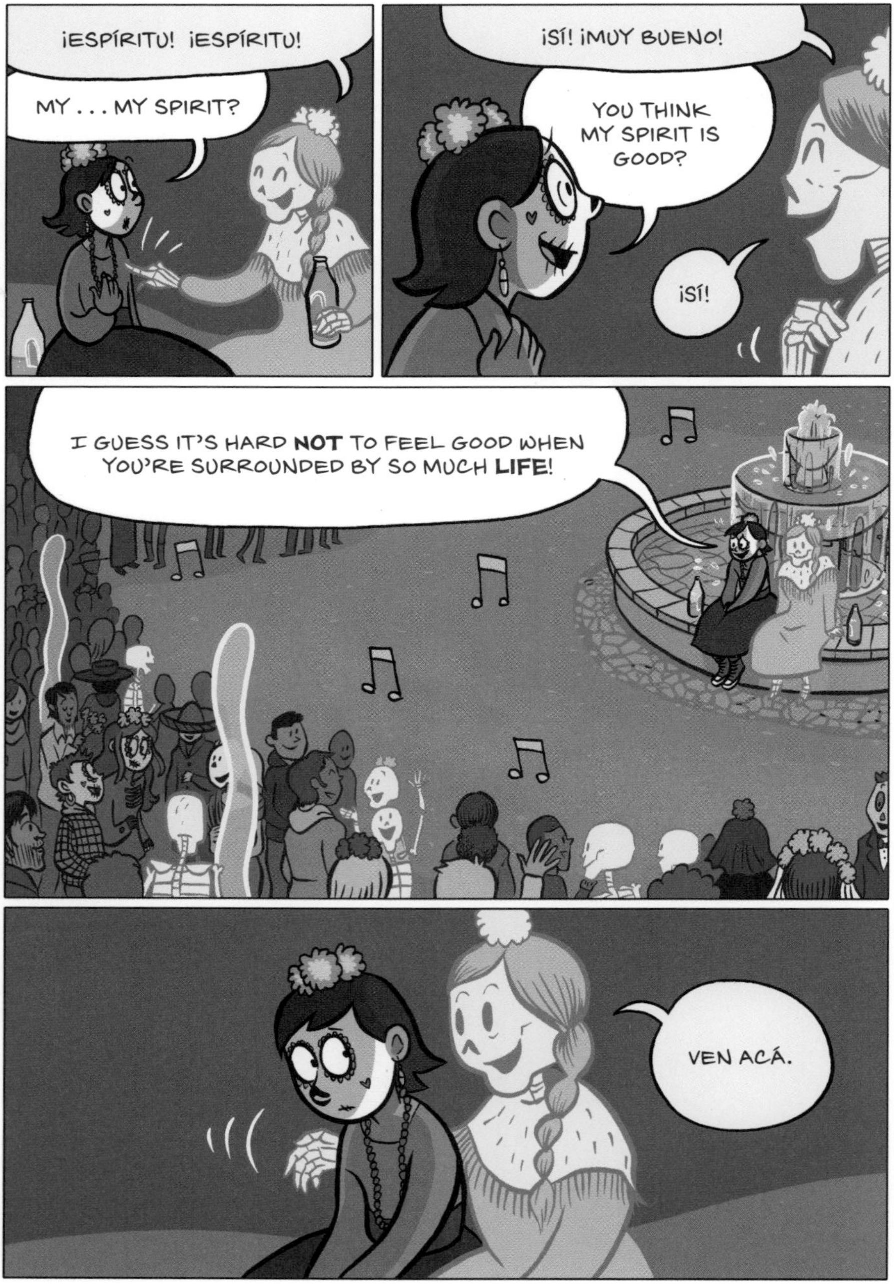

¡ESPÍRITU! ¡ESPÍRITU!
MY . . . MY SPIRIT?
¡SÍ! ¡MUY BUENO!
YOU THINK MY SPIRIT IS GOOD?
¡SÍ!
I GUESS IT'S HARD **NOT** TO FEEL GOOD WHEN YOU'RE SURROUNDED BY SO MUCH **LIFE**!
VEN ACÁ.

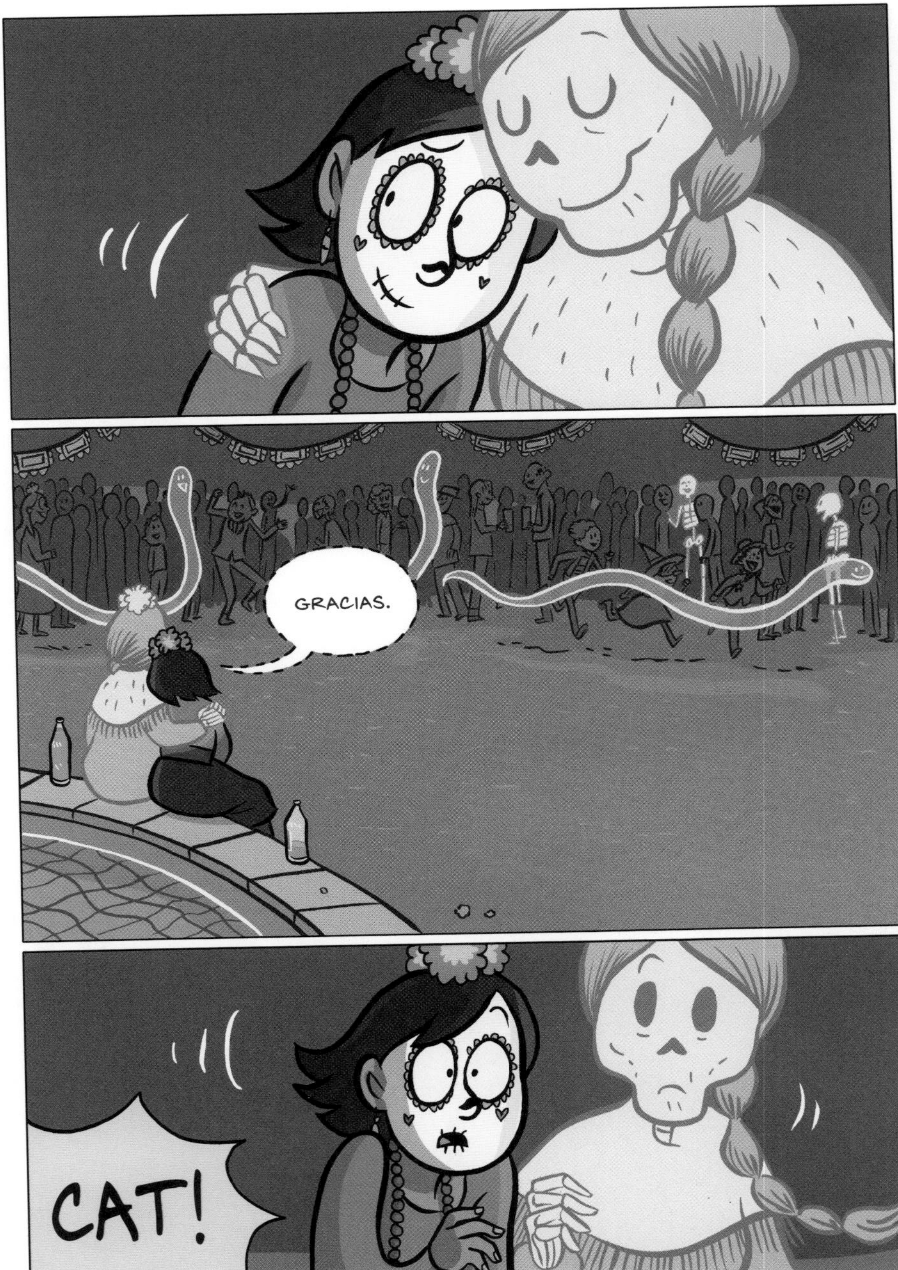
GRACIAS.
CAT!

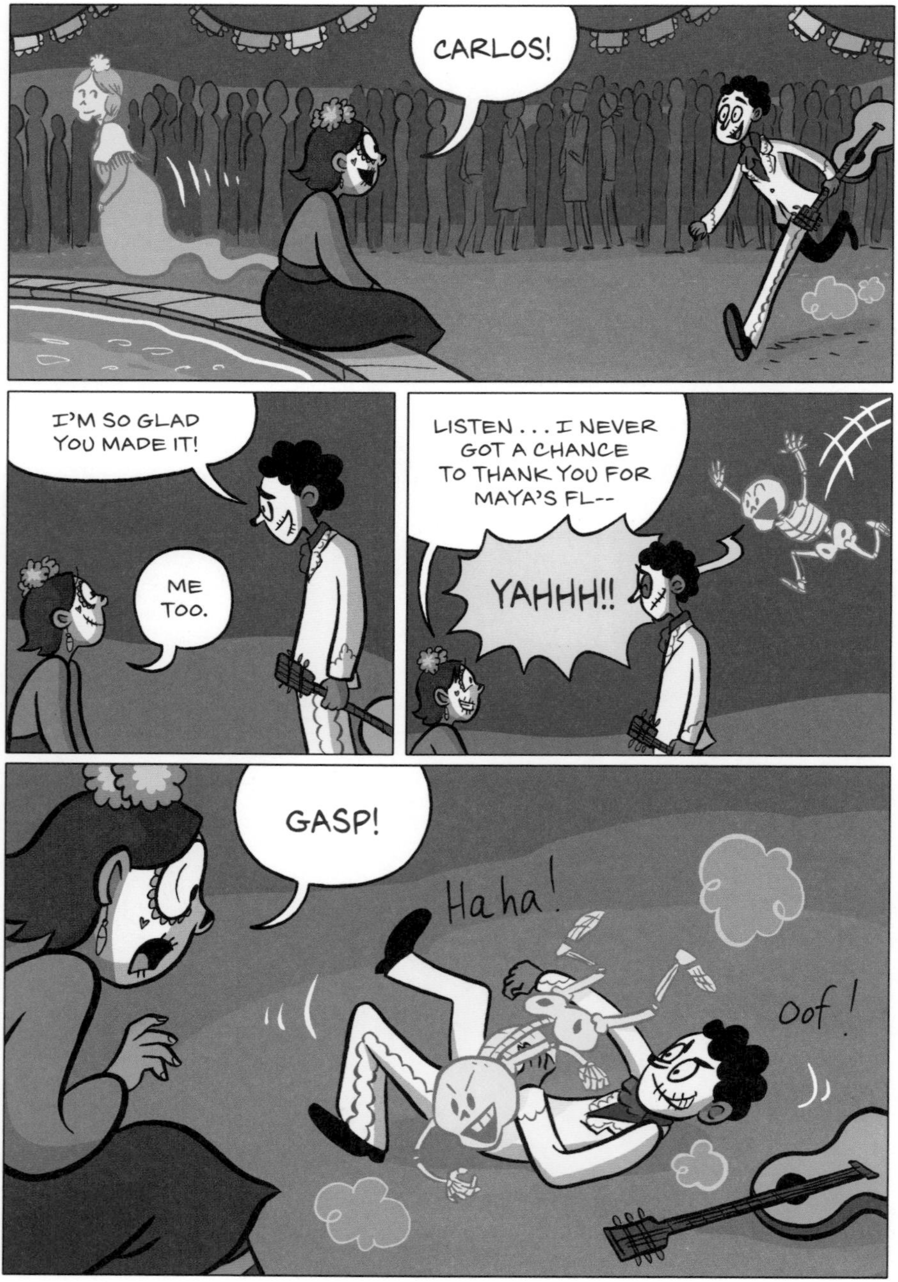
CARLOS!
I'M SO GLAD YOU MADE IT!
ME TOO.
LISTEN . . . I NEVER GOT A CHANCE TO THANK YOU FOR MAYA'S FL--
YAHHH!!
GASP!
Haha!
Oof!

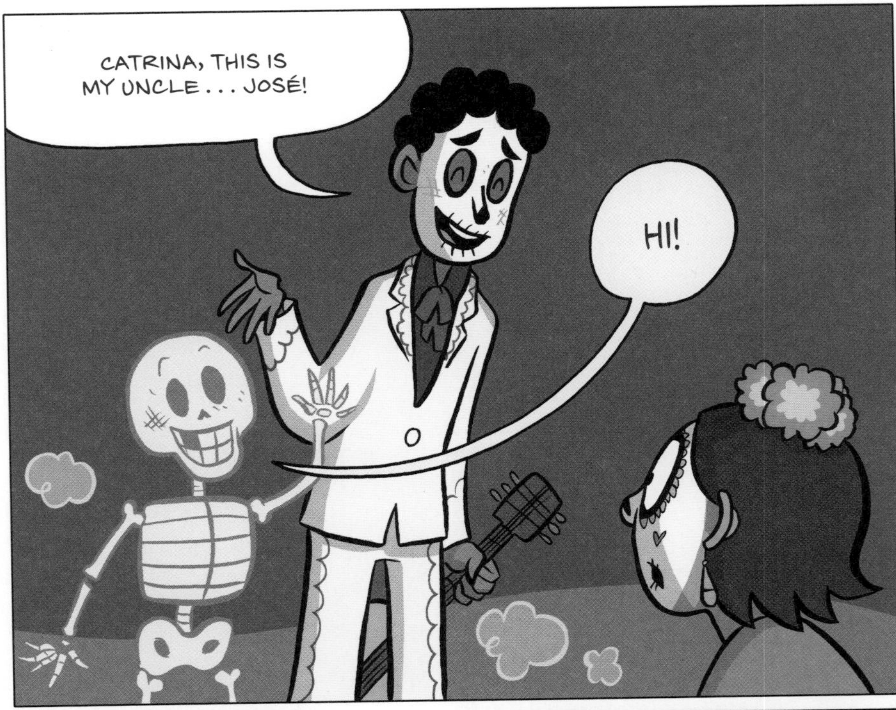
CATRINA, THIS IS
MY UNCLE . . . JOSÉ!
HI!

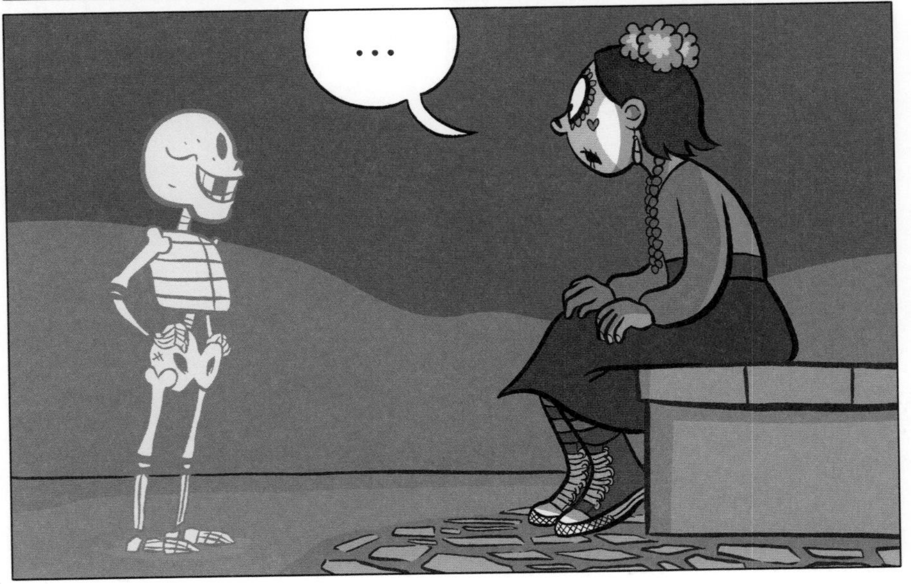
. . .

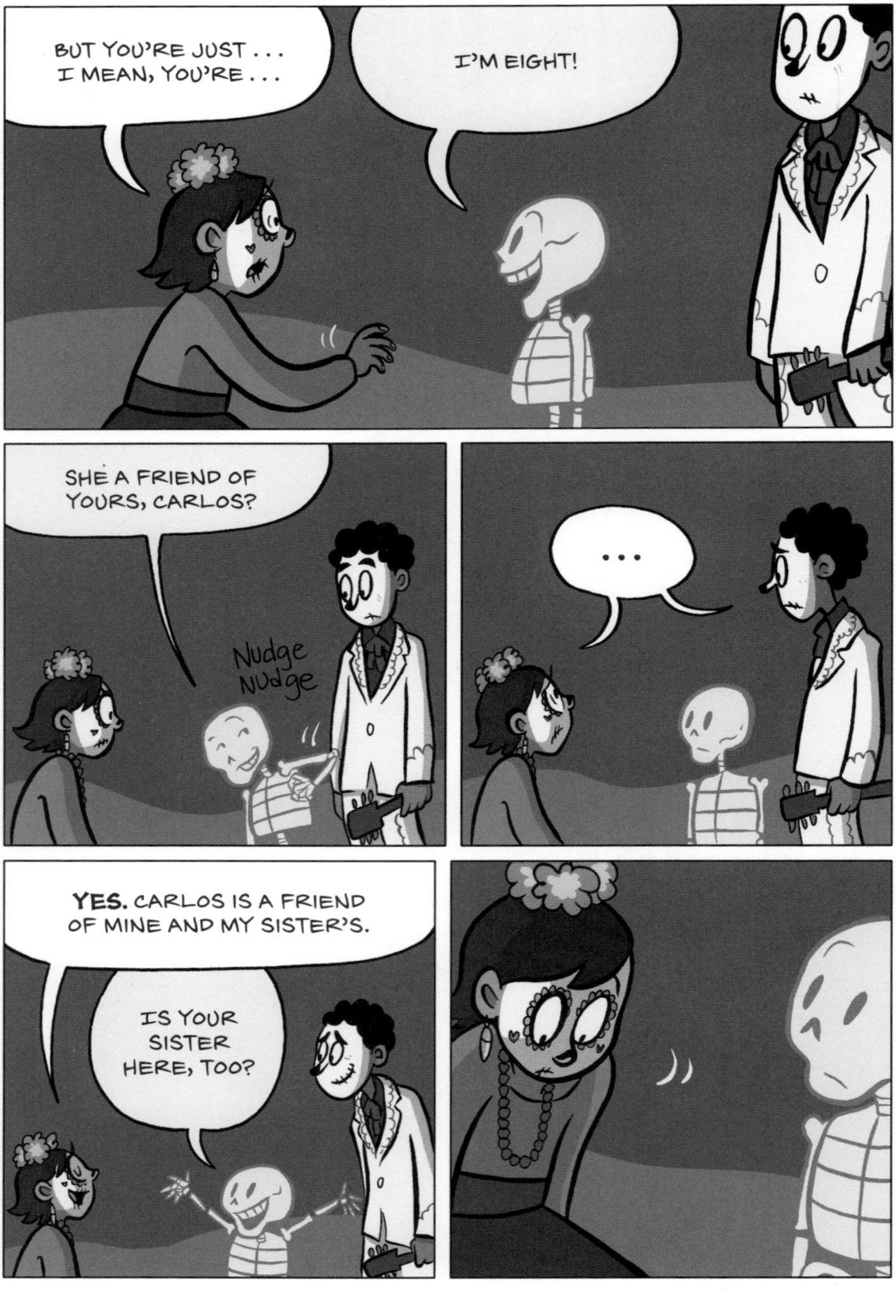
BUT YOU'RE JUST . . . I MEAN, YOU'RE . . .
I'M EIGHT!
SHE A FRIEND OF YOURS, CARLOS?
Nudge Nudge
. . .
YES. CARLOS IS A FRIEND OF MINE AND MY SISTER'S.
IS YOUR SISTER HERE, TOO?

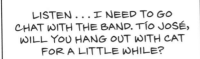

LISTEN . . . I NEED TO GO CHAT WITH THE BAND. TÍO JOSÉ, WILL YOU HANG OUT WITH CAT FOR A LITTLE WHILE?

¡SÍ!

Salute!

HOW DID YOU DIE, JOSÉ?

I DUNNO.

YOU DON'T REMEMBER IT AT ALL?

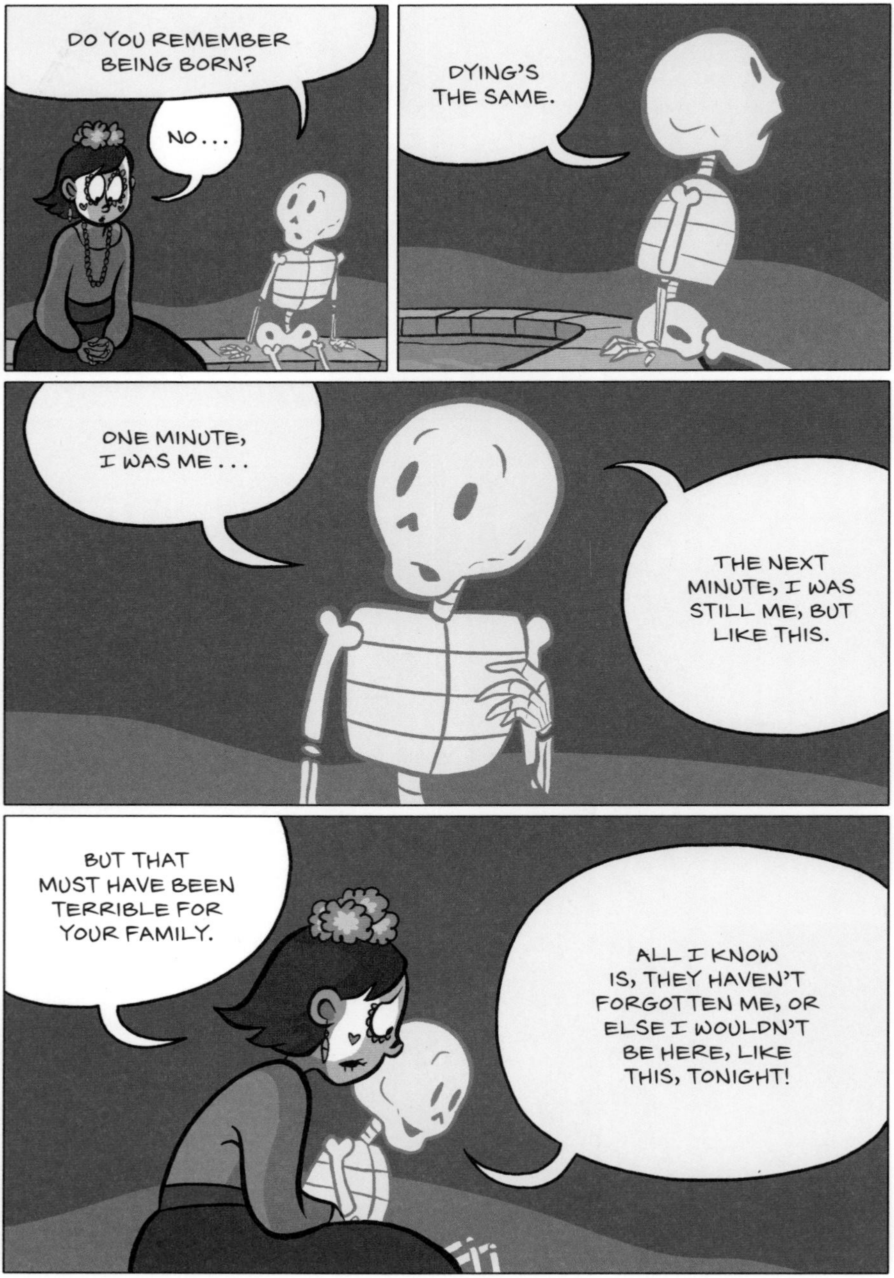
DO YOU REMEMBER BEING BORN?
NO...
DYING'S THE SAME.
ONE MINUTE, I WAS ME...
THE NEXT MINUTE, I WAS STILL ME, BUT LIKE THIS.
BUT THAT MUST HAVE BEEN TERRIBLE FOR YOUR FAMILY.
ALL I KNOW IS, THEY HAVEN'T FORGOTTEN ME, OR ELSE I WOULDN'T BE HERE, LIKE THIS, TONIGHT!

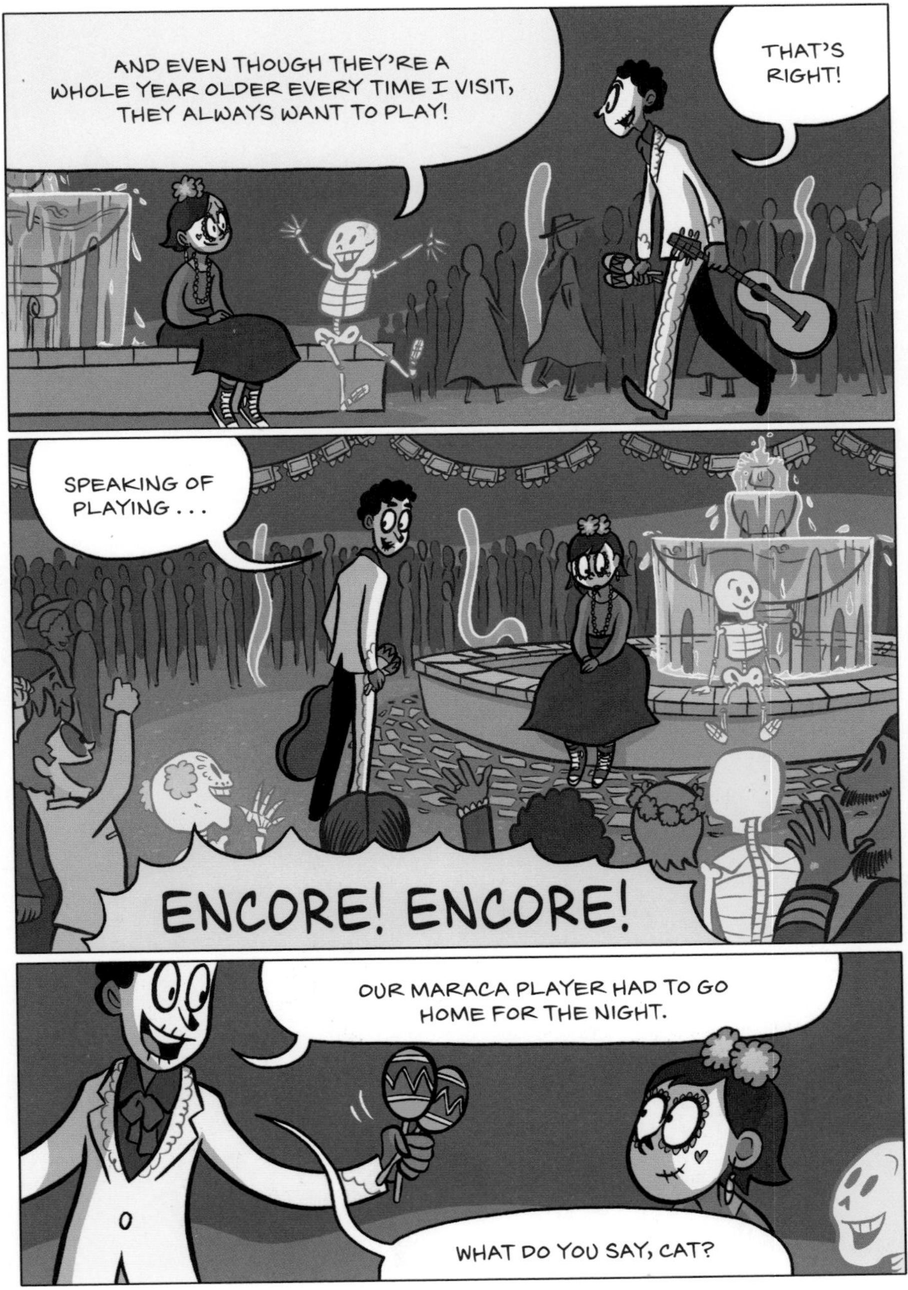
AND EVEN THOUGH THEY'RE A WHOLE YEAR OLDER EVERY TIME I VISIT, THEY ALWAYS WANT TO PLAY!
THAT'S RIGHT!
SPEAKING OF PLAYING . . .
ENCORE! ENCORE!
OUR MARACA PLAYER HAD TO GO HOME FOR THE NIGHT.
WHAT DO YOU SAY, CAT?

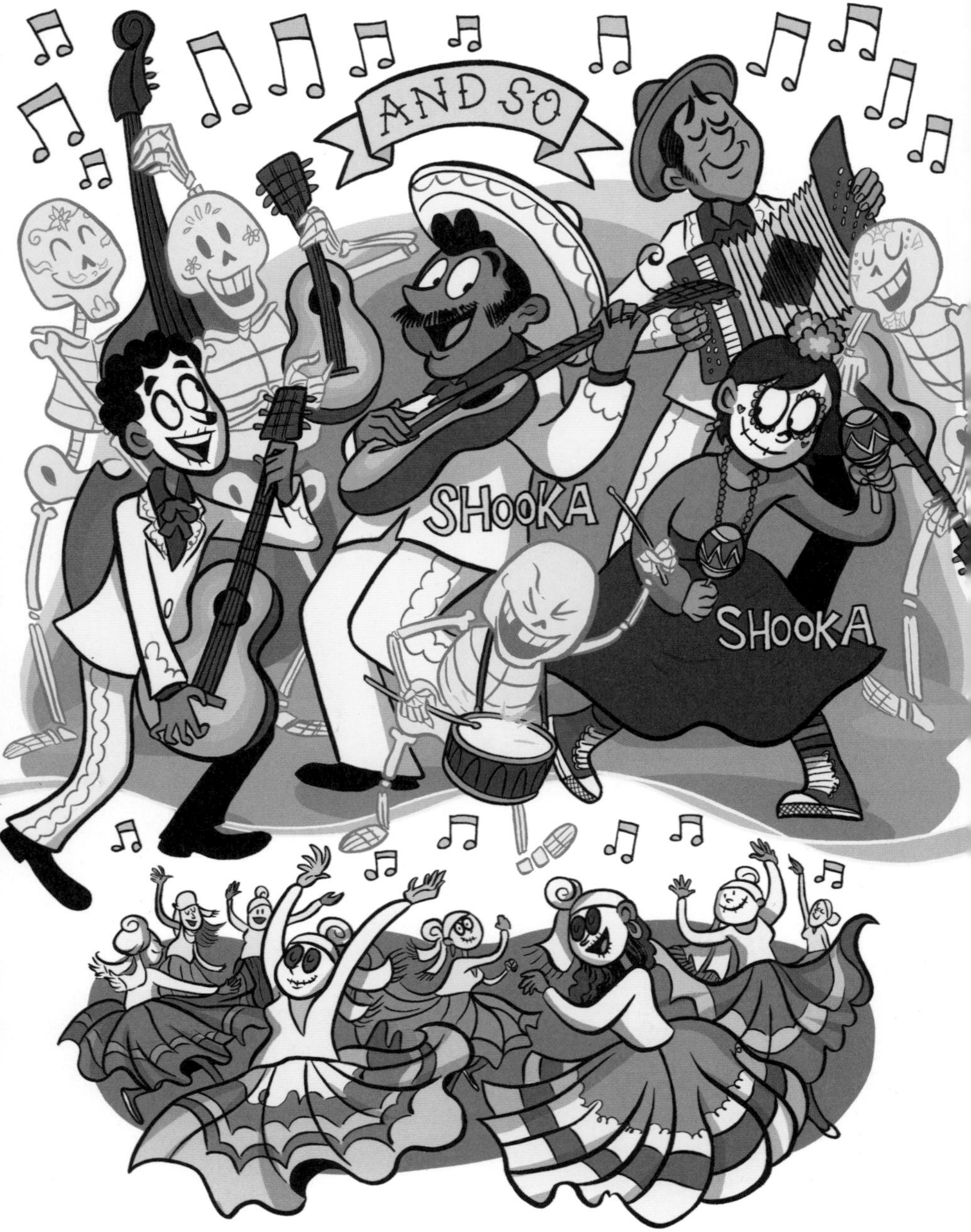
AND SO
SHOOKA
SHOOKA

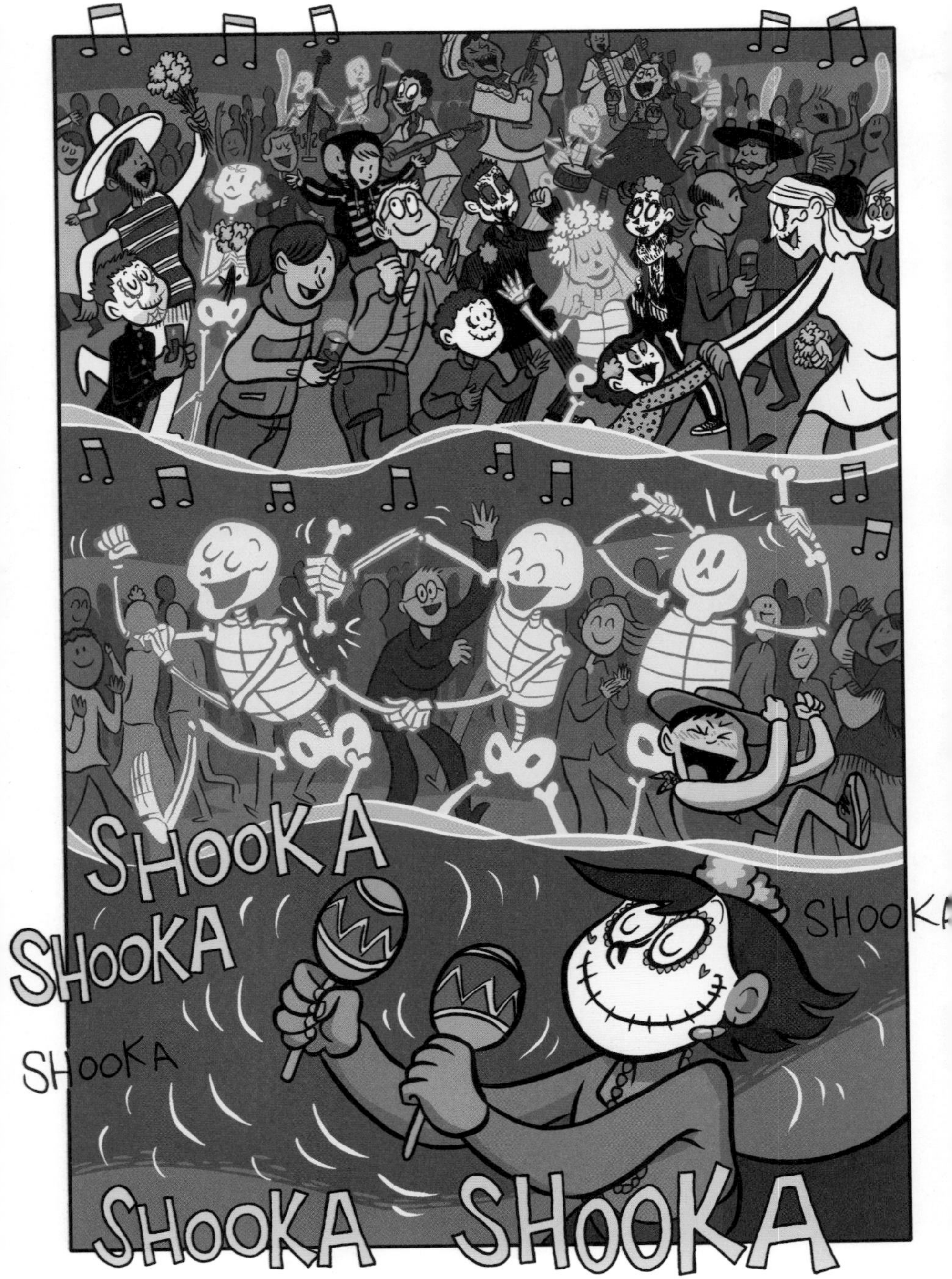
SHOOKA
SHOOKA
SHOOKA
SHOOKA
SHOOKA
SHOOKA

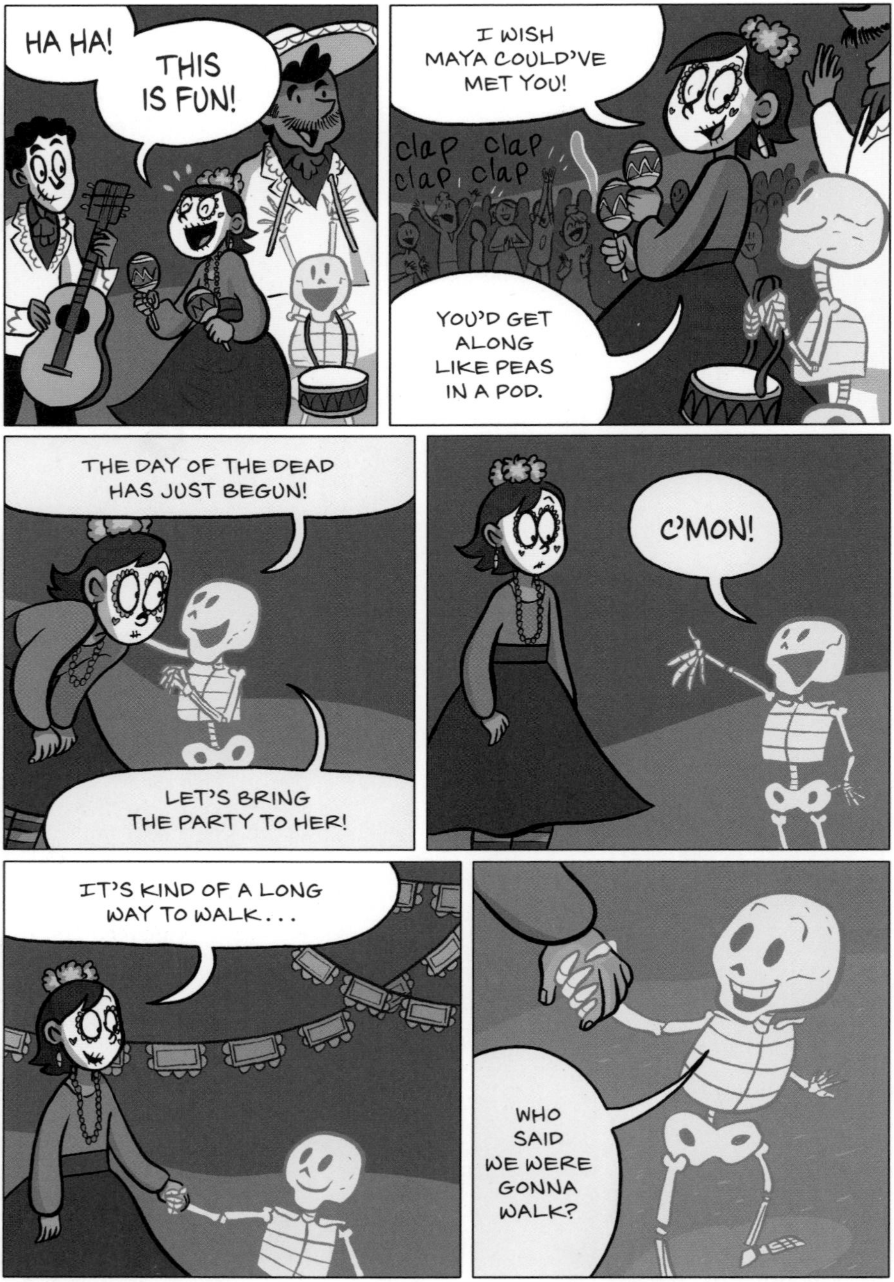
HA HA!
THIS IS FUN!
I WISH MAYA COULD'VE MET YOU!
clap clap clap clap
YOU'D GET ALONG LIKE PEAS IN A POD.
THE DAY OF THE DEAD HAS JUST BEGUN!
LET'S BRING THE PARTY TO HER!
C'MON!
IT'S KIND OF A LONG WAY TO WALK . . .
WHO SAID WE WERE GONNA WALK?

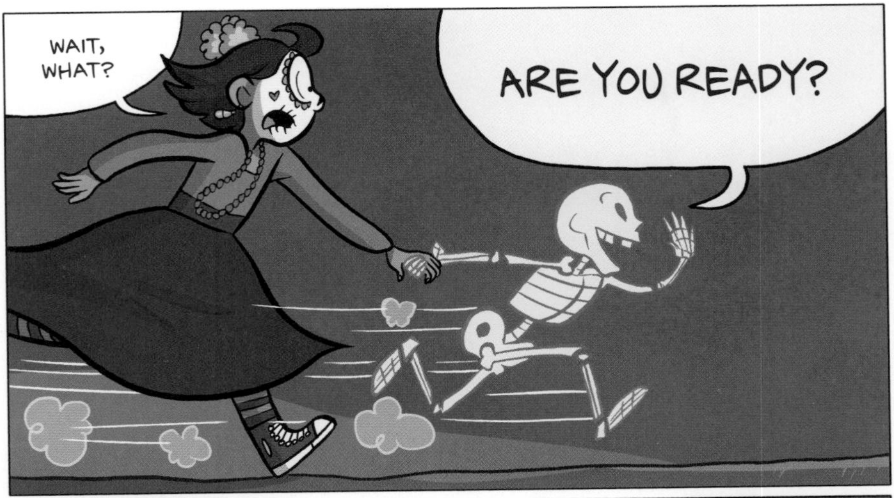
WAIT, WHAT?
ARE YOU READY?

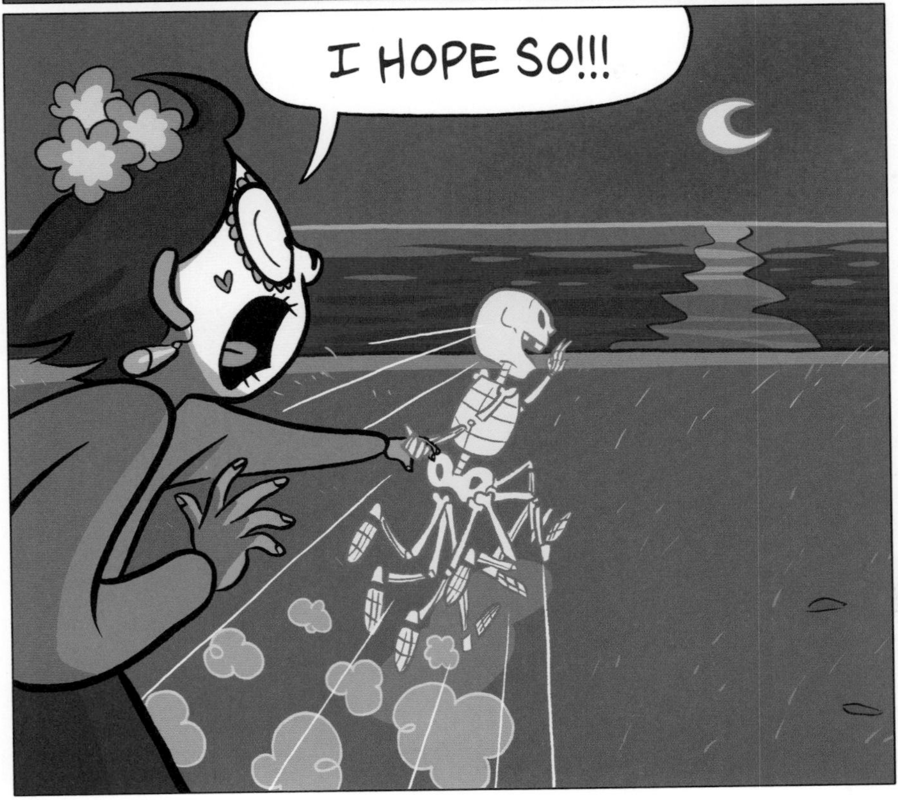
I HOPE SO!!!

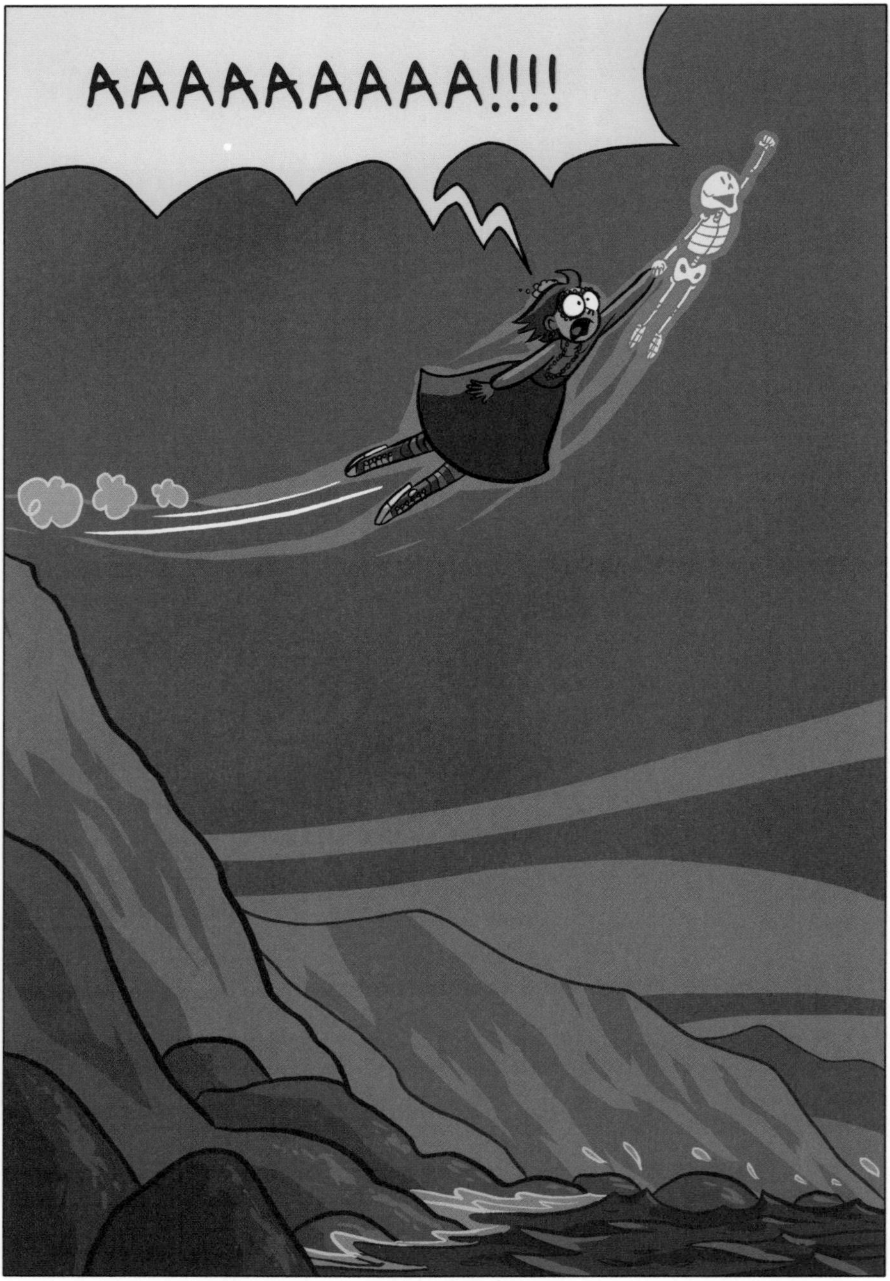
AAAAAAAAAA!!!!

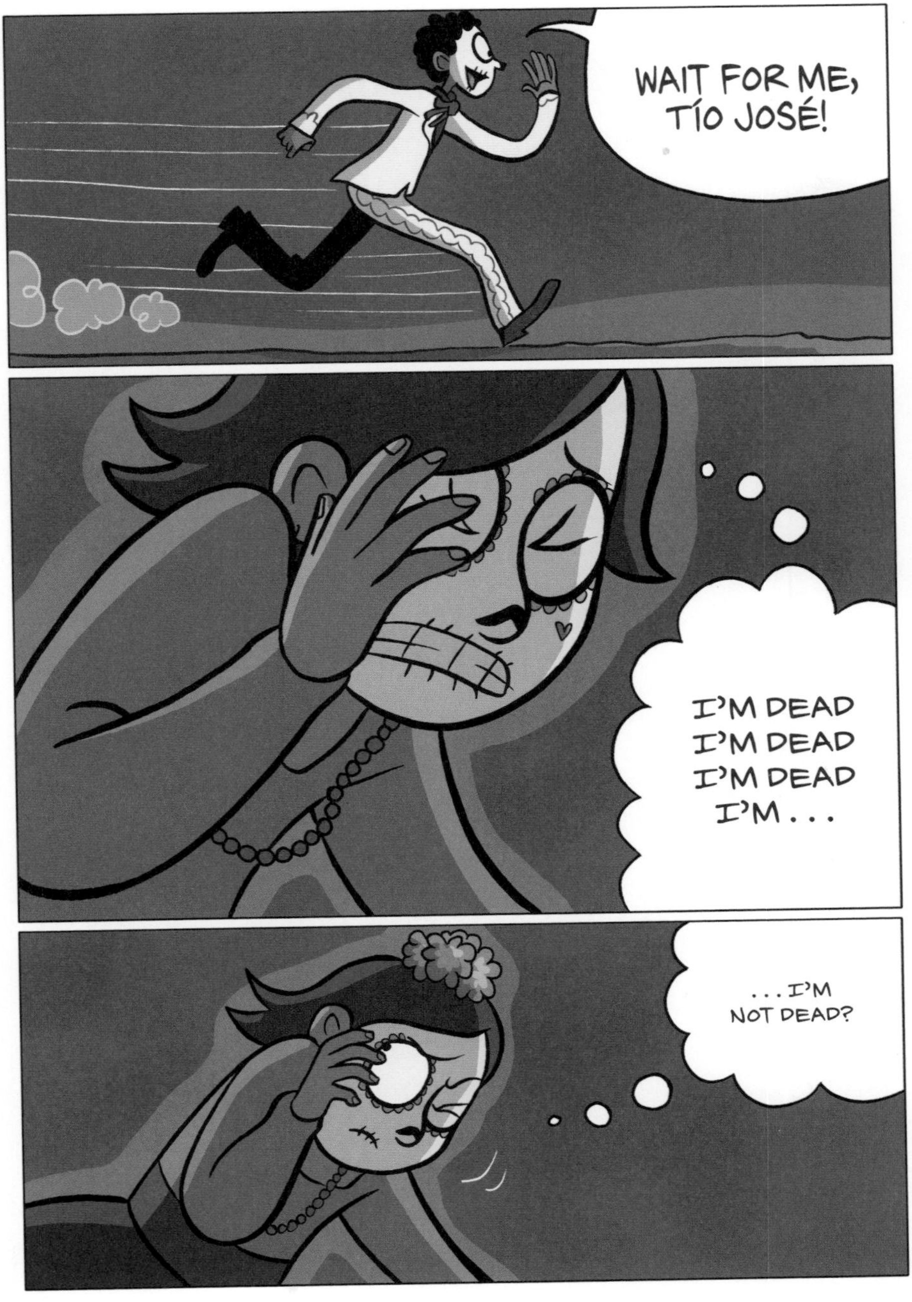
WAIT FOR ME, TÍO JOSÉ!
I'M DEAD I'M DEAD I'M DEAD I'M . . .
. . . I'M NOT DEAD?

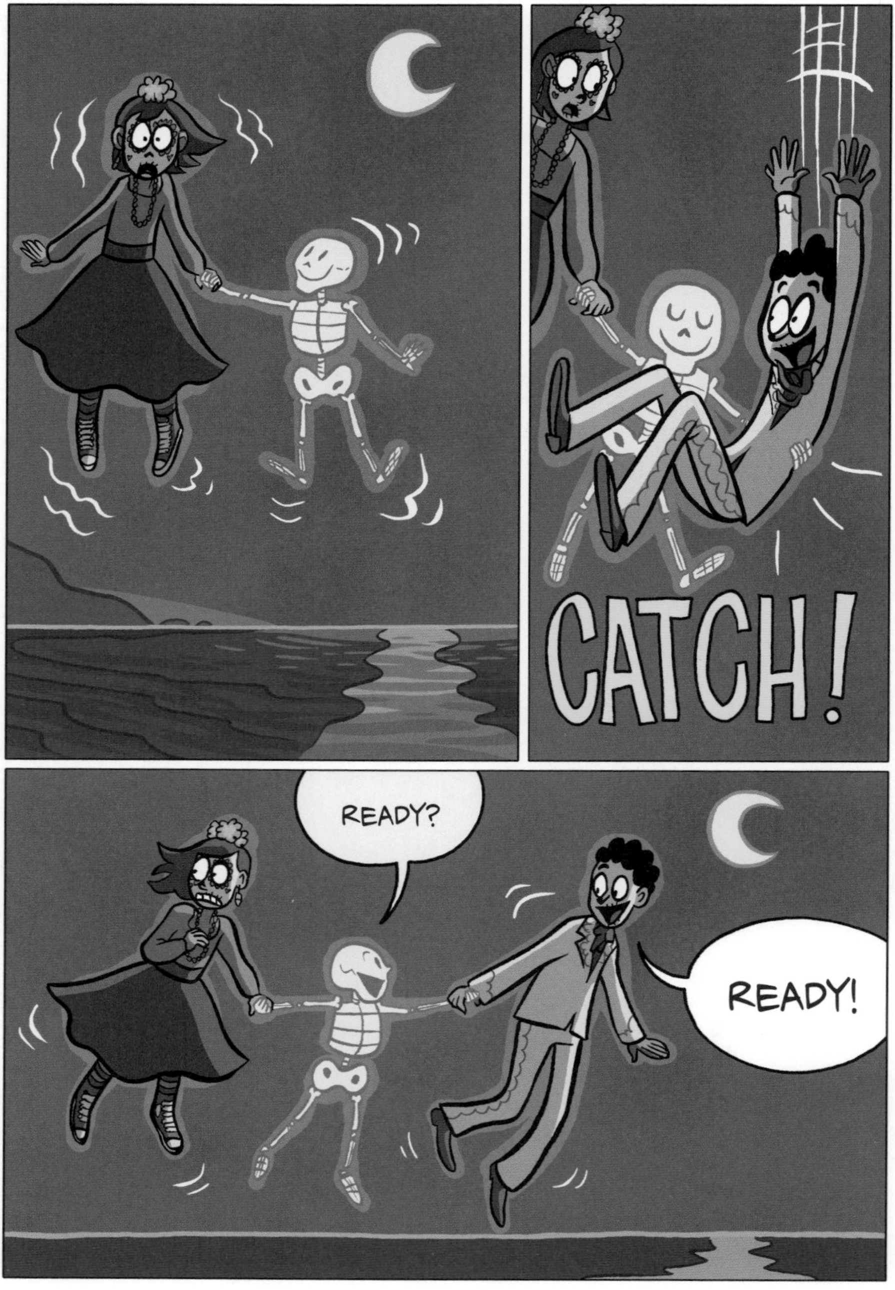
CATCH!
READY?
READY!

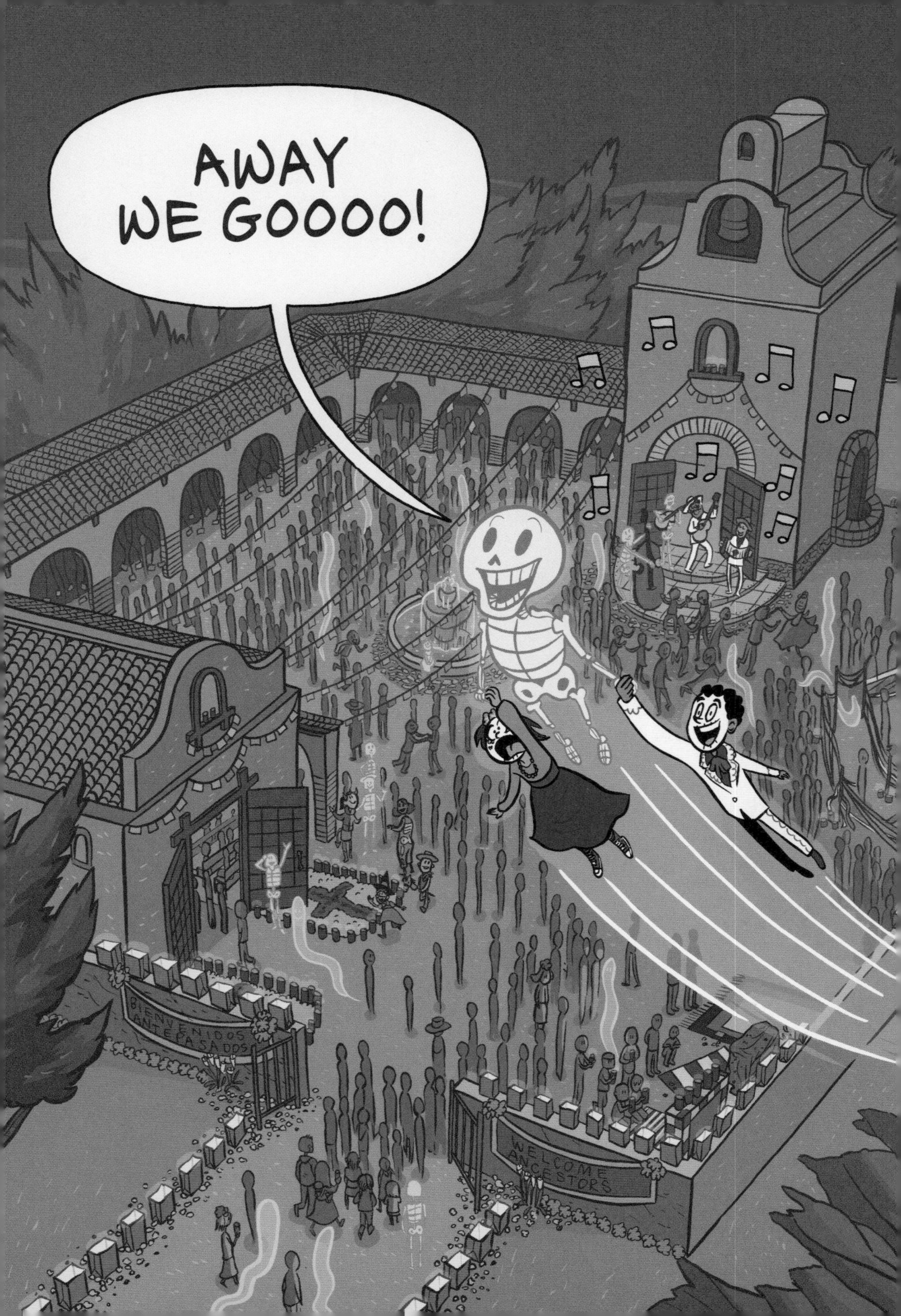
AWAY WE GOOOO!
BIENVENIDOS ANTEPASADOS
WELCOME ANCESTORS

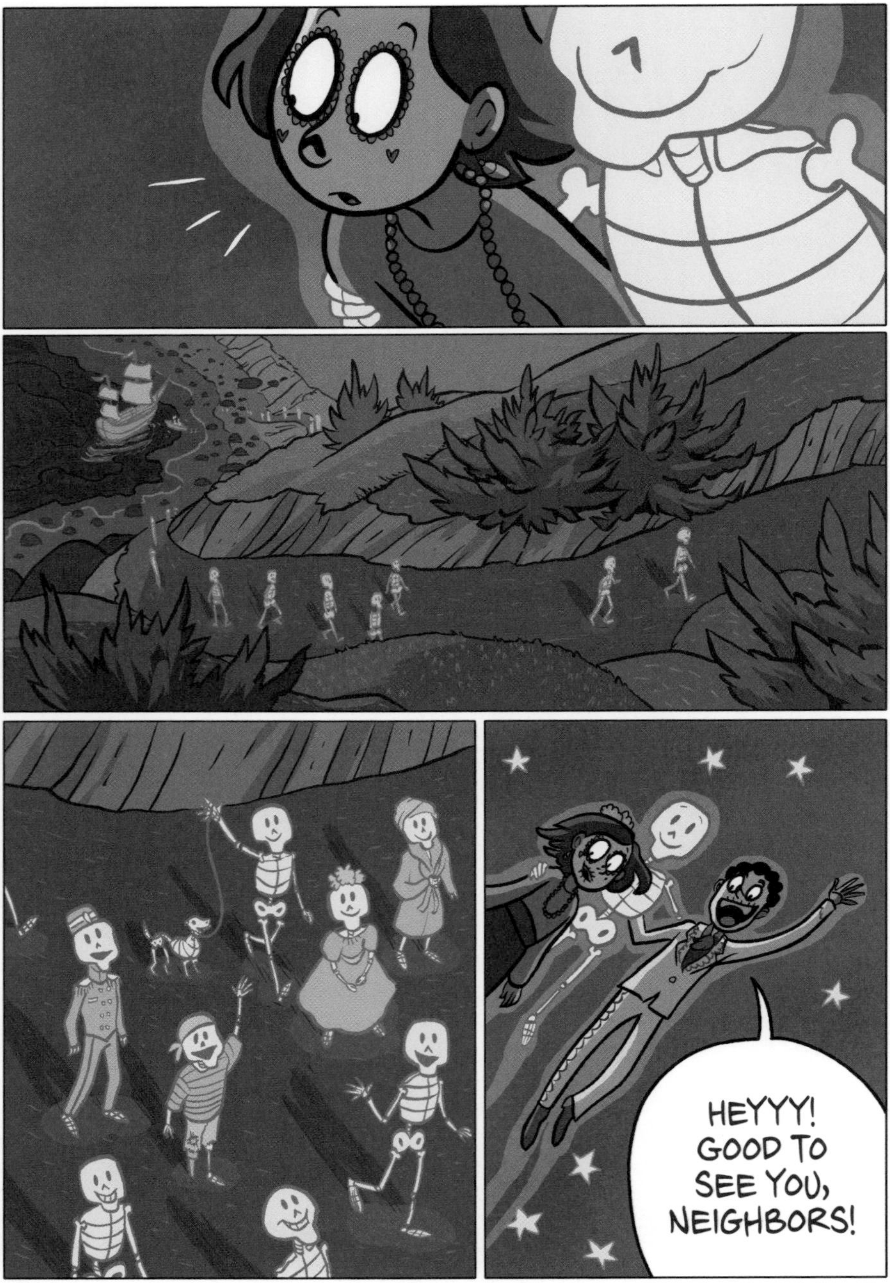
HEYYY!
GOOD TO
SEE YOU,
NEIGHBORS!

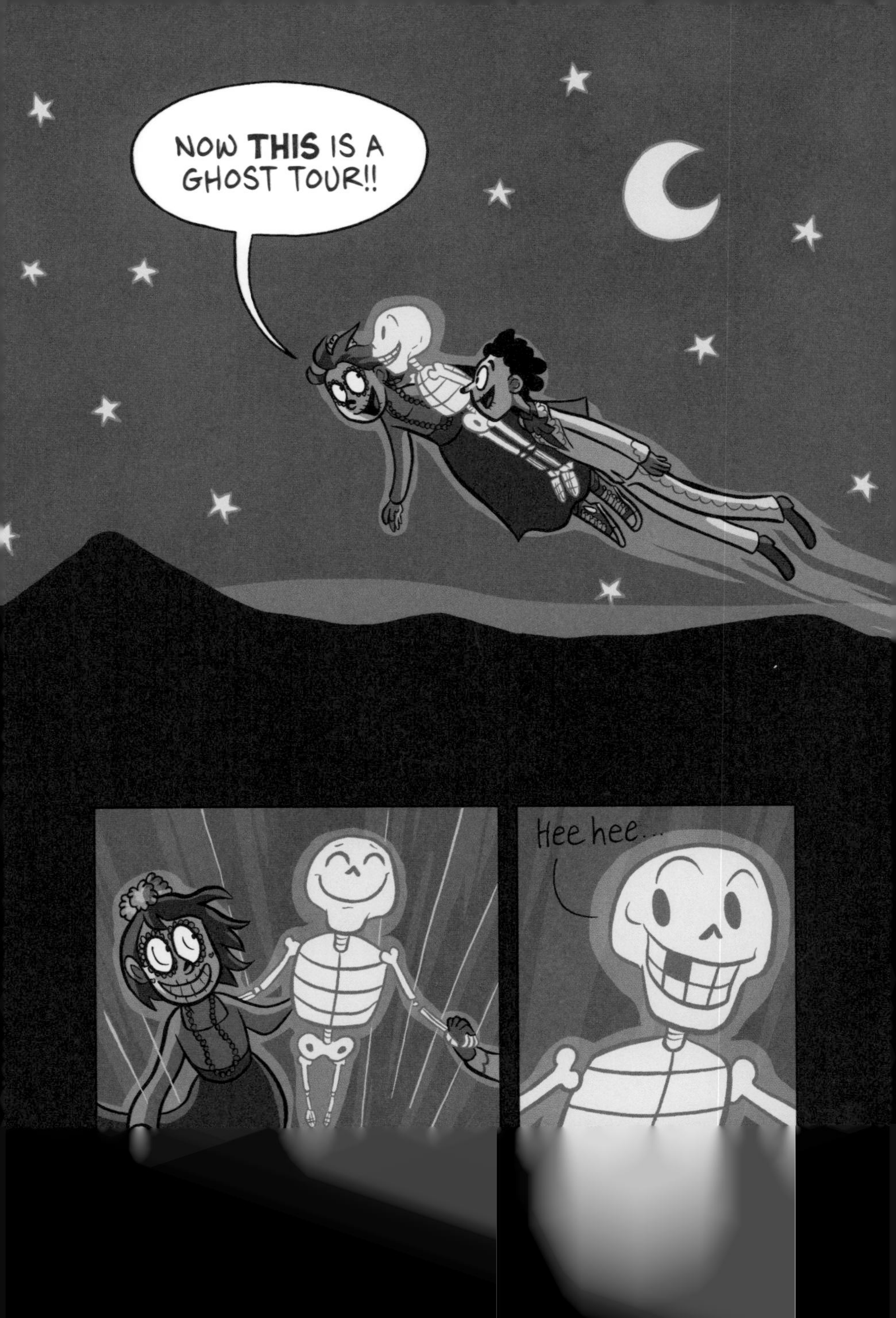
NOW THIS IS A GHOST TOUR!!
Hee hee...

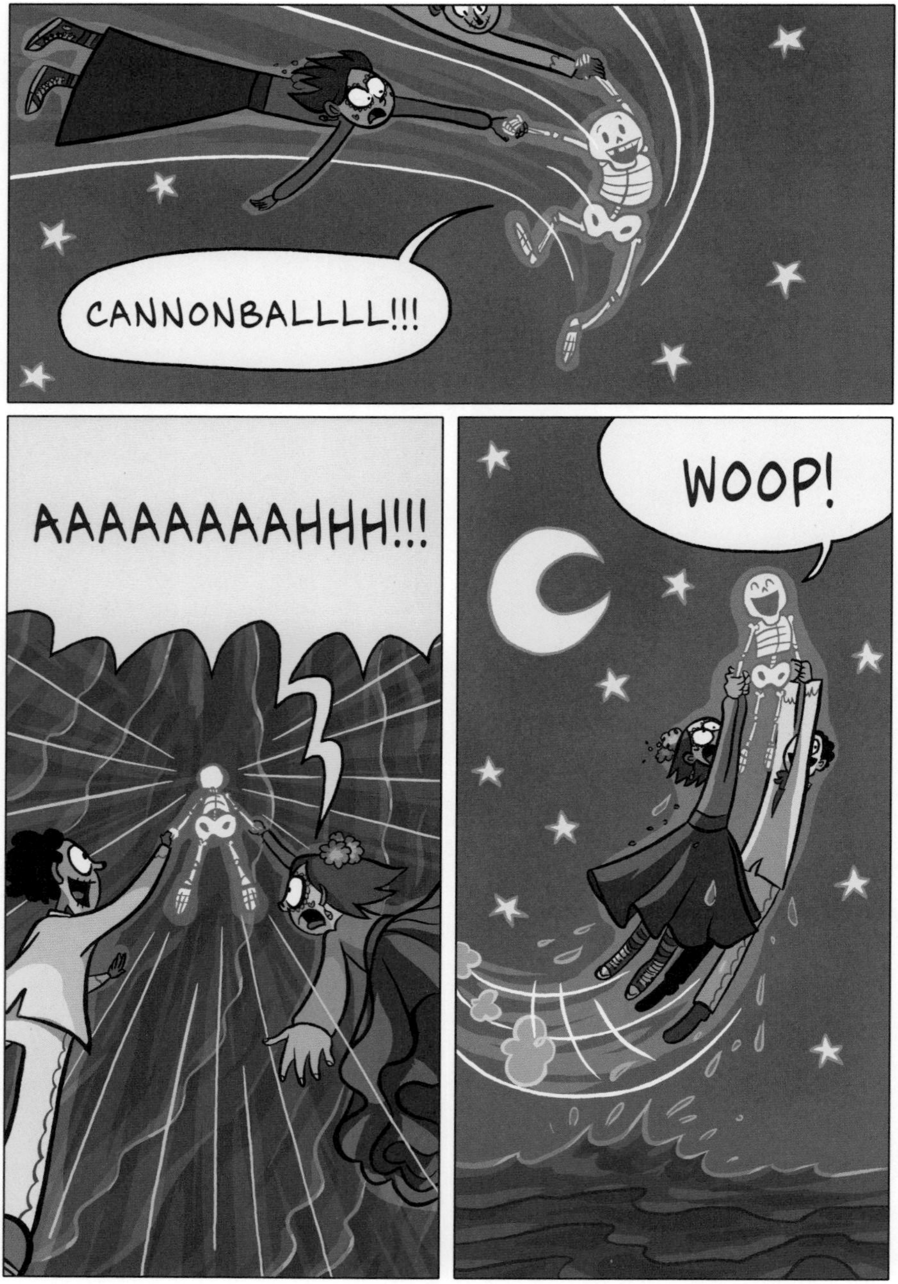
CANNONBALLLL!!!
AAAAAAAAHHH!!!
WOOP!

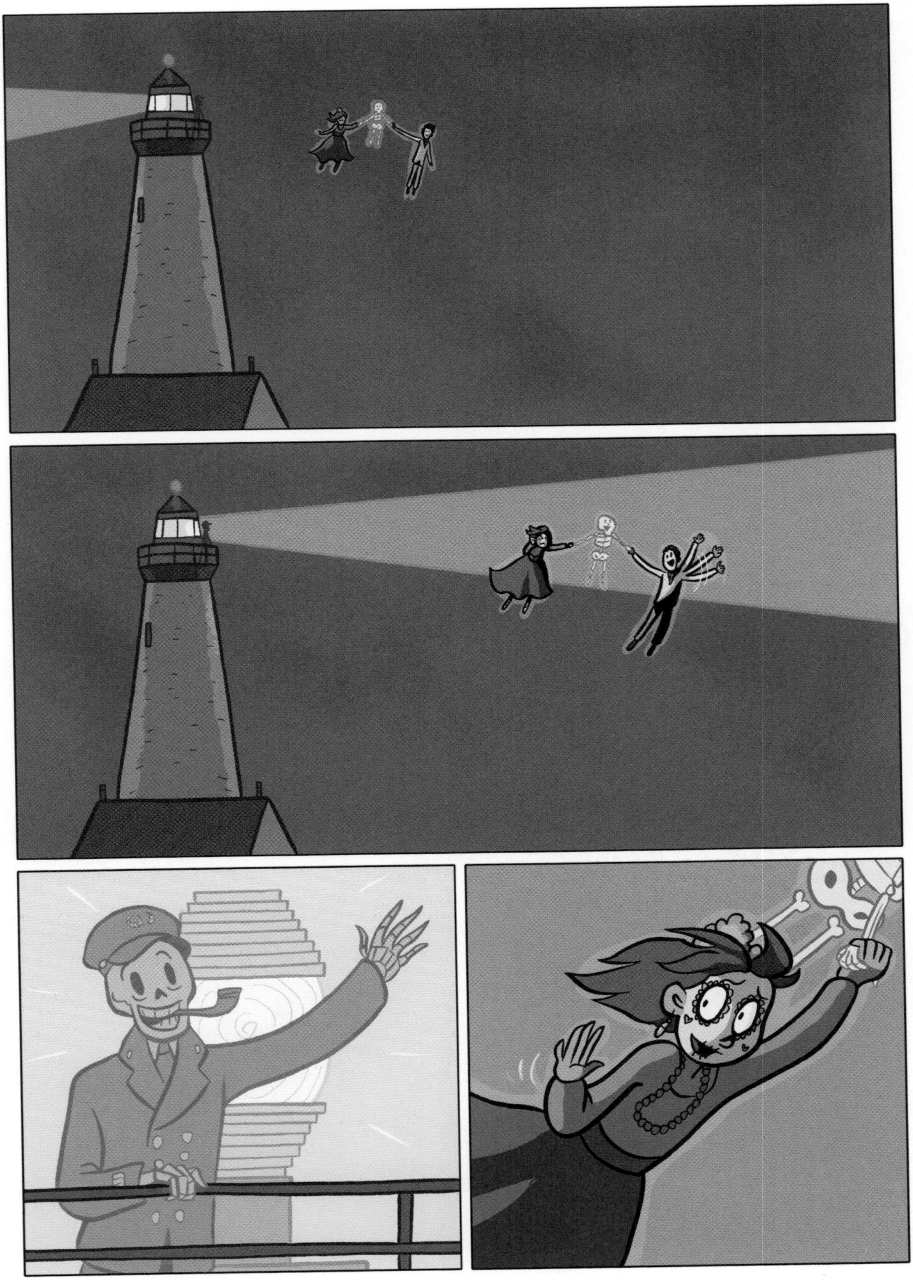

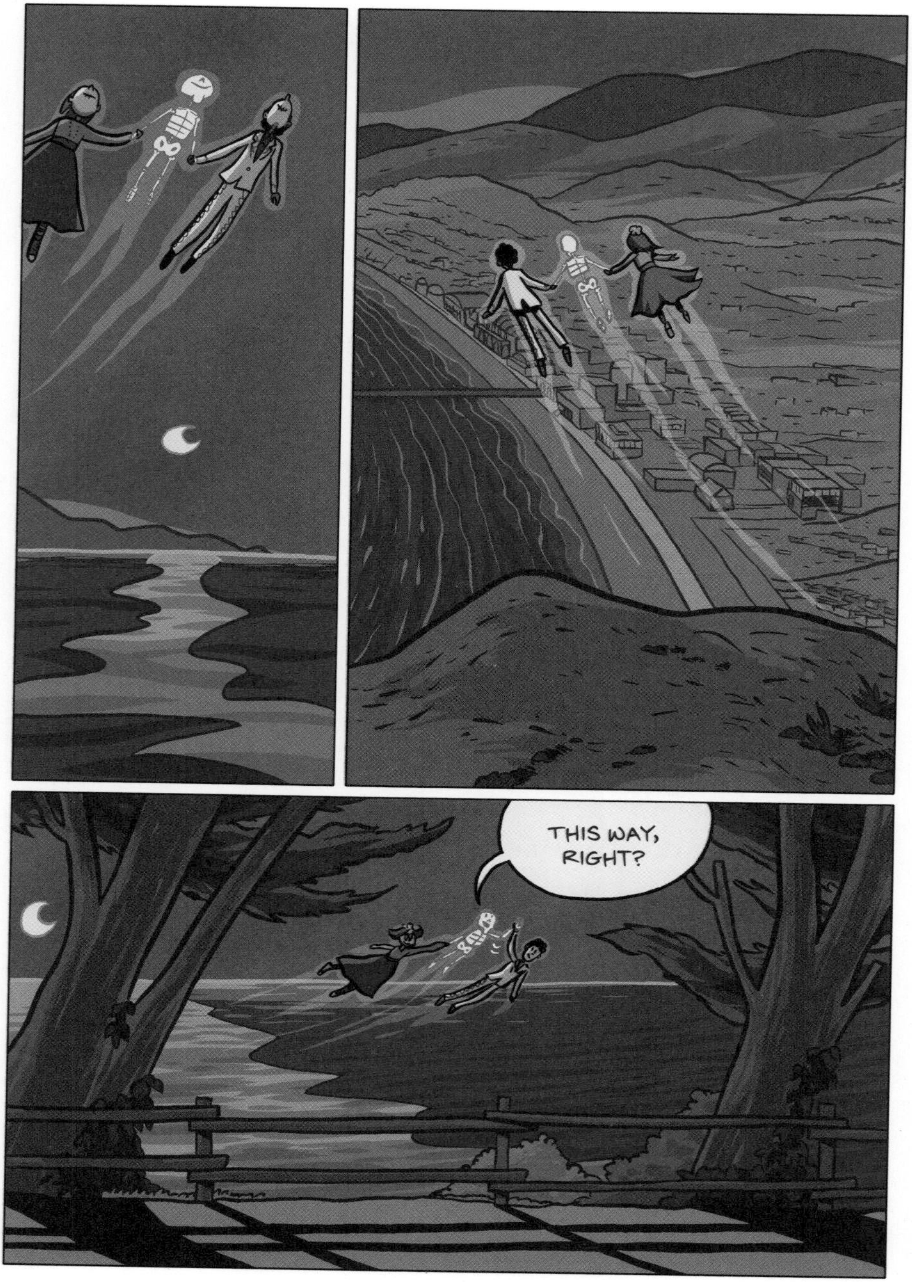
THIS WAY, RIGHT?

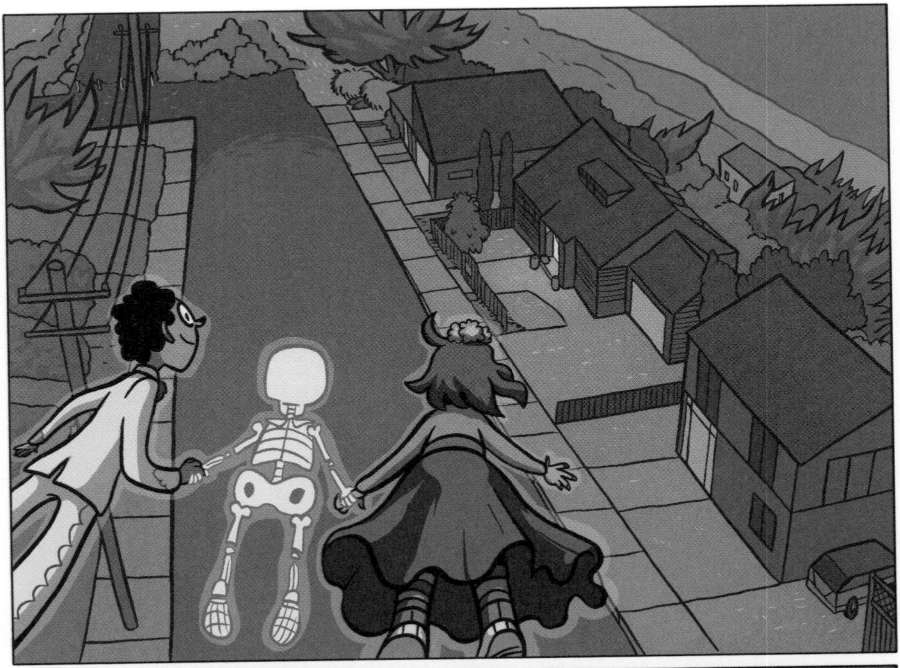

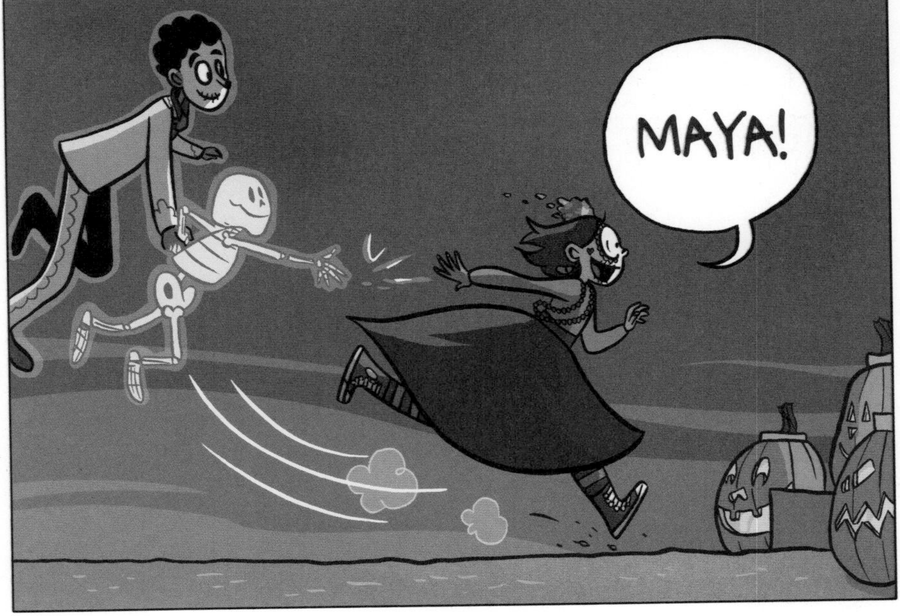
MAYA!

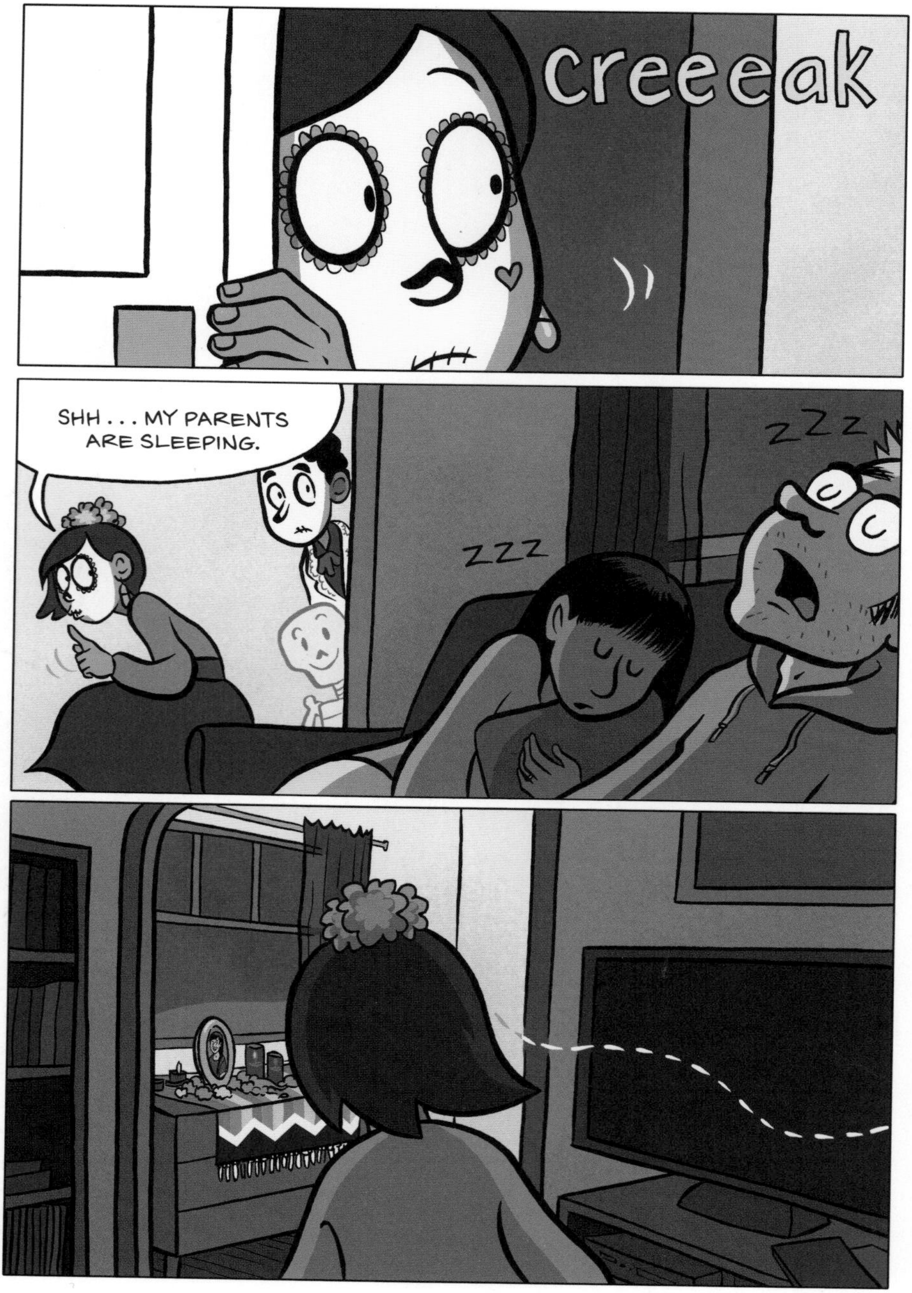
creeeak
SHH . . . MY PARENTS ARE SLEEPING.
ZZZ
ZZZ

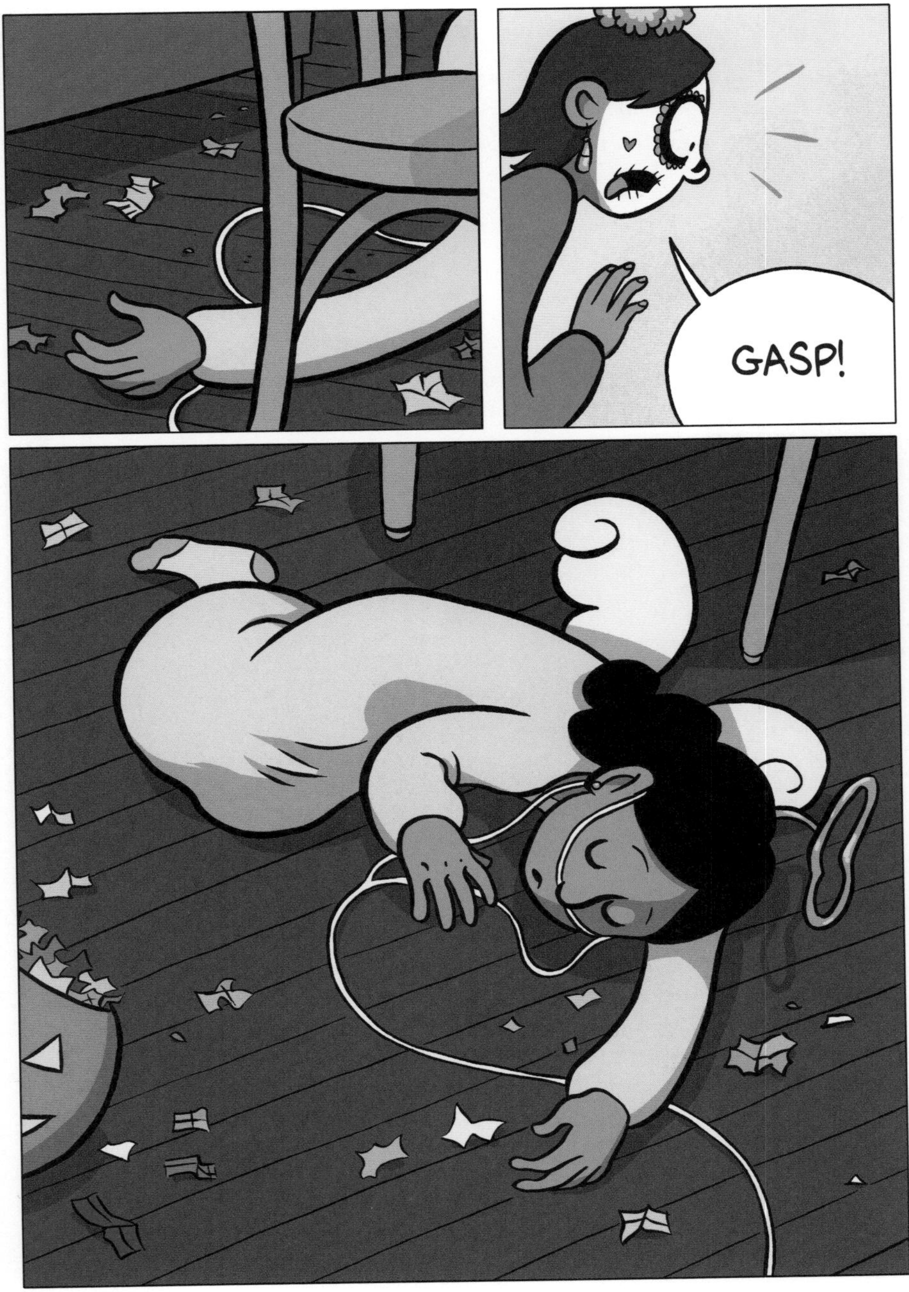
GASP!

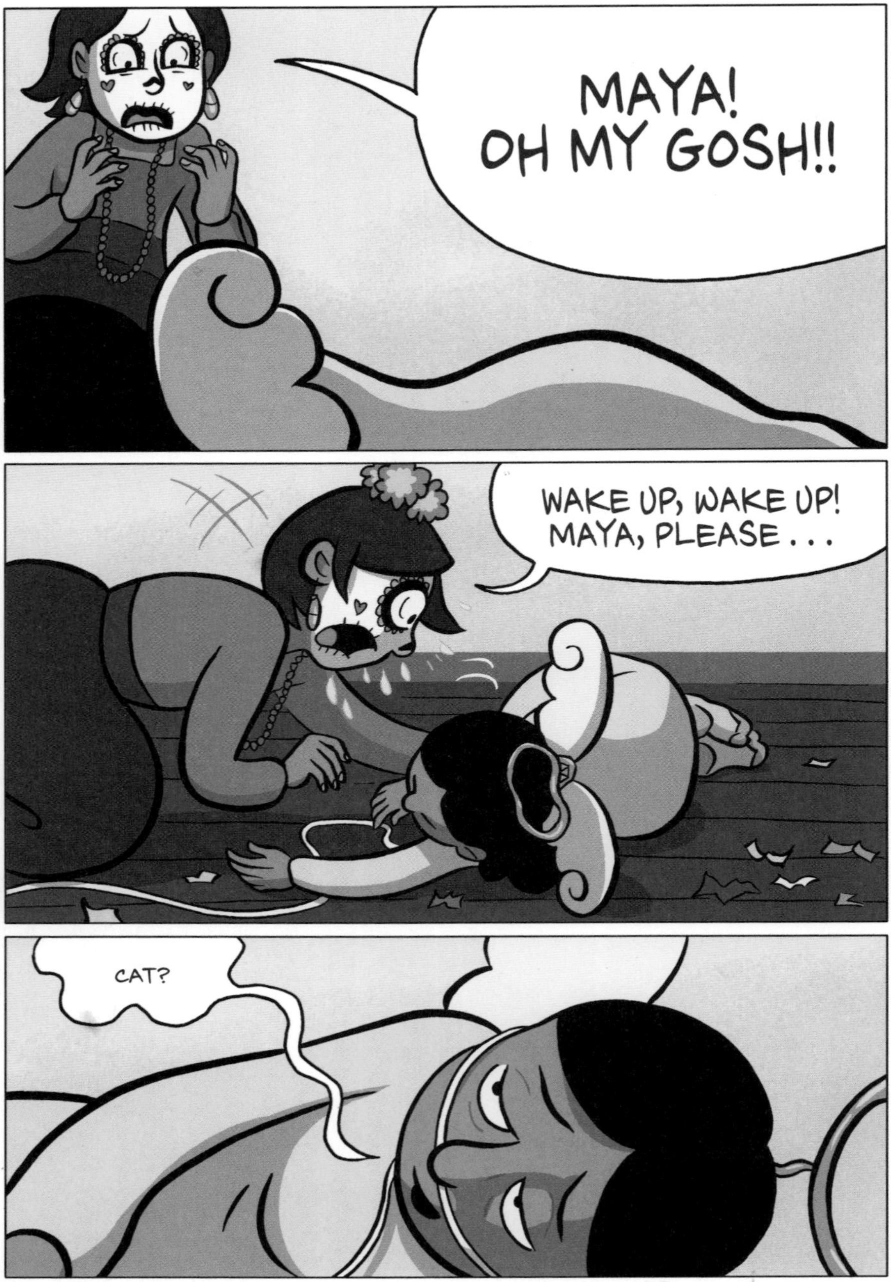
MAYA!
OH MY GOSH!!
WAKE UP, WAKE UP!
MAYA, PLEASE . . .
CAT?

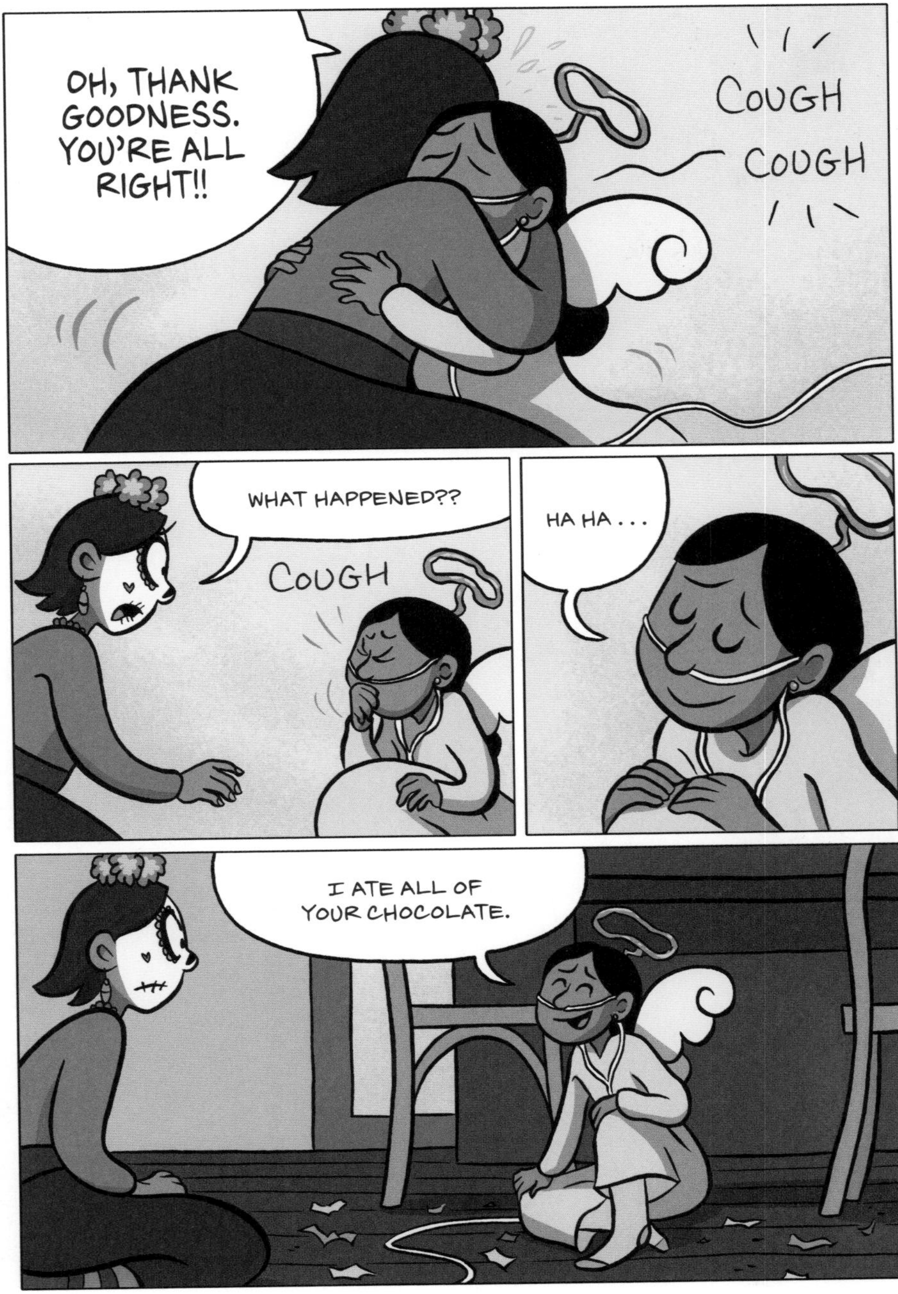
OH, THANK GOODNESS. YOU'RE ALL RIGHT!!
COUGH
COUGH
WHAT HAPPENED??
COUGH
HA HA . . .
I ATE ALL OF YOUR CHOCOLATE.

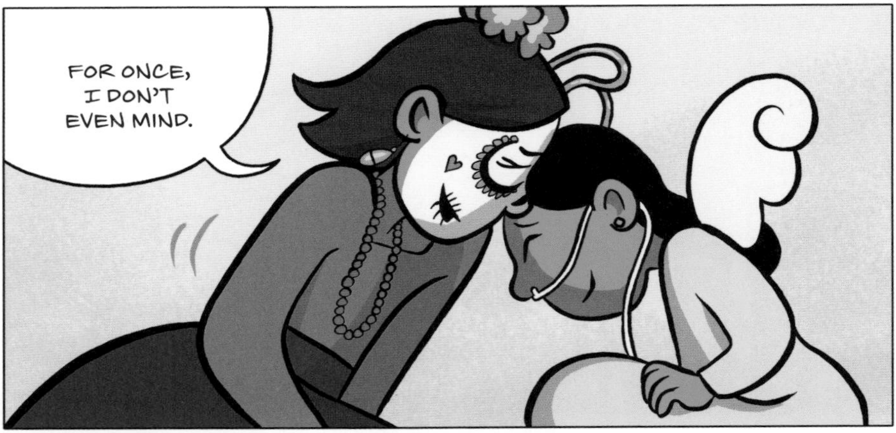
FOR ONCE, I DON'T EVEN MIND.

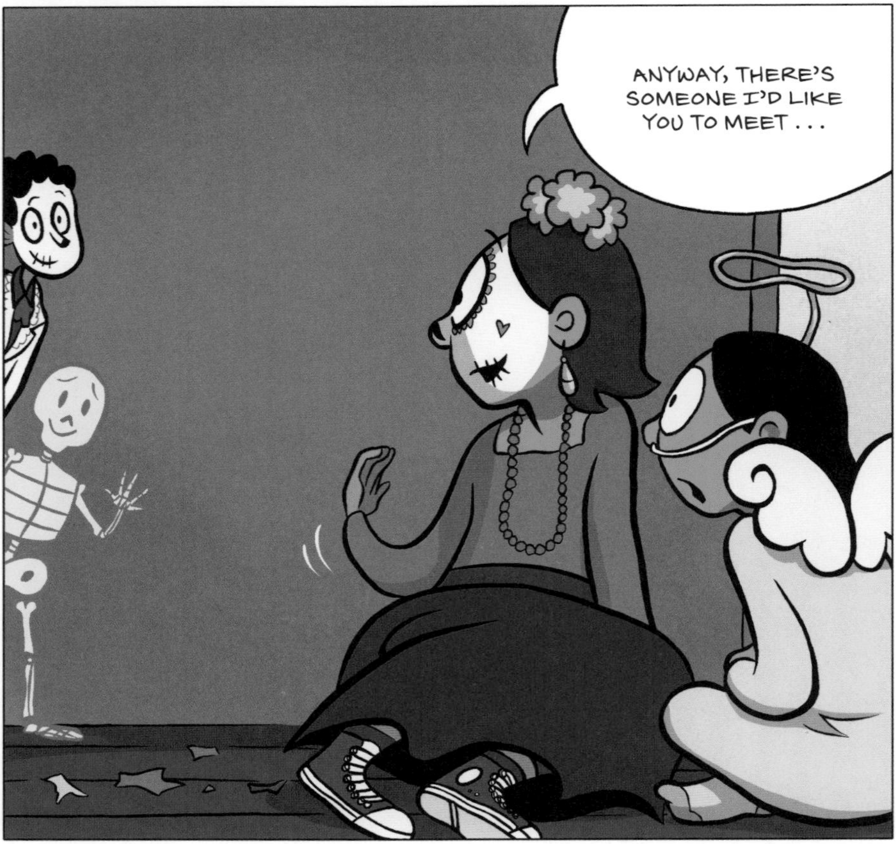
ANYWAY, THERE'S SOMEONE I'D LIKE YOU TO MEET . . .

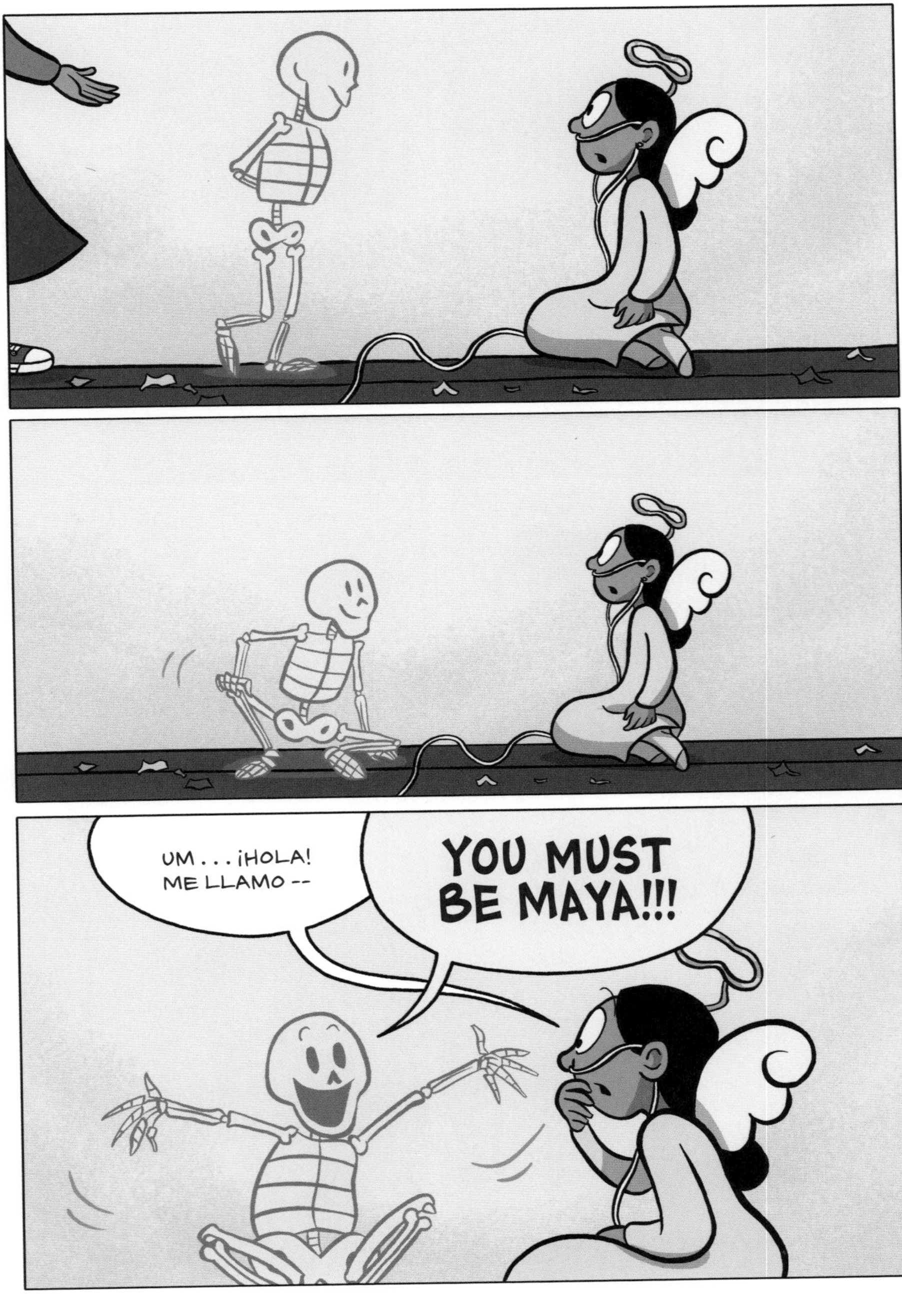
UM . . . ¡HOLA! ME LLAMO --
YOU MUST BE MAYA!!!

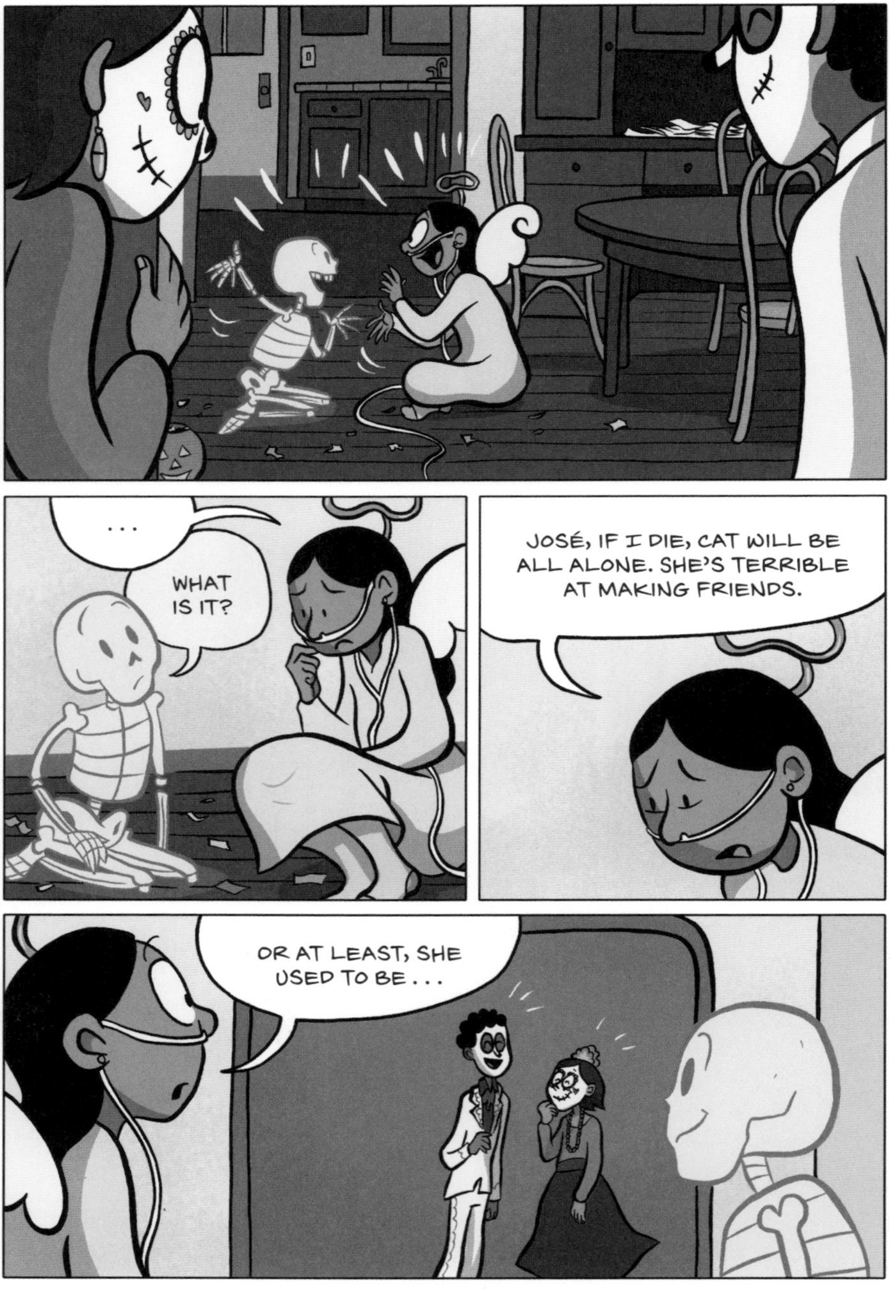
. . .
WHAT IS IT?
JOSÉ, IF I DIE, CAT WILL BE ALL ALONE. SHE'S TERRIBLE AT MAKING FRIENDS.
OR AT LEAST, SHE USED TO BE . . .

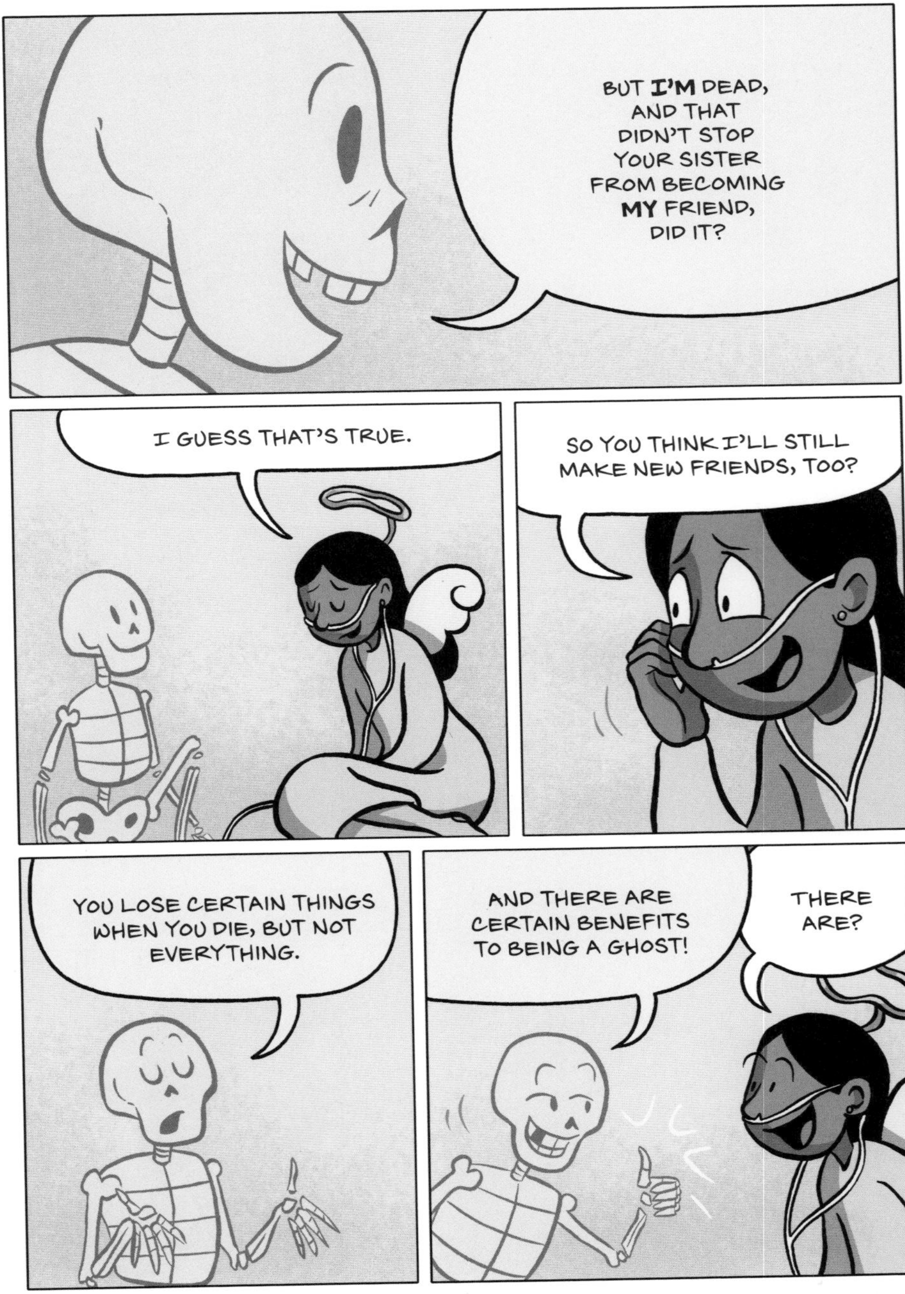
BUT **I'M** DEAD, AND THAT DIDN'T STOP YOUR SISTER FROM BECOMING **MY** FRIEND, DID IT?
I GUESS THAT'S TRUE.
SO YOU THINK I'LL STILL MAKE NEW FRIENDS, TOO?
YOU LOSE CERTAIN THINGS WHEN YOU DIE, BUT NOT EVERYTHING.
AND THERE ARE CERTAIN BENEFITS TO BEING A GHOST!
THERE ARE?

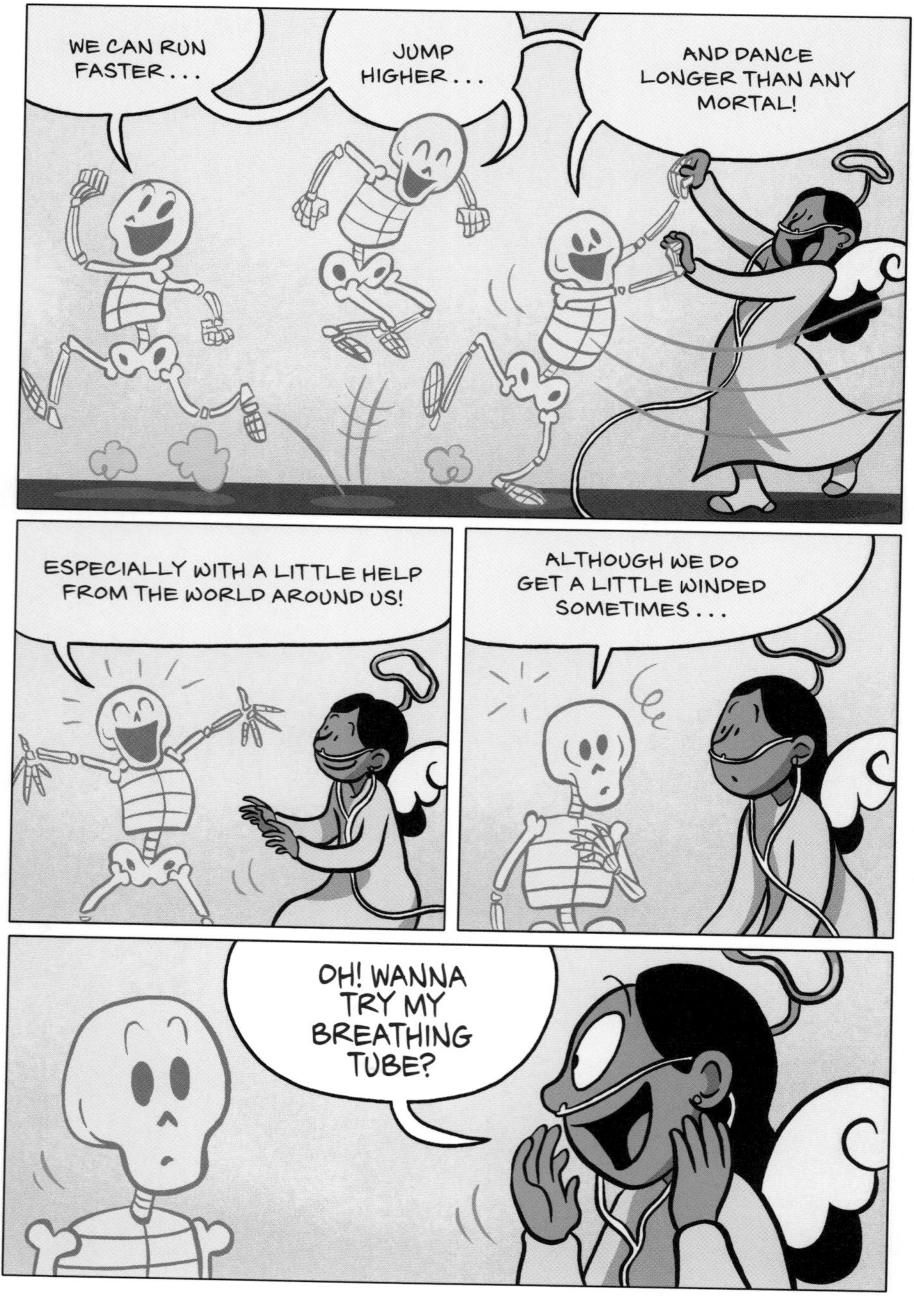
WE CAN RUN FASTER . . .
JUMP HIGHER . . .
AND DANCE LONGER THAN ANY MORTAL!
ESPECIALLY WITH A LITTLE HELP FROM THE WORLD AROUND US!
ALTHOUGH WE DO GET A LITTLE WINDED SOMETIMES . . .
OH! WANNA TRY MY BREATHING TUBE?

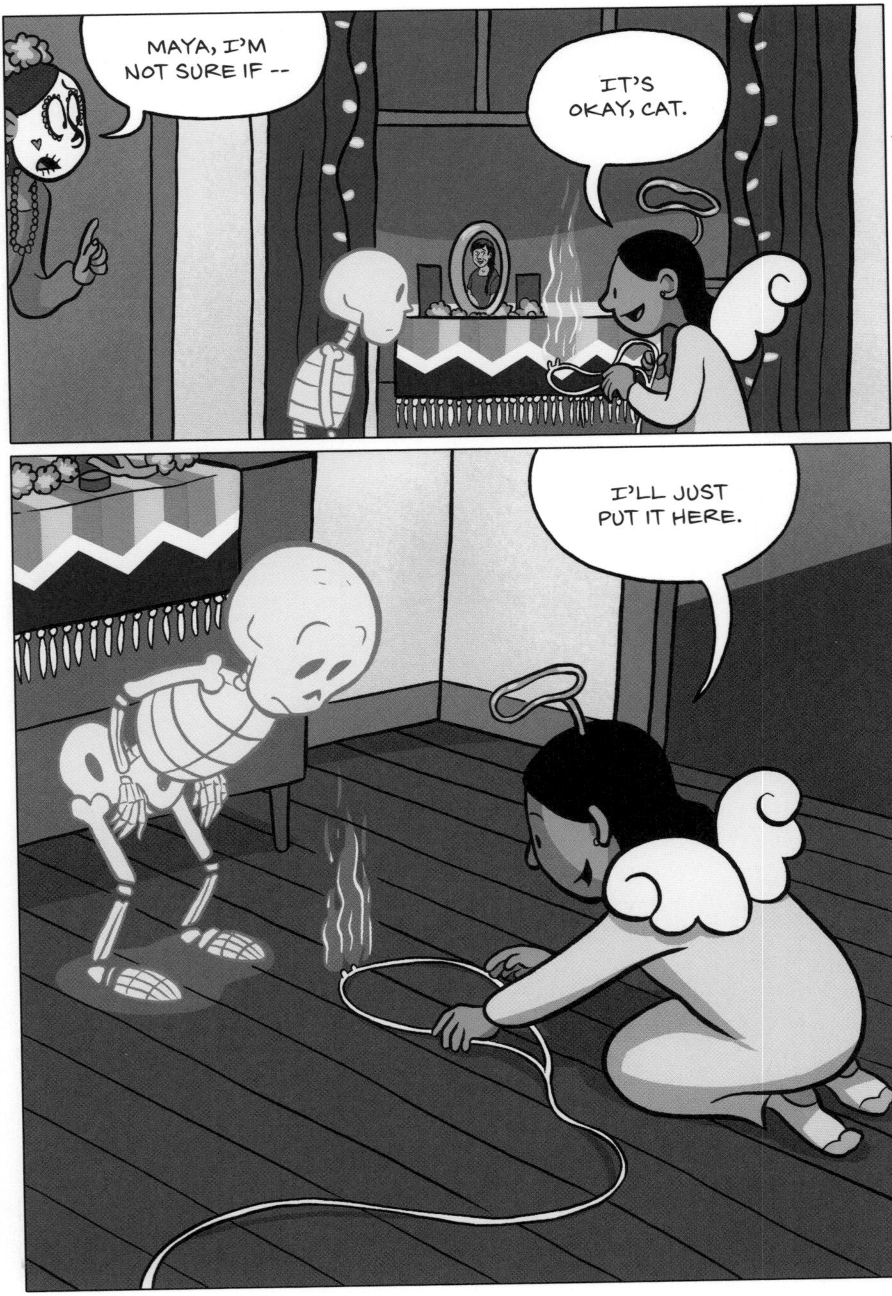
MAYA, I'M NOT SURE IF --
IT'S OKAY, CAT.
I'LL JUST PUT IT HERE.

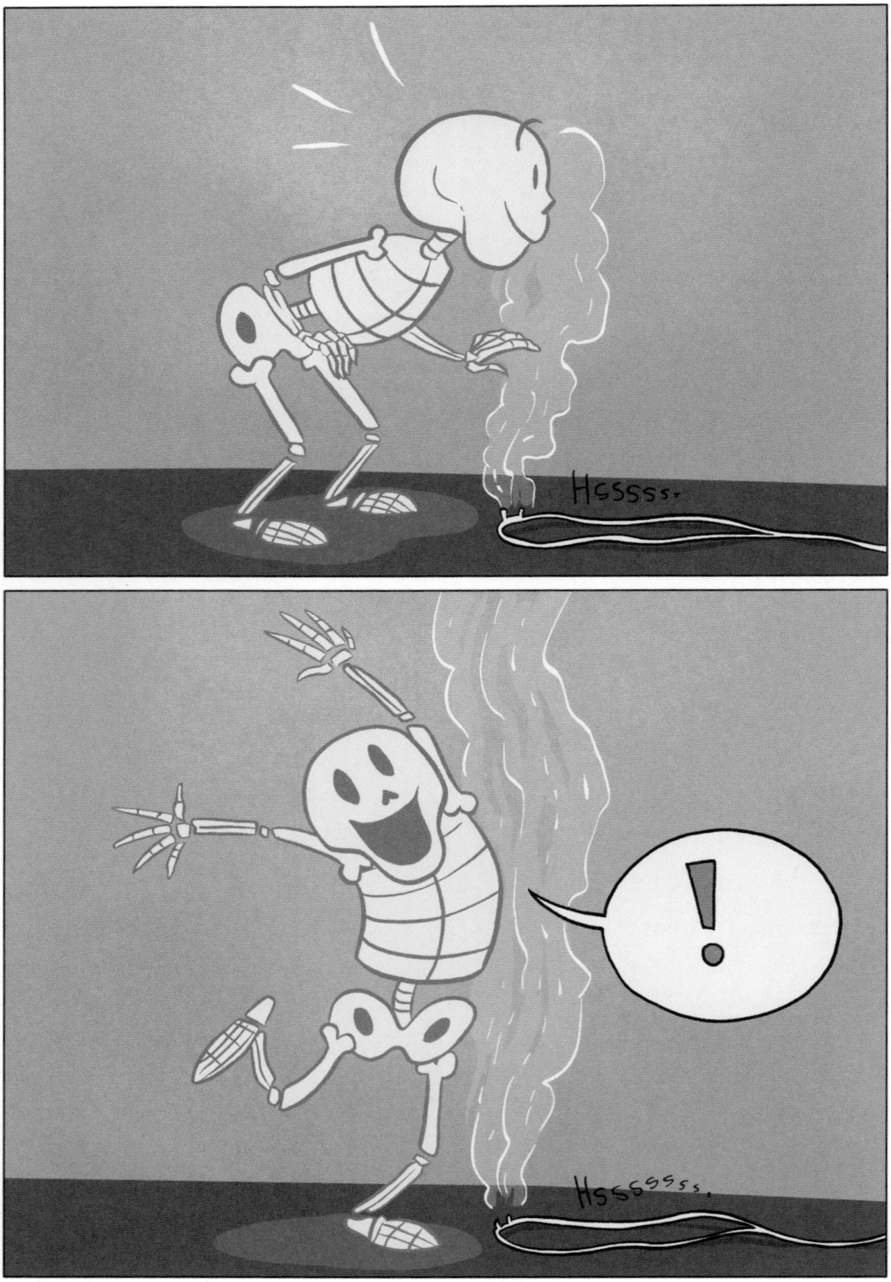
Hsssss.
Hsssssss.
!

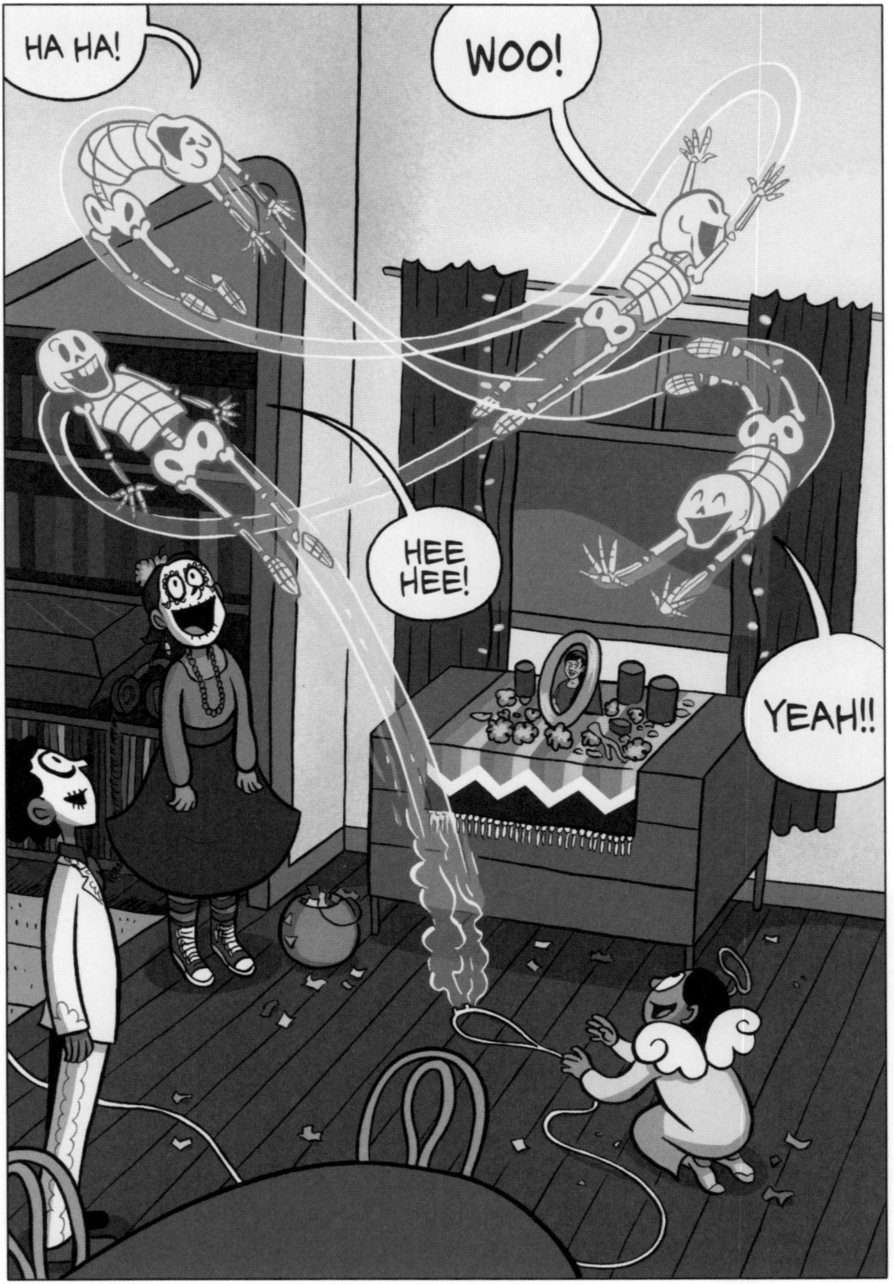
HA HA!
WOO!
HEE HEE!
YEAH!!

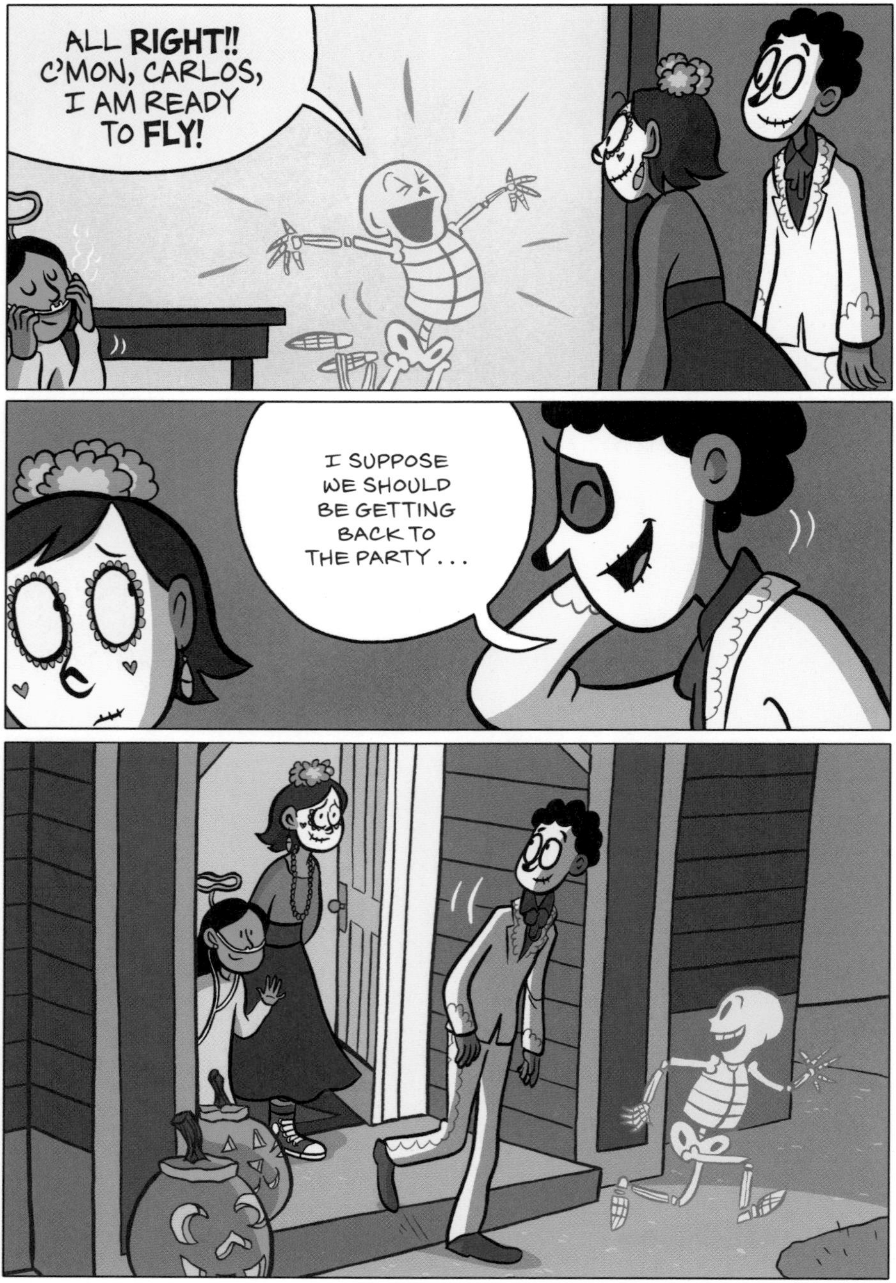
ALL **RIGHT!!** C'MON, CARLOS, I AM READY TO **FLY!**
I SUPPOSE WE SHOULD BE GETTING BACK TO THE PARTY . . .

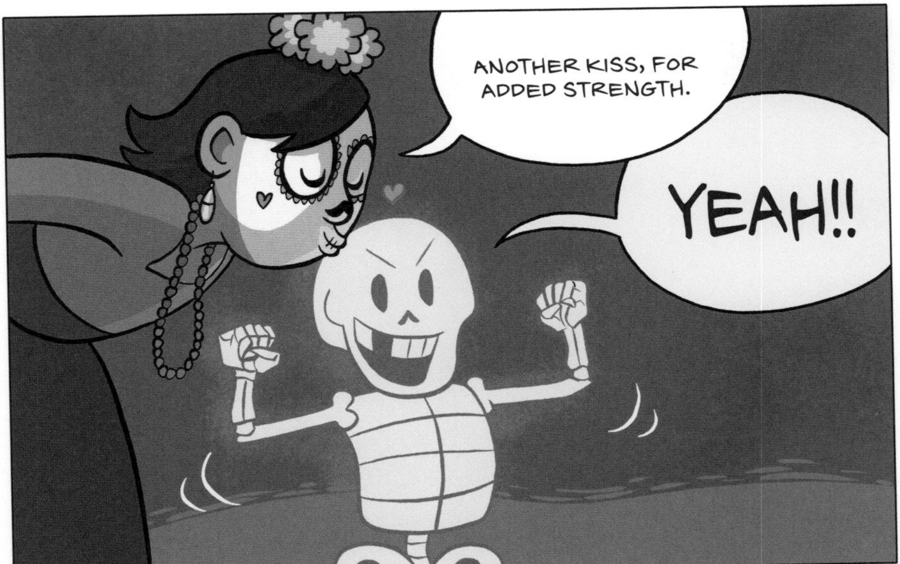
ANOTHER KISS, FOR ADDED STRENGTH.
YEAH!!

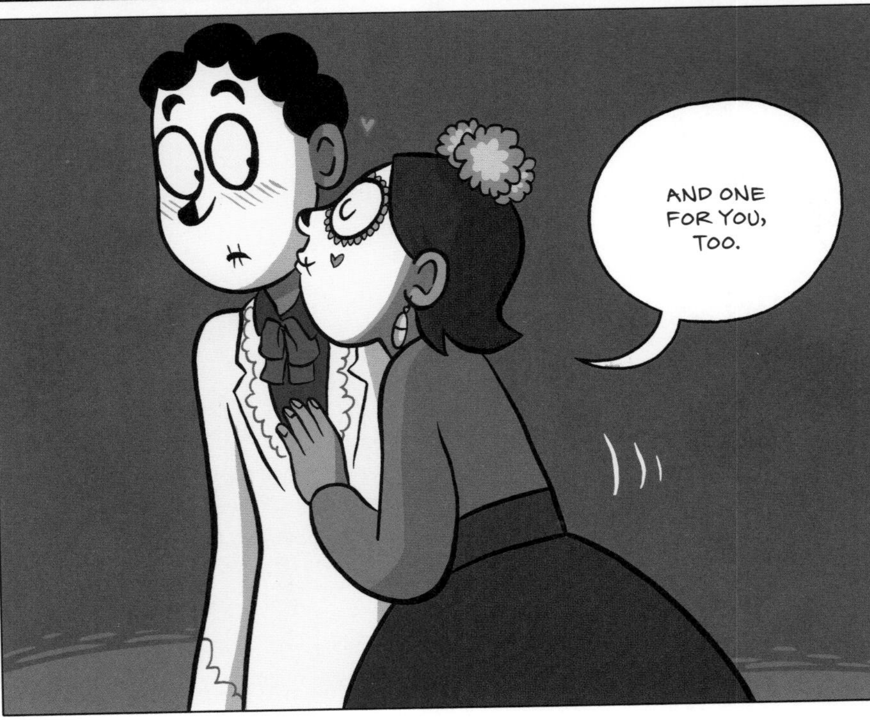
AND ONE FOR YOU, TOO.

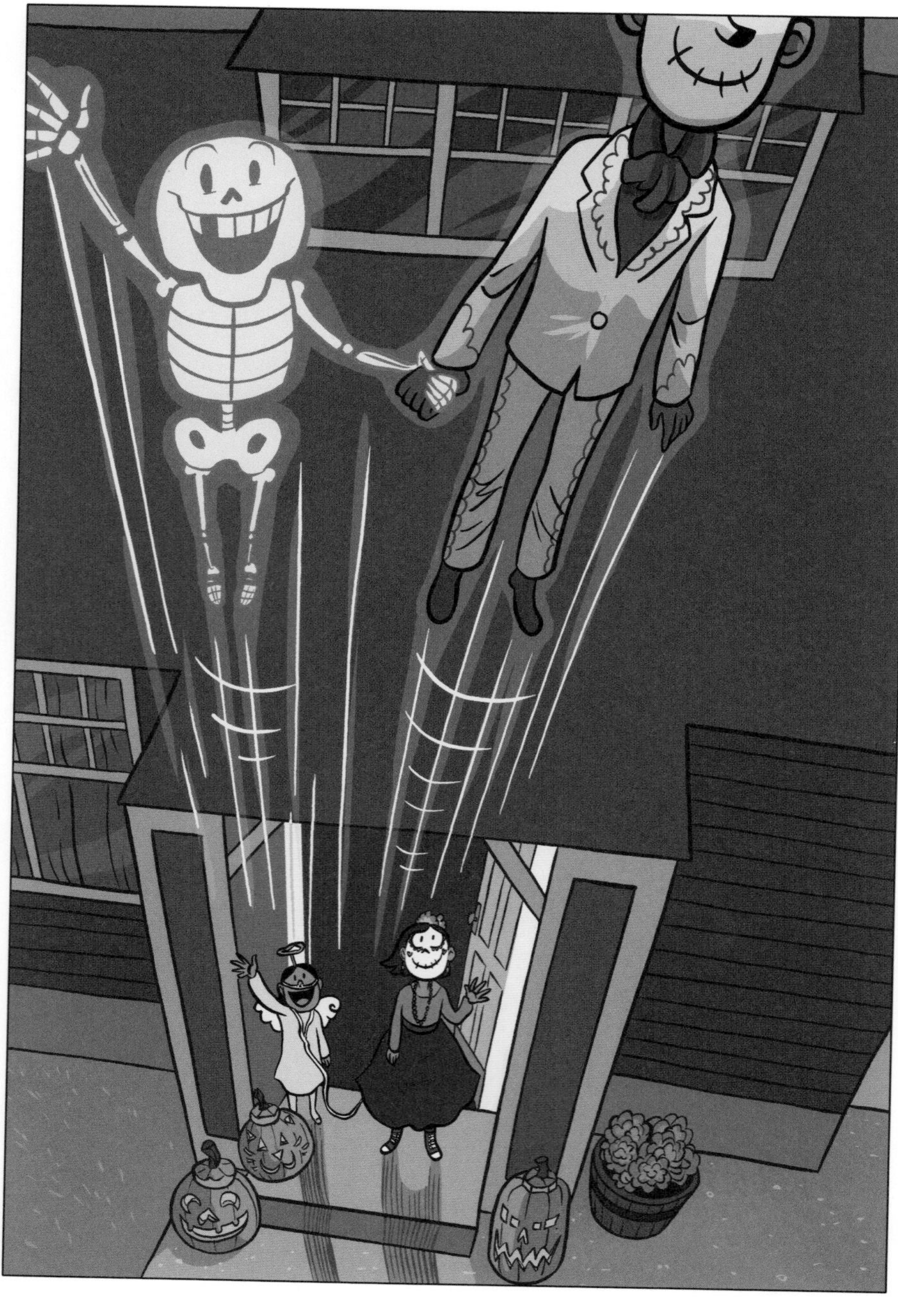

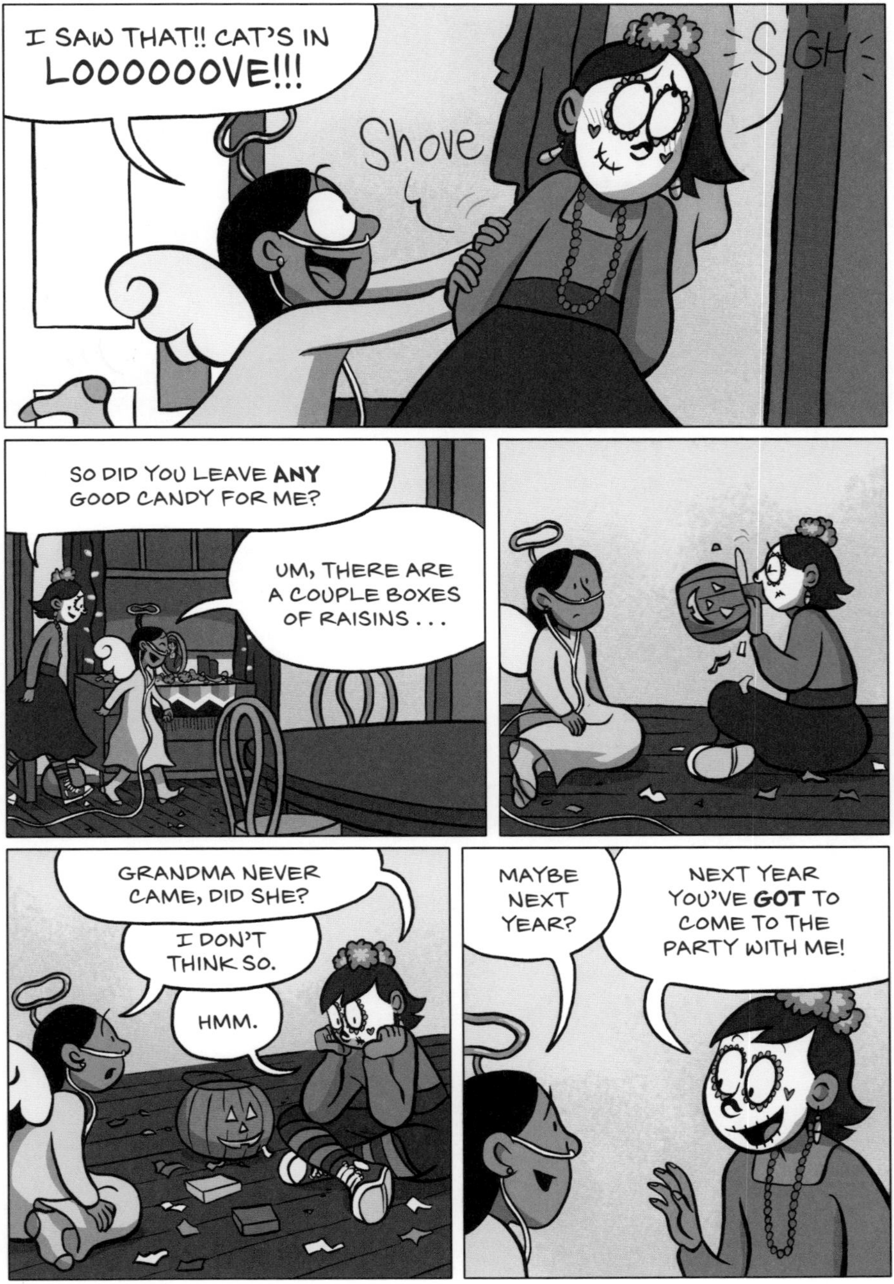

I SAW THAT!! CAT'S IN LOOOOOOVE!!!
Shove
SIGH
SO DID YOU LEAVE ANY GOOD CANDY FOR ME?
UM, THERE ARE A COUPLE BOXES OF RAISINS . . .
GRANDMA NEVER CAME, DID SHE?
I DON'T THINK SO.
HMM.
MAYBE NEXT YEAR?
NEXT YEAR YOU'VE GOT TO COME TO THE PARTY WITH ME!

I MET THE CUTEST OLD LADY . . .
Riiiiip!
Raisins
AND YOU WOULD NOT BELIEVE HOW TALENTED CARLOS'S **DAD** IS!
SCRATCH
SCRATCH
SCRAAAATCH
DO YOU HEAR THAT?

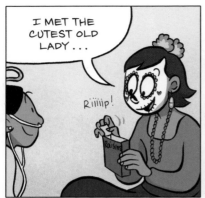

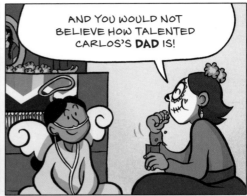

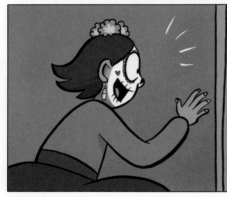

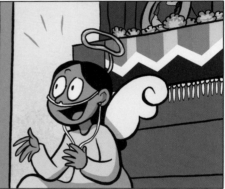

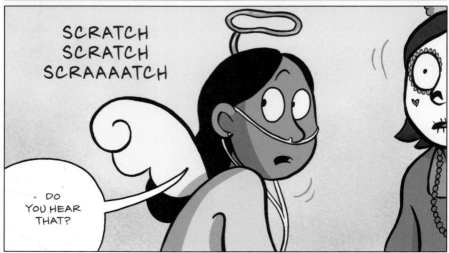

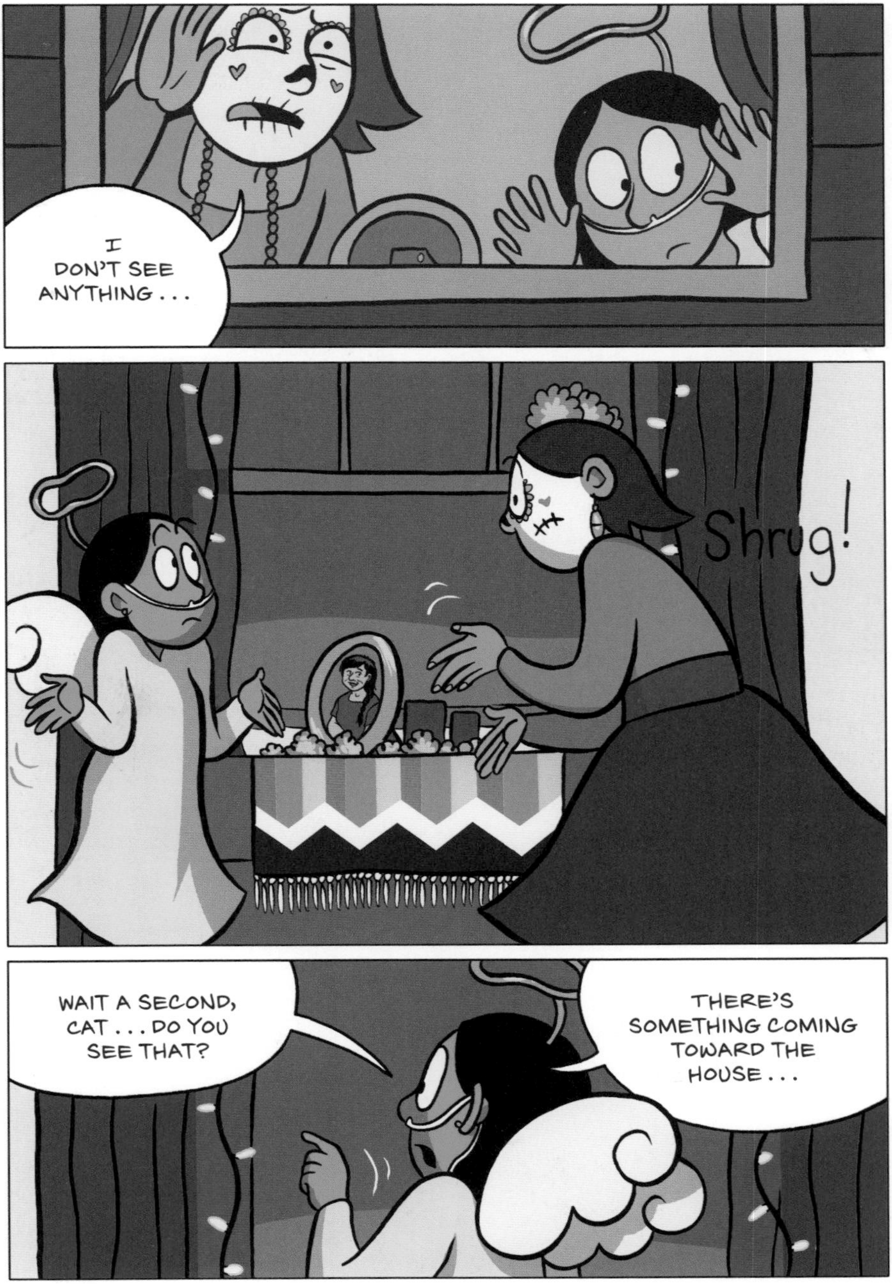
I DON'T SEE ANYTHING . . .
Shrug!
WAIT A SECOND, CAT . . . DO YOU SEE THAT?
THERE'S SOMETHING COMING TOWARD THE HOUSE . . .

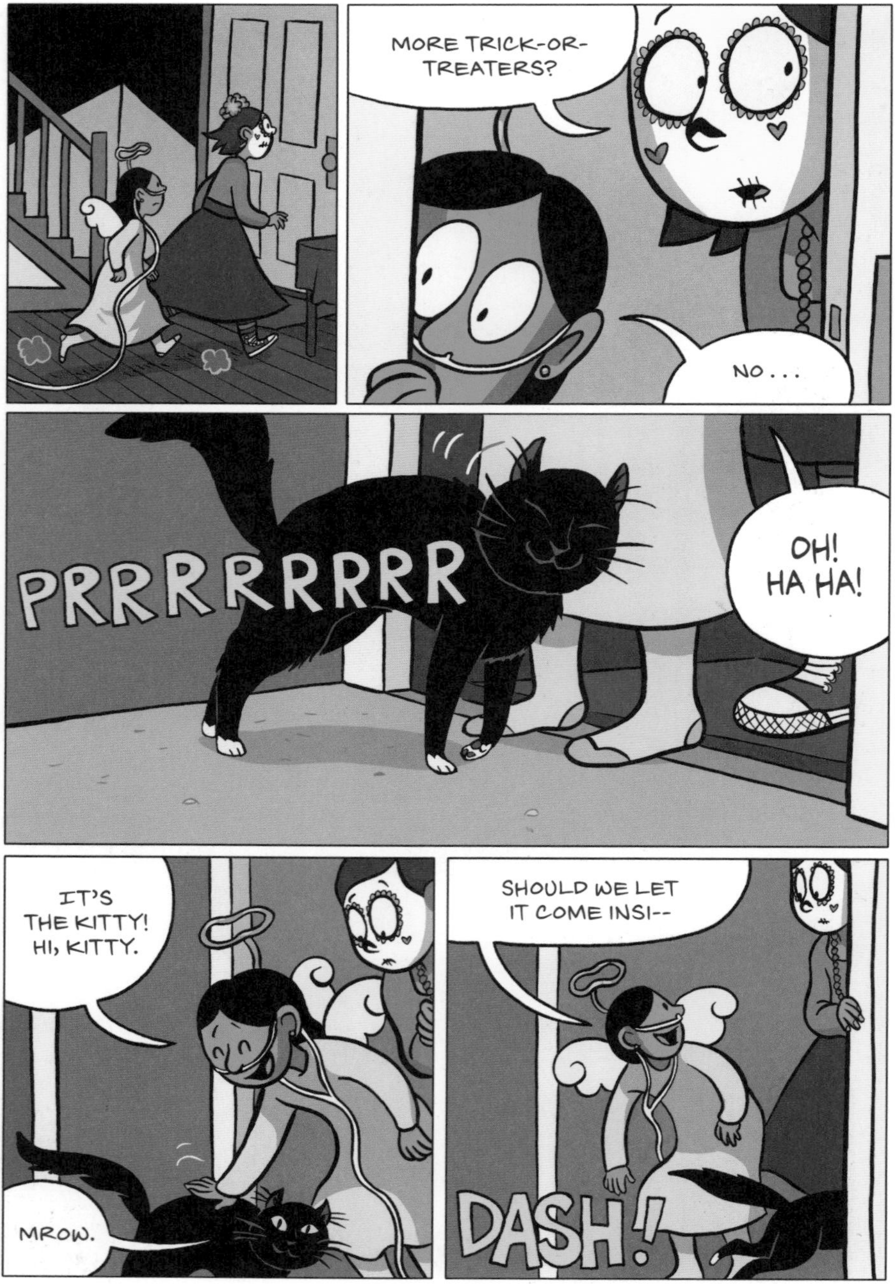
MORE TRICK-OR-TREATERS?
NO . . .
PRRRRRRRR
OH! HA HA!
IT'S THE KITTY! HI, KITTY.
MROW.
SHOULD WE LET IT COME INSI--
DASH!

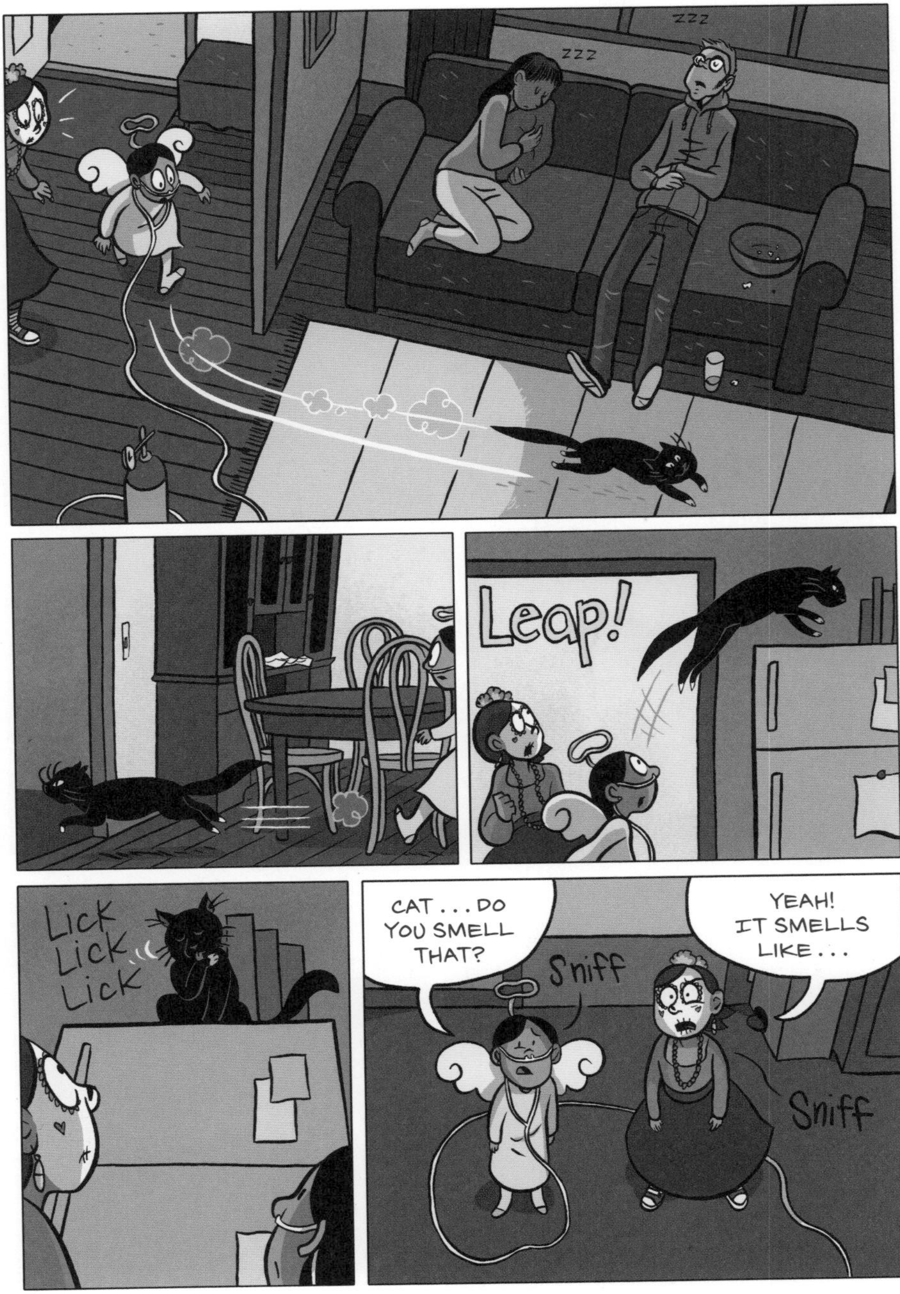
ZZZ
ZZZ
Leap!
Lick
Lick
Lick
CAT . . . DO YOU SMELL THAT?
Sniff
YEAH! IT SMELLS LIKE . . .
Sniff

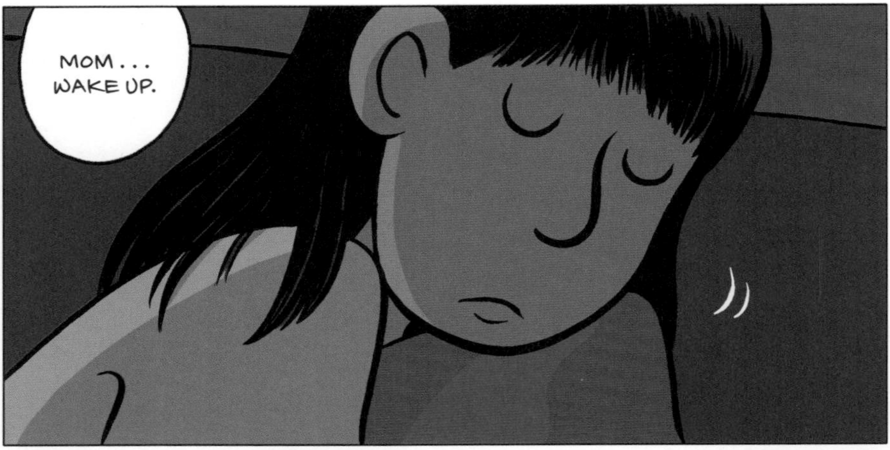
MOM . . .
WAKE UP.

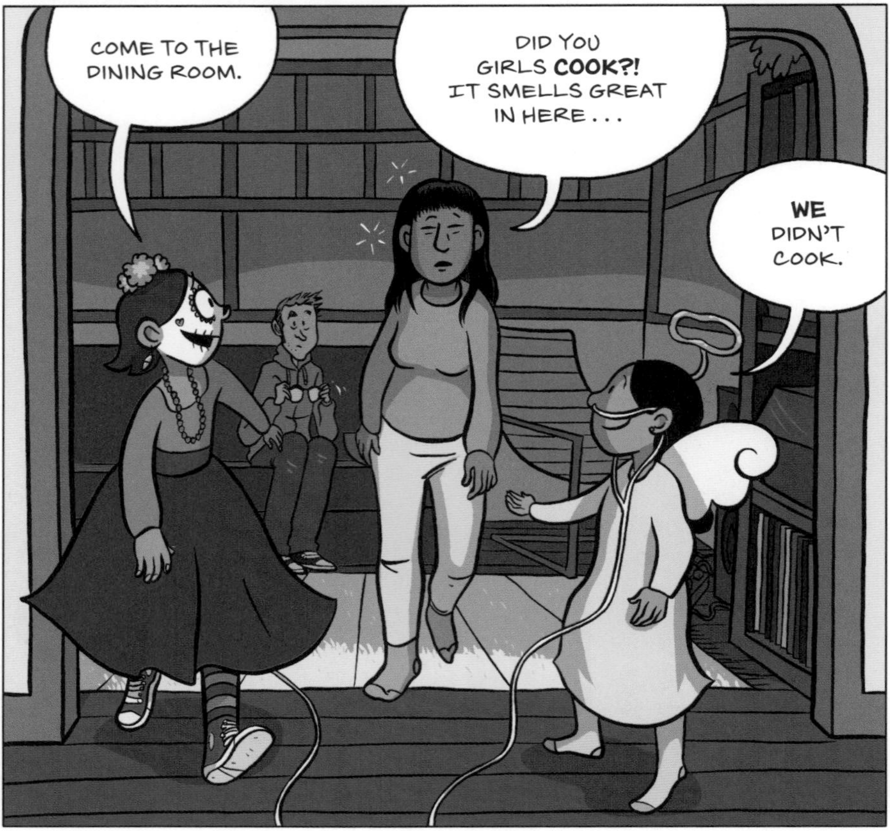
COME TO THE DINING ROOM.
DID YOU GIRLS **COOK?!** IT SMELLS GREAT IN HERE . . .
WE DIDN'T COOK.

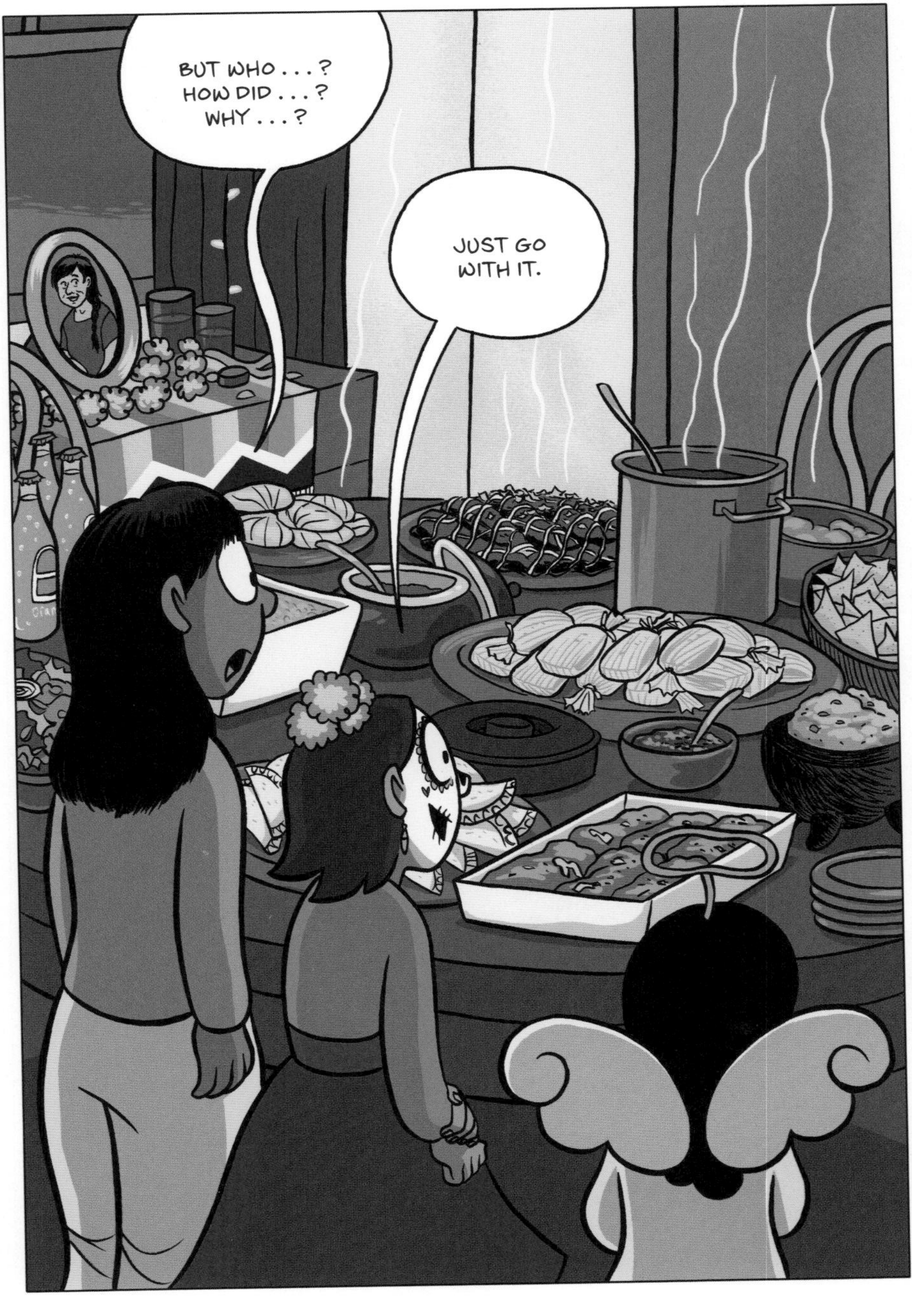
BUT WHO . . . ? HOW DID . . . ? WHY . . . ?
JUST GO WITH IT.

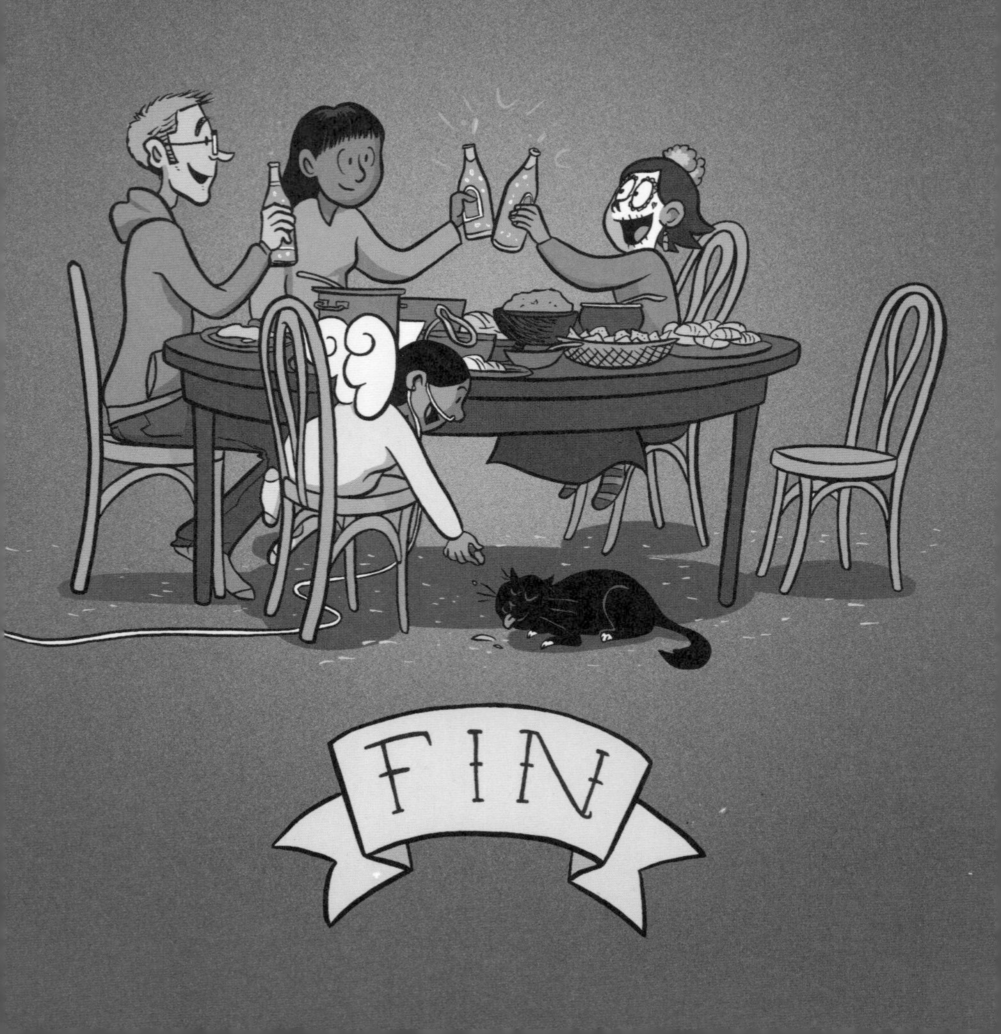
AND SO WE DID.
FIN

A FEW NOTES ABOUT
GHOSTS

BAHÍA DE LA LUNA

Bahía de la Luna was inspired by foggy coastal Northern California, where I grew up. I've always had an appreciation for the windswept coastline, the gnarly cypress trees, and especially the seaside town of Half Moon Bay, which is famous for its artichoke fields, pumpkin farms, and cheerful, laid-back Halloween vibe. I wanted Bahía de la Luna to feel like that, and the characters who live there to reflect the laid-back, gnarly, slightly haunted atmosphere.

DÍA DE LOS MUERTOS

Día de los Muertos, or Day of the Dead, is an ancient tradition that is now largely celebrated in Mexico and throughout the world. Instead of mourning the loss of loved ones, Mexican culture chooses to celebrate and honor the dead each year at the beginning of November, building altars (ofrendas) in homes, parks, and cemeteries, and decorating them with flowers, food, photographs, and other personal items. Although Day of the Dead represents the afterlife, there is something undeniably joyous about it!

I was very fortunate to attend San Francisco's annual Day of the Dead celebration during the course of creating this book. Thousands of people came together to dress up, build altars, light candles, and remember their loved ones. It was one of the most beautiful, respectful, and moving experiences I've ever had. Many of the visuals from the celebration scene in *Ghosts* came directly from that night, as I sat, sketched, and observed everything and everyone around me. The process of creating a book is not unlike letting go of the things that haunt your past. Making peace with your ghosts is as profound as the idea of life itself. And at the end of the day, love transcends life and death.

Me in Day of the Dead makeup

CYSTIC FIBROSIS

Cystic fibrosis is a genetic disease that causes thick, sticky mucus to build up in the lungs, making breathing difficult and leading to frequent infections. Some of the treatments Maya endures in this story are the vibrating vest designed to break up the mucus in her lungs (making it easier to cough out); extra nutrition delivered through a port in her belly while she sleeps; and, eventually, a breathing tube to administer more oxygen. Scar tissue can build up in the lungs following infections, reducing the space available for air to pass through. In some cases, CF patients need to undergo lung transplants. While there is no cure, improved treatments for CF have greatly extended the life expectancy of patients. I chose to write about cystic fibrosis because breathing is a huge theme in this story. Ghosts can't breathe, and Maya can't breathe very well herself. Cat has normal lungs, but she is often anxious and sometimes needs to be reminded to stop and breathe deeply. You can learn more about cystic fibrosis at www.cff.org.

SKETCHBOOK

These sketches were done in 2008, eight years before the publication of *Ghosts*! The characters, their story, and this environment have existed in my head for a very long time.

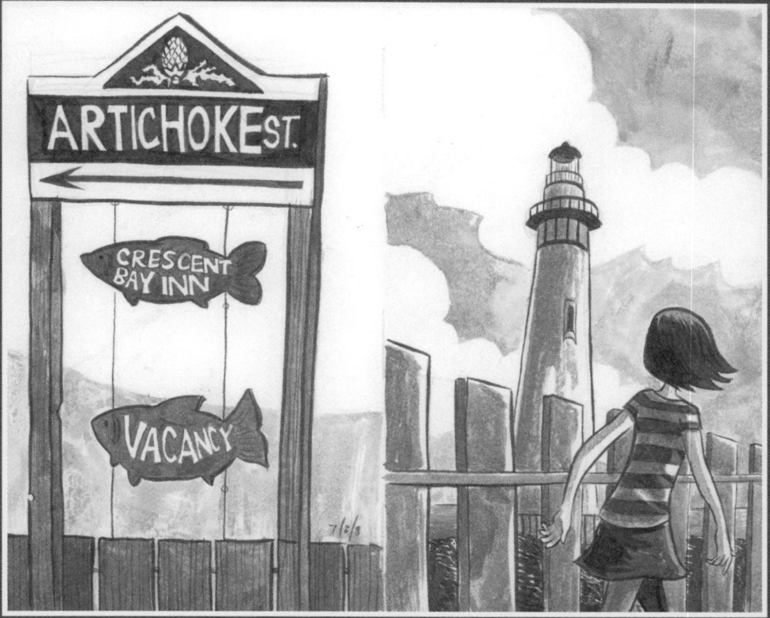
ARTICHOKE ST.
CRESCENT BAY INN
VACANCY

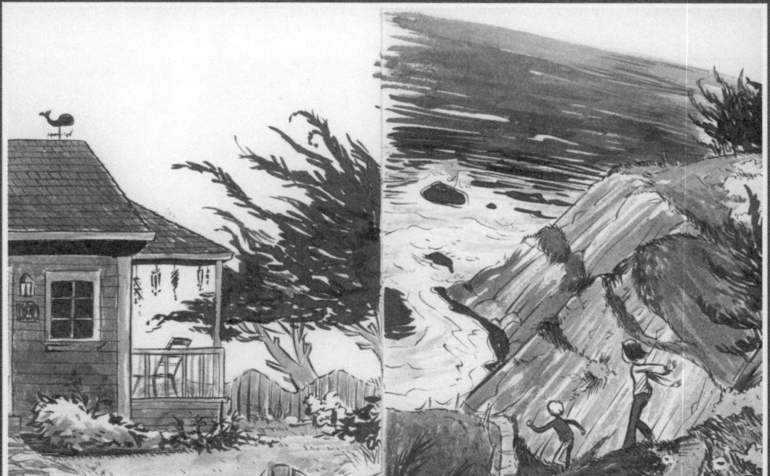

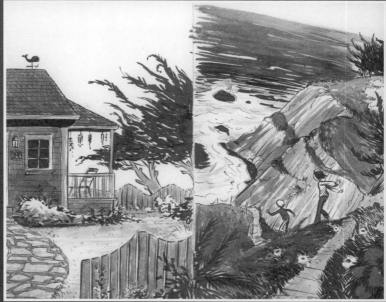

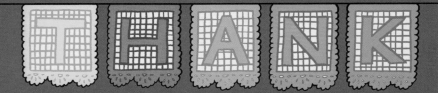

THANK

This book drew a lot of inspiration from my cousin Sabina Castillo Collado, whom we lost to cancer when she was thirteen. Sabina was one of the most inspiring kids I ever met: spirited, joyful, and not interested in letting her illness define her or slow her down. She is greatly missed and will never be forgotten.

Sabina's parents, Suzanne and Dioni, and her siblings, Sophia and Adonis, also blew me away with the depth of their love for their daughter and sister. They are incredible people and I wish to thank them for everything they are and everything they do. Special thanks to Sophia for being one of the coolest big sisters I've ever known.

Thanks to Dave Roman and the Cuevas, Roman, Rigores, and Fernandez families for their support. Special thanks to Tammy Diaz Cuevas for talking tamales with me.

The cystic fibrosis community, especially the brave families who posted their stories online, was a constant source of inspiration as well as a great resource for understanding.

My editors, Cassandra Pelham and David Saylor, nurtured this project from the ground up and helped me down the winding path that leads from one ocean to another. I can't think of two better people with whom to wander the windy hillside that is creating graphic novels.

Thanks to Phil Falco, Sheila Marie Everett, Lizette Serrano, Tracy van Straaten, Lori Benton, Ellie Berger, Bess Braswell, Antonio Gonzalez, Caitlin Friedman, Michelle Campbell, Emily Heddleson,

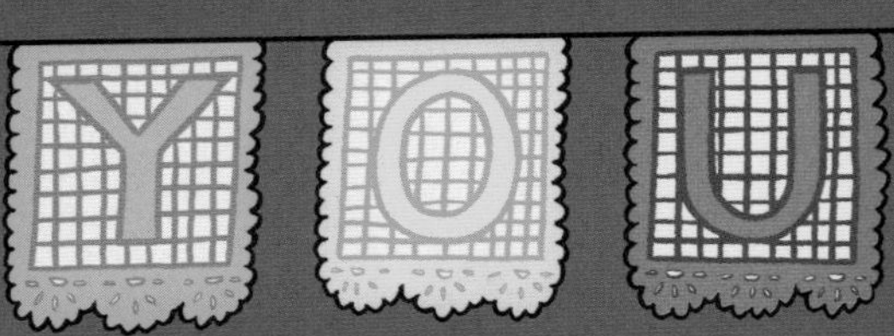
YOU

and the rest of the incredible team at Scholastic. I love working with all of you.

Braden Lamb deserves an extra-special round of bone-rattling applause for the coloring of my art for this book, translating my notes and reference for the atmosphere of Bahía de la Luna into stunning Technicolor. And muchas gracias to Braden's team of assistants, Shelli Paroline and Rachel Maguire!

Additional thanks to my studio assistants, Alexandra Graudins and Kristen Adam, for providing so much help, never-ending good cheer, and cookies; my wonder agent, Judy Hansen; ace letterer Jenny Staley; Sofia Vasquez-Duran, for talking health and medicine; Jewels Green, for her thoughtful insights on cystic fibrosis; and my friend in all things art, introspection, and skeletons, Ashley Despain.

Thanks to the authors, artists, filmmakers, and photographers who inspired me to think about spirits and magical realism and history and delicious food. Thanks to the librarians, booksellers, teachers, comics community, and everyone who has supported my work so wholeheartedly. Thanks to the state of California, my lifelong muse. Thanks to my family, who don't seem to mind living in the fog; I'll bear it if I have to, as long as you guys are here. Thanks to my friends, who are a continual source of love, support, and ideas. I'd be lost in the dark without them.

Finally, an orange soda toast to my readers, young and old, who are endlessly amazing.

–Raina

ALSO BY
RAINA TELGEMEIER

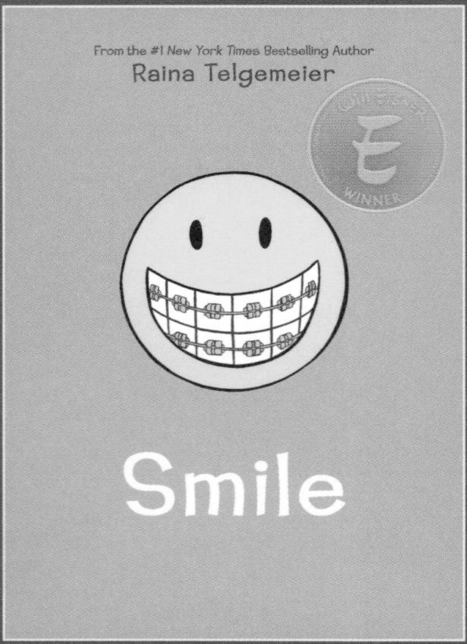
From the #1 New York Times Bestselling Author
Raina Telgemeier
WINNER
Smile

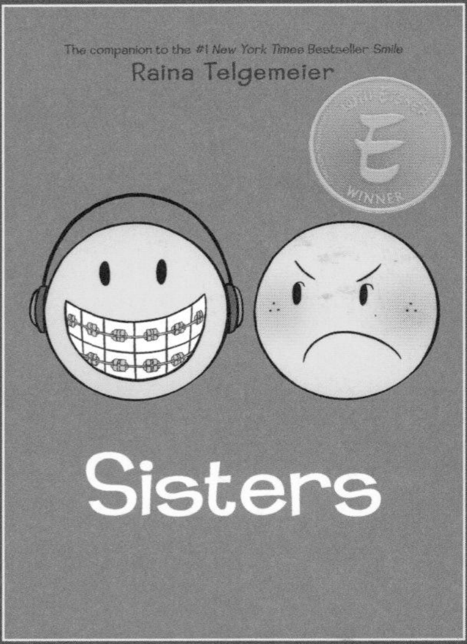
The companion to the #1 New York Times Bestseller Smile
Raina Telgemeier
WINNER
Sisters

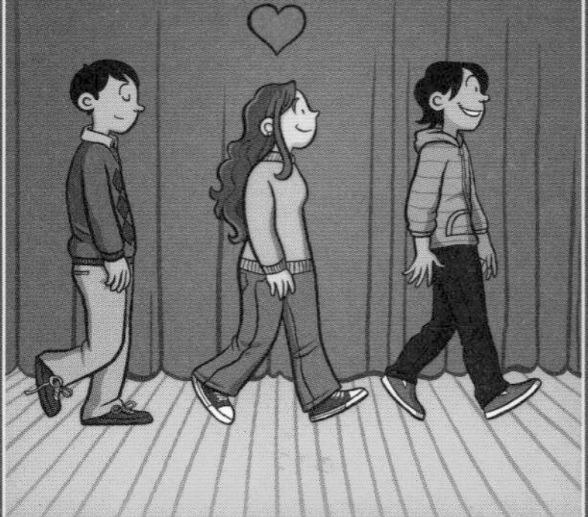
FROM THE #1 NEW YORK TIMES BESTSELLING AUTHOR OF SMILE
RAINA TELGEMEIER
DRAMA

BY ANN M. MARTIN AND RAINA TELGEMEIER

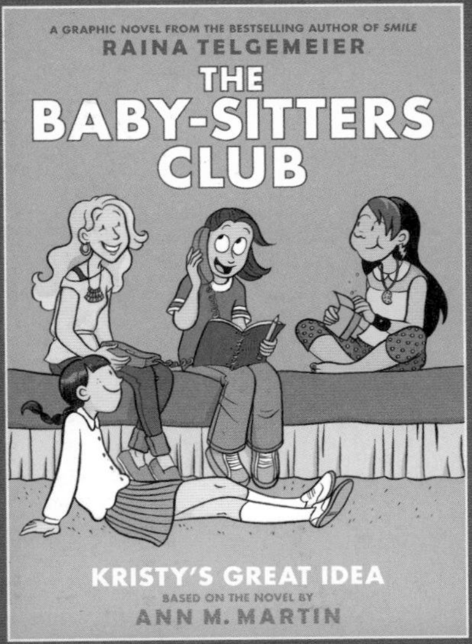
A GRAPHIC NOVEL FROM THE BESTSELLING AUTHOR OF SMILE
RAINA TELGEMEIER
THE BABY-SITTERS CLUB
KRISTY'S GREAT IDEA
BASED ON THE NOVEL BY
ANN M. MARTIN

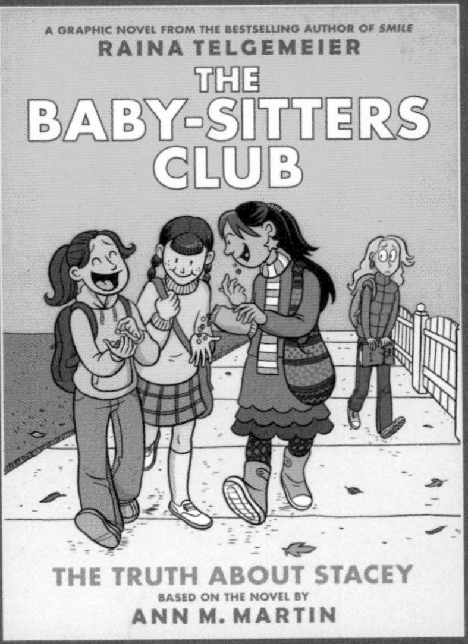
A GRAPHIC NOVEL FROM THE BESTSELLING AUTHOR OF SMILE
RAINA TELGEMEIER
THE BABY-SITTERS CLUB
THE TRUTH ABOUT STACEY
BASED ON THE NOVEL BY
ANN M. MARTIN

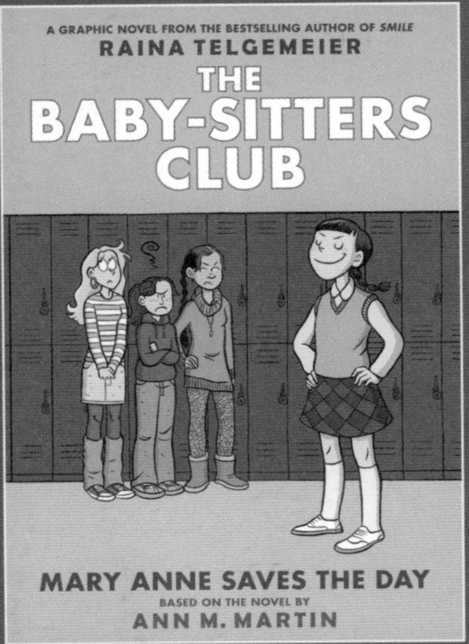
A GRAPHIC NOVEL FROM THE BESTSELLING AUTHOR OF SMILE
RAINA TELGEMEIER
THE BABY-SITTERS CLUB
MARY ANNE SAVES THE DAY
BASED ON THE NOVEL BY
ANN M. MARTIN

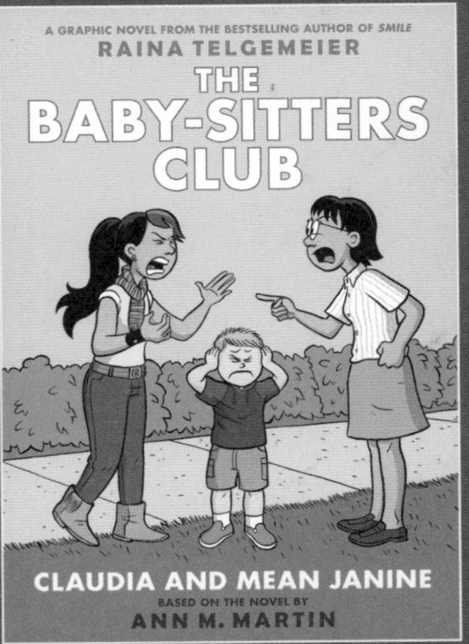
A GRAPHIC NOVEL FROM THE BESTSELLING AUTHOR OF SMILE
RAINA TELGEMEIER
THE BABY-SITTERS CLUB
CLAUDIA AND MEAN JANINE
BASED ON THE NOVEL BY
ANN M. MARTIN

RAINA TELGEMEIER is the #1 *New York Times* bestselling, multiple Eisner Award–winning creator of *Smile* and *Sisters*, which are both graphic memoirs based on her childhood. She is also the creator of *Drama*, which was named a Stonewall Honor Book and was selected for YALSA's Top Ten Great Graphic Novels for Teens. Raina lives in the San Francisco Bay Area. To learn more, visit her online at www.goRaina.com.